CIVIL TERROR
GRIDLOCK
BOOK 1

CIVIL TERROR
GRIDLOCK

A JAKE BENDEL THRILLER

J. LUKE BENNECKE

J. Luke Bennecke
www.jlukebennecke.com

Jaytech Publishing
PO Box 421
Beaumont, CA 92223
www.jaytechpublishing.com

Ordering Information:
Quantity sales. Special discounts are available on quantity purchases by corporations, associations, and others. For details, contact the publisher at the address above. Orders by U.S. trade bookstores and wholesalers. Please contact Jaytech Publishing at www.jaytechpublishing.com.

Printed in the United States of America

Publisher's Cataloging-in-Publication data
Bennecke, J. Luke
Civil Terror: Waterborne / J. Luke Bennecke
p. cm.
    ISBN (paperback): 978-0-9657715-2-8
    ISBN (ebook): 978-0-9657715-1-1
1. The main category of the book — Thriller — Suspense.

First Edition-Revised

10 9 8 7 6 5 4 3 2 1

Interior design and typesetting: Stewart A. Williams

Dedication

To all civil engineers young, old, and no longer with us: thank you for providing the bedrock for modern civilizations worldwide.

"I was originally supposed to become an engineer, but the thought of having to expend my creative energy on things that make practical everyday life even more refined, with a loathsome capital gain as the goal, was unbearable to me."

—Albert Einstein

FACTS

1 Every year in the United States, traffic congestion causes over $450 billion in lost economic productivity.

2 93% of all fatal car accidents in the United States are caused by human error.

3 Between 30,000 and 40,000 people are killed in car accidents in the United States every year.

4 As of Spring 2019, there are at least forty major corporations working on self-driving car technologies.

STATEWIDE TRAFFIC COLLISIONS KILL NEARLY 1,800 MOTORISTS IN CALIFORNIA

Los Angeles, CA – At least 1,800 people died yesterday in traffic accidents across California in what Caltrans officials are referring to as a "technical glitch," according to a representative from Governor Fairchild's office.

"At approximately four o'clock yesterday afternoon, what appears to be a freak technical glitch in the Statewide Intelligent Transportation System (SITS) caused over 7,000 traffic accidents throughout the state," the state representative added. "The timing of tens of thousands of signalized intersections throughout California, typically handled by local agencies, was taken over two months ago by the SITS. The Super Six are looking further into this unfortunate and regretful incident."

The Super Six, led by civil engineer Dr. Jake Bendel under the direction of the US Department of Transportation, are responsible for the implementation of a separate, nationwide self-driving network known as the "Sûr System," or SS, and are generally considered the "Top Gun" of transportation, legal, ethical, and psychological experts in the country.

Dr. Bendel, who resides in Upland, was unavailable for comment.

CHAPTER 1

JUNE 9, 2023
Los Angeles

Deep inside the Federal Building, FBI Special Agent Jose Cavanaugh huddled with several other agents around a flat screen TV, listening to the distorted ramblings of a female reporter as crackled audio came and went. The bottom of the screen displayed an ABC-7 logo and read 4:09 p.m. The Sky-7 copter, which provided the source of the feed, swerved right to avoid hitting one of the other dozen aircraft hovering above the unfolding freeway scene in West Los Angeles, mere blocks away.

"Carnage," reporter Nicole Freemonte said. "From up here, we're looking down at an apocalyptic scene of twisted metal, smoke, and chaos along seven miles of the 405 freeway." Her voice, normally pleasant, comforting, and professional, had deteriorated into that choking sound people make when they experience gut-wrenching pain, trying not to break down at the sight of true terror. "Thousands of vehicles lie in a mangled sea of destruction that is, from what I'm told by our fact-checking crew, incomparable to any traffic accident in the history of the US."

Cavanaugh shook his head. *First the statewide SITS nightmare, and now this.*

People struggled, crawling over lifeless vehicles, waving their arms to garner attention from the souls suspended above them.

Nicole continued, "To get a better sense of the magnitude of what appears to be a terrorist attack on thousands of innocent civilian drivers using the new Sûr System, let's turn it over now to our reporter on the ground, Bobby Jones. Bobby?" She sounded relieved to pass the attention to a different reporter.

The reporter stood on the shoulder of the 405 freeway, facing south, wearing a white dress shirt and blue tie with slicked-back hair and thin-rimmed glasses. The bloodbath behind him filled the majority of the frame. Sweat trickled down his brow, and he wiped his forehead. A woman cried in the background. A shriek rang out from an unseen man, "Help me!"

"Nicole, the scene down here is pure chaos. In all my years of reporting, I've never—" A truck-sized fireball exploded a few hundred yards behind the reporter, rattling the camera. Bobby ducked, turning his head. A fraction of a second later, a booming clap of thunder forced him to his knees.

"Jesus, that's the second explosion in five minutes," Cavanaugh said, leaning forward to turn up the volume on the TV.

The cloud behind Bobby mushroomed as he straightened up and looked around, smudges of charcoal on his right shoulder and left cheek, his microphone shaking in his hand. "We, uh, sorry, I . . ." he cleared his throat, laughing under his breath. "We're here on-site at what reminds me of"—he paused and raised his eyebrows— "a war zone. That explosion came from one of dozens of tanker trucks caught in the pileup." He extended his trembling arm. "Miles and miles of tangled cars and trucks sit motionless here on the 405 freeway. The scene is like one giant junkyard of death and destruction. Emergency crews are skirting the perimeter, trying to tend to the wounded, but I'm told they're having a difficult time getting to the inner lanes."

The camera panned away from Bobby and zoomed in to an upside-down green Smart Coupe with a caved-in roof. At first, the shot appeared fuzzy, but when the cameraman focused the lens, it revealed the partially decapitated head of a woman. The camera jerked away, back to Bobby.

Cavanaugh muted the TV, shook his head. "Too late."

✳

August 10, 2023

Jake designed the Sûr System to save lives, but some bastard had gone and weaponized the damned thing.

The SITS nightmare three months ago was only the beginning. The terrorists cloaked themselves well. Even the papers reported it as a glitch. Jake had a theory. SITS had been a test run. A warmup.

It made the second attack in June, the one using the Sûr System, that much worse. And, when no one had answers, they needed someone to blame. So Jake had ended up here.

Wherever 'here' was.

From brilliant engineer to suspected terrorist. Just like that.

The interior of his eight-by-eight room reminded Jake of a prison cell, with gray paint flakes clinging to the tops of the walls. A fly buzzed, landing on Jake's nose, but he remained still, his mind focused on how to stop the killing. He knew the Sûr System inside and out. Someone must have set up a back door into the code.

Jake's mind shifted focus to Cynthia, his wife of twenty-five years. He missed the way her hazel eyes sparkled when she smiled. They had never been apart longer than two days. Until now.

The fly buzzed away, then Jake sat upright on the clumpy, two-inch thick mattress and inhaled the scent of charred wood from the sooty dress shirt he'd worn since his arrival six days ago. Feeling abandoned, he assumed the FBI had forgotten to get him a change of clothes. Or they didn't care.

Standing, his back cracked as he stroked his stubble. A sense of determination devolved into frustration, made its way down to his hand, and balled into a fist before he punched a hole through the drywall. *Pain is good*, he thought, craning his head downward to his bloodied, shaking fingers.

After closing his eyes and leaning against the wall, clouds of depression swirled inside his tired brain, mixing with distant memories of his wife dancing in her favorite yellow dress, the curls in her hair bouncing whenever she tipped her head back to laugh. With his palms pressed against his eyes, he imagined the faces of the thousands of people killed by his Sûr System.

He resumed doing calculations in his mind, imaginary code floating in front of his face, like a personal hologram, courtesy of his semi-photographic memory. A gift and a curse. As a member of the Super Six, he'd worked countless hours on the algorithm, with his memory protecting key pieces of code.

Sirens suddenly screamed throughout. With emergency strobe lights flashing, Jake hustled to the door and yanked on the handle.

"Roger that, getting him now," yelled the ex-football-playing, beer-gutted agent jogging toward Jake's room.

Jake put his hands over his ears and yelled. "Looks like I finally won the lottery."

"Bomb threat. Gotta move your ass down to the basement."

A bruise on Jake's upper arm jolted with pain as the agent clamped on, manhandling Jake down the hall. Sleep had been hard to come by, with unresolved issues colliding in his brain of the SITS nightmare, his family, the Sûr System attack and the reasons behind his pseudo-incarceration. The passageway turned right, taking both men down several flights of stairs before dead-ending at an oversized metal security door. A box near them buzzed, and the massive steel door clicked.

The agent swung open the door, but Jake hesitated, darkness staring back at him. "In you go, Dr. Bendel," the agent said, shoving Jake, who staggered into the bunker, tripped, and crashed down into a small wooden table, hitting his head.

"For your own safety." Lights flickered on before the door shrieked and slammed shut, jolting Jake's bones.

After shaking his head, a floating image appeared in the

air above him of Cynthia, wearing her yellow dress. He briefly wondered how hard he'd hit his head but decided he didn't care and spoke to her shakily. "Help me, baby. I need you more than ever."

"You know what you need to do, sweetheart. But wait for the right time," she said, her voice as smooth and calm as ever.

CHAPTER 2

Jake wiped a warm liquid from an angry cut above his eye. Blood.

He studied the four cracked concrete walls around him. "Not much of an upgrade," he mumbled to himself, looking around.

The alarm sirens and lights stopped and seconds later keys clanked on the door, then it swung open with a loud screech. He squinted toward the doorway. A man, dressed in a black suit with a white shirt and a slim black tie, stood next to the manhandling agent. The stranger had the presence of a handsome leader, with his chiseled jaw, high cheekbones, deep penetrating eyes, and tan skin. *A man in a suit always has something to sell you.*

Jake backed himself into a corner, arms across his chest. "I'm stuck in a bomb shelter and now one of the guys from X-Files shows up. Great." No response. He took a step forward. "Where's my wife?"

Suit-man flashed his picture ID and shield and responded, "Dr. Jake Bendel, I'm Special Agent Cavanaugh with the FBI.

We received a credible tip someone had planted a bomb at this facility with the intention of neutralizing you."

Jake studied the credentials, then looked up at Cavanaugh. "You mean . . . kill me?"

Cavanaugh shifted his weight, cocked his head, and narrowed his eyes. "Yes."

Jake uncrossed his arms. "Isn't a safehouse supposed to be … safe?"

Cavanaugh looked to the ground, nodding. "We'll have to get to that later."

"Regardless, I'm a civil engineer. I design and construct roads, bridges, interchanges, stuff like that. Nobody would want to kill me."

Cavanaugh paused, rubbing his chin. "That may be true, but you seem to be the one responsible for one, two, possibly three, terrorist attacks."

"Bologna. I didn't do anything. And why hasn't anyone come by and told me all this until now? I've been in this damned place for almost a week."

"I know, and I apologize. We've been a bit, well, distracted."

Jake furrowed his brow, frustration coming to a head after a week in isolation. "Then tell me why you're holding me here like some goddamned criminal." He crossed his arms and took a wide stance, contemplating how someone with his notoriety, strong level of patriotism, and friends in high places could possibly be shunned to some random outpost. He needed to get the hell out of there and make sure his family was safe.

"You're not technically a prisoner, Dr. Bendel. You're being held here for your own safety." Cavanaugh turned to the other agent and waved his hand. "That'll be enough. I'll take it from here." Extending his hand to shake Jake's, he said, "I know you have a ton of questions for me."

"Again, let's start with exactly where 'here' is," Jake said, trying to act tougher than he felt. His ribs cried out with pain at every spoken word.

"You're in a secure location."

"Jesus. Let's rewind a minute and come back to reality. First of all, I don't know what in God's name a 'secure location' means." Jake thought for a moment and raised his eyebrows. "I'm assuming this is a safehouse."

The agent nodded once. "A secure, secret location. That makes this bomb threat all the more troubling. I'm honestly not sure how the anonymous tipster even found out about this place. I suspect we might have a leak, but that's my problem, not yours."

"Okay. Tell me how my wife and daughter are doing."

"Your country appreciates all you've done," he said. "I would've come sooner, but couldn't, not with the heat on us politically to find the people responsible for the attacks. And now with this bomb threat . . ." Cavanaugh said.

"You didn't answer my question."

"I know you must be pretty confused and upset, and I'm afraid I have some bad news. Let's sit down." They sat on two plastic chairs. "Dr. Bendel, I'm afraid your wife has been killed. I'm very sorry. Her body was found at the fire where you received your award. We suspect foul play."

Jake struggled to suck in oxygen as his vision spun around

and around and around. It took him a long time—perhaps seconds, perhaps minutes, he had no idea—to form the next words. A pain throbbed in his chest. In a broken whisper, he said, "Carlie. I—I have to tell Carlie. Someone has to tell Carlie."

His daughter, Carlie, was a mature, free-spirited, loving, and intelligent twenty-five-year-old drama queen who'd worked full time in the theater department at Cal State San Bernardino since she'd completed her undergrad degree. With the terrorist attacks and Jake's weeklong stay at the Hotel-FBI, he'd been worried about her and his wife between calculations.

Jake remembered filling her childhood with ample family time, picnics at the park, camping trips to Big Bear, soccer games on Saturday mornings, and more. The family of three had enjoyed spending time with one another and Jake knew that he and Cynthia had been exceptional, loving parents who had raised a strong woman, but he knew Carlie would be a mess.

He remembered his wedding day, how happy Cynthia was. Her curly blonde hair, smooth skin, and her smile—oh, her smile. The urge to fight something—anything—grew strong in his belly, growing stronger each passing second.

"Your daughter has been, well, we'll get to her in a minute. I'm afraid there's more bad news."

Jake stood, flooded by more memories of his wife, the amazing, stunning, gorgeous, playful way she looked at him the moment she said "Yes" to his marriage proposal oh so long ago. *No!* "There must be a mistake. I was just with her at the gala. We were drinking and dancing and ..." Jake's memories of that evening a week ago faded into an abyss. He had no recollection of coming to the safehouse. Did someone drug him?

"We believe the fire at the convention center was intentional. A targeted attack."

"Targeting what?"

"Not what. Who. I believe you were one of the targets, Dr. Bendel, so I need you to focus." Jake, with tears forming and threatening to break free, lower lip quivering, turned to Cavanaugh. "Look, the press received copies of videos, photos, and documents that seem to prove you had a grudge against the federal government, the liberal agenda, Democrats, and a host of other organizations. Most of the guys here at the bureau think you're involved." Jake's heart thumped and climbed up into his throat and when he tried to inhale, he only choked, coughing. "The press and public have already convicted you as a terrorist and I'm one of the few people on earth who knows you're innocent. I think it's a bunch of Deep Fake crap, but haven't been able to prove it yet."

Jake beat a fist onto his chest to coax his lungs to expand. After several seconds without air, he finally drew in a massive inhale and bent over, still coughing, gagging on the right-left-combo of bad news.

Cavanaugh continued. "Each of the major news networks received some pretty damning evidence that proved you were responsible for major crimes, the largest being the attack on the 405, but also you paying off state employees to gain access to the network mainframe, and audio evidence with the

Federal Highways administrator about killing people using the self-driving system. All the recordings were studied by industry experts and determined to be legitimate."

Shaking his head, he said, "Unbelievable."

"But I'm here to enlist your much-needed expertise. You're gonna come work with us as part of a clandestine operation. I've already worked out all the details—we've even faked your death—and will be your primary handler. I can't tell you how critical your involvement is to helping us stop these guys before they strike again."

Jake wiped his eyes, then stared into the agent's stoic brown eyes, trying to figure the guy out. Up until a week ago, Jake's beliefs in the strength and righteousness of the federal government were intact. He loved his country, but after what he had been through, his faith had been shattered like a broken mirror and he had no desire to pick up the pieces. Too much government. Too much abuse of power. Too much waste. *How could such an incompetent group of idiots find the people responsible for the attacks?*

Since his incarceration at the safehouse, Jake had been consumed with coming up with a plan to get out, identify and locate the backdoor to the code, and plug the hole in order to prevent the same thing from happening again. Now he also needed to prove his innocence, which took a back seat to wanting to find his wife, care for her, love her, tell her everything would be okay. He struggled to stay focused on the tasks at hand, willing himself to push his instincts for Cynthia aside, convincing himself he'd have more time later to grieve. His guts wrapped up tight inside his belly and the various conflicting thoughts wrangled deep in his mind. This Cavanaugh guy could help get him the resources he needed to make that happen, even though Agent Wonderful could probably care less about who's actually responsible. *No, I gotta get to a PC and fix this. Me. All by myself. Without this Cavanaugh guy.*

"For your own safety, I need you to come with me right now." He motioned toward the door, but Jake took a step backward suddenly feeling how uncomfortable his dress shoes were.

"The last thing I remember was attending the awards gala at the Long Beach Convention Center with my wife and the other members of the Super Six. Then I woke up in this so-called safehouse."

The other agent reappeared with a clean blue-and-white-striped shirt, pants, socks, and sneakers. "Here," Cavanaugh said, "put these on. You'll feel better."

Jake uncrossed his arms and accepted the stack. He slid the stained shirt and pants off his bruised body and worked a pair of loose-fitting jeans onto his legs before buttoning the golf shirt and slipping on the pair of socks and running shoes. The feeling of clean clothes reminded him of the comforts of home but quickly faded as images of his wife and daughter again consumed his thoughts. Jake swallowed and followed the agent out of the bomb shelter to a dim locker room.

"This is a med tech. She's gonna get you patched up before we leave," Cavanaugh said, motioning to a petite woman standing next to him. "I'll be right back," he said before exiting the room.

The medical technician stepped toward Jake and he got a

whiff of rubbing alcohol. In less than a minute, she had wiped dried blood from Jake's face and bandaged his forehead.

The obese agent cuffed Jake's hands in front of him. The handcuffs were the Peerless brand, the same he'd played around with as a young boy.

Two men, one on each side of Jake, escorted him several dozen yards, with various doors opening and closing. They ascended dozens of stairs, up a steep incline before entering an elevator, as Jake wiped several Cynthia tears from his cheeks.

Wonderful. Another tight, enclosed space, he thought. His motion sickness always kicked in when he rode in elevators. A vivid memory came into focus of his six-year-old self being thrown into his mother's dryer before they changed dryer doors to open from the inside. The babysitter's boyfriend, aka the neighborhood bully, had held the door shut with his leg while laughing, and then he pushed the "ON" button. Crying and screaming, Jake had spun around several times before vomiting all over himself. He hit his head on the inner flap and the concussion knocked him out, but he remembered the event like it happened yesterday.

His palms dripped with sweat, his insides twisting and gurgling, as he leaned against the wall of the elevator and continued breathing in through his nose, out through his mouth.

The elevator doors creaked open and he stumbled forward with his two escorts for several seconds before they all stopped. The smell of dirt and horse manure wafted past. An agent's hand guided Jake's head into a vehicle, ducking to miss the door jamb. But Jake, at six-foot-three-inches tall, bumped his knee on the floor as he entered an SUV. *Thanks for the help, jerk.*

Agent Cavanaugh verbally dismissed the other men.

Between heavy breaths, Jake asked, "Where the hell are we going?"

"Calm down, Dr. Bendel. We're just taking a short drive."

Jake thought he heard his wife's voice and, for the briefest of moments, imagined her sitting next to him. "Cynthia?" No response.

Jake shook his head. *I must be hallucinating. Try talking.* He said to Cavanaugh, "You mentioned earlier about attacks. Plural."

"You need to trust me."

Jake shifted in the back seat and paused. "Of course I'm supposed to trust you. Maybe you're the one who caused the leak. You're your own mole. Or the one who tried to blow me up. No way I'm gonna be blackmailed into working with the FBI." Jake knew he had a weak negotiating position, but gave the civil-rights angle a try. "I'm an innocent American citizen and, the last I checked, I have rights."

"Not anymore. Since Congress passed the Homeland Security Act in 2002, a ton of rights for American citizens disappeared. Poof. Gone. This is no longer as free a country as most people think, but it does give us more tools to catch terrorists. Especially if they're labeled an enemy combatant."

"Let me guess. I've been labeled an—"

"Yes, but either way, we're not here for a civics lesson."

"Thank God."

The car hit a bump in the road and swerved to the right.

Jake struggled to keep from rolling onto his side.

"What I can tell you is that your colleagues from the Super Six project, all five of them, are dead, which means there's no one left to corroborate your story. If we make one false move, the media will put the FBI in their crosshairs, too, and blame us, like they did with you. That's unacceptable."

CHAPTER 3

While sitting in the rear of the speeding FBI SUV, Cavanaugh's news bludgeoned Jake yet again. "No." He lowered his head in disbelief, thinking about his coworkers at the Super Six. "Those were my friends." He pictured each of their faces as memories flashed in his mind of their work together over the last several years. Like when he and Dr. Feenster, the tall, blond, athletic mechanical engineer, had the same idea at the same exact time about the communication towers, and they went out drinking that night to celebrate. Or way back at the start, when he first met Mr. Stenner, the security expert, and they didn't hit it off with each other and were in constant conflict until their heart-to-heart discussion that cleared the air. From that moment on they were best buddies, going to each other's Christmas parties, summer barbeques, and family get-togethers. In all, they were part of a successful team.

Grief drained his motivation as only grief can. He scratched his jaw. "How'd they all die?"

"We don't have time to get into details right now. Let's stay focused. There was another attack I don't think you're aware of."

Son of a bitch. With pursed lips, he asked, "With the Sûr System?"

"Thank God, no. Exactly one week ago, on four August, there was an attempt on Archbishop Cardinal Mahony's life, the same day as the attempt on yours. At 6:00 p.m. the Archbishop was riding in a limo on the I-10 freeway, heading west, south of the Staples Center, when there was an accident similar to the CDM attack."

"No idea what you're talking about. 'CDM?'"

"That's what everyone's been calling the I-405 attack on 9 June. It's an acronym for three Latin words, *Celer, Desino, Mortis*, which roughly translates to fast, stop, death. Some mucky-muck Harvard professor came up with the term and used it during an interview a couple weeks after, and it stuck. I guess because the drivers on the freeway were traveling fast and were forced to stop in a hurry. Now, everyone's calling the 405 incident the CDM attack. Most people don't even know what CDM stands for."

Their SUV hit more bumps in the road, but this time, Jake managed to sit straight.

Cavanaugh continued. "Only three vehicles were involved, one belonged to the Catholic church, but the bishop survived. The media referred to the incident as the Miracle on Tuesday."

Jake's mind searched its recesses for information.

Cavanaugh continued. "Now tell me more about the algorithm you worked on."

Jake paused a moment. "I designed major parts of it."

"Dr. Bendel, I don't understand any of the technical details, and since you're the only surviving member of the Super Six, I want to know how, in less than ten seconds, seven miles of traffic on the I-405 turned into one huge-ass clusterfuck."

"What day did the Mahony attack happen?" Jake asked, ignoring the agent's request.

"4 August. Tuesday."

"Exactly the same day as the fire at the Long Beach gala. If my calculations are correct, today is the tenth." *Which means I was stuck in that damned safehouse for six days.* "I wonder if there've been any other attacks that might be related."

"Four attacks so far. Five if you include the fire at your Long Beach gala, but we haven't officially linked the incidents. The first was the green lights incident on May 5, the one that killed about eighteen hundred people at various roadway intersections throughout California. Caltrans is sticking to its story about a technical glitch with the SITS, but we don't buy it."

"The other five members of the Super Six and I investigated that," Jake said. "Instead of alternating red and green, the intersections all turned to simultaneous green lights. Since drivers thought they had the right of way—BAM—massive collisions. I'll bet you have stronger evidence that might lead to finding who hacked into the system and caused these accidents on purpose."

"Working on some theories."

Jake swallowed down a thick chunk of dried saliva. "Doesn't make sense to me that whoever is responsible for the attacks is going after smaller targets. I thought crazy people normally morphed into stronger aggressors, getting ballsier with each attack."

"That's a scenario we've considered but don't have an answer to yet."

"Other than the Deep Fake material, is there any specific evidence that proves I'm the bad guy?" Jake felt the inner turmoil irritating his stomach.

"No. But the videos are pretty convincing. Based on them, you were involved in the planning and implementation of both of SITS and CDM attacks."

Jake nodded. "Both of the attacks. Wonderful." His panic jumped up to a new level. Tears formed in his eyes. *Men don't cry*—his dad's voice blazed at him.

The sound of high-speed wind made its way to the rear of the vehicle as Jake watched the freeway and desert surroundings zip past. "We anticipated and prepared for hacking attempts. There should've been no way for anybody to bypass the security protocols for the federal mainframe where we stored the code, let alone tamper with the algorithm. The best cyber-security experts in the world worked on it," Jake said, not believing what Cavanaugh was telling him.

"People are like sheep. They believe what they see on TV, whether it's right or wrong. Nothing based on science or facts matters to them, only opinions. Fact: you were framed, but the masses didn't see your side of the story, they only saw what the media showed them. Therefore, in the minds of three hundred million people, you're guilty."

"Un-frickin'-believable." Jake buried his head in his clasped hands. "I've been trying for years to help millions of people I've never met, and now these same people think I'm guilty because of some crap they read in the press."

"Welcome to America."

"The Super Six group that I worked with consisted of myself and five of the most elite scientific and engineering experts in the country. We were tasked by the president via the US Department of Transportation to lead a team to develop an implementation strategy upgrading America's human-controlled vehicular transportation system—freeways only—to a fully automated one. The new, national self-driving network had been named 'Sûr System,' which more or less means 'Safe System' in French. Not that you'd know any French."

"I know all that and matter of fact, I do."

"Good for you. Two reasons justified the need and purpose of the proposal: first, to prevent accidents and save the lives of thirty to forty thousand people killed annually in traffic accidents, and second, to eliminate all traffic congestion throughout the United States, which the team calculated would be a multi-trillion-dollar steroid injection to the US economic engine. Too much technology already existed *not* to implement it. The nation's leaders saw it as a bold and politically unfavorable move, but the benefits outweighed the costs by multiples of a hundred."

"I'm well aware of your role, Dr. Bendel," Cavanaugh said with increased volume, half-craning his neck toward the rear seat. "The press started referring to your system as the 'SS' and have been making Nazi wisecracks."

"No," Jake said, clenching his jaw.

Jake remembered his stomach churning when he watched the news about the attack later referred to as the CDM, apparently. Six thousand people—dead—same as a small war. He recalled dozens of helicopters hovering above the carnage on live TV. "And that was just the seven-mile stretch of I-405 between the 101 and I-10," he said in a hushed voice. His head felt like it had marbles bouncing around inside. The Super Six initially thought the accident had been caused by some kind of technical hiccup. "Right after the first accident happened, I calculated about a hundred and seventy-five thousand cars and trucks traveling there that day, all with the standard computer-controlled, two-foot gap between them." Jake clasped his hands together in his lap. "Vehicles that close to each other and moving at precisely sixty-five miles per hour would've never been possible without the network algorithm and the autopilot systems that our team and other driverless car companies developed."

The nationwide system had been set to self-driving mode or "automatic" control in late April, and the corresponding benefits stunned even the most ardent opponents. Results had proved far better than expected. In a typical month of May, about three thousand people would have been killed nationwide on America's freeways. This most recent May, however, only eighteen people were killed, a 99.4 percent decrease. Economists were hustling around trying to calculate the financial benefits to the various industries that used the highways, like the trucking industry and anything related to shipping. Local drivers were amazed at how fast they could get from one side of Los Angeles to the other, at any time of day, and without the added stress or risk of a possible car accident.

The sound of a motorcycle, maybe a Harley, zoomed by them on the left. The cool air from the air conditioner felt good on Jake's skin.

"There's absolutely no way someone could have hacked the mainframe that controlled the traffic flow," Cavanaugh said.

"And you're basing that assumption on what? You play first-person shooter games with your kids, and now you're some kind of computer expert? Who the heck told you that?"

No response.

"When it comes to cyber-security, mathematically speaking, nothing's foolproof," Jake added. "Christ, you're the FBI, you already know this, but there's always a way. I know. It's highly unlikely with the security systems we put in place, but possible."

"Meaning what?"

Speaking through his teeth with forced restraint and frustration, Jake replied, "Meaning I'm sitting here in the back of some car, handcuffed, with a theory that explains what happened and who's behind what you're referring to as the CDM attack. Not that I have a choice, but I'd prefer to work on my own, without the FBI. I need to get to a computer to find out if the safeguards we built into the system worked as designed."

"Soon, Dr. Bendel."

"Besides the SITS, CDM, and attacks on the Cardinal, were there others?"

Cavanaugh exhaled. "Two others. The fourth attack occurred on 30 June, three weeks before the attack on the bishop, which I'll get to in a second. Not sure if you remember those five buses that careened off the road at the Del Mar Racing track. Of the seventy-six people on board the buses, thirty-four were killed, and twenty-four thoroughbred horses were also taken out. That happened on 21 July, three weeks ago from tomorrow."

Jake shook his head and shifted in his seat.

"The attack on the bishop's life was the fifth incident and it happened on 4 August, again, one week ago," Cavanaugh said. "And the fourth one was on 30 June, an Airbus plane crashed into the tower at San Bernardino International Airport. The FBI hasn't officially connected these events. They're all pretty different and, quite frankly, random."

Jake furrowed his brow. "You tell me how the hell the incident involving the racehorses is related to roadway fatalities and an attempt on a religious figurehead."

"To be honest, I'm not a hundred percent sure if this incident is related to the others, but it feels connected. If they are related, I'm worried. It's too much of a coincidence," Cavanaugh said.

"Not seeing any pattern." Jake pictured the timeline in his head:

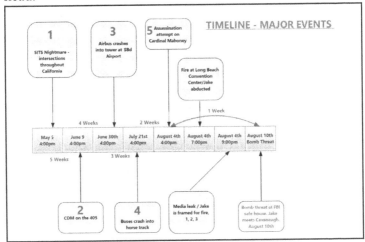

"There isn't one, not at first glance. But assuming they are related, whoever or whatever is responsible is getting more and more confident each time."

Jake scratched a sudden itch atop his head. Images of Cynthia coughing, choking, crying, suffering . . . he'd had enough.

"You're the goddamned FBI." He pointed his finger at Cavanaugh. "It's your job to figure out who's behind this crap. I'm a civil engineer, not a cop, not a spy. You have a bazillion people at your beck and call. Why the hell do we pay all those goddamned taxes if you want private citizens to do your job for you?"

"Tell me your theory, Dr. Bendel."

With a bitter chuckle, Jake said, "Nice try."

Cavanaugh slammed on the brakes, forcing Jake's body to smash into the seat in front of him as Cavanaugh exited the vehicle. A half-second later, Jake's door opened and Cavanaugh sat next to him.

"You were unconscious when I grabbed you from the convention center fire that killed your wife, five friends, and fourteen other people. None of those people made it out alive, but you did, thanks to me. Me. Now everyone thinks you're dead, except the conspiracy theorists."

"I get it. I think."

Cavanaugh patted Jake on the shoulder. "I've been working my ass off to help you and figure this out, Dr. Bendel, and I'm sticking my neck out and really need your help."

Out of breath, Jake said, "I'm sorry. I just . . ."

Cavanaugh exited and stood, leaning back in. "I'm trusting you, now I need you to trust me."

Jake nodded, Cavanaugh got back in and they drove off.

In a professional tone, Cavanaugh said, "For what it's worth, we held a funeral for you last Saturday and over five hundred people attended. You were well-liked."

A smile inched to one side of Jake's face.

"Initially," Cavanaugh continued, "there was rampant speculation in the media that you survived and were on the run. Not sure how that information leaked out, but either way, without a body to prove your death, we had our work cut out for us. For the most part, we managed to get things under control by doing our standard 'no comment' routine and supplying those media hounds with alternative forms of evidence to get them off your trail."

"This is a nightmare. I need to wake up. A bad dream, that's all."

CHAPTER 4

Viktor sat on an old wooden chair in the living room corner of his log cabin nestled deep in the evergreened foothills of Sugarloaf, three miles east of Big Bear Lake in Southern California. A dying fire crackled in front of the bare feet of the balding, white-haired man. With his arms crossed over a loose-hanging white cotton undershirt, he swayed back and forth.

No sane person needed a fire in August.

Viktor Johnston continued rocking his sixty-two-year-old tanned body while turning his head to squint, looking outside through a dull, calcified windowpane. Instead of the dead grass and summer flowers that any normal person would see, a hallucination of snow drifted down to earth from a mad sky. In Viktor's eyes, three feet of God's powder, the same color as his hair, had fallen on the ground. An apparition of his dead mother, who'd raised him to be a good Christian boy in rural Texas, took shape on a nearby hill. She wore a pink-and-orange-flowered dress. A thin layer of snowflakes gathered on top of her shoulders and curly brown hair. He made eye contact with her, and a sense of calm came over him.

Still rocking, streaks of black running throughout his gray beard, he relished the warmth and sound of the fire as it crackled, but pondered the reality of his mother's opaque image outside.

His head pounded with pain, so he unfolded his arms and rubbed the temples of his once handsome face. He opened his eyes, arched his back, looked up, and laughed. A moment later, he squeezed them shut, smiling as bubbles of saliva oozed down his chin and beard.

With his head cocked back, his eyes popped open again and he stared at the stained wood ceiling. Arms stretched wide, he cried out to his god, "I've done everything you asked, taken care of it all. Please, Lord, make this intolerable pain stop."

Over the years, four separate incompetent doctors had diagnosed him as a psychopath, but he knew there was nothing wrong. His god spoke to Viktor using different voices because Viktor was a genius. Special.

Today the voice of his god was relentless, booming louder and louder, commanding Viktor to stick with the plan, to bring this country to its knees and make Americans suffer. *Kill the sin-worshipers. Kill the infidels. Kill them all.*

Viktor relished knowing about the secret modifications to the SS algorithm. And the upcoming attacks. Oh, the genius behind his perfect plan, four years in the making. Despite the unbearable pain in his skull, he smiled and nibbled on his lower lip.

Some days he felt invincible, like the world was in the palm of his hands, ready for him to manipulate any way he saw fit. Other days, when he spent sunrise to sunset in bed or sitting in a chair as he did now, Allah's voice would shout louder than ever. Crazy loud. Like standing next to a moving train filled with drill sergeants. His god enjoyed reminding Viktor of the unmet expectations his mother had for him. "Auditory hallucinations" a therapist had called them over thirty years ago. *Whatever.*

Only one way existed to make Allah's voice stop: cooperation. Do as he instructed. Whenever Viktor ignored the voice—which was rare—Allah would force him to self-mutilate as penance. Sinners must be punished—severely—so it behooved Viktor to acquiesce to his demands. Scars covered Viktor's arms and back, a result of his previous noncompliance with commands from Allah. If Viktor questioned Allah's commands, Allah was quick to remind him his soul would face eternal damnation in Satan's grasp unless he complied.

Concepts of right and wrong had been twisted and contrived in his conscience. The US of A needed a prescription-strength enema to flush out the sin-worshipers and infidels. Viktor had the right medicine to cure the ailing country, and he wanted to do his part to ensure the infidels suffered. After all, that was Allah's wish.

He stood, inhaled a lungful of stagnant air, waited for the brief dizziness to pass, then walked to his bedroom. On the floor next to his bed lay an old iron and oak chest. He spun the correct combination on the five-number lock and opened the lid to reveal a dozen cardboard boxes full of history. He picked up the one labeled "Syed," rummaged through the contents, and pulled out a yellowed envelope with worn, tattered edges dated four years ago. The letter, from someone who claimed to be his true brother, contained an email address and a request to meet.

Viktor remembered how he had first met the man outside a Pomona mosque. At their third meeting, the man, Syed Rezwan Farook, had worn a white kurta with long sleeves. His black beard was trimmed short and neat over smooth olive skin, and his face showed signs of many hours in the sun. "As-Salaamu-Alaikum, my long-lost brother," the man had said, extending his hand to shake Viktor's.

"Peace be onto you, too."

With steady eye contact, Syed had said, "I understand you still have concerns over the validity of my claim that we have the same mother and father. Perhaps this will help." Syed pulled out an old photograph, a handwritten birth certificate, and an old paper that looked like a contract written in Arabic, which Viktor had learned years earlier as part of a temporary engineering job in Egypt.

Viktor had studied the documents and recognized the woman, with her green eyes and raven hair, in the photo. Goosebumps popped up on his forearms and he felt a strong connection to her, even though, if the man's claims were correct, Viktor had been sold as a six-month-old baby.

"You were going to have a DNA test done. I don't see a report here," Viktor said.

Syed then opened a different folder and produced a full-page clasped orange envelope that contained two semi-opaque papers from a report, each with graphs of lines, bars, and dots. He'd overlaid one on top of the other. A perfect sibling match.

With a thick Arabic accent, the alleged relative said, "You see, my brother, we are related. Allah has given us this DNA test to confirm the truth, and this contract here is the one signed by our father when you were sold to your American family over sixty years ago." Syed had then opened his arms and welcomed a hug from Viktor, and the two men embraced.

Since that meeting, the faith of Islam had marinated deep into Viktor's soul and overshadowed—even erased—his earlier Christian beliefs. His Caucasian mother, who would have despised any sort of killing, had beat the love of Jesus Christ into him, but the prophet Mohammed had beat it out.

On occasion, Viktor queried Allah for his insight as to the reasons and wisdom for terrorizing the infidels. Each time, the same response from Allah: the time had come to purge the American society of Satan's flock from within. He relished in the privilege and honor of bathing in the Glory of Allah for already completing five glorious terrorist attacks. Viktor had done a commendable job, Allah had told him, but the best was yet to come. Many more must die for the cause. His mother had appeared in the kitchen, shaken her finger at him, and told him she was disappointed.

Praise Allah.

Viktor returned the letter to the trunk and closed the lid. He said to himself in a hushed voice, "If those atheist bastards thought the CDM attack was bad, six thousand of those American infidels banished from existence with one click on my cell phone, wait till they see what I have planned next. Will be fucking beautiful."

He wiped the saliva from his chin as he walked in a circle

and laughed. Who could stop him? Those six so-called scientists were dead. What a bunch of morons. Even that arrogant, pompous-ass civil engineer, Jakey Boy, the one Viktor's media friends framed for everything, had died.

Viktor had enjoyed toying with Jake the same way cats chase red laser dots, so he'd experienced short-lived feelings of regret after hearing Jake's death confirmed. Although glad the asshole could no longer threaten the ultimate plan, Viktor missed the game. He missed—

"Viktor. Viktor. Shame on you," Allah boomed, louder than ever. *"Shame on you. You know what happens when you take pride in MY accomplishments!"*

Viktor covered his ears and dropped to his knees. "No, no. I'm sorry, I'm sorry." Tears welled up in his eyes.

He rose, ran as fast as possible back to his corner and sat down on the little wooden chair.

The voice added, *"Do this now and do not get caught, Viktor. With the Super Six gone, I will send a message the world will never forget. Give the infidels a wake-up call. We will prevent the further weakening of the moral spine of your country. I will run the show. Our next act will set the world on edge, Viktor. Do not let me down."*

Tears streamed down his cheeks, and he stood and ran around in circles, arms swinging. With all his heart, he wanted to quell the voice.

Viktor couldn't take anymore yelling. Time to check out.

He slammed his head hard against the wood-paneled wall. His forehead split open on the first try. On the second try, he gave his brain a jolt strong enough to take him to the brink of concussion. He wiped the liquid trickling down his cheeks. Blood mixed with tears. One thought crossed his mind before he knocked himself out on the third bang:

Death. Death to 'em all.

CHAPTER 5

While seated in the rear of a government car, Jake tried to take his mind off his wife. And Carlie. A simple memory, one of the last times his wrists had been handcuffed, popped into his head. As a young boy, he'd enjoyed playing with his friends and practicing breaking out of cuffs with simple tools, like a paperclip or bobby pin. Unfortunately, these tools were unavailable at the moment. Even if he had one, little good it would do with him locked inside a car with an armed agent at the wheel. Plus, he had absolutely no idea of his location or their destination. *Figures.* They'd been treating him like a criminal. After all, he was the one who'd enabled the terrorists in the first place. His book published eight years ago about the theories and practical tips on the design and implementation of self-driving cars had helped spark the transportation revolution.

The unmistakable crushing sounds of jets and the buzzing of turboprop engines filled the air. The vehicle stopped, another man in a suit opened the door, guided Jake's arm to help him exit the vehicle, and escorted him across the tarmac toward a Gulfstream G450 jet.

Ten yards from the car, Jake stopped walking. "No way. I'm not going in there, I still feel sick."

Cavanaugh came up from behind and tried to calm him down. "Yes, you are. We'll just be in the air for a little while." He nudged Jake, and they stepped up the jet bridge and walked to the back of the plane. "Sit down."

Jake sat in a rear holding area of the plane behind a closed door. There were four seats. He and Cavanaugh sat in two of them. The two windows were closed and the plane smelled new. *Government tax dollars at work.*

The thundering sound of jet engines whirred away. The airplane rolled forward, prepared to taxi, then stopped. Jake remembered how most fatal aircraft crashes occur on take-off, and his stomach moved toward his backbone. *Another small space.* So far, the FBI had only succeeded in making him sick. He tried to focus his thoughts on engineering. "Runways for all airports require consistent designs," he recalled Professor Everton telling his transportation-design class one day.

The plane stopped at what could likely be the hold line on the tarmac while the pilot waited for clearance to take the active runway and depart. Jake felt a surge, closed his eyes and pictured the plane as it accelerated down the runway. He envisioned the craft rotating and lifting off the ground.

Images of his wife popped back into his head, and another round of dread hit him. He gritted his teeth and banged his head on the back of his seat. What he wouldn't give to be with Cynthia, resting safely at their second home in Pasadena, holding each other tight in the swimming pool out back, and drinking glasses of chilled Chardonnay from their favorite Central Coast winery.

He opened his eyes and boomeranged back to reality. He

welcomed the dizziness and hoped the plane would crash. End it all right now. Be with his wife again and kiss her sweet lips.

Fifteen minutes into the ride, a forcible shock hit the plane, it dropped, and Jake flew up from his seat, slamming the tops of his thighs into the seatbelt. Someone spoke over the loud-speaker. "Agent Cavanaugh hold on tight. Looks like we've got some turbulence. It's going to be rough for a bit."

An involuntary, low-pitched guttural noise emanated from Jake's mouth as his body convulsed. He couldn't hold back. Puke ejected from Jake's mouth at sixty feet per second, smack dab onto the wall in front of him.

Cavanaugh jumped back, hitting his shoulder on a baggage bin. "Jesus, God, what the hell?"

Jake sensed a small piece of food crawling down his bearded chin as he assessed whether more vomit needed to escape.

Cavanaugh wrinkled his nose and stood to open the door. "Clean yourself up." He threw a handkerchief at Jake before exiting. Jake assumed Cavanaugh went to get cleaning supplies to mop up the mess but didn't see him again for an hour and a half. This left Jake alone to look at and smell the former contents of his stomach as the unending storm tossed him around the entire trip like a ragdoll inside that clothes dryer from his childhood.

They descended and finally touched down in one of the hardest landings Jake had ever experienced.

Cavanaugh returned to the holding area. "Let's go."

After cleaning himself up in the tiny bathroom, they exited the G450, entered a black SUV, and sped away from the airport. In his head, Jake broke down the equations and assumptions that went into the algorithm math, as he recalled a snippet of the presentation he gave to the President of the United States when the Super Six project first launched. How far he'd fallen since then.

With humans at the controls, a limited number of vehicles (about two thousand per hour) can fit through any particular point in a standard traffic freeway lane within a given amount of time. But with computers running the show, what we engineers refer to as the "capacity" of the freeways is increased by a factor of five, and we can make traffic accidents a thing of the past. In California alone, there are over fifty thousand lane miles, so our plan would add the equivalent of about two hundred and fifty thousand lane miles. Since the cost of constructing one lane mile is about two million dollars, automating the freeways in California would be, at a minimum, the equivalent of spending about five hundred billion dollars in freeway upgrades, all without the hassle of going through the environmental process or land acquisition, and at a fraction of the cost.

Nationwide, the economic benefits had been fantastic. Also, in the first month the system was active, the lives of several thousand people were saved. His mind turned inward to Cynthia. *I must have had blinders on. How much more can these incompetent bureaucrats possibly screw this up? If my sweet Cynthia was murdered, whoever killed her is gonna die. Jesus, I'm gonna find him and beat him to death with my bare hands. I don't need to work with some bureaucracy to do what I need to do.* He must have been so focused on saving lives and eliminating traffic congestion that he lost track of what was truly important to him. *I sold the president on an idea that probably and ultimately killed my wife. Great. Real genius, Jake. Hopefully the system is turned off, set back to manual mode and back to the dark ages, so no more terrorist attacks are possible.*

They had driven an hour through desert landscapes when Cavanaugh said, while looking in the rear-view mirror, "Shit. We got company."

The roar of a revving car engine preceded a ramming of the rear of their car, whipping Jake's head back. He shoved his fists down on the seat for leverage, then craned his neck around. A black pickup truck swerved behind them, accelerating before plowing a second time into the back of their SUV, crushing the rear taillights and splattering pieces of red and white plastic across the highway. The rear windshield exploded, giving Jake an unmistakable view of the attacking driver who, with his white knuckles gripping the steering wheel and an angry frown pasted below his dark glasses, continued to push the FBI SUV in an attempt to flip them over.

CHAPTER 6

"Faster. Go faster!" Jake yelled as blurred images of Joshua trees and desert scrub brush zoomed past.

"Already doing ninety," Cavanaugh said as he yanked their car to the right, missing a white delivery truck by inches. Their rear-end fishtailed, tires screeched, and Cavanaugh nearly lost control, but he pointed the wheels in the direction of the swerve and shimmied the wheel to straighten out the SUV. With his shoulder, he wiped the sweat from his brow and kept a solid grip on the wheel.

"Get off this damned freeway. We're sitting ducks out here." Jake turned to see a smoke plume from burned rubber beneath their SUV. The sunglasses-wearing driver stuck his hand out the window, but before Jake could register the man's action, three distinct pops rang out that sounded like M-80 firecrackers. Two holes punctured the rear door and more glass fell away.

"Holy crap, Cavanaugh. They're shooting at us."

"You think?" Cavanaugh hunched over. They zipped by a yellow semi so close Jake could read the bumper sticker on the trailer that read "Haulin' Ass" as it passed out of sight under his forearm. He felt the metal-on-metal scraping against his door. Another near miss with death. The assailants fired four more shots while Jake tried to stabilize himself in the back seat by latching onto the door handle.

A militarized black MD 500 helicopter, similar to the one he flew in years ago with the Highway Patrol as part of the planning for a new freeway in the High Desert, dropped out of the sky a hundred feet in front of them, flying too low to be a news chopper. The hovering beast fired multiple rounds from its onboard Gatling gun. The shots missed Cavanaugh's car but punctured the gas tank of a passing orange Volkswagen Beetle. The ensuing explosion flipped the poor bastard twenty feet in the air. The orange mass landed on its hood and skidded down the highway, entombing the driver.

"Grab your balls, Jake!" Cavanaugh veered right through cattle fencing that lined the freeway shoulder. The car jumped off a dirt berm, and the back of Jake's neck slammed into the ceiling. The heavy engine of their SUV forced the front of the vehicle to dip down while the rear floated ten feet above the ground. They landed at a forty-five-degree decline, crashing the grille of their SUV into a paved frontage road, which buckled the hood. They skidded and hobbled thirty yards before the rear tires slammed to the ground.

Jake tried to grab hold of the front seat to prevent himself from flying out the back window.

The helicopter fired more rounds. Bursts of steam shot out from underneath their SUV hood as dozens of bullets punctured the front half of their ride, forcing Cavanaugh to skid to a stop at a nearby gas station, a cloud of blazing smoke trailing behind them. Flames erupted from under the hood, licking the tops of the two crinkled front fenders. "Quick! Get out and hide behind that trash bin." Cavanaugh exited with his side-arm pulled.

The pursuing truck attempted the same maneuver onto the field at over a hundred miles an hour, but rolled when it hit the berm and tumbled end-over-end four times, ejecting two occupants before landing upside down.

Jake stumbled toward the rusted green three-yard metal trash bin and plopped down behind it. The pungent smell of sewage hit him as he noticed a trail of black gunk oozing from the bottom of the bin onto the boiling-hot concrete. A bobby pin lay submerged in the middle of the trash juice. Jake looked around, picked up the pin, wiped it on his pant leg, and went to work on his handcuffs.

Cavanaugh hustled toward the enemy's wreckage and, based on his body language, discovered both men had been killed, likely on impact. He stood in a Weaver stance and fired several rounds at the helicopter, forcing it to flee the scene. The sound of the helicopter faded away to the east and footsteps approached Jake.

"Roger that, agent is on scene. Send the M.E." Cavanaugh offered his hand. "We're all clear; you can come out now."

Jake squinted and paused for a moment, pondering the recent events. He put his hand up and let Cavanaugh hoist him to his feet. Jake handed Cavanaugh the unlocked handcuffs. "I want to know who those guys are and why they were shooting at us."

Cavanaugh took the handcuffs and rubbed his chin, his head flinching back slightly. He held up the cuffs and looked at them with a furrowed brow before tucking them into his pocket. "So do I. News must've leaked that you're still alive—but they knew our route too." Cavanaugh holstered his weapon. "Only someone inside would've known that."

Before he knew it, Jake found himself sitting in the back of a local police squad car. Over the next half hour, while they waited for a new FBI vehicle, the local sheriff and a dozen law enforcement officers arrived, taped off the crime scene, took statements and photos, and performed their investigation. Cavanaugh helped with the coordination efforts but kept a constant eye on Jake.

The engineer exited, stood and stretched his legs as he walked around. Clean, hot air filled the early afternoon blue sky. Extremely hot. Desert hot. Like 115 degrees. Sweat prickled his forehead and armpits.

He approached Cavanaugh, looking around the desert landscape. He recognized the location and roads. "I'm guessing we're up in the High Desert area of Southern California, just off the I-15, maybe near Victorville."

"We're almost done here. Go sit back down in the patrol car. I don't want anyone to see your face."

"You could always put a hood on me."

Cavanaugh locked eyes with Jake. "Don't test me, Dr. Bendel. Once our new ride arrives, we're gonna take a trip down to the Federal Building in LA. I want you to meet a few people and while we drive, you're going to share details of that theory of yours."

When their replacement vehicle finally arrived, a black Chevy Tahoe, both men hopped in. Cavanaugh fired up the engine and floored it, kicking out sand behind the right rear tire as they accelerated south. Jake's forehead dripped with sweat, and he knew his face was beet red. As the cool blast of air-conditioning pelted his face, he let out a sigh.

"Your file indicated that you're a published author," said Cavanaugh.

They have a file on me?

"I wrote the book after my daughter left for college because I felt empty inside, as though my job as dad had come to an end, and I didn't like the feeling. I wrote to keep my mind off it. Plus, I hoped the book might help reduce my karmic debt, so to speak, if it ended up saving lives."

"Whatever. Guess you never know in life. Either way, you're lucky to be alive. That's twice now I've saved your life."

Jake was still on the fence. "If we're going to work together, I need you to get me in front of a terminal at the FBI mainframe, so I can gain access to the actual server where the transportation algorithm is hosted."

The agent flashed a confident smile. "You're gonna meet a couple of friends of mine at the bureau; we'll see what we can do."

A cell phone rang as they entered the I-15 freeway. "Special Agent Cavanaugh." As Cavanaugh listened, his face grew troubled. "Are you sure? Wilson?" Pause. "No. No, I'm on my way."

Cavanaugh flipped a switch on the dashboard that activated the running lights and sirens. The tires barked and Jake's body slammed against his seat as they accelerated up to over a hundred miles an hour.

"Sounds like an emergency," Jake asked.

"I'll trust you with what's happening, but only if you agree to start trusting me."

Jake thought for a second. The guy did save his life. *What the hell.* Jake nodded. "Fine. Tell me."

"Another agent, a friend of mine named Wilson, is holding my boss hostage, threatening to kill him."

Jake looked out the side window. "You sure have a wonderful work environment set up for me there. Can't wait to join your little circus."

"I'm not sure why, but Wilson's demanding to talk with me. Every second counts."

CHAPTER 7

Despite the arctic air blasting Cavanaugh's face, beads of sweat dripped down his cheeks as the duo exited the 405 at Wilshire Boulevard. *Hope we make it to before Wilson does something stupid.* Cavanaugh had been friends with Wilson for almost two decades and, for the most part, the guy had a solid set, but every now and then he'd come up with these crazy conspiracy theories.

Cavanaugh parked.

"You're coming upstairs with me. Keep a low profile," Cavanaugh said as he and Jake exited the vehicle.

"Walking around in broad daylight like this seems like a great start," Jake replied, hoping Cavanaugh would get his hint at sarcasm.

Half jogging toward a large nondescript building that looked like a giant, gray generic air-conditioning unit, Cavanaugh said, "Some of these people would love nothing more than to have Dr. Bendel's head mounted on a spike. We'll take care of you soon, but gotta focus on this Wilson situation."

They dashed toward the x-ray machine at the security

desk. In a low tone, Cavanaugh said almost in a whisper to Jake, "With the potential mole, I don't trust anyone. Stay close to me." Cavanaugh winked at the security guard, who had a blank stare on his face as though he were in a trance, and grabbed hold of Jake's upper arm. "This is an emergency. He's with me, Frank. He's already been stripped and cleaned." The security guard blinked several times, turned his head toward Cavanaugh, then nodded and waved them through the machine.

Cavanaugh glanced at a newspaper on the guard's desk and scanned the headline in large, bold print, "L.A. STILL STUNNED BY CDM."

Soon they were inside a secure room on the first floor where five agents stood huddled around a stainless-steel table. Cavanaugh slammed the windowless door shut.

"Talk to me, guys," Cavanaugh said.

"Who the hell's this?" One agent pointed at Jake.

"He's with me. Doesn't matter. Tell me what's going on with Wilson."

"He's up on the fourth floor with a gun to Shankle's head. He says he knows what caused the CDM attack," another agent replied.

Jake crossed his arms.

"What are our options at this point? What's the strategy?" Cavanaugh leaned forward, giving an intense gaze to each agent.

"The hostage negotiators haven't been able to get anywhere with him. Wilson wrote half their damned playbook, anyway. He's not threatening to hurt anyone else. We think he snapped.

He's demanding to talk with you and only you, so I think we need to get you up there and see where it leads. Any other reason you can think as to why he'd do this? Maybe he's got a grudge against you?"

"No way. We went through the academy together, play golf on weekends. He's a good friend. If he wants to talk with me, he's gonna talk with me. I like your strategy. Let's go."

The group entered a clean, shiny elevator, and Cavanaugh pressed button number four. A short upward journey later, they exited into a sea of gray cubicles. The office area smelled of new carpet and fresh paint, which, for an old building, was like putting lipstick on a pig. Cavanaugh led the small team to a conference room walled with bulletproof glass, a long oval table in the center, and twelve chairs.

Cavanaugh pointed to the center of the room. "Sit here, and no matter what happens, don't move." He locked the door from the outside.

Wilson stood about twenty yards away, near the perimeter of the building in front of a window-covered expanse. Cavanaugh recognized the obese, curly-haired fifty-year-old man in Wilson's choke-hold with a pistol held several inches away but aimed at the man's temple. Tears streamed down Wilson's face as he yelled, "Cavanaugh. Come on, man. Disarm yourself and get over here now."

Cavanaugh edged along a cubicle aisle toward Wilson until they stood twenty feet from each other. Taking his time, he reached into his holster, slid out his weapon, and placed the gun onto a nearby desk. He put both hands in the air as he maintained eye contact with Wilson. "You okay, Shankle?"

Cavanaugh asked.

The big man rolled his eyes. With a bright red face, he choked out the words, "Oh, yeah, just another day at the park."

"What do you say we let these other people outta here?" Cavanaugh said to Wilson.

Wilson looked around. "Fine. Get 'em outta here."

Cavanaugh waved his arm and dozens of employees, who had been standing as shocked spectators, herded themselves to the stairwell and exited the floor.

"Wilson, why don't you let Shankle go so we can talk? Just the two of us, and maybe—"

"No. No fucking way, man."

"Okay, then maybe you can just put the weapon down. You're gonna—"

"No." He jammed his weapon deep into Shankle's meaty cheek. "You're gonna listen to what I have to say first. Then maybe I'll drop my weapon."

"Sure, man, whatever you say."

Wilson's chest pumped in and out. He tilted his head down toward his shoulder and wiped the sweat from the brow of his purple face onto his shirt. "We're on the wrong team, Cavanaugh. The wrong team."

"What do you—"

"We signed up to be the good guys, and now we're killing innocent Americans. This is like the fucking definition of a conspiracy come true."

"I understand you're upset, Wilson. Take a deep breath. Tell me what you're talking about. I honestly don't know what you mean, but want to understand. Help me so I can help you."

"The fucking CDM attack, man. We're in on it. We, the FBI. We killed those Super Six people."

Cavanaugh glanced around, down at the ground, then back at Wilson. "No way. Look over there. We have Dr. Bendel in the flesh. He's the last of the Super Six, but he's here in the conference room." Cavanaugh pointed at Jake. "I'm working to get to the bottom of this."

Wilson's eyes widened and he shot a glance toward Jake. He cocked the gun and drilled it into Shankle's temple. "You told me Bendel was dead."

Jake gulped, stood straight and made eye contact with Wilson.

Cavanaugh responded. "No. Now why don't you put down the—"

"Goddamned Shankle buried me, man. I'm a field agent. He moved me down to the Surveillance Specialists team. After twenty years in the field. I didn't deserve that shit."

Cavanaugh put his arms straight out in front of him, palms facing Wilson, and looked at Shankle, then back at Wilson. "Okay, let's talk about that."

Wilson yelled, "Dr. Bendel. Run. Run while you still can."

Shankle elbow-jabbed Wilson in the gut, but as he tried to get control of the weapon, a round fired into the large window behind them, splintering it. As the two men struggled and grunted, the gun fell to the floor. Shankle pushed Wilson backward, toward the cracked glass. Wilson's back slammed against the pane, and a million shards of glass exploded outward. Wilson tripped on the ledge and fell through the window opening. He yelled an obscenity as his body hurtled out into the open air.

Jake's eyes widened. He shoved his shoulder into the door, it flew open, and he bolted to Cavanaugh, who was leaning over the ledge with his right arm extended, clawing and pulling Wilson back onto the window ledge.

"I got you, man. Don't let go," Cavanaugh grunted.

Shankle dropped to the landing and kneeled, grasping his chest and coughing for air, while Cavanaugh struggled to rein in his old friend who hung from the ledge by his left hand.

Blood spurted from Wilson's neck like a geyser as he dangled in the gentle breeze.

Cavanaugh leaned out further and managed to get a firm grasp on Wilson's forearm.

Jake butted up against Cavanaugh and leaned out to help pull the man in.

"Let the traitor fall!" Shankle yelled.

The fresh blood made everything slippery. Some spurted into Cavanaugh's eyes and he winced. Jake was unable to get a hold of anything.

Wilson stared up at both men, but with the loss of blood, his consciousness was slipping away. "Conspir . . . Sh . . . Sh . . . Shank . . ." was all Wilson could muster before his suit tore and he slipped from their hands.

CHAPTER 8

Jake and Cavanaugh leaned out the empty window of the FBI building, watching Wilson accelerate toward the ground as he plummeted four stories before landing on the sidewalk. Cavanaugh let out a primal scream, while Jake pressed his fists to the sides of his head, at the sight of Wilson's mangled body.

Several other agents had rushed in to help, but it all happened too fast.

"Get back in the conference room," Cavanaugh said to Jake, then clasping his bloody fingers behind his head and walking around in a circle. "Of all the screwed-up things. Goddamnit." He shook his head. "Shankle, you didn't have to do that. You knew he wasn't gonna shoot you."

"Don't give me that shit," Shankle said. "He was gonna take me out and then go postal on the rest of you guys. I just saved your life." *Cough, cough.* "You should be thanking me."

"This isn't over," Cavanaugh said. "You just murdered a good man."

Shankle took a slow, determined step toward Cavanaugh and stood toe-to-toe. "My office. Now."

✳

Cavanaugh followed his boss into the elevator and up to Shankle's twelfth-floor corner office, a despised hellhole Cavanaugh was quite familiar with, having been the subject of insubordination on two previous occasions. The two men walked in, then Shankle slammed the door behind him, not giving Cavanaugh a chance to sit.

"You're off the case. The CDM attack, you're off," Shankle said.

Cavanaugh put his hand on his forehead and spun around. "You can't do that. We're this close to nailing these bastards." He made a pincer symbol with his fingers.

Shankle smiled. *Cough, cough.*

I've had it with that damned nervous cough.

"I want you here," Shankle said. "Work on whatever the hell Wilson was into. Figure it out. This could be a political nightmare for us. I need you to stay focused." He walked over to his desk and sat, locking his hands behind his head. "And don't you ever talk to me that way again in front of staff or I'll have you picking up trash in downtown New Orleans for the next two decades."

Cavanaugh stepped to the door and placed his hand on the knob. "Bendel needs to stay with me as his handler."

Shankle shook his head. "Not on your life. Bendel's assigned to Special Agents Kirrin and McCallister effective now. You'll have nothing more to do with that pain-in-the-ass engineer."

With a tight jaw and harsh squint, Cavanaugh flung open the door and left.

Cavanaugh knew he was on a short leash, but the greater good demanded he let protocol fly in the wind. At great risk of ruining his career, he decided to ignore Shankle's direct order.

CHAPTER 9

Jake sat in the FBI conference room, his toes and the tips of his fingers numb. He had never witnessed someone die in front of him. Had he not passed out at the Long Beach fire he might think differently, but no, this was his first experience with death in real-time. He wondered how many other people in that office had experienced that type of terror. From the drooping shoulders and looks of dread on their faces, not many.

Cavanaugh poked his head in the room and motioned for Jake to follow him. "C'mon, Bendel. We're getting out of here."

He burst through the door to the stairwell. As they descended the stairs, he said, "On behalf of the FBI, I would like to apologize to you for what you just experienced. I thought I could talk him down."

Following close behind Cavanaugh, trying not to trip on his heels, Jake said, "How the hell is that wimp-ass Shankle guy your boss?"

"No idea, but he's not only my boss, he's the assistant director in charge of this entire office."

At the ground floor they stopped at a vending machine, grabbed two cups of coffee, and went into a soundproof room with tiny foam pyramids coating the walls. Cavanaugh bent over, put his hands on his knees, stood back up, and finally stopped moving to look up at the ceiling tiles.

Jake crossed his arms. "What did Wilson mean before he fell when he said 'Shank?' Maybe Shankle?"

"I don't know yet. He said there's a conspiracy here, which is consistent with my theory about a mole, but it can't be that simple. Maybe Shankle's part of it; maybe Wilson lost his mind. Not sure. Here, Dr. Bendel, please sit down." He motioned to an orange plastic chair and sat at the round metal table.

"I'm good," Jake said, still standing. "If that's true, how do we know we can trust this guy? I don't want him coming after me, trying to neutralize . . . or whatever."

"You're learning, that's good, but that's not how it works around here. You leave him to me. Now, as much as I'd like to indulge your questions, let's not forget one thing: I'm the law here. You're the engineer. Are we clear?"

"Guess I'll sit down after all."

"I'm afraid we need to get back to the investigation of the CDM attack. We're estimating there've been over fifty billion dollars in total economic damage so far. Over six thousand dead. Double the death toll from the nine-eleven attack."

"Thought it would be more, but still a lot," Jake said, looking at the floor as he rubbed his temples.

"I've just been ordered to hand you and this case off to two other agents, but I'm only going to do so officially. So, on the books, you're going to play along with whatever the new agents want you to do. You and I will still work together on this, but you gotta help me keep it under the radar. We need to find out what's going on sooner than later and before we step in any piles of Shankle shit."

Jake nodded, taking a sip of coffee.

Cavanaugh pushed his cup away, stood again, and leaned against a wall. "Fill me in on your theory. Hold on, I need to ask you a personal question. Oh, and you might want these back. I swiped them from my desk. Been keeping them handy for you since the fire." He handed Jake a his wallet—stuffed full of hundred dollar bills and a few twenties—and a gray fedora and his black-mirrored Oakley sunglasses.

Jake thought about the last time he wore his trademark fedora—at the Long Beach gala with Cynthia—and a chill went down his spine. He'd been wearing one for decades. He felt naked without it. He thought of Cynthia. "Thank you."

"We're the FBI, Dr. Bendel. Not some Nazi regime, not that you could tell the difference with the press referring to your system as the 'SS.'"

Jake put the hat on. "You've already said that."

Cavanaugh poked his tongue lightly into his cheek and took a long breath. "Moving on. I've been with the bureau for twenty-six years now, and in all those years I've never, not once, come across a civil engineer. So please pardon my ignorance, but I have no idea what a civil engineer is. I looked up online what you guys do, but I'd like to hear from you."

Jake normally admired the simple question. He'd answered it many times during career-day fairs for students, but right now he'd much rather focus on finding his daughter.

"Be brief. We don't have much time."

Jake put his concern for Carlie aside. He decided to let his internal guard down and explained, "Civil engineers do two things. First, we provide the foundation for a thriving, productive, and successful civilization. Hence the word 'civil.' Second, in a very real sense, we're the exact opposite of terrorists."

"Not sure I follow."

"We design and construct bridges, houses, buildings, roads, power systems. We also provide clean water for people to drink." Talking about civil engineering made him feel good, comfortable, and real. "Without these things, our civilization would fail. And what do terrorists do? They try to blow those things up. Terrorists work at tearing down society, ripping apart what the engineers build. They create the polar opposite of a civilized society. Their mission is to destroy the physical things that bind us together as a nation and inject fear into the minds of the masses."

Cavanaugh nodded, sat back in a chair, and stared at his paper coffee cup as he spun it in circles. "Never thought of it that way."

Jake continued, "Most Americans have absolutely no idea what civil engineering is. There are no thriller novels with a civil-engineer protagonist. They're all about you guys—law enforcement or firemen or teachers, pilots, lawyers, doctors, or whatever. No movies either. None."

Jake's love for civil engineering gave him the energy to keep talking. "In fact, in most other countries, from a social hierarchy standpoint, civil engineers are typically ranked at the top, right up there with doctors and lawyers. But here in

America, nobody even knows we exist. Pretty sad, especially considering all we do for society. I mean, I personally designed and oversaw the construction of two of the interchanges we drove on earlier today. The water we're drinking in this not-so-tasty coffee comes from a water distribution system I designed twenty years ago when I worked for the Department of Water Resources."

"Enough of that, I get it. You can hop down off your soap-box now." Cavanaugh's phone pinged a text.

"Fine. Let's focus on finding Carlie." Jake adjusted his hat.

Cavanaugh looked up from his phone. "Trust me, she's one of the pieces I'm juggling right now and I'm sure she's all right, but I thought it might be helpful for you to talk about a topic you're familiar with. You can continue this lecture about civil engineering later."

Jake crossed his legs. "I thought you had a couple other agents you wanted me to meet."

"You're right. We gotta get back," Cavanaugh said. The two stood, exited the room and walked back upstairs to the fourth floor.

By now the crime-scene techs were working the entire area. Four men in white jumpsuits fiddled about by measuring distances, sweeping pieces of evidence into plastic baggies, and labeling spots on the floor where the Wilson incident occurred.

The two men entered conference room number 407 on the opposite side of the building.

As Jake sat, a woman entered. "Can we get you anything?" Jake turned to her. "Any kind of painkillers."

The woman nodded and stepped toward the door.

"While you're out there, send in agents Kirrin and McCallister," said Cavanaugh.

The woman returned with several uniformed officers. "Agent Cavanaugh, this room's scheduled for a meeting. Shankle said the police could use it, so we need you two to move to a different room."

Cavanaugh rolled his eyes, stood, and his phone pinged with another text. He read it as they followed the woman down a hallway. Cavanaugh opened the door to a new conference room.

The woman handed Jake a double-dose of Advil and a bottle of Arrowhead water. "I'll go get the other two agents," she said, and walked away.

Jake shoved the brown discs into his mouth and glugged half a bottle of water while thinking about Carlie. He grabbed a handful of trail mix from the bowl on the table, sat in a chair, and continued. "While we wait, I'm getting back on my soapbox. When you were young, like eight or nine, what did you want to be when you grew up?"

"A fireman," Cavanaugh answered. "It seemed really cool to me to ride in the fire truck, put out fires, and help people. My favorite TV show at the time was *Emergency*, especially since that show was based right here in Los Angeles County. But my real dad was murdered when I was nine, and the police in Venezuela where I'd been raised until that point did nothing. To this day, I have no idea who killed my father. Anyway, we moved here to LA and, as I got older, I found myself watching more police shows, and that sort of changed what I wanted to do. I guess ever since high school, I wanted to work in law enforcement to make a difference. Both my degrees are in criminal justice. I'm in this a hundred and ten percent and never want anyone to feel like they are dealing with incompetent police."

In Jake's ignorance, he hadn't thought about FBI agents having college degrees. Made sense, though. "Okay, so you wanted to be a fireman, then a policeman. What were the other options that you remember your teacher or counselor telling you were out there as far as careers?"

"Well, it was those two, and then I guess a teacher, doctor, lawyer, pilot . . . and that's pretty much it, I think."

"Typical," said Jake, shaking his head, disappointed. "Sounds like nobody explained to you what engineers do." His attitude toward Cavanaugh had improved. Sparks of trust flickered in his mind toward the man.

Two men entered the room. One of them said, "Sir, we need to talk. Now."

CHAPTER 10

In the conference room, one of the agents had bleached-blond hair and the one on Jake's left had an odd-looking, exceptionally long nose jutting out from his face. Both agents showed Jake their photo IDs and shields and introduced themselves as Special Agents Kirrin and McCallister.

Jake stood, noting reduced pain and returning strength as the meds kicked in. His hands shook less.

Kirrin and McCallister stood about as tall as Jake, wore dark suits, one blue, the other brown, and skinny ties. Jake realized he had never been in the presence of three FBI agents before. Intimidating. Not at all what he imagined and not the stereotypical government agents by any stretch of the word. He wondered if the two new men had families, what their stories were.

"Okay, from this point forward, I'm going to be your primary handler," said Agent Kirrin with a strong, annoying nasal tone in the man's voice. "And Agent McCallister here will be your secondary. We understand Cavanaugh has a theory about someone named Viktor Johnston as the leader of a terrorist cell here in Los Angeles, but our instructions are to do a quick check into him and, if nothing pans out, head in a different direction. Cavanaugh will no longer be working this case. We are well aware you worked on the Sûr System."

Jake's ears perked up and he darted a look at Cavanaugh. "Viktor's a suspect?"

"You know him?"

"Oh, yeah. We hired Viktor as one of the associates at the Super Six because of his brilliant mind and his extensive experience in the fields where we needed expert help, from civil engineering and telecommunications to psychology, sociology, networking. He also knew a ton about intelligent transportation systems, how they're used, whose ideas they came from, leaders in the field, et cetera. And from talking with others on the Super Six team, he was very helpful, very knowledgeable. We all embraced his support and collaborated heavily with this guy. To be honest, he was like an honorary seventh member of the team, that's how good he was, but sort of a loose cannon. He—well, we had to let him go after he made some bizarre threats. Mostly against me. Not sure why, but he always seemed to hate me. I tried to overlook some of it but eventually it went too far."

Before Cavanaugh could reply, Kirrin nodded, saying, "Good, but right now, he's only a person of interest. Tell us more about the Super Six project."

"But if Viktor is—"

"Dr. Bendel, please, we'll talk about Viktor next, but now we need you to focus on getting us up to speed on the SS," Kirrin said.

Jake looked at Cavanaugh, who said nothing.

"Fine. On a national level, the benefits of the SS were estimated to be in the trillions of dollars annually. And this doesn't take into consideration the enormous economic boost our nation will benefit from once people no longer have to wait idly in money-wasting traffic congestion. We're talking several more trillions of dollars of economic benefits." Jake looked down at the gray pile carpet and remembered looking at a Google Map of Los Angeles during rush hour one day. Solid red and dark-red squiggly lines everywhere, each representing a slow-moving virtual parking lot on the freeway. The map also had several dozen little icons, one for each traffic incident. "At that time, before Caltrans had implemented the Sûr System across California, commuters took hours to drive from one side of Los Angeles to the other in heavy traffic."

Kirrin wrote notes into a tiny spiral, handheld pad. "Thank you. Now, getting back to Viktor. We have a lead on one of his accomplices. If we can find the guy, known in cyber-circles as Ivory Snow, he might lead us to Viktor. While we're doing what we can on our end of the investigation, we want you to make some calls. Reach out to some of your friends in the industry and ask around. Quietly." He looked at Jake. "We understand you had some kind of relationship to Viktor, is that correct?"

"Of course. You already know this. He was one of the engineers on my team on the Sûr System project. The guy's a total creep, but I don't understand how he's connected here."

"You're going to help us investigate this. While you do, it's extremely important to proceed with a low profile and to keep in mind the clock is ticking."

"You tell me how the hell I'm supposed to reach out to my friends if they all think I'm dead." Jake considered the strong possibility that these two novice agents hadn't thought this all through and he might be stepping into a pile of incompetent shit. He trusted them about as much as a used-car salesman on a Monday morning. "I don't understand why Cavanaugh is off the case. Everyone thinks I'm dead, apparently most people want my head on a spike, my wife is dead, and my daughter is missing, but nobody seems to know much about that either."

The men remained stoic. "We've set up a safehouse for you a few blocks away. Once you're there, you make your calls and lay low for a few days until we can figure this out. We're working on a plan," said McCallister, the dark-haired agent, as he put his chin up and pushed out his chest.

Jake's mind had been racing like a cheetah in pursuit of its prey, but suddenly collapsed mid-stride. "Great. So now I'm just supposed to sit around and magically make it rain with a phone." He shook his head. "No, I need to talk to people face-to-face. In the field."

Cavanaugh jumped in. "Let's not get ahead of ourselves here. Jake, nobody's asking you to sit on the sidelines." He shot an angry glare toward Agent Kirrin. "I think what Agent Kirrin is trying to say is we should try to use your supposed death to our advantage. We'll go bad-guy fishing."

Jake's eyes darted between Kirrin and Cavanaugh, and he said, "You're the FBI, and this is a terrorist you're dealing with. I thought this is what you guys do. I'm on board with helping out as the bait, but don't you have some kind of secret way to flush terrorists from their hiding place?"

"Of course we do, Dr. Bendel," Kirrin said. "We've tried several other strategies, but most of the folks involved are dead now, so we're having trouble finding leads. Plus, the Sûr System mainframe itself is on lockdown, and our guys aren't able to access the files for analysis. We keep running into dead ends."

Jake knocked around more ideas inside his head, but after a few seconds of silence, Kirrin slammed his hand on the table. "This isn't some kind of goddamned game. People are dead, and if we don't find some answers soon or if the press gets wind you're still alive, more will die. Period. End of story."

Jake stood and snapped back, getting into Kirrin's face. "How about some frickin' answers about my wife and daughter, huh? I'm not going anywhere until you tell me what the hell happened to them. Right. Now." He paused and looked at each agent as he waited for a reply. They looked at one another but did not respond, so Jake continued. "Look, I want to help, but I'm a civil engineer, not a spy. I'm trained in how to build bridges and roads, not find terrorists. That's your job. My effectiveness will be limited, and you know it." Jake took several steps and sat in a different chair. They stared at him like hot-headed football coaches at a quarterback who'd thrown a third interception.

Cavanaugh chimed in. "There's no guarantee your plan about going after Ivory Snow will even work. Who knows, maybe he isn't even alive."

"Ivory Snow is out there," Kirrin said. The agent pulled his right hand out of his pocket and waved it toward the world outside the building. "We received an encrypted ping yester-day, so we know he's out there, but by the time we mobilized the tracking software, he'd already bounced his signal off more routers in different countries than bunnies living in Hugh Hefner's mansion. Couldn't triangulate his location," the man said, still speaking with deafening volume.

A small piece of paper had fallen to the ground when the agent pulled his hand out of his pocket. The agent hadn't noticed it. Jake fought the urge to look down at the paper and kept his eyes focused on the agents. "Okay, so you do have some hi-tech FBI way of getting to him. Go with that and bring him in for interrogation and I'll help."

McCallister uncrossed his arms, put his hands on his hips, and shook his head. He took a calming breath and moderated his tone. "Not possible. Hate to say this, but the guy's outsmarted our tech. He's using a cyber-cloaking system that's years ahead of what's available to us in-house. We need some-one who's got a relationship with him to help us find his actual physical location and bust his sorry ass."

Cavanaugh glanced at the two agents and spoke to Jake. "You can either do what these agents ask and work with us as our hip-pocket informant, or I can take you back to the safe-house. Don't make me take you back to the small, dark—"

None of this crap was part of the civil-engineering curriculum at Cal Poly.

"Great. Damned if I do, damned if I don't," Jake said, shift-ing in his chair, thinking hard about a decision that could end up getting him killed while possibly helping him exact his revenge and save God-only-knows how many lives. "I'm supposed to be grieving for my wife and searching for my daughter right now, not dealing with all this."

The three agents, all with their arms crossed, stared at Jake.

The pain meds finally kicked in fully. He reeled in his anger and thought of his wife with that twinkle in her eyes when she smiled. *Worst case, someone recognizes me, the bad guys find out and I die, but I'd get to be with Cynthia again.*

"Here's a burner phone with my number already entered," said Kirrin, handing him a brand-new Android cell. "In case you come up with any ideas at the new safehouse."

"Gentlemen, may I have a word with Dr. Bendel alone?" Cavanaugh asked.

McCallister thought for a moment. "Two minutes," he said, holding up two fingers. "Then he's on his way to the local safehouse." The two men exited the room.

"Sorry about that, Dr. Bendel. I had to make them think you're going to the safehouse."

"I am." Jake cleared his throat. "That's what they just said I'm—"

Cavanaugh shook his head and jutted out his chin. "No, you're not. I'm going to give you a vehicle and want you to do some digging on your own. I don't trust those two, especially after the bomb threat. I think they're working with Shankle, but I have no evidence. Yet." He grabbed the phone from Jake and punched in a cell number. "You call *me* with updates."

Jake sat to let this new information soak in for a moment.

"Dr. Bendel, I'm sticking my neck out for you, because I have a feeling you're going to be an integral part of helping us stop the bad guys, but considering what happened this morning with Shankle and Wilson, and the bomb threat, everything has to be strictly under the radar."

"Under the radar. Explain."

Cavanaugh leaned in and said, half-whispering, "Assistant Director in Charge Shankle isn't buying Viktor as a suspect or my theory this is all homegrown domestic terrorist crap. His sources are telling him it's some towel-head organization from Syria, not Viktor. You and I are going to be operating strictly off the books here, you understand? If these two other agents or anyone else gets wind of what we're doing and they find out you're alive and working with me, I'm out on the street and you're in federal prison for the rest of your life."

Wow, this guy goes for the throat. No soft sales pitch here.

Jake certainly didn't want to go to prison, especially not with all the work he needed to do to gain access to the SS mainframe, find Carlie, and help Cavanaugh track down Viktor. He knew Viktor well, but further debated with himself how much he wanted to risk.

So this guy's going rogue, not following the chain of command. This is exactly what I need right now.

"If your FBI intel points to Viktor Johnston as a key player in this and we can prove it, I can help. I'm totally in, Agent Cavanaugh, and I trust you, but I really need to talk to an old friend of mine. He's been like a mentor and father to me. I want . . . I *need* to run this by him for leads."

The agent looked at Jake and sighed. Cavanaugh then glanced at the clock and Jake's eyes followed: 12:54 p.m. "Fine, but time is of the essence here and I can't tell you how important it is for you to maintain a low profile while you're out there. Keep the number of people you contact in your investigative efforts minimized. Is that clear?"

"Crystal."

"Keep that phone on you at all times so we know where you are. There's a tracking app installed."

"A tracking app? What for?"

"Dr. Bendel," said Cavanaugh, "I'm tracking you for your own safety, a precaution. If anyone sees your ass alive, you'll be in danger. Hell, you're already in danger. Every minute you spend outside this room is a significant risk to you. Keep the goddamned phone on."

"Once I'm done talking with my friend, you need to get me in front of a computer with access to the SS mainframe so I can get to my files."

"I have an iPhone, will that work?"

Jake laughed. "Are you kidding me? This isn't some mobile app, I need access to the mainframe."

"Whatever, we'll have to cross that bridge when we get there. Now for a car," he reached a hand into his pocket, "I'm going to loan you mine." He handed him a set of keys. "Even though we're working under the radar, the process of formally issuing a federal vehicle to you would be a huge red flag, and Shankle would be all over us. Tell me what your next move will be after you talk with your mentor friend," Cavanaugh asked.

Jake smiled. "I just told you. I need access to a real computer. I'm going to get some help from a genius friend of mine to hack in. The guy will run circles around the best cyber experts in this building."

"Not sure that'll be much help, but okay," Cavanaugh said. "Stay here for thirty more seconds then head back to the stairwell." He stood and exited the room.

Jake swooped down and, with a clammy palm, grabbed the piece of paper the agent had dropped onto the floor. Without looking at it, he jammed it into his pocket.

CHAPTER 11

Jake disappeared into the sea of cubicles on the fourth floor of the Federal Building and counted to thirty in his head. Ducking, he peeked around the corner of an empty cubicle and saw Kirrin and McCallister walking toward the conference room. After they passed him, he snuck out into the hallway and darted into the stairwell.

Cavanaugh stood there waiting for him, wearing a clean shirt and coat. "C'mon, follow me," he said, motioning with his arm.

Jake followed Cavanaugh down to the second floor. A sign read: "Gym / Locker Room". Cavanaugh said, "Jake, I want you to shave that beard off."

"No way. I've had a beard ever since I graduated from Cal Poly. It's part of my look."

"Not anymore. By concealing your identity, we'll make it easier for you while you're ghosting. If we're right about Viktor, even he won't recognize you."

"Good point." Jake ran his fingers along his facial hair, shaking his head in disbelief. He thought about how Cynthia had always enjoyed running her fingers through his beard and how it tickled her lips. "Get me a razor."

Cavanaugh fumbled around in his gym bag and handed some tools to Jake, along with another change of clothes. After grabbing a quick shower to clean up and rinse Wilson's blood from his hands, he threw on his trademark jeans and white golf shirt and checked out his overall appearance in a full-length mirror. He grabbed the scissors, clipped his beard, and shaved off the rest with a fresh, sharp razor. Cavanaugh nailed it. Without the beard, Jake looked thinner and ten years younger.

"Now I want you to go out to the parking lot, stall C4 is where my vehicle is parked. I'd give you my personal car, but it's in the shop. Call me if anything happens. We have a strict policy against issuing vehicles to civilians, but I'm making an exception due to the paramount importance and the high stakes involved. It's a risk, but it's on me, so whatever you do, do not turn on the red-and-blue flashing lights or siren. Those are reserved for law enforcement personnel only. Now get the hell out of here, and call me when you're done with your little mentor meeting."

Jake nodded as he shook Cavanaugh's hand, then hustled down to the basement of the building and over to the spot where Cavanaugh's vehicle was parked. He had expected a shiny new black Dodge Charger or an SUV identical to the one in which he'd ridden with Cavanaugh, but instead he found a gutless black compact Ford. An older model. He noticed no trace of the new-car smell when he entered, but the dashboard did have a switch to turn on the forbidden red and blues.

He pushed the start button and headed south on the 405. After what seemed like hours in the putt-putt mobile that would have taken mere minutes in a Dodge Charger, he merged onto I-10 east toward Cal Poly Pomona.

Jake reminisced about his first days on campus as a freshman. They'd told him the school was founded in 1938 as California Polytechnic University at Pomona, or Cal Poly Pomona if you're a local. It had been consistently ranked as one of the top engineering universities in the nation. The lecturers had informed him how the engineering students would learn their craft from well-educated and experienced professors about topics like chemistry, physics, strength of materials, thermodynamics, structural analysis, hydraulics, and a ton more than the average human could stuff into their brain. He remembered his thermodynamics professor telling the class that this was where they would all learn to think like engineers and become effective problem solvers, a skill that had proved valuable over the years for Jake. He had used his problem-solving skills to save lives before by analyzing and making improvements to dangerous road conditions, but never anything on such a grand scale as helping the FBI stop a terrorist from killing civilians. There could not possibly be an uglier, more deadly problem for an engineer to solve.

Over the course of his studies, Jake had developed a strong bond with his advisor, Professor Mike Everton, a structural engineering guru and his daughter, Paige Terner, was a good friend of Jake's. The man was fun and lively, and everyone on campus knew his reputation for drinking beer at the local salsa bar and smoking pot at the beach on weekends.

In Jake's encrypted email sent from his burner phone to his old advisor, he'd requested the secret meeting to discuss a "very important" issue in the Engineering Meadow outside Engineering Building 9 and had advised the professor not to tell anyone Jake was alive. To convince the professor that the real Jake Bendel had written the email and verify its legitimacy, Jake had given Everton the code number they used back in the day: A36-101. This number represented an inside joke between the two men.

Jake parked and tried to remember Carlie's cell to send her a text. Before the fire, if he wanted to get hold of her, he'd click the "Carlie" button on his iPhone and never paid attention to the actual number. Fortunately, her number was similar to his with the same area code and first three numbers. If only he could remember the last four. He closed his eyes and the digits popped into his head like looking at a photo.

Using his FBI-issued Android phone, he typed in a text message:

Hi, Carlie Barlie . . . take a deep breath . . . this is crazy and you won't believe this, but I'm still alive, need to meet ASAP where you had your freshman orientation at CSUSB. That was a good day. Love, Dad

He checked his appearance in the mirror and startled himself, half expecting to see his reflection with a beard still on his face. Worried somebody might recognize him, he pondered whether to wear his hat, but as he stepped out of the car, he placed his favorite gray fedora on his head of thick, dark blond hair, slid the pair of black-mirrored Oakley shades over his steel-blue eyes, and walked toward the civil engineering buildings.

He passed a mother and teenaged daughter walking in the opposite direction. "You're not driving on any more freeways, young lady. You're grounded until they tell us it's safe to drive across town again." The girl hunched her shoulders and slowly shook her head.

The comment stopped Jake in his tracks as he absorbed the impact, for better or worse, his work had on everyday folks.

Jake took in the scent from nearby eucalyptus trees to calm his nerves, knowing the risk of meeting with his old friend in public. But as Jake walked farther and entered the Meadow, the secluded place reminded him of the many walks in the past together with Professor Everton as they pondered life, civil engineering, and the universe.

Jake approached an old man waiting under an expansive oak tree with a broad canopy. The professor, now in his mid-seventies, stood a few inches shorter than Jake. He had straight white hair, a small potbelly, emerald-green eyes, and a warm smile that endeared people to him. Jake wondered if the guy still toked it up out at the beach on the weekends.

"Professor Everton. Been a long time."

Professor Everton smiled. "Well, I'll be a monkey's uncle. Jake Bendel in the flesh, sans the beard. Striking look, I must say, although I wouldn't believe it if I wasn't standing here shaking your hand, seeing you with my own two eyes. I have so many questions, oh, my goodness."

"Sorry to have to meet you under these circumstances, but

it's for the best. I'm in a bit of a bind."

"I'm assuming all this secrecy has to do with you being dead. I saw the news last week and I even went to your funeral on Sunday. Really shook me up. Not every day one of your former students is killed, let alone see them alive a short while later. You must be tryin' to give me a heart attack."

"Sorry, Professor, I—"

"I'm just bustin' your chops." The professor winked and let out a brief laugh. "Other than that cut above your eye, you look pretty good."

Jake would normally have laughed too, but not today. Not with his wife gone. "I'm sorry, Professor, just not in the mood for joking today." He felt another set of tears come up on deck, teetering on his lower eyelids, ready to break free, but he wiped them away before they had a chance to dribble down his cheeks. "According to the FBI, Cynthia died in that fire in Long Beach, the blaze was apparently supposed to kill me. Long story, I don't want to—"

"I'm so sorry to hear that. Working with the FBI, eh? Do you want to come into my office for a wee bit and talk?"

Jake stopped, considering the offer. "Yes. That's very generous of you, but after being cooped up in a safehouse, I need this fresh air and sunlight. Plus, I'm running short on time. Maybe once the storm blows over."

"Fair enough."

"One thing that's helping me cope with my grief is staying focused on trying to figure out what the hell is going on. I'm certain if I track down who's behind these terrorist attacks, I'll end up finding out who murdered Cynthia."

"How is your daughter taking all this?"

"We don't know where she is. But the FBI says they're trying to find her. She's a big girl. She's smart, so I'm hoping she's okay, but I am worried. I should be heading out to San Bernardino to look for her, but since she hasn't responded to my text and I need to talk with you, I'm here." Jake scanned the area for potential threats, former colleagues who might recognize him, fans of his book, friends. Nothing out of the ordinary. Normal college kids wandering to and from their classes, but with a depressing vibe woven into the campus atmosphere. As they walked, all the students were looking at the ground or up at the sky, slowly, with less purpose than he remembered. Most stared off into the distance, not talking with each other, quiet, even the groups.

"That CDM attack was the worst news I've ever heard, to be honest, worse than the San Bernardino shooting where several of my good friends were killed. And right here in our own backyard. The media kept blabbing on that you were involved, but I didn't believe them. I want you to know that, Jake. Not for one gosh-darned minute."

CHAPTER 12

Jake looked deep into the professor's eyes. "The FBI has a working theory that there have been several other attacks related to the CDM. Remember the algorithm you and I worked on several years ago for analyzing the structural integrity of old bridges?"

"No."

"Yes, you do. The one where we discerned steel-plated girders had issues with the reinforced concrete box structures." He looked at the professor as the wheels turned.

"Ah, yes!"

Jake started along a worn path in the grass, put his hand on the professor's upper arm and walked toward the other side of the field. "Here, let's walk while we talk." He clasped his hands behind his waist. "I developed a similar networking algorithm while I was working on the Sûr System with the Super Six. The FBI thinks the attacks are all being coordinated by someone or some group and involve the algorithm."

The professor strode at Jake's side. "If I remember, we based ours loosely on a core Euclid algorithm. Not sure how that would work with a network of vehicles."

"Correct, but"—Jake scanned the area again for anyone who might recognize him—"I had a plan worked out in my head during my six-day stint at an FBI safehouse, but now that I'm here and one of my engineers is involved and my wife and team are dead, I have no idea where to start. I told myself that if I ever got out, the first thing I'd do is come ask you about a story you shared with me a long time ago."

The professor crossed his arms, put his right hand under his chin, and nodded.

"You told us once that you worked with the FBI. Helped them solve a crime? You're the only person I know who ever did anything with the FBI."

"Goodness, that was, like, thirty years ago. Not sure how much help I can be, but,"—he shook a stern finger at Jake— "before I answer your FBI question, I'm interested in your numerical analysis. The engineering details of that transportation algorithm you helped develop and how it works."

A jumbo jet flew overhead, no doubt on its way to land at LAX, the major L.A. airport a few dozen miles west. They both looked up for a moment. Jake thought back to his brief hellish ride on that damned FBI plane.

Jake wanted to hear the professor's story about working with the FBI, but it felt good to talk. "My book went into great detail about how, at that time, there were between thirty and forty thousand fatalities every year in traffic-related accidents. I was talking with some colleagues one day at lunch about how crazy it seemed that a modern society tolerated traffic congestion and accepted, without question, so many people dying every year on our roadways."

"With you so far," said the professor.

"It's insane. We had all the technologies we needed, like GPS, self-driving cars, automatic backup systems, finely tuned gyroscopes, supercomputers the size of a dime, infrared sensors, but nobody had taken the initiative to come up with a way to connect these technologies into one overall system to allow people to move along the freeways without fear of dying or suffering endless hours of congestion delays."

"Interesting," said the professor, nodding. "And the book you wrote was about how to do this?"

"Well, sort of. Again, nobody wants to read a technical thesis about the gritty details of fully automating cars and trucks on freeways." He put his hands in his pockets and shrugged. "Unless they were having a hard time going to sleep, 'cause that would certainly do the trick."

They both chuckled. "Anyway, I was out jogging on the beach one morning, and it hit me like a ton of bricks." A wave of seagulls flew overhead, cawing in unison. "I gave myself a magic wand and went on the basic premise that we could retrofit all vehicles made after a certain year to fully automate their driving for less than two thousand dollars. Like having a robot with advanced software control their cars. Technically, that would automate each of the cars driving on the road."

"You mean the way Google was doing at the time?"

"Yes and no. Google was looking at it from only a one-car standpoint, which was a good start, but to get the maximum benefit we'd need all the cars and trucks moving on the free-ways as a networked system in order to have them moving safely at the same speed with only a two-foot gap between vehicles. Either all the cars and trucks have to be on the network and controlled by the system, or none. We can't mix robots and human drivers. One or the other, not both. Picture a moving parking lot of vehicles going sixty-five miles per hour. Super-efficient stuff, but with certain risks that needed to be identified and mitigated or eliminated."

"There's no way humans could've made that happen without the assistance of computers and advanced technologies," the professor said.

"Exactly." Jake stopped walking and turned to the professor. "The algorithm was the missing piece to the puzzle. It's what handles these risks for us, makes the system operable and safe. It considers over a hundred different variables, including, for example, the mass of each vehicle, which determines the momentum depending on the speed. It also calculates a safe distance between the car in front and behind based on—"

"The engine's size, horsepower, and acceleration capabilities, which are more of a factor when the vehicles are traveling uphill than downhill," said the professor, nodding his head and putting his hands in his pockets. Jake chuckled at how he learned some of his mannerisms from the professor.

"Precisely." Jake guided their journey off the freshly cut grass and onto a cement sidewalk. The hum of freeway traffic roared in the distance. "There were also legal and human psychological factors that needed to be considered as part of the overall process, all of which indirectly affected the algorithm."

"You mean things like what does the vehicle do if the driver falls asleep and it's time to exit the freeway or if there's a flat tire or an engine failure? How does the network adjust the flow of vehicles to accommodate these changes?" the professor asked.

"That's a huge oversimplification, but yes. There's more to the tech, but that's it in a nutshell. The algorithm handles all these factors, variables, and contingencies. We had five of the brightest minds in the country working on it, plus me, and about three hundred staff, including a man named Viktor Johnston. When we finished, the feds rolled out the system in record time thanks to the president's federal funding initiative."

"Ah, yes. Where she offered the tax incentive to vehicle owners and trucking companies to essentially pay for half of the upgrade for each vehicle. I remember most people jumped on that. Small price to pay for eliminating traffic congestion from their commutes. I believe you mentioned it as a recommendation in that speech you gave her. What an experience that must have been."

Jake nodded. "Check that off the bucket list, for sure. But either way, the existing freeway systems needed relatively minor physical upgrades here and there to allow for the communication between the vehicles and the mainframe computers. So after a phased rollout, within two years the vision was realized and we started saving lives. No more traffic accidents and no more traffic congestion. We finally made it into the twenty-first century. Better late than never, I guess."

"On the surface, all quite reasonable. So don't take this the wrong way, but you gotta tell me what the hell happened. Fifty-seven hundred drivers don't get killed because of a technical glitch. Caltrans had already used that as the reason for the SITS nightmare, so their cover story was total malarkey."

Jake tilted his head back and looked up to the tops of the palm trees nearby. "It's over six thousand now."

The professor let out an audible exhale and tugged on his ear.

"Even though we embedded advanced security protocols in the code and specifically anticipated hackers getting in and causing chaos, I shouldn't have to stand here and tell you a death toll. This should not have happened. We had the most cleverly designed, impenetrable, cyber-secure network on the planet. Better than what any bank has by a factor of thousands. Clearly, we left a hole somewhere."

"Okay, my turn." The professor paused, leaned toward Jake, and raised an eyebrow. "I'll give you the unedited version of my story, one I've never told anyone else. Until the early 1980s, civil engineering designs and calculations were all done by hand, or maybe with a slide rule or simple calculator. Everything we did to design hydrology flows, the treatment of water, construction of hydroelectric dams, roadways, and the structural analysis of houses, buildings, and bridges was all done without the use of computers. Cal Poly was one of the first universities in the country to develop software for civil engineering applications."

Jake crossed his arms and took a wide stance to focus on what the professor was telling him.

"Right around that time, during the infancy of the computer

revolution, someone caused a panic with these new things called computer viruses. Was a big deal." He motioned behind them with his thumb, pointing to the past. "No one had ever heard of such a thing. Industry experts didn't even know what to name them. There weren't any types of anti-virus software either. It was kind of a Wild West of the computer industry."

Jake kicked a small rock and watched it dribble down the sidewalk in front of them. "I remember pirating games when I was younger. That's what got me hooked on computers, to be honest. We didn't have any computer classes; we just learned by doing."

"Exactly. While you were off shooting aliens on a monitor with green dots, we developed a software program to help structural engineers do beam-, column-, and foundation-design calculations, all with desktop computers. That was huge back then. Nowadays, just about everything is done with computers. I mean, look at our phones. They're more of a handheld computing machine than a device to talk to another person with, but we still call them phones."

"I'm getting lost, professor. Tell me what this all has to do with the FBI."

"Right, sorry. I tend to go off on tangents when I speak. Hazards of the job."

Two crows cawed in the distance. They sounded distinctly different than the earlier seagulls. *Would be nice to be a bird and fly away.*

Everton continued. "We'd completely debugged the software and, to my surprise, it ran quite well, but then we noticed a problem. The program kept freezing. The disk drive was going nuts, and we couldn't figure out why. None of us had ever seen anything crashing like that before. We initially thought the computer itself had a malfunction, but that wasn't the problem. When we drilled back into the code, we stumbled onto a glitch that—and we didn't know it at the time—was put there by one of the associate professors helping us with the software. The man's name was Dr. Marion Engel. A real piece of work, that guy. I'll never forget his name because, in my own ignorance, I'd always thought of Marion as a girl's name. Anyway, turns out the son of a bitch had infected our software program with a virus he created. When we ran certain lines of code, the system would attack itself and start to delete critical files on the floppy."

"That was before the internet and networked computers," Jake said. "You must have shared floppies."

A strong breeze blew through the eucalyptus trees, and a large chunk of branch came crashing down near a student couple holding hands. They jumped off the sidewalk to safety, and several other students rushed in to make sure they were all right.

"Damn you're smart, Jake. My theory was his virus infected a disk and replicated its malicious code and automatically integrated itself into my program. Then when I used that particular disk, the virus loaded onto my rudimentary hard drive, where it replicated and wrote itself onto other disks I was using for my program. It infected everything I was working on."

Jake made a slow, disbelieving shake of the head before he noticed a redheaded woman in the distance walking along the perimeter of the Meadow. He stopped, put his hand across his brow to block the glare of the sun, and although she reminded him of a former girlfriend, he determined she must be a student. His mind wandered back to Cynthia, and a fresh wave of grief washed over him, but he continued his walk alongside the professor as two students passed them, mumbling to each other. " . . . going to tear down all the freeways. Nobody is safe anymore, and . . ."

"Everyone around here seems to be in some kind of trance. Like walking zombies," Jake said.

"It's gotten worse this last week, been like one long nightmare. Some of my older friends had bomb shelters constructed in the sixties, during the cold war, and they've been holed up inside since the CDM attack. There are a lot of scared people out there, Jake. The whole city is terrified."

All because of something I helped create.

"I heard on the news the 405 has been completely shut down since the attack," the professor said. "Caltrans is still mopping up the mess, and they say it will take at least another week before all of the 175,000 cars and trucks are hauled away. There was significant damage done to roadside signs, guardrails, and other parts of the freeway. Trees on the side of the road are charred black, and there are thousands of soot marks on the pavement of the seven-mile stretch where vehicles caught fire."

Jake shook his head again. "I'll bet the insurance companies have been overwhelmed with claims and a bunch of them will have to declare bankruptcy. The hospitals were probably inundated with patients."

The professor nodded. "Yep. All of them set up triage

centers to handle the incoming wounded. The morgue has been farming out work to other county coroners' offices to deal with all the dead bodies. With the 405 shut down, all north-south traffic was rerouted onto other north-south free-ways, like the I-5, all of which turned into parking lots. A lot of people stopped driving on the freeways and have started taking the subways, but now those are inundated with commuters. Driving anywhere around here these days is impossible. Worse, you walk along the streets and everyone is in a trance, like you said, walking zombies. Never witnessed anything like this before."

"Not cool."

"Anyway, back to my story," the professor said, continuing to walk. "We were watching the news one night and they were talking about how certain large companies—I mean huge companies like IBM and the big banks at the time—were having similar problems with their computer systems. I wondered if there was a connection but didn't think much of it at the time. Marion's virus used polymorphic code with a dormant phase to help keep itself hidden. At the right time, the virus deleted valuable data permanently, which caused some companies to lose enormous amounts of money, at least digitally. Billions of dollars evaporated because of a computer virus. First time I heard the phrase 'cyber-attack.' First of its kind. Until then, those guys were just called crackers. The loss of money created such a panic that it caused the stock markets to crash. A couple days later, I thought about it more, and my gut instinct told me that our software glitch might be related to that corporate attack."

"That's when you called the FBI?" Jake asked, looking around for any familiar faces or anything that might seem suspicious to his untrained eye as they walked through the park.

"Not exactly." The professor rubbed the back of his neck. "I made some calls to the police to report our relatively small incident on the outside chance a connection existed. Before I knew it, two FBI agents showed up in my office asking me questions. The FBI was not keyed into the computer scene at that time, so after I disproved their initial assumption of me being a suspect, they asked for my help to solve the crime. I'll never forget their term for me: they called me a 'hip-pocket informant.' One of the agents was polite. The other was, pardon my French, a total donkey's ass. Young fella by the name of Shankle."

"I know the feeling," Jake said, as he raised his eyebrows and looked at the ground in front of him.

The professor nodded. "I showed them our software program, how it worked, and the weird virus code embedded inside. They did an analysis and determined the virus had the same digital signature as the one that did all the financial damage. They asked me who I thought might be responsible for the virus in my program, and when I told them I shared disks with Dr. Engel, they quickly diverted their attention to him."

Jake made a circling motion with his hand. "Let's get to the point, Professor. Time's of the essence, and I need to get going to find Carlie."

"Here's where the story gets weird, my friend. When the

FBI went to question him, he wasn't in his office, so the agents flashed a warrant to the secretary and seized his computer as evidence. A few hours later, after I rifled through the files on his machine, I found the smoking gun that proved Engel was the one behind the virus. I couldn't believe it. Right here at Cal Poly, there was a guy who single-handedly caused companies to lose billions of dollars in stock value and created panic across all sectors of the US economy."

"I don't recall the story being that detailed and involved," Jake said as he narrowed his eyes.

The professor rubbed behind his ear again as he looked upward, gathering his thoughts for what to say next. He smiled at Jake. "Well, most of the students and faculty know the incident involved the FBI, but there's only a handful of us who know the gritty details. Long story short, the feds tracked him down a few days later, but he managed to escape. Never found. Was a shame, too. He had a wife and three sons."

"Seriously? The guy disappeared after causing all that damage? Wonder what motivated him to create the virus."

"Turns out he'd caught his wife having an affair with their best friend, and her dad was some high-level executive at one of the companies hit with the virus. Engel sent floppy disks with the virus on it to the companies, and when they loaded them, the virus replicated itself onto their hard drives and other floppies. The geniuses at the FBI figured it was his way of getting back at the corporations. A twisted revenge. But he didn't expect to get caught."

"Maybe some mental illness too."

They both stopped walking. The professor rubbed his chin

and rolled his eyes up, back, and forth. "Affairs can get really ugly. I'll bet the guy was whacked out of his mind."

Jake swallowed. "Tell me about it. You don't happen to have a picture of your buddy Marion, do you?"

"I have digital and hard copies of all the old yearbooks. The faculty photos are all there. Come with me."

The two men walked back toward the professor's office, but before they entered, Jake stopped and checked his phone to see if Carlie had responded to his text. Nothing.

"You gotta remember that back then the term 'terror' was not really a household name per se, not like it is now. We used to refer to those guys as whacko religious nut jobs who blew themselves up for their causes."

Jake scanned his surroundings, catching the eye of two young students leaning up against an otherwise empty hallway wall, who held his gaze for longer than expected. He wondered if they recognized him.

The professor unlocked his office door and opened it. "Sometime in the early nineties, several years after Engel disappeared, I started hearing the term 'cyberterrorist' on the news."

His office looked like a paper bomb had exploded several years ago and nobody had bothered to clean it up. Several stacks of books and reports, some over a foot high, littered the old man's desk. Everton walked to the corner between two bookshelves, squatted down, and after a few moments found a yearbook for the year in question.

"Ahh, here's what we need," he said, stepping toward Jake. He held the hardbound book in his hand and thumbed through the pages. A moment later, he pointed a bony finger to a small grayscale photo of a man. "That's him. Right there. Marion Engel."

Jake's eyes widened. *He looks exactly like Viktor.*

CHAPTER 13

Groggy, Viktor blinked as he lay on the floor in a fetal position. The old man awoke from his blackout, clueless to his whereabouts or what he'd been doing prior to losing consciousness, as was typical of such episodes. Smoldering hot embers crackled in the cabin fireplace, casting faint hues of red-and-orange shadows across the wall in front of him. He moaned, rubbed his temples, and with a hunched over back and head drooped low, struggled to sit upright, panting, trying to catch his breath. *Goddamn those fucking headaches.*

He studied the dim room's interior. Nothing looked familiar, so he focused on figuring out the date and time, but the walls were bare—no paintings, wallpaper, or decorations, save for a large, colorful, six-foot-by-four-foot map of the United States pinned to a wall. In a burst, his memories returned. *August 10. Afternoon. Big Bear cabin.*

The monster map showed dozens of cities circled in red ink and hundreds of colored pins stuck across its entirety where maximum damage would be inflicted with the impending attack.

Blood rushed to his head as he stood, cracked his back, and walked to the map. He mumbled under his breath, "These people. I hate them all. This joke of a country is done with its run of world domination. We'll stop it dead in its tracks. Too many morons, homos, atheists—anyone who's not Muslim deserves to die." He smiled, scratching his balding head. "Those apes have ruined the world, but I'm gonna fix that. Starting with those arrogant civil engineers. They killed my family and all deserve to die." He nodded in agreement with himself and relished the thought of how imminent the next attack was.

Leaning forward to get a closer look at the Southern California area on the map, he eyed the pin stuck into Los Angeles, and his mother's voice reminded him how all good Christians need to obey the laws of our Lord and Savior, Jesus Christ; that our purpose on this planet is to create wonderful children and to lead a happy, healthy, productive life filled with love and compassion for all living things. But before she could finish, the deep booming, echoing voice of Allah eclipsed her tender voice. The Muslim god spoke inside Viktor's head. "Do it, Viktor. Finish what you started. Kill that senator bitch and her friends. Kill 'em all."

He pressed his palms lightly on his cheeks as he agreed with Allah's voice.

Viktor recalled the car crash that had changed his life when he was fifteen years old. He'd suffered a massive blow to his head, and his mother died in the accident. Prior to the collision, Viktor had been known by his family and friends as a relatively happy young man. Psychologically, he had functioned as any normal boy, free from the voices of Allah and his deceased mother. Since that time, however, his headaches had become unbearable as they grew in strength, adding piles of anxiety during most of his waking hours. He struggled to put the memory out of his head before it triggered another blackout, but he failed.

Violent spasms forced his body to the cabin floor as his brain scrambled on a hot skillet. He felt nothing but the pain of sharp needles poking his skull from within. After a few moments the seizure ended, the shaking stopped, and he drifted into a light trance. Drops of warm liquid oozed from his left ear as he relived the car accident with his mother that had solidified his criminal intellect.

Viktor's stepfather, the one who'd initiated the adoption back in the 1950s, had died in a separate car accident two years prior to Viktor's accident. Mildred, Viktor's mother, had found their Baptist church helpful in dealing with the grieving process. She'd blamed herself for her husband's death, but the roadway conditions were flat-out dangerous. Any civil engineer worth his snot would have designed a better road.

As part of the church-recommended reconciliation process, she devoted her entire existence to Jesus Christ. From that point forward, she considered herself a good Christian woman. She traveled alone to attend church services every day except Sundays, when she forced Viktor and her other two teenage sons, Viktor's stepbrothers, to join her.

He relived that tragic accident.

Fog had licked the treetops in the distance on that unusually cold and dreary Sunday morning in January on the rural outskirts of Houston, Texas. Viktor's younger brothers had come down with colds and stayed home, but the Lord's message could not wait! It was a sin to miss church and Mildred and her eldest son were late for the first service at church that fateful day.

As she roared along on the open road in their lime-green 1967 Buick Skylark, Viktor noticed his mother speeding fifteen miles an hour faster than the posted speed limit of twenty-five. Concerned, he said, "Mom, I don't think we're supposed to be going this fast. In my driver's ed class at school, they say it's unsafe to drive this fast, especially during such cold weather because there might be ice on the road."

She glanced toward him, smiled, and responded in an urgent tone, "The Lord Jesus is here looking out for us." Viktor swallowed hard, trying to embrace the words of his loving mother who created a safe cocoon for them in which to travel. He grabbed ahold of the door handle anyway, a wave of foreboding washing over him.

As she spoke to Viktor, her eyes turned away from the road, and at the same time, a packing truck headed their way hit black ice, spun, and headed straight towards them. After the large vehicle emerged from the shroud of gray moisture, Mildred slammed on the brakes. They crashed into the side of the truck doing forty miles per hour and skidded underneath it.

Within a fraction of a second, their cocoon of safety exploded, the roof of the Skylark collapsed around the Engel bodies, shearing apart from the rest of the vehicle before coming to rest under the truck.

The decapitated head of Viktor's mother lay in his lap, staring up at him, eyes wide open. The steering wheel had collapsed her chest cavity inward all the way to her backbone. Reddish-black blood streamed from her neck like a small volcano, with steaming-hot life spurting out from her torso onto the seat and Viktor's motionless body.

His frontal lobe had taken a massive blow, specifically his prefrontal cortex. With a bashed-in head, his eyes stared forward like a blind man. His left eye twitched as he sensed his own warm blood trickling out of his head, down his cheek, and onto his neck. Somehow, he remained conscious long enough to create memories of the accident. Clear as a raindrop, the image of his mother's headless body etched itself deep into his memory. He lapsed into a coma and remained there for seven days. He awoke in a downtown Houston hospital.

Young Viktor spent the next ten years in and out of mental hospitals. He heard voices, including one of his mother, which started out somewhat quiet. He initially ignored her, taking no action when she gave him instructions.

His two stepbrothers, teens themselves, but natural offspring of Viktor's adopted parents, placed the blame for their mother's death squarely with Viktor, so they never visited him. Not once. Later in fact, as adults in their twenties, they seemed to take quiet enjoyment in persecuting his every move by not paying the hospital bills on time, sending him threatening letters, and lying to him about his mental health. Somewhere along their troubled teenage years they'd learned hatred and racism. They saw him as a foreigner. A raghead. They harbored deep anger toward him. Over time, Viktor's love for them disappeared, replaced by rage.

A half-inch-wide, pink-and-purple scar wrapped around his entire head from above the bridge of his nose up to the top of his skull and back down behind his left ear.

On occasion, during his bouts of religious weakness and under the influence of alcohol, he'd have a one night stand with some stranger and whenever he caved in and committed these acts of lust, God's voice would order punishment, telling Viktor to cut his forearms.

Every. Single. Time.

Knife, razor, broken glass . . . didn't matter. The more blood that flowed, the faster the Lord would forgive him. Viktor would think to himself, *I'm a good Christian boy. God will forgive me. I didn't sin, wasn't my fault, was the booze.* The erotic desires would always subside after the cutting ritual, but eventually the entire lustful process would reignite and start fresh. This pattern of torment repeated for the next several decades. The purple, white, and pink scars on both forearms were too numerous to count.

Eventually, Viktor had made a deal with God. On the day he would eliminate his two brothers from existence, God shouted at Viktor louder than ever before: *Murder those two sons of bitches and I promise to make your sexual desires disappear.*

Viktor wanted to go to heaven and sit on the knee of Jesus, and he desperately wanted the sexual sins to cease, so he took the deal—anything to purify his soul in the eyes of the Lord Almighty. God told Viktor taking another man's life was a lesser sin than pre-marital sex, so for the sake of the salvation of Viktor's soul, he needed to commit fratricide.

Viktor held up his side of the deal. His two brothers shared an apartment and late one warm summer night, Viktor approached the twenty-two-year-old while he slept, covered the man's mouth with his hand, slit the neck from ear to ear and watched without emotion as he bled out. The middle brother, two years older than the youngest, must have heard a noise and came running into the room. He almost got away, but Viktor pulled a 0.38 pistol from behind his waist and shot the other jerk twice in the back. His brother fell to the ground beneath a large doorway and begged for his life. Viktor walked up to him, curled his lip, stroked his throat and grimaced. "Say hi to Mom," he said as he pointed the revolver at his brother's face and pulled the trigger.

Despite all the violence, those goddamned sexual urges returned the very next day and were stronger than ever. The voice of God had tricked him. *God is a lying sack of shit! How could He—*

Viktor woke up from his nightmare. As time moved on, differentiating his dreams from reality had become more of a challenge. He wondered if he had killed those six thousand people on the 405. *Did I dream that?* He smiled and shook his head. That was me. *I killed them for real.* All me.

He stood and, with the headache gone, his thoughts turned to his stash of porn mags in the bedroom. When he finished getting the poisons out, he went through his cutting ritual to purify his soul, fumbled for his cell phone and dialed his pilot. Time to fly to San Luis Obispo.

CHAPTER 14

"You look like you could use a cold beer. Or ten," the professor said, patting Jake on the back.

Jake put the yearbook down and they headed toward the pub near the center of the Cal Poly campus, careful not to be seen.

"The Marian Engel guy might have been the first cyberterrorist, who knows?" Jake said before an idea popped into his head. "The FBI is reluctant to get me in front of a mainframe terminal, so my next move is to hack into their system to review the networking algorithm that the Super Six developed. Since the 405 attack, I've suspected there's malicious code hidden deep inside. I went over and over and over the code in my head while at the safehouse and figured out exactly where to look. But now it's more than a hunch. I know it's there. I can practically see where they hid it."

The smell of jasmine flowers permeated the air as they walked down a winding narrow sidewalk littered with dead cypress-tree leaves. When they approached the pub, Jake opened the door for the professor, and they walked toward the bar. The cool air felt good on Jake's face, and the smell of freshly popped popcorn helped put his mind at ease. He remembered sharing a bag of popcorn with Cynthia on their first date.

"I don't understand. Why do you think you can find it when nobody else did?" the professor asked.

Jake stopped and looked up at the television in the corner as a newscaster said, ". . . the food supplies are being protected by armed guards, and we're being told by the Governor's office not to worry, not to panic . . ."

Jake shook his head and turned back to the professor. "Because I wrote the original code for that particular part of the algorithm. The other members of the Super Six would know too, but they're dead. I'm it. If there's terrorist coding in there that doesn't belong, I'll know. But I haven't seen the code since we signed off on it nearly two years ago, so I need to get a recent version of the source-code files and analyze it line by line."

The professor rubbed his hand on his head. "It's my understanding that the final source code is locked securely in a certain server farm, a databank in downtown Los Angeles."

Jake's eyes widened with surprise. "A minute ago you sounded like you had no clue how this all worked. How'd you know that?"

"This old man has his ways. Ever since that incident with Marion, I've been, uh,"—he leaned in for a whisper—"helping the feds here and there." He winked and leaned back, nodding with a smile.

They ordered two draft beers, wandered to an empty table

in the corner, and sat.

"Sounds like my instincts to talk with you were spot on, Professor."

"Indeed. I'm assuming you have someone to get you access to the database, which I hear is on lockdown."

"I know just the guy," Jake said. The song "Baby Come Back" by the group Player came on—one of Jake's favorites—over the ceiling speakers and reminded him of Cynthia. "The crazy part isn't breaking into the databank. The crazy part is that this is even necessary. I don't get it. I don't understand why some people kill and do the evil things they do."

"Ah, yes, the million-dollar question," the professor said. "Y'know, I've studied many different religions throughout my life, from the eleven major denominations of Protestantism, to Catholicism, to Buddhism, Taoism, Deism, Atheism, Hinduism, Sikhism, and, of course, Islam. And I've talked with many, many spiritual leaders about this very same subject."

"Jesus, Professor, you rattle off religions like they're going out of style."

A cute young lady brought their beers in glass mugs with the Cal Poly logo on the side. With jittery hands, she set their cold refreshments down, gave a forced smiled at Jake, and left. Jake took a much-needed swig of brew, closed his eyes, and enjoyed the plethora of good memories associated with drinking ice cold beer on a hot summer day.

The professor took a sip of brew. "What I'm about to tell you is not about religion. People often confuse spirituality with religion. They think they're the same thing, but in reality, they're two different but overlapping concepts. Spirituality is inherent in every animal and every human. It's necessary for life— "

"I get it." Jake checked his phone again for a reply message from Carlie or an update from Cavanaugh. Nothing. "I really need to get back to the FBI."

Jake took another glug of beer and set it down on top of a Cal Poly Pomona coaster. He remembered how much he missed his university days when drinking, women, and academics were all he had to concern himself with. Life was so simple back then.

The professor nodded. "To some people, their life views are anywhere from miserable and hopeless to frightening and demanding. They see God, no matter what their religion is, as an entity that is anything from despising and vindictive to punitive and vengeful. To me it's a sad existence, to be honest, but that's their place along the path of spiritual development. They don't even know they are in a lower realm of consciousness because they have no other frame of reference. They haven't been taught that there is light out there."

"Huh. I've never thought about seeing things that way before." Jake's brain bombarded him with details of the crushing amount of work he needed to do to find his daughter and reveal a terrorist plot, but this lecture might help him form a strategy to deal with his guilt. Jake leaned forward. "Sounds like you've got it all figured out, Professor."

The professor slapped his hand on the table and grinned. "I forgot how fast you pick up on things." He held up his beer mug and gave 'cheers' to Jake.

I wonder if the professor is high. Jake stood, threw a

five-dollar bill onto the table, and said, "I gotta get going. Let's head back to the quad." They stood and walked out of the pub, up the winding sidewalk and toward the grassy quad.

A skateboarder zipped past them and almost knocked the professor down. Jake's quick reflexes moved the professor out of the way. The skateboarder yelled back, "It's the end of the world, man! Yeah!" He laughed, put his arms up over his head like a football referee after a team scored a touchdown.

"Dumb-ass kid."

"Not his fault," the professor said. "Everyone is suffering in their own way."

The two walked toward the peak of a small grassy hill.

The professor continued. "Try to remember, the concepts of good and evil are also manmade constructs. Everything is relative and subjective. Is a lion evil for devouring a gazelle on the grassy plains of Africa? To the gazelle, maybe. But to the lion, it's needed to survive, and it's perfectly natural."

Jake thought about this for a few paces before saying, "My car's just over there. Before I go, I want to get your opinion on this." He pulled the scrap of paper, with numbers and dots written in blue ink, from his pocket and handed it to the old man.

"I'm guessing passwords or vehicle registration numbers. Might be IP addresses too, but not sure. I recognize the first three numbers. They're the same as some of the servers here at Cal Poly in the server farm toward the center of campus."

Jake agreed and took the paper back.

"Take care and don't do anything irrational, Jake."

"You know me."

"Exactly," the professor said with a smile.

They had walked no more than fifteen steps away from each other when they both stopped as their cell phones received emergency notifications.

CHAPTER 15

Two days before the Sûr System went live in early May, Peter Mauricio whistled as he worked in his cubicle on the fifth floor of the Caltrans building in Sacramento. The offices of Intelligent Transportation Systems were empty save for Peter, who stayed late to finish editing his final draft of the report, "The Self-Driving Network – Success or Failure?"

He sipped his calorie-laden vanilla latte, feeling guilty about blowing his diet because he and his wife, Janel, had an argument earlier in the day about his out-of-control obesity. The resentment toward her grew stronger with every sip. His thoughts drifted to plans for the weekend with his best buds from high school, where they'd fire up a poker game in the mancave of his Lake Tahoe log cabin, crack open a new bottle of Old Grand-Dad whiskey, and barbecue his favorite recipe of onion-packed burnt burgers.

Out of nowhere, the thunder of loud footsteps approached,

vibrating the floor as three black-bearded men stormed into his cubicle, yanked his chair out from under him and forced him to the ground. He landed on his sizeable belly and felt a knee in his back before his chin exploded onto the carpet.

Peter fought to escape but found himself trapped like a lamb in a slaughterhouse. Ice-cold hands gripped his forearm. Adrenaline surged through his veins and he struggled for air. They pulled him up, but the grip of someone's arm squeezed the bureaucrat's neck, while a hand covered his mouth, muffling cries for help. The spilled latte cup soaked its contents into the low-pile carpet.

In seconds, the three men had positioned Peter's lower right arm onto the laminated desktop. From a duffel bag, the tallest of the abductors retrieved a chrome hatchet and showed it to Peter as the cubicle's florescent lighting reflected off the surface of the razor-sharp edge. The combined scents of Old Spice cologne and man-sweat drifted into Peter's nose. Tobacco stains littered the man's grin.

Peter fell into an abyss of pure terror and lost control of his bladder. With urine dribbling down his khaki pants, his eyes stretched open wide and heartbeat throbbing in his ears, he struggled to stay conscious.

"Fifteen seconds, Syed. Hurry," one of the two assistants said with a thick Middle Eastern accent.

Syed raised the hatchet and thrust down onto Peter's innocent wrist. An immediate jolt surged up Peter's arm as the cutting tool sliced through flesh, muscle, and bone, making a crackling, ripping noise. The hand sat in a pool of crimson, dangling by several uncut nerves before the assailant took a second unwavering whack to completely sever it from Peter's forearm.

Vital fluid spurted from the open wrist across the inside of the cubicle. Syed pulled out a clean white cloth from his bag and wiped splatters of blood from his face before grabbing the hand and tossing it into a plastic baggie. As blood dripped from the hatchet, Syed also stashed it into the duffel bag, along with Peter's dead hand, and zipped the bag closed.

With life draining from Peter's body, the skin on his arm took on the shade of a snowflake, and his abductors dropped him to the floor.

Syed pulled a mini buck-knife from inside his pocket and looked at his partner, who nodded. "Five seconds remain. Do it and we have mission accomplished."

The trio viewed the grisly scene for the briefest of moments before Syed leaned over Peter and, in one clean swoop, slit his victim's neck from ear to ear.

As his vision tunneled black, Peter pictured the face of Janel and thought how stupid he'd been to harbor animosity toward the woman he loved. He took one final look down at his arm and checked out for good.

CHAPTER 16

A red light flashed on Jake's secret FBI Android phone as he walked back toward the Cal Poly parking lot. The severe-weather-alert text message informed him that thunderstorms were approaching the area and a flash-flood warning had been issued for the Los Angeles basin.

The phone had only two numbers programmed into the contacts. He dialed one.

Cavanaugh answered. "Jake, you need to finish your meeting. We don't have much time."

"About that, I'm concerned there might be a bigger game here. We've only seen what's going on in California. We've been assuming this is an isolated incident and the systems in other states have similar firewalls and security measures in place, but what if they—"

"—have been hacked as well," Cavanaugh finished his sentence.

"Exactly."

"I'll reach out to some of my contacts at the bureau in other states and see if they've received any similar accident reports or noticed anything suspicious with the system."

Jake walked another hundred yards and finally reached the Ford. "Anything new on the Shankle front?" He entered the car and a blast of 150-degree air blew upward into his face.

"No."

"How about my daughter?"

"Nothing."

Jake sat in the vehicle, turned on the a/c, and pondered his next possible move. He wanted to drive out to San Bernardino and find Carlie, but she still hadn't replied to his text.

His mind switched to the code. He needed Dave Trainer. "I'm going to try to track down an old . . . um, programming friend of mine. Last time we saw each other was a few years ago when he worked at Caltech. Will check in with you in a bit." Jake lifted his arm to press the "ON" button for the Ford.

"What's his name?"

Jake cringed and hesitated before starting the engine. "I need you to trust me. It's a risk, but a minor one. I'm keeping a low profile, just like you said."

An annoyed growl came through the phone. "We have new information from the attack I need to share with you, but not over the phone. You need to come back in."

"If I don't meet up with my friend, there's no way we'll find any more clues. This is critical. Give me three hours, and I promise I'll come back in."

Pause. "Two. Check back with me in two hours." The call ended.

Before pulling out, Jake sent Carlie a copy of his previous message and added the word "URGENT."

✳

Jake parked and walked along the tree-lined campus pathways to the IT department of Caltech. The California Institute of Technology enjoyed its location in the heart of Southern California. Formerly named Throop University, it churned out some of the best engineering and scientific minds in modern times. Most people referred to it as Caltech, a professional center for some tremendously talented faculty and students.

Along the brick and concrete walkways, he caught the smell of freshly cut grass but noticed how unusually solemn the students appeared. Same as at Cal Poly. Eerie, subdued. He had visited this campus numerous times throughout his career and remembered students were typically laughing and enjoying themselves. Not today. Not with the recent attack so fresh in the hearts of every living soul.

A blonde student cried on the chest of her friend, with mascara streaming down her cheeks. Two other students moped along the leaf-strewn sidewalk, shoulders hunched over, seeming to carry the weight of the world. He detected that raw, zombie-like fear in the eyes of everyone he passed.

He thought about the small piece of paper in his pocket he'd snatched from the FBI office, pulled the tiny parchment from his pocket and studied the eleven digits.

As he walked toward the IT building, he glanced up and his eyes caught a redheaded woman walking toward him. She wore a dark blue dress, matching high heels, and studious-looking glasses. Nearby, several boys stumbled when they saw her too, craning their heads like owls. Another student spied the beauty, head tilted downward, eyes focused on the woman, and slid his sunglasses a bit down on his nose.

Apparently, the zombie effect hadn't impacted everyone.

But Jake's insides stirred. He definitely recognized her. He stuffed the paper back into his pocket.

Crap. The last thing I need right now is to bump into my ex-girlfriend. I should turn and walk the other way.

No. Too obvious.

After all, dead men typically didn't walk around college campuses. He realized how dangerous it could be—foolish even—for him to be out in public like this.

As the woman approached, Jake tried not to stare. Instinct kicked in, he tilted his head down so the fedora covered his face, and he put his hand up for extra coverage.

She started to smile at him, but then her eyes semi-squinted through her glasses. "Jake?"

He ignored her and proceeded forward.

She grabbed the back of his shirt. "Jake Bendel? Holy shit." She flung her hair over her shoulder and let go, as her face flushed red. "What the hell? They said you were killed in that fire last week." She tilted her head and raised her eyebrows in disbelief.

So much for Cavanaugh's advice about keeping a low profile. Jake had no idea what to say. With his wife's death so fresh, the last person on earth he wanted to talk to was Bridgette Trukowski, the woman who'd seduced him eighteen months earlier into having a three-month affair. "I'm sorry, Bridgette, I can't talk right now."

She stared at him with a crinkled brow. "It's me, Jake. What do you mean you can't talk? We haven't spoken in what, like a year? Maybe more?" She put her chin up and exposed her pale neck.

"I . . . uh, I'm in the middle of something important and I—sorry," Jake said, again taking a step to move past her.

With catlike speed, she grabbed his arm. "Oh, no you don't, mister. You're not getting away that easy."

For a moment, he argued inside his head whether it would be best to talk. Tell the truth. *Lies get you into trouble.*

"My wife died last week in the fire," Jake spurted, as if the news might free him from this awkward situation.

As much as he'd tried to bury his infidelity and forget the affair happened, Jake recalled how his marriage to his wife had been on the rocks for several years. The three-month affair he'd ended fifteen months ago with the woman standing in front of him added fuel to his rising internal inferno. Cynthia's soul had been a bundle of kindness wrapped around a gentle spirit. She'd forgiven him, and they'd attended weekly counseling for a year to work on strengthening their marriage, their connection. With his love for her rekindled and optimism for their future together, he had looked forward to a long, healthy partnership with her. Now seeing Bridgette for the first time in over a year, the pain rekindled what he'd endured during that period of his life.

Bridgette gazed into his eyes as he waited for her to respond. A stiff breeze blew through the eucalyptus trees behind her.

I'm in mourning for my wife. I loved my wife, I still love my wife—

"I know," she finally said.

He remained silent.

She ignored his lack of response. "Jake, let me help you with whatever you're working on. I went to your funeral for god's sakes, but you're here, now, which means . . ."

She paused, looked him up and down, and crossed her arms across her chest.

"I'm waiting," Jake said.

She squinted her eyes. "Somehow, the government is involved. You were looking at a piece of paper in your hands when I approached. It's in your pocket. Show it to me."

"I can't do that."

"This has to do with the CDM attack. Or at least the Super Six project you were working on when we had our fling." She put her hand to her forehead and wiped back her bangs.

Jake shook his head, looking around like some paranoid fool.

Her forced smile disappeared and the frustrated look returned. She apologized and gave her condolences and said, "Tell you what. When you come to your senses, call me. I've been working here at Caltech now for the last year and would love to see you and catch up on everything that's been going on. I'm an associate professor in the Physics Department and"—she looked at her watch—"I'm late for a particle physics class right now." She glanced down at her bag of books.

Dammit, Jake, focus. Cynthia loved you and wouldn't want you talking with Bridgette like this. You need to find Dave. There's too much on the line. Stop dickin' around and get going.

Jake gulped. "I gotta run," he said and darted north on the pathway.

The combination of perfume, hair products, and skin lotion had clogged his mind. Before his biology had a chance to take over, he shook his head and walked until he finally arrived at the IT building.

He pushed through the old oak front door. The smell of musty air and old books filled his nose. He jogged up the dark marbled staircase as his footsteps echoed throughout the chamber. On the third floor, he strode into a quaint reception area. One of the walls had a metallic Caltech logo mounted at eye level with the words "IT Department" below. He shivered, trying to shake off the arctic breeze swirling around.

An obese black woman cried silently, staring at a photo on her phone. He said, "Excuse me, I'm looking for someone and was hoping you could help me." He flipped through various piles of business cards in a holder on the counter as she wiped tears away and composed herself slightly. "Who you lookin' for?"

"Guy's name is David Trainer. Dave."

She shook her head. "Don't ring a bell." Her face contorted as she rolled her chair toward her desk.

"David Trainer, the last name spelled 't-r-a-i-n,' like a choo-choo train, but with 'e-r' at the end. He worked here about, oh, nine or ten years ago, in this department, as a freelance coder."

"Well, I been workin' here two years, and I ain't heard of him," she said as she clicked away on the keyboard, squinting. "Let me check the roster for the rest of the school. Maybe he transferred to another department."

If I can't find Dave, I'm totally screwed. He's my only lead.

While Jake waited, he checked his phone for a return text

from Carlie. Nothing.

A black-and-gold nameplate sat on top of the reception-ist's desk: Janel Mauricio. He didn't recognize her name or face. While flipping through the business cards, one read "V. Engel" and he remembered Professor Everton's story about Marion Engel.

His phone buzzed. Cavanaugh.

"Jake, we gotta meet. Something big just happened and we need to talk," said the agent.

"Found it," said Janel. "Says he used to work here, but—"

Jake looked at her and put his hand over the phone. "Just a sec," he said with a wink and turned around to talk with Cavanaugh.

"Tell me."

"Can't. Too risky."

Jake rubbed his temple. "Okay, I'm at Caltech right now. I'll be there in less than an hour." He hung up and turned back to Janel. "Sorry about that."

"As I was saying, his employment was terminated about three years ago. Says he quit. I have a forwarding contact phone number if you'd like to maybe give him a call."

Jake exhaled a sigh of relief.

He punched the number into his phone and thanked the secretary, who quickly covered her face with her hands. Without hesitation, he inquired about her sullen look. "Pardon my asking, I hope I'm not out of line, but are you all right?"

She maintained her downward stare, wiped her forehead and closed her eyes. "I recently lost my husband. He worked for Caltrans and was murdered at work, but nobody will tell me anything. Then we had that CDM. Four of my close friends was killed and a bunch more injured. Everyone in the county knows at least one person involved. Last few months been like living a damned nightmare, and we can't wake up." She began to shake with sobs.

Jake grabbed a box of tissues from the countertop and handed it to her. "I'm sorry to hear all that, ma'am, I seriously am. I've worked with a ton of good people at Caltrans over the years. What was your husband's name?"

"Peter. Peter Mauricio. He was on a special assignment in Sacramento. He worked for the Office of Intelligent Transportation Systems. He supposed to be up there another two weeks, then come back home here with me. We was gonna take a vacation to Sedona, Arizona, with our two boys and now . . ." Sobs of sadness filled the office as she cried even harder.

Jake recognized the name now. They had worked on different ends of a few projects relating to self-driving cars, but he'd never met the guy. "I knew Peter. From what I remember, he was a dedicated, trusted worker at Caltrans. He'll be missed, for sure."

A tiny smile found its way into her cheeks and she looked up at him. "I'm supposed to be at home getting' my life back together, but I can't. No way I stay home in an empty house with the boys at school. But it's kind of you to say you knew my husband. Thank you."

"I'm sorry to have to leave you like this, but I have a meeting to get to that I'm already late for. My condolences to you and your family. I'm truly sorry." Jake tipped his hat to her as he left.

Once outside the building, he dialed Dave's number. The line rang a few times and went to voicemail. Typical Dave, never answered the phone. Goddamnit, Dave. Then he remembered he was on an FBI phone. Of course Dave won't pick up. Jake ended the call without leaving a voicemail but instead texted a coded message to his old acquaintance about *meeting for pizza and dancing at the usual place.*

He walked back to his car, sat down, and waited for Dave to return the text.

The emotions of the day weighed on his eyelids like a steel beam. Fuzzy flashes of bright blinking lights obscured his view of the other cars in the parking lot and the rustling trees beyond. *Time for some help from my old friend Mr. Caffeine,* he thought.

Limp with exhaustion from lack of sleep and those beers with the professor, the motivation for caffeine took him along East California Boulevard to Starbuck's next to the Fillmore Station. A red Porsche 911 was following him so he made three unnecessary turns at random stop signs to confirm. It followed. His heart pounded in his chest as he dialed Cavanaugh for help, but the call went to voicemail and he hung up.

Jake parked and walked to the entrance door, trying not to give away his knowledge he was being followed. The Porsche pulled in and parked, but the tinted windows obscured a view of the driver's face. In line to order his favorite drink, a mocha latte with soymilk and a double shot of espresso, Jake noticed on the wall next to the pricing signs at the rear of the order area, a three-foot diameter homemade wooden sign that read "I-405 We Will Never Forget." Hundreds of signatures were scattered across the board and red, white, and blue flowers were glued to the perimeter. Jake hung his head and thought about the SS, wondering why someone would weaponize his invention and take so many innocent lives.

The lady in front of Jake finished her order and he stepped up to the counter, but instead of receiving the typical welcome greeting from the young man behind the register, a blank stare came over the man's face as he looked over Jake's shoulder through the full-height window.

"Excuse me," Jake said to the stoic.

The guy shook his head. "Sorry," he said, ruffling his fingers through his hair. "Welcome to Starbucks."

Jake ordered his latte and gave the name Jose.

While waiting in a corner, he glanced at the cell phone of a young, hunched-over girl as she drank her beverage. She was Facebooking someone and chatting about the CDM. With her puffy eyes and stooped posture, Jake could tell she had cried recently. He assumed she knew someone killed or injured in the CDM attack.

Jake rubbed his eyes with his palms as his mind raced, questioning the red Porsche outside, whether the terrorists knew he was alive, if they'd take the risk of shooting him dead right there in broad daylight or maybe spray the entire place with machine-gun fire to eliminate any possibility of Jake living. His hands shook, but he put them in his jeans pockets and tried to play it cool.

Finally, the guy at the counter called "Jose." Jake picked up his source of caffeine and returned to the corner, but as soon as he did, a rail-thin, petite, blonde-haired woman approached him from his right. He caught her out of the corner of his eye, and when he turned to face her, he realized who had been following him.

CHAPTER 17

The man referred to by his hacking friends only as *Mr. Sanchez* drove into the CSU San Bernardino parking lot F, an area designed for on-campus residents. His dark gray GMC 2500 truck rolled past Carlie's red Prius and he parked several stalls away. From behind his tinted windows, he scanned the area for life, but that early in the morning the lot was dead. Perfect.

He reached across the seat, picked up a beige backpack and unzipped it. He stuck his arm inside and carefully slid out the tiny bomb the size of a large matchbox. With the exception of a flip switch attached to the outside, all the contents—the Semtex, wiring, cell-phone receiver, detonator, and lithium-ion battery—were stuffed inside the black plastic enclosure. With the bomb in his hands, he snapped the lid open and admired the work of his brother, Syed. More than enough to neutralize the Bendel girl.

After checking his surroundings a second time—clear—he exited his truck, walked to Carlie's car, and knelt down on the driver's side to study the undercarriage. Finding a hefty part of the steel frame underneath, he lowered his hand, reached out, and placed the box near the beam. The neodymium magnets sucked the bomb upward, pinning it to the steel. He flipped the switch and a tiny red LED started blinking.

Sanchez grinned with satisfaction as he stood, dusted off the knees of his American jeans, and walked back to his truck.

Dumb bitch will never know what hit her.

CHAPTER 18

While sitting at a small round table inside Starbuck's, Jake stared up at the woman standing next to him.

"Like. Oh. My. God," Paige Terner, Jake's long-time friend whispered with wide eyes and slid into the seat next to him. "You're supposed to be dead. Like Jimmy Hoffa dead." She covered her mouth and glanced around the shop to make sure nobody else heard her.

He scanned the room full of various folks sitting at other nearby tables enjoying their caffeine infusions, working their laptops, and scrolling through Facebook pages, ignoring the unofficial Jake and Paige reunion. With a tentative smile that grew as the surprise soaked in, he asked, hushed, "Did your dad call you?"

Only fate would bring his old friend into his life when he needed help the most. She was one of the most intelligent people he knew, with two degrees in mechanical engineering and an IQ off the charts. Over the years he valued her loyalty and warmth as a friend and had watched with admiration as she'd moved up the ranks in the engineering world at a phenomenal pace.

"You told *him* you're still alive, when were you gonna tell me?" she asked, leaning toward him to keep her voice low, even though the echoes of the other patrons were almost deafening.

"Been a little distracted."

"I've been following you like some stalker since you were at Cal Poly. I saw you get into your car and it totally freaked me out. I thought I was seeing a ghost." She rolled her eyes. "Maybe I am."

Jake shook his head. "Nope, still here. Flesh and blood for now, at least."

"Which begs the all-time most-consuming complicated question ever: what the hell?"

Jake smiled, moved in toward her even closer and spoke directly into her ear. "Paige, I'm gonna tell you a secret, and I need you to keep it between you and me, okay? I trust you."

"You got it, boss. Lips are sealed tighter than a cat's ass." Paige had been a struggling comedian for the past year or so. Sometimes her jokes were funny; other times . . .

They'd met each other over two decades ago while at Cal Poly. Somewhere during her climb up the career ladder, however, she'd lost the zest for life. She'd had what many would consider a moderately healthy engineering career and made good money, but the daily grind and stress had taken their toll on her. She'd felt constantly irritated but had no idea why, so eventually she went to see a therapist. Turns out Paige was bisexual. She'd wrestled with her feelings since puberty, because she grew up in a Judeo-Christian society that relentlessly shunned homosexuality of any persuasion. She had buried her sexual urges for other women, which had caused high levels of internal stress for her, along with an anxiety disorder, nervous tics, and a heart murmur.

After the bisexual epiphany, Paige had realized she'd only stayed in mechanical engineering for so long because of other people's expectations, not because she loved it. So she'd quit her mechanical engineering job and struck out as a stand-up comedian. No more trying to get ahead. All she wanted to do was make people laugh.

The smell of fresh-brewed coffee permeated the entire place as time seemed to tick-tock its way by Jake faster than normal.

After sipping his piping-hot drink, he scanned the room once more to make sure nobody had noticed them talking, and continued to whisper. "I feel like I'm losing my mind, but talking with you is helping. Guess I could use some of your dark humor to help keep me sane. And that powerful brain of yours might help us solve a few mysteries." They had collaborated on various engineering projects throughout the years and made a good team. By understanding how his mind worked, what motivated him, what his inner fears were, she kept him balanced and stable.

"Holy crap. Hold on a second, captain. I, like, gotta wrap my head around you still being alive." She buried her face in her hands.

Jake stood and nudged her elbow. "Let's take a walk," he said, motioning to the door. He kept his head down, face hidden behind the brim of the fedora, as they exited the coffee-house and meandered north along the gum-strewn sidewalk toward a train station. The hot summer air filled Jake's lungs, but he smelled the beginnings of a thunderstorm.

Looking at the ground, he said, "Some people are after me. The entire country will be after me too if the media finds out I wasn't killed in that fire."

"We need to call the police."

He chuckled. "No." She stopped walking and gave him a much-needed hug and a peck on the cheek.

"Fine, but I was totally devastated when I heard you'd been killed in that fire," she said. She cocked her head to the side. "You don't look so good. Can't blame you, of course. Several of us were interviewed by the FBI, local PD, and people from government agencies with acronyms I've never even heard of."

"What did they want with you?"

"Guess they thought we were part of the CDM attack," she said as they continued north on the sidewalk. "But they mostly wanted to know about you and my relationship to you and some of the other members of the Super Six."

"That's right, you knew Dr. Feenster, the mechanical engineer we worked with on the retrofit."

"The rumor mill is saying the CDM attack was an act of terrorism."

Jake paused, looked at her, and agreed. "It was."

Her jaw dropped. "You gotta be shitting me."

"I can't tell you how hard this is for me to swallow, having an actual terrorist attack here in California. I mean, we developed the algorithm to save people, not kill them."

She blinked several times. "The CDM attack scared the

crap out of everyone. It brought in a cloud of depression, and it's been floating over everyone since. Never want to go through something like that again. This is the USA. We're not supposed to have shit like this happen to us, especially not in California."

"Cynthia's dead."

She stopped, cocked her head and patted him on the shoulder. "I read about it in the paper before I attended your funeral. I, uh, don't know what to say." She gave him another hug. "You need to tell me what the hell actually happened."

"From what I can tell, someone spiked the drinks of Super Six members, including mine, with some kind of sleep-inducing drug. At least that's what my guy at the FBI is saying. Then fires erupted in several spots inside the building and I remember looking at Dr. Feenster. The room was spinning and I lost track of my wife. I was exhausted, couldn't keep my eyes open, and then blacked out. Each of the other five experts passed out. The ones who didn't drink didn't get drugged, so they got out safely. Fourteen people, including Cynthia, died. I'm the only one of the Super Six members who survived; the other five are gone. And I'd be dead too if the FBI guy hadn't pulled me out before I suffocated from smoke inhalation. I can still taste the burning ash."

"Horrible."

"Agreed, but right now I need your help to keep me focused on what I'm working on. Help me keep my emotions in check." Worried someone might be watching them, he spied his surroundings and Paige mimicked him. He put his mouth next to her ear. She smelled like orange blossoms. "We have an opportunity to try to get the guy who murdered Cynthia and make things right. When I met and talked with your dad earlier, he gave me some good advice."

"Haven't seen my old man in weeks; been busy working the comedy circuit. Was on my way to see him when I spotted you and started following."

"He's doing well, I suppose. Getting old, though, but that happens to all of us eventually." A couple blocks up the road was an In-N-Out Burger joint. He smiled. "You look like you could use a good burger."

"Starving." She licked her lips. Paige had always been exceptionally thin, but she loved to eat and had the highest metabolism of anyone he'd ever met. "Maybe we should use the drive-through."

"I don't want to go back for our cars. Plus, we need some privacy and I'll bet my car is bugged. It's a loaner from the FBI. You go inside and order."

They talked more about her dad as they walked toward the restaurant. Jake told Paige his order and handed her a twenty. He wanted to prevent too many people from seeing him, so he went to a remote corner of the outside seating area and sat. A few minutes later, Paige arrived with their chow.

"Paige, I'm about to tell you some seriously disturbing stuff. I don't need to remind you it's super important you keep everything to yourself. You understand?"

"Aye aye, captain. I, like, cross my heart and hope to spy."

Jake chuckled, not so much at the humor, but more for the lack of humor—the attempt, at least. He went on to tell her about everything since waking up in the safehouse. He intentionally dumped more onto Paige than any normal friend could take, but he knew she could handle it.

As he spoke, he remembered the day her therapist had asked her whether she would rather be a wealthy engineer with cancer or a poor, healthy comedian. She had realized she despised her engineering career. The time had come to move on. She'd quit her job, taken classes on how to become a comedian, and had performed on the Hollywood stand-up circuit ever since.

When he finished filling her in, she took a bite of burger, wiped her mouth, and said before swallowing, "We gotta figure out our next move, man."

A thin smile inched to the side of Jake's face. He liked how she referred to their current dilemma as a shared journey. He certainly did not have the stomach to go through this ordeal all by himself.

His phone vibrated with an incoming text from Dave. It read:

okay, dude, if you are who you say you are, what's the name of our fave restaurant and beer?

Jake replied:

Roberto's. Budweiser on tap. Special pizza.

"You remember our buddy Dave Trainer, right? In Pico Rivera?" Jake asked.

She nodded. "Seriously? I remember Dave," Paige said, "but geez, like I haven't talked to him in ages." After stuffing the last morsel into her mouth, she crushed the burger wrapper with both hands and tossed it into a nearby trash dumpster.

Another text appeared on Jake's phone:

meet me at my house in 1 hour the address is . . . And if this is some kinda trick, I'm gonna blow your fucking head off

He showed it to Paige and they both laughed out loud. "Good ol' paranoid Dave hasn't changed a bit, but he's the best hacker I know. Let's go see him before he has a coronary. I'm not sure what else you have going on the next day or so, but it would be great if you could help us find some answers."

"That's gonna be tough. I'm booked tonight at Dodger Stadium for a comedy gig, then I'm flying to New York tomorrow to do the Jimmy Fallon show, then the night after that—"

"Shut up," he said, giving her a shove.

Jake's phone rang. Cavanaugh.

"Oh, crap, I'm supposed to be heading back to meet with my FBI handler." He declined the call.

They walked back toward Starbucks and stood next to the Ford. The phone rang again.

"You should probably answer that," Paige said.

"It's the FBI. I don't want to talk with them right now."

Paige chirped the alarm on her Porsche. "Should we take my car?"

Jake took a beat. "No. I'd feel safer in the FBI car."

"Done. Guess we can come back and get this later, assuming nobody steals the tires."

"You sure?" Jake asked.

"No, but helping you is way more important than some stupid car."

They hopped in the Ford and within five minutes of getting on the 210 freeway, slammed on their brakes before hitting a sea of red lights as screeching noises and burning rubber filled the air.

"There's not supposed to be any traffic congestion on the freeway." Jake's phone rang again. Cavanaugh. This time he answered, wondering why his two handlers hadn't bothered to check in. "Never thought I'd say this again, but I'm stuck in traffic on the 210. What in God's name happened?"

"I'll fill you in when we meet. I'll text you an address."

"I have a meeting set up in forty-five minutes with my programmer guy. I need more time before I come in," Jake said.

"While you were out, we came up with a possible motive for the terrorist attack," Cavanaugh said. "Don't take too long with your guy. We need to talk and we don't have much time on this."

Jake's phone buzzed.

CHAPTER 19

While the lazy peach-colored sun melted into the Los Angeles skyline, Jake and Paige drove smack dab into the middle of a nightmare Jake hoped to never see again: gridlock. Up until that point, the Super Six algorithm and Sûr System were still in full effect, but sometime between the time Jake had driven to Starbucks and now, the Sûr System had been officially shut down. The only way this could have happened was for some high-ranking official at the federal level to order a shutdown. *Two hundred billion dollars invested in the system. Now it's turned off. Great.* Every ounce of sweat and dedication from the hundreds of people working to eliminate traffic fatalities and congestion over the last several years all useless at that point.

Yet the more he thought about it, for the first time in his life he relished the congestion, and his bitterness turned to dim delight. A part of him wished his system would have never been brought online. Thousands of people, and probably his wife, might still be alive. *Maybe computers weren't destined to control our lives. Maybe I was irresponsible to allow this to happen. I wanted to save lives, not end them.* But since humans have been driving on roads, people have been the primary cause of car accidents, not the roads engineers designed and constructed. People.

And now my software.

With humans once again in control of their own vehicles, no further large-scale terrorist attacks would be possible. At least a pinhole of light in an otherwise dark scenario.

He thought about Carlie and wondered why she hadn't replied to his texts. The strength of his negative thoughts grew. No way he could stay sane if he lost the two most important women in his life.

"I have a question," Paige said.

"Here we go," he replied, hoping a conversation would help keep his mind off the pain and confusion.

"Why didn't someone come up with your system of self-driving vehicles sooner? I mean, like, we've had cruise control since the eighties, computers were sending ships to Mars, so they could have made it more of a priority earlier. Didn't you tell me once that like forty thousand people die each year in car accidents? That means every ten years the same number of Americans are killed as in World War Two. That's totally crazy."

A loud crash jolted them from their conversation as Jake slammed on his brakes in response to the car in front of them coming to an abrupt stop.

"Great. Just what we need." Jake watched the driver in front of him exit his white Toyota Camry, pound his hands on the hood, and walk toward the yellow Nissan pickup truck he had just rear-ended.

Jake unbuckled his seatbelt to exit the car, but Paige grabbed his arm.

"No, you stay here. Let me go see if they need some help." Paige opened her door and, with her hands in the back of her jeans pockets, walked toward the confrontation.

A few minutes later, she came jogging back. "The airbag in the front car popped and the woman in the passenger seat is unconscious. I'm calling 9-1-1."

"We can't afford to get into any entanglements," Jake said.

"But we can't just sit here. Let me call and give them a fake name. We need to get an ambulance out here ASAP."

"Of course. Go. Go!" Jake felt his heart rate increase. He was already late getting to Dave's house with the unexpected traffic, and he knew Cavanaugh would explode if he called with another delay.

If cops came to the scene, or worse, a news crew, he risked screwing up his low profile. He tried to stay focused as he stared at the accident in front of them.

Paige ended her call and sat back in the car. "Tell me more about the self-driving tech. I need to know." She did what she'd done a thousand times before: got Jake talking about engineering. That always helped to calm him down.

With a glassy stare, Jake said, "Right. Theoretically, it's been possible for quite some time, but the extraneous potentialities needed to be worked out. On the technical side, it's complicated, but to oversimplify, there are three things needed to fully automate driving."

Steam erupted from the Camry in front of them. The driver was still in a frenzy, walking around in a small circle, looking at the ground, muddling his hair.

"Let me guess. Gas, brakes, and steering," Paige said, guiding Jake back on course.

Jake rubbed the jeans on his thighs. "Exactly. With cruise control, the rate of fuel the fuel injectors spray into your pistons is adjusted based on your speed and transmission gear. So if you set the control to sixty-five miles per hour and you're only going sixty-three, the computer instructs your engine to add more gas so you accelerate until the desired speed is reached. That's the first thing you need."

Distant sirens echoed through the area as two more good Samaritans arrived on the scene to help tend to the lady in the white Camry.

"Totally got it so far."

"Around the turn of the twenty-first century, we started seeing cars come with computers that also controlled the braking systems. This is the second thing you need. Computerized braking systems are more complex, because a built-in intelligence works together with software and hardware. They enable the car to use radar-like sensors and sort of 'see' what's in front of the vehicle. The system calculates the strength of braking based on the relative distance of an object ahead." Jake played back a video in his mind of the collision in front, how it would have been avoided if the proper amount of braking had been applied within a calculated timeframe. These braking factors and much more were included in the massive SS algorithm. "Considering the current speed and other physical factors, when an automatic braking system is activated, people don't need to use their feet to control either of the pedals. They only need to steer."

"I'm guessing the steering, the third piece, was the tricky one."

The screech of the approaching sirens cracked through the air. In Jake's side mirror, the red-and-white flashing lights of an ambulance strobed toward them as the vehicle drove on the shoulder. Jake debated whether to do the same with the lights in his Ford, but what would people think if they saw a police car speeding away from an accident? He needed to get to Dave's house to fix the code so accidents like this would stop happening.

"Right again. The experts who designed the steering and navigation component of the self-driving experience had to consider a crazy number of factors, dump it all into a complex algorithm, and make sure that the car stayed where it was supposed to. You wouldn't want it to drive you off the road and into a tree."

She nodded her head slowly. "Makes sense."

The ambulance parked next to them, but before the paramedics hopped out, Jake took the risk and flipped on the red-and-blue lights, pulled forward onto the inside shoulder, and tried to squeeze between the Camry and the guardrail. He scraped the left side of the tiny Ford and gritted his teeth, knowing how pissed Cavanaugh would be.

Once past the accident, Jake pulled back out into the number one lane, turned off the flashing lights, and accelerated toward Dave's house.

"That was fun. A lot like dating Tom Cruise, I would imagine," Paige said. "Tell me more about the tech."

He knew she was trying to keep him calm. Good thing, too. He paused before continuing. "Go back in time when they first came out with GPS units to help us navigate from one place to the next. You'd be driving along and the stupid GPS would tell you to drive through the middle of some lake in front of you. Didn't know any better."

She laughed. "Yeah. I remember driving to a seminar at Cal-Berkeley once, and the computer told me to head toward San Francisco instead of toward Berkeley. Totally wrong direction."

"That was pretty sophisticated tech, but it still had bugs. It's one thing to erroneously tell someone to drive through a lake. It's quite another to actually drive someone through a lake."

She shook her head. "You gotta be totally a hundred percent perfect with the navigation tech you worked on."

He nodded. "We used a combination of GPS, cell-phone pings, and a proprietary system of tracking signals to get one hundred percent, not ninety-nine point nine nine nine. One hundred percent."

Half a mile past the accident, they ran into more traffic and plodded along the freeway like a snail on sandpaper.

"This is ridiculous. Let's take the local streets," he said, exiting the freeway and taking the back roads toward Dave's house. The local arterials moved along much better than the clogged freeway, which helped shave off drive time. A few blocks along, he was so lost in thought he almost struck a pedestrian jaywalking mid-block.

Paige put her hand on his shoulder. "Deep breaths, Jake."

Jake let out a heavy sigh. "Speaking of the human factor,

even with those three technologies mastered, there were social, philosophical, ethical, and legal questions that needed to be addressed as well."

"Ahh, you mean like the hypothetical situation where the self-driving car is cruising along and something weird happens like that idiot pedestrian?"

"I've missed you, Paige."

She smiled. "I can imagine a scenario where, like, the computer has to make a split-second decision whether to hit the pedestrian and save the driver, or avoid the pedestrian, crash the car, and risk killing the driver. Which is the correct decision for the computer to make? And who's liable for the death: the car, the driver, the manufacturer? The computer? Can a computer be liable for that kind of accident?"

"You're missing the big picture. Those are only a few of the questions we answered as part of our committee. Hundreds of variables and thousands of possible scenarios were studied and analyzed by the brightest minds in the country. We studied each one independently and as a whole. We determined beforehand where the precise liability would fall if such an accident were to occur."

Street lights flickered to life as Jake passed a shady liquor store with several loiterers outside. One had a pistol tucked into the back of his pants, making no attempt to hide it. The men all turned toward Jake and stared as he drove by. "Dave's house must be close," Jake said.

"Seems like there'd be no simple answer," Paige said. "The attorneys, lawmakers, and insurance companies should have figured out a way that worked best for everyone."

"Now you're talking. In fact, the hardest part was getting everyone to the table to discuss the issues. Coming up with the solutions together after that was just a matter of time."

"Never heard of that happening before. Imagine, like, government experts and officials actually being efficient and productive for a change," Paige said with a wink.

"I know. Call the presses," Jake said, chuckling.

Jake remembered he still had the piece of paper the banana-nosed agent had dropped back at FBI headquarters.

They stopped at a red light. Jake retrieved the scrap of paper from his pocket, handed it to Paige, and told her where he got it. "Got any ideas?"

"IP addresses," she said, handing the paper back.

"Your dad agreed. He thought they might also have to do with vehicle registration. I'm gonna have Dave punch them into his computer and see what happens."

Paige looked at her phone. "Google Maps says if we stay on this frontage road to the 605, we can be at Dave's house in Pico Rivera in ten minutes."

Jake turned left and headed down the final stretch of road as the thump-thumpity-thump of a low-rider, a 1964 Chevy Impala that had been lowered to the ground, with shiny chrome bumpers and wheels, cruised past on his right. He forced his frustrated brain to turn back to the task at hand and tried to focus on his evaluation of the algorithm, but he remembered a car show he'd taken Carlie to once when she was little, and could only think about her.

With Paige's directions, Jake drove along the surface streets to Dave's house near a municipal golf course. He parked the car adjacent to a freshly cured concrete curb and gutter that encircled the entire cul-de-sac. He stepped onto the alligator-cracked asphalt pavement and took several steps before he realized Paige was still in the car. He walked to her side and she rolled down the window.

"I don't feel right," she said. "My intuition's telling me we're being watched."

Jake scanned the quiet neighborhood. Nothing. "Don't be ridiculous. We're several blocks from that liquor store. A few blocks can make a big difference. A kitten would be safe here. Come on, we don't have much time."

Paige rubbed the back of her neck and exited the car.

The two made their way toward the front door of a shoddy, cookie-cutter California bungalow house that looked straight out of a 1940s movie.

Tired palm trees swayed in the evening breeze, and Jake smelled the scent of gardenias from the neighbor's yard, which reminded him of Cynthia. That was the flower he used to bring her when they dated.

He stepped onto the front porch, and Paige rang the circular doorbell surrounded by a tarnished brass ring.

As the door opened, a stocky man in his late thirties with a French-fork beard and a shiny bald head stood in the doorway. Based on the man's bulging waistline, Dave had eaten one too many large pepperoni pizzas. His softball-sized eyes peered through Coke-bottle lenses, while he stuffed a large bite of burrito into his mouth and grinned, revealing a tiny piece of refried bean stuck in his teeth. "Jake, you son of a bitch. It is you. Holy fucksticks. I totally bought the conspiratorial propaganda that you were dead. If I hadn't seen ya here with my own eyes, I wouldn't believe it. Total living, breathing fucking conspiracy, man."

"Been hearing that quite a bit lately."

"Hope you're not bugged. This is a bug-free house, my friend," Dave said, scoping out the neighborhood to make sure nobody was watching them.

"Of course not. I need your help with some time-sensitive coding that's right up your alley."

Dave nodded. "C'mon in," he said as he bowed to Jake like some kind of pseudo-servant. The constant skeptic and worrier, Dave gave the outside a final suspicious scan as he closed the door.

He chomped the last few morsels of burrito and swallowed before he turned to his two guests. "Wow, Paige Terner, here in my house. I can't believe this. You probably don't remember me, but we met like a ton of years back. I saw you in a Groundlings show a couple of weeks ago and couldn't stop laughing for, like, three days. Tears the whole way. Had I known you were coming, I would've cleaned up. Sorry for the mess."

Jake surveyed the interior landscape for a piece of furniture that resembled a chair or couch beneath piles of pizza boxes, magazines, newspapers, and crumpled up Del Taco bags. The air smelled stale, like old gym socks.

"Looks like the maid's had the last few decades off," Paige said, tossing an old McDonalds bag to the side with her foot. "Jake's the one who needs your help. Show him the paper." She motioned to Jake.

Jake gave the paper to Dave.

CHAPTER 20

"Definitely IP addresses," Dave said.

With one swoop of his arm, Dave cleared away an entire swath of trash on his couch. "Diagnosed with mild agoraphobia six months ago, so I don't leave the house much. Only for certain jobs, but even those are a struggle to get my ass outside."

Once settled as best he could, Jake looked at Paige for support. She nodded at him.

"Serious question, Dave. When was the last time you danced with a government network?" Jake asked.

The term "dance" had been the inside term they both used when they hacked computer systems—they tried not to use the actual term "hack" anymore. They considered it overused, cliché, and misunderstood by most people outside their world.

"We talkin' something simple or something worth my time?" Dave asked as he rubbed his ear, then licked his lips, squinted, and smiled.

"You know what I mean." Jake smiled back. "I want to make sure the tools in your toolbelt are still sharp."

"Please." Dave rolled his eyes. "But if these numbers are, in fact, IP addresses to what I think, we're looking at felony charges if we get caught. Plus, the media reported you were killed, so this has gotta be some crazy-ass shit." His face burned with curiosity as he glanced at Paige. "She's cool with this, right?"

"Absolutely." Jake waved his hand to dismiss the notion. "I'm sure you've heard about the Super Six and the networking algorithm we developed."

"Rings a bell." Dave tapped his fingers on top of the desk.

Jake brought Dave up to speed. "Believe it or not, I was framed for those deaths on the 405 and several other so-called accidents, and I'd really like to clear my name, but first we need to find out who's behind this mess. So" —he looked at Paige, then back at Dave— "I need access to the federal main-frame system where the algorithm is stored. I'm willing to bet those IP addresses will take us there."

Dave took a deep breath, sat back, and crossed his arms on his chest.

Jake added, "I think someone planted a back door into the live code—made it past all of the security protocols we imple-mented during the QA process. I need you to help me find the backdoor and any other altered code so we can try to catch the bad guys before they hurt anyone else."

Dave's brows knitted. "Don't tell me the FBI is in on this gig."

"Kinda sorta," Jake said, as his head bounced around like one of those bobble-head dolls. "That's not all. After we hack into the mainframe and figure out how to shut down the back-door, we'll need to do some separate research on a lead they gave us. Someone called 'Ivory Snow.' Need your help wading into the dark Net. Apparently, he's some kind of dancer who's involved in all this."

"You're my friend and all, Jake, and we've known each other forever, but if the feds are involved, no way I'm helping. None." His face looked like a kid at Christmas who didn't get the present he wanted. "Anything else, I'm there for you, man, but this is a duck-shit storm, man. Plus, I'm theoretically clean now. My dancing days are over. I work for the good guys, and the last thing I need is to get caught by the feds doing some illegal bullshit."

Jake nodded. He thought this might happen.

"We're on the good guys' side, Dave, we really are. My FBI contact is in our corner on this, but we don't have time to deal with all the protocol baloney. The time between attacks has been diminishing one week per attack, and they've all occurred on Tuesdays, so if my assumptions are correct, they'll rear ugly heads again tomorrow. And I'll take the blame for this if it goes sideways, I promise."

"I don't know, man. I got caught a few years back, and those jerk-offs put the fear of God into me and turned me from the dark side to helping find other dancers. They said if I so much as 'think' about going back, I'm looking at twenty large. And they don't have Roberto's Pizza in prison, man, you know what I mean? I gotta have my Roberto's every week. I'd never make it in there. You want me to risk going to jail to save the lives of people I don't even know? Dude, there's already too many people driving around as it is." Dave looked away from Jake and crossed his arms. "Definitely not."

"You don't mean that. Three thousand people die every

month on US freeways without the SS. That's a lot of people. Tons more could die if we don't get into the system and shut down that backdoor. This is white-hat hacking and you know it."

Dave wet his lips and pressed them together. "Tell me you're sure about this."

Jake nodded. "Mostly sure."

He bit, Jake thought. *Now if I can reel him in.* "Think about the greater good. We could help you prove to the feds that you were a key ally on this. Score you some points with a judge and get you out of hot water."

Dave looked at Paige, over to his monitors, back to Jake, and shook his head. "And if I get caught, you take the rap? The whole enchilada. Like I was never involved at all."

"Yup."

"And I saw on the news your wife's dead. I'm assuming these bastards killed her."

"Right again." Images of Cynthia flashed in Jake's mind and a tiny tear tried to well up in his eye, but he made it go away.

"Done. Screw those guys, man." He turned toward his computer and started typing. "Rattle off those IP addresses to me." Jake read the numbers and Dave typed them into an open Python coding window. A moment later Dave confirmed it. "Yep, this is the IP for the federal mainframe in downtown Los Angeles."

Jake's fingers touched his parting lips and he asked, "How in the world do you know that?"

Dave gave Jake a sinister grin. "Look here," he said,

pointing to the monitor. "This is the access point for their server. Just need to run a few custom proprietary dancing programs I use to bypass their username and password login scripts. Might be how the terrorists are getting access too. We'll see in a sec."

"Looks like we came to the right guy." Paige hopped on one of the unused computers and opened the login screen.

"Tell me what you think you're doing," Dave said to Paige.

"Start researching Ivory Snow." She started typing.

Dave let out a bark of laughter and nodded slowly. "A comedian and a dancer. I like you." He gave her the password.

After thirty minutes, Dave slouched in his chair as his confidence waned. "Man, these guys are good. It's taking me way longer than I thought to get through the multiple layers of authentication. Triple firewalls, but not a problem to slice through 'em."

He tweaked two of his go-to programs by inserting customized references to specific lines of code and maximized the correlation between random bits of data and potential access keys. Over the next several hours Paige explained to Jake how Dave was using various computer programs on multiple devices, all designed to anonymously penetrate even the most secure systems.

Jake's FBI burner phone rang. Cavanaugh. He ignored it and looked at the time on the phone and realized he was four hours past the deadline to meet Cavanaugh. He touched his ribs and abdomen. Still major soreness from when Cavanaugh pulled him from the fire and when he tripped inside the bomb shelter. With the caffeine rush wearing off, and if his eyes could talk, they'd scream at him how much they wanted to slam shut. He needed sleep, but with this crisis and Cynthia's memory as motivation, he dug deep, finding reserves to continue.

Dave clapped his hands and said, "We're in. We're totally in." He typed like a madman as streams of data poured onto the monitors.

Jake knew his way around the files and folders inside the server and figured out the critical piece of code had to be somewhere in either section sixteen or seventeen. *If I was a devious criminal, I would have hidden a backdoor right there.*

He pointed to the file folder he'd seen in his mind, section seventeen, the one he hoped contained the back door code. Dave clicked on the folder to open it. Inside were several files and the actual algorithm itself. Dave opened that file, and the contents of the algorithm spilled out onto the main screen. Of course, this was only a tiny portion of the overall code that the Super Six had created.

As the two men searched through several thousand lines of code, Jake homed in on a portion that did not match with everything else. Like a cat creeping forward to stalk its prey, he leaned over Dave's shoulder and squinted at the monitor while Dave scrolled through the code line by line.

"There. Stop. Right there. You see it?" Jake impatiently pointed to a spot on the monitor. "Right there, starting on line 1776. Section seventeen. Sick bastards."

"Looks like totally normal code." Dave put his finger on the screen to keep track of each line. "Wait, this string of data here doesn't match up with the sequence of numbers. What the hell?"

Paige slid her chair over from the other computer and joined them. "Tell me you guys found the backdoor."

"Jesus, that's sneaky. Stealthiest damned back door I've ever seen. They buried the back door inside the algorithm itself. Genius, really. Those few lines of code unlocked the entire control system that ran the automated software. And the intelligent traffic systems too," Jake said.

"Dude, it's totally camouflaged in there. Wow." Dave's eyes widened. "Whoever put that code in there's a genius. It's concise and totally hidden. I'm not used to being outdone on the dance floor."

"I found a clue here too," Paige said as she sat up in her chair. "You guys should get a printout of that for your buddy at the FBI."

She showed them some info on Ivory Snow, then Dave blurted out, "I'll do you one better. I can tell you how often this sweet-ass gem of code has been accessed and by whom." Dave sounded uppity-up as he whacked away at his keyboard, eyes scanning the screen. "Okay, here's a list," he said, scrolling . . . scrolling. He copy/pasted some encrypted text—what would appear to a layperson as random characters—into a de-encrypting window which converted the gibberish into legible text. "Looks like an address in Big Bear has accessed this shit four times in the last six weeks."

Cavanaugh called Jake again. This time, Jake answered.

"Jesus Christ, Jake," Cavanaugh said, "I'm sweating bullets over here. Not sure you understand the meaning of a deadline. Tell me you're all right and you're on your way. McCallister just sent out a team to track you down and haul you back in here. If they find you in my car and figure out what we're doing—"

"Yeah, yeah. Listen, I'm here at my buddy's house and we just figured out how the terrorists accessed the system and got an address in Big Bear. Need you to buy us some more time."

"Here, let me get a screen capture of this," said Dave.

"Jake. Jake, come here," Paige said, bouncing up and down in her chair and waving him over. She pointed at a name on her monitor.

Jake leaned in for a look. He blinked, processing.

"Cavanaugh, I have to go. I'll fill you in when we meet."

Outside Dave's Pico Rivera house, the hum of freeway noise filtered its way through the stucco walls to the engineer, hacker, and comedian.

Paige hung up her phone and, as she pulled up a new window on her monitor, Jake jerked his head back. The screen looked like a regular internet page but opened inside a software program called Tor, an acronym for *The Onion Router*. It reminded him of the early internet pages from the mid-1990s that displayed mostly text with a few images scattered here and there, all on a nifty gray background.

"That was the second of my two former professors," she said. "They owe me bigtime, so I called in a favor from each one. Here." She pointed to the screen. "You can see I've been able to hack into a special site on the dark web. There's a list of illegal hackers for hire who think their identities are anonymous, but they're not. I thought I'd try to see if your guy is in here somewhere. Figure he's got to pay the bills somehow when he's not working for our terrorist friends."

"Wow, I'd heard of the dark web before, but had no idea such a list existed," Jake said.

Dave gave a smirk. "Amateur."

"I don't pretend to be a dark web expert," she said, "but there's an entire other internet out there most people don't know about. We're using special software and hardware to access it, and it's not for the faint of heart. Some of the sites have some pretty sick shit."

"You mean like porno stuff or—?"

"No," Dave butted in. "We're talking actual rape vids, kiddie porn, snuff vids of people getting killed."

Paige shook her head. "Like I said, pretty sick shit."

"What are you doing with access to that kind of stuff?" Jake asked, worried his friend might be getting in over her head.

Dave put his hands up. "Let me be clear: I have no inclination whatsoever to interact with any of the sick crap out there, and believe me, there's some seriously disgusting stuff available."

"But this is where everyone goes to avoid Big Brother," Paige said. "It's also where criminals hang out. The software uses layers, or onion software, to cloak the actual sites. The tool I'm using here is a program Dave wrote himself that tricks servers into telling the users their data is encoded, but in reality, it's not, and their information is right here. Like an onion peeler." She pointed to the screen again and continued typing. "Should be a matter of an algorithmic search at this point."

Jake turned his head slowly to Dave, his eyebrows raised. "I guess whatever you gotta do. Fight fire with fire."

"Exactly. Dave's got a kick-ass dancing getup in full protection mode, so anyone out there peeking back at us will think we're someone else. In a different country. On a different IP address. No one can detect our presence. True digital stealth."

Paige sounded confident, the way Jake remembered her. He watched over her shoulder, thoroughly mystified with their journey deep inside the underground world of computer mischief. Throughout the night, she worked with Dave to create a new algorithm that cross-referenced banking info with the date, time, and location of all the Ivory Snow incidents—what she referred to as digital "footprints"—and several other variables.

Finally, the word "Ivory Snow" popped up on the screen with a name next to it.

CHAPTER 21

Sixty miles east of Los Angeles, at the Big Bear Municipal Airport, Viktor grabbed hold of the cable railing of his Beechcraft King Air C90gti, climbed up the steps, and ducked to enter his plane. He sat in the rear seat and was untangling his seatbelt when his phone pinged with a new text.

With the dual props spinning, making chopping noises outside, Viktor started to read the text, but his pilot turned around and interrupted to inform him they were ready for takeoff. As the sky arced with a hue of azure blue, a few white clouds strolled off in the distance.

A pilot himself, Viktor knew the Federal Aviation Administration had classified the Big Bear airport as "uncontrolled," which meant it did not have a control tower with live air traffic controllers spouting directions at the pilots, telling them where to fly or helping them to avoid collisions. Pilots self-announced their position at critical junctures, such as when they were five miles out or making a turn from downwind to the base legs of the landing pattern. With a runway elevation of 6,752 feet, landing and taking off could be particularly challenging for novice pilots because of the thinner air which reduced lift on the wings and minimized thrust created by propellers. On a hot day like this one, some of the smaller aircraft would be unable to take off.

But Viktor's Beechcraft would have no problem battling the thin air. The plane had enough thrust to get airborne within a scant two thousand feet, less than half the length of the asphalt runway. The craft reminded Viktor of himself. No matter what the physical challenge, he would always overcome it.

Needing some time to gather his thoughts, he told his pilot to wait. *My FBI mole must be trying to cover something up.* Why had he informed Viktor they never recovered Jake's body from the fire? Something was wrong. He sensed it, closing his eyes to envision a possible trap for Jake, if he was alive. The I-710 freeway. Under construction. Perfect place to lure the infidel, but Viktor needed confirmation Jake still had breath in his lungs. After ten more minutes of plotting, he instructed the pilot. "Okay, t-t-take off when you're ready. I'll get the door." With his headache gone, a manic episode had crept its way into his being, giving him energy on top of energy. His stability and confidence had returned. Nobody could stop him.

"Roger that, Mr. Johnston," the pilot said as he finished adjusting the altimeter to the appropriate barometric pressure.

Wait till those stupid fools find out what we have in store for them.

Viktor stood, pulled the side fuselage door closed, then

sealed the lock. He sat back in his favorite beige leather seat and glanced at his Android phone. *What the hell?* He noticed the text message had come from the federal mainframe in Los Angeles. The phone-home feature his partner had secretly built into the Sûr System algorithm via a "reveal" code in line 1776 had sent Viktor a notification that someone appears to have accessed the mainframe from an address in Serbia. *Probably the FBI*, he figured. *They've searched through the mainframe before, those idiots.* Viktor had confidence in his work to bury the terrorist code.

Viktor tilted his head to the side, blinked several times, curious, then tapped the screen a few times to determine the true location of where the access originated, but the system refused to reveal the location. Blocked. The intruder knew how to cloak their IP address. "Nice try," he mouthed to himself. He ran his "deep override" program and a new set of GPS coordinates popped up.

Pico Rivera, California.

He ran a different customized app he had personally developed to automatically cross-reference the GPS coordinates of government vehicles with an ID database they stole the prior year. The app searched for a few seconds until a map popped up on his screen, displaying a parked car belonging to the FBI about a hundred feet away from the coordinates of the breach. *Clever,* he thought, *but not clever enough.*

Viktor knew from experience difference in IP locations was no coincidence. *Why the hell would the FBI park a car in Pico Rivera? Unless they hired someone to access the federal mainframe house using a cloaking program? To trick me that they're in Serbia?* He nodded. *Jake Bendel?*

He pulled up a different screen inside the same custom app, one he had designed for Allah and this specific purpose. Allah had instructed him to develop the app over a month ago, although he did not understand why. But now he knew. Using his own cloaking mechanism, he could tie, undetected, directly into FBI video feeds from up to three weeks in the past. He gazed proudly when it opened.

Viktor tapped various buttons on his phone. He entered yesterday's date and the time of the breach, then watched a video with an orthographic aerial photo of a cul-de-sac near a golf course. He zoomed in so that five houses showed on the screen. A black compact Ford had a camera icon on top, which meant it had a recorded dashcam video from the same time. With the tip of his finger, he pressed "play" and watched the video as it happened at that time.

He watched from the camera view behind as someone approached the house, someone who walked like Jake Bendel. A short blonde person walked next to him. Viktor had a hard time discerning precise details, but he'd studied Jake's walk on several prior occasions. It was somewhat unique, the way his right foot pointed inward.

Viktor squinted while cocking his head, fixing his gaze on the man walking up to the door of the house at the end of the street.

Is that Jake? No way. My guy at the FBI would have told me.

Viktor harbored a boiling animosity toward Jake. Jake's passion for highway design reminded Viktor of how both his parents were killed in car accidents caused by crappy engineering. Civil engineers have too much power. Especially arrogant ones like Jakey Boy.

If Jake's alive, that changes everything, Viktor thought as the plane ascended through 12,000 feet on its way to a 16,500-foot cruising altitude at a heading of 2-9-0 toward San Luis Obispo.

Viktor had planned and executed the Long Beach fire himself. The FBI investigated the fire and officially reported every member of the Super Six had been confirmed dead. But were they?

If Jake is alive, the others could be alive too, which could screw up the entire next phase of my plan.

Viktor's intellect and professional connections had provided him ample opportunities to plant the evidence condemning Jake for the CDM attack. He marveled at how low the proverbial bar had dropped when it came to ethics within the journalistic community. Opinions were everything to the ignorant masses and facts meant nothing. A few credible anonymous tips here and there, sprinkled with a few seconds of damning video footage—doctored *deep fake* vids, of course—and within two days Viktor had successfully manipulated all major national newspapers and TV news stations into believing Jake Bendel was guilty.

Viktor thought how wonderful and simultaneously tragic that he lived in a country that touted the greatness of theoretical liberty, but in reality allowed the press, the "fourth branch of government," to essentially convict an innocent man of crimes he hadn't committed. Not random, relatively harmless crimes, but horrendous ones.

Viktor shook his head, bringing himself back to his manic

reality, then dialed a number on his phone. He looked out the window, down to the combination cloud-and-smog-infested Los Angeles basin below.

"Hello?" a female replied.

"W-w-we have a situation. J-J-Jake Bendel m-m-might still be alive." Viktor watched the clouds slowly moving outside his window.

"He is," the woman confirmed.

Viktor's eyes widened. "How the hell do you kn-kn-know for sure?"

"Can't discuss over the phone. Need to meet."

"Okay, but until th-th-then, go to a house in Pico Rivera and watch a v-v-vehicle for me. Bendel might be there. I'll text you the address. Just watch for n-n-now. Do not engage, repeat, do not engage. Understood?"

"Roger that."

"Gotta be careful how we do this. If it is him, we need to find out who he's working with and what he knows about our p-p-plan. He might still have access to the Sûr System database, and I d-d-don't need him finding our backdoor and fucking everything up."

"Yes, sir, discreet locate only. I'll sit on the house and observe and record. Will send you anything that happens."

"I need to make a stop up north, then I'll contact you t-t-tomorrow to arrange the meeting." He ended the call then texted the address to her.

Cruising along at over three hundred knots, Viktor notified the pilot, "We have a change of course."

"Yes, sir?" he asked, with a British accent.

Viktor cocked his head to the right, unbuckled his seatbelt, and stepped toward the captain. "You look f-f-familiar. Have you flown me before?"

"Yes, sir. Once. I believe we flew together to Mexico."

Viktor nodded. "Ah, yes. I recall you d-d-did a marvelous job getting us away from those drug-cartel assholes."

"Thank you, sir. I was surprised none of the bullets hit us, to be honest."

"Me too. I meant to give you some hazard p-p-pay back then. You go ahead and put yourself down for a five-thousand-dollar bonus on this trip."

"Yes, sir. Thank you, sir," the pilot replied through a smile.

"Now, once we're f-f-finished in San Luis Obispo, fly me to LAX. And call in a limo to pick me up."

Viktor sat back in his seat, wondering if all the details had been finalized for tomorrow's main event with *the queen*. Viktor mindlessly massaged his earlobe as he planned the details of Jake's trap. *If that nosy engineer didn't die the first time, I'm going to make damned sure he dies an epic death the second time.*

He dialed another number on his phone. The line rang twice, and a man with a deep voice answered. "Hello?"

"As-Salaamu-Alaikum, Mr. Sanchez."

Mr. Sanchez, aka Ivory Snow, was born Ali Rezwan Farook in Syria twelve years after his brother, Syed Farook, who had been born fifteen years after their oldest brother Mohammed Rezwan Farook. This made Ali the youngest of three brothers.

A year after his birth, his parents sold him on the black market, too, because of their severe impoverishment and need for food and shelter. On the outskirts of Mexico City, Mr. and Mrs. Francisco Sanchez purchased their new baby boy.

After their son's second birthday, the Sanchez family immigrated illegally to California. As the young Sanchez boy grew into a smart, handsome man, he had trouble identifying with his past. His good looks and social gifts took him relatively far in life. He had the ability to manipulate any girl he wanted. This skill set came in handy when Viktor called upon him to get close to a female target. "Carlie Bendel was easy to manipulate. Like a tame kitten," Mr. Sanchez had told Viktor.

He had not known about the existence of his two other brothers until Syed had tracked him down four years ago. Syed originally contacted and convinced Mr. Sanchez that Allah had a grand plan for the two brothers, one involving working with and financing a creative genius named Viktor Johnston, aka Mohammed Rezwan Farook, their oldest blood brother. Viktor knew he could trust Mr. Sanchez when the time came for him to do his part.

Syed had informed Mr. Sanchez that Viktor Johnston had also been sold as a child. The three Farook brothers had bonded in their quest to win the jihad against the American infidels.

With a hint of a Mexican accent, Mr. Sanchez greeted his brother boss. "Wa-Alaikum-Assalaam, Viktor."

"How are we p-p-progressing with the Victorville operation?"

"Excellent, my brother. We were successful at getting inside the Caltrans right-of-way. Everyone assumed we were part of the construction crew, exactly as you'd anticipated. Nobody even stopped to ask what we were doing there. We planted the device exactly where you specified, at the base of the bridge column."

"Get to the point."

"Of course. Completely out of sight. It's truly an honor to work under the light of Allah with you on this. We—"

"Sounds like we're all s-s-set, then. Tell me about the jamming devices," Viktor demanded.

"Individual testing for those is complete and we have placed all but two. They'll be finalized and tested as a network early tomorrow morning, plenty of time for the event. In fact—"

"Expected casualties?" Viktor asked.

"The device is in perfect place to inflict damage of the maximum."

"Praise Allah. Maa'aas-alaama."

"Maa' aas-alaama."

CHAPTER 22

Dave leaned over Paige and pointed to the name. "Bingo." He clapped his hands. "M. Sanchez. No idea who the hell that is."

"So the guy has a real-world name of M. Sanchez and goes by the cyber name of Ivory Snow. This could crack the case wide open for you, Jake," Paige said.

Jake said, "It might, if we weren't forced to work under the radar like this. Does the site give any information other than the guy's name? There's probably a million guys with the name Sanchez. We need to narrow it down."

Paige's fingers whizzed inhumanly across the keyboard like the digits of a crazed lunatic.

"Try to tweak your search parameters so it cross-references that name with Viktor Johnston," Jake said.

She moved the mouse cursor around, clicked a few times, and hit more keys. A fresh hit showed up on the screen. "Looks like . . . Yeah, okay, there's a reference here to someone named

Viktor, but not with the last name Johnston. Someone named Viktor Engel, spelled with a 'k', just like Viktor Johnston, so that's something."

Jake snapped his fingers. "I saw that last name on a business card at Caltech. Somebody named Viktor Engel works in their IT department, where you used to work, Dave." He turned to Paige. "And your dad said a guy named Marion Engel used to teach at Cal Poly back in the 80s, but disappeared after the FBI found out about a cyber-attack he orchestrated. Not sure how this all fits together and I don't know if that helps us find M. Sanchez, but it's a start."

Jake realized a whole new problem. If this Viktor Engel guy saw him today at Caltech . . . *What if the guy is part of the terrorist plot?*

He continued. "I'll bet you a dollar Viktor Engel is Viktor Johnston is Marion Engel. All one and the same."

They all glanced at each other.

"No way," Dave said. "Too much of a coincidence. Plus I don't remember anyone there with that name, and I knew everybody."

"I'll get you a printout of this," Paige said. "It's pretty much all I can find on these two guys anyway. Everything else is, like, over-the-top secret. Ain't nobody gettin' in there." Paige grabbed the printout and handed it to Jake, who did a fist pump.

"We gotta go." Jake gave Dave a strong hug, a challenge due to his friend's bulbous stature. "Thanks for everything. I'll be in touch, and remember, please do NOT, under any circumstances, tell anyone I visited you here, at least not until we find out what the hell's going on."

"No promises," Dave said with a wink. "My next call is to TMZ."

As they walked to the little Ford, Jake felt his FBI cell phone vibrate in his pocket. He assumed it was Cavanaugh because he'd failed to check in for several hours, but it might be Carlie. Jake chirped the unlock button on the car's alarm remote and tapped the phone to view the message from the blocked number:

Next time you surf, Check your Brown board with 1.5

Jake stopped mid-stride, staring at the confusing text, and blinked rapidly. *What the hell?*

CHAPTER 23

AUGUST 11,
8:55 am

The woman, wearing a long blonde wig, sat quietly in the Corvette down the street from Dave's house, watching Jake through binoculars. She called Viktor. "Jake just got your text. Totally dumbfounded."

"Yes. Excellent."

"How did you know Jake had a phone, let alone know the number?"

"Our man inside the FBI has been k-k-keeping tabs on Jake's handlers, two loser newbie agents. It's one big beautiful mess over there. His old handler, Agent Cavanaugh, has gone off the grid and will probably end up dead before long, but he gave Jake a burner phone he thought nobody else knew about. Fortunately, our guy did know and g-g-gave me the number in an encrypted text. I have no idea how Jake s-s-survived that goddamned fire, our guy hasn't told me yet. He kept this fact from me until now and his consequences will be severe."

She followed as Jake drove Paige back to Starbucks where her car was, dropped her off, then headed toward downtown Los Angeles. He parked two blocks away from the FBI building and made a call.

When the woman had discovered that Viktor had convinced—probably blackmailed—a man inside the FBI to be a part of their team, she had admired her leader even more. She knew her infatuation with his vision and leadership would likely be her downfall, but she didn't care. She was in this for the big score. As Thomas Jefferson put it so eloquently over two centuries prior, "The tree of liberty must be refreshed from time to time with the blood of patriots and tyrants. It is its natural manure." The woman was willing to give her patriot blood to nourish the tree of liberty for her great country.

She didn't agree with Viktor's Muslim beliefs for waging battle, or, as some of the guys in the cell put it, *jihad*, the final holy war. But she did agree with Viktor one hundred percent that the country had gone to the dogs, so she was in this for the change, not the fanatical religious reasons Viktor used. Like most Americans, she witnessed Washington political gridlock caused by too much bureaucracy and an infestation of narcissistic, aggrandized career politicians running the circus instead of strong, capable leaders. The federal and state governments were bloated beyond belief, and wasteful spending had infiltrated all forms of government like a cancer. Too many people sucking from the public tit. If nothing sparked drastic change soon, she foresaw a path that ended in the death of her beloved country.

Where's the next Kennedy? she wondered. *Roosevelt?* She

knew the US had grown weak and ripe for another country, possibly China, to seize any reasonable opportunity to invade.

She checked in with Viktor every hour as she contemplated and reaffirmed the various motivations for her actions. She loved the man despite his insanity. Hell, she loved his insanity because that's what would bring her country back.

*

After parking a few hundred yards away from the downtown Federal building, Jake used the FBI phone to call Cavanaugh, but before he could get a word in, Cavanaugh blurted out, "Dr. Bendel. You're two blocks away from me. Stay right where you are. I'll be there in three minutes."

There's definitely either a tracking bug in this car or on this burner phone.

CHAPTER 24

Cavanaugh normally worked in his office on the fourth floor, along with 174 other special agents, professional staff, intelligence analysts, language specialists, and surveillance experts. The perimeter offices—the premium locations for the veteran lawmen—offered views of the other buildings in the downtown Los Angeles area. He'd worked for the bureau for over twenty years, so he should have had a perimeter office by now, especially since his wife hated it when he risked everything to do "the right thing," which he tended to do often, even if doing the right thing stressed the hell out of his newly promoted boss, Assistant Director in Charge Sam Shankle. Cavanaugh was the unofficial administrator of the office; his actions demanded respect and his friends were abundant. ADIC Shankle was an arrogant and egotistic man who used fear to control his staff. Cavanaugh loathed the man and most of Cavanaugh's colleagues wouldn't care less if Shankle dropped dead of a heart attack. Fortunately, Cavanaugh's experience and seniority allowed him to cover his tracks as he went about his business by coordinating the investigation off the reservation.

Cavanaugh did his best to practice patience, although he became frustrated at times with incompetent people and inherent inefficiencies of a federal bureaucracy. On the whole, his career had moved in the right direction, even if that dick-head Shankle objected when Cavanaugh ignored protocol as an excuse to help someone do the right thing.

As he walked toward his black Ford, he wondered whether involving Bendel was the right move. *Maybe he can't help us. What if everything is, in fact, random and unrelated? Or what if some Middle Eastern terrorist group is behind this like Shankle says it is?* Or perhaps there's an even more sinister explanation.

What if Shankle's just an ass?

✳

Dozens of palm trees swayed with the morning's warm summer breeze in front of the Federal Building, the epitome of modern government architecture. To Jake, the structure was aesthetically pleasing but built like a tank even though some integrity had failed yesterday with Wilson's death. Jake wondered how many employees knew a new window had been installed. Today was business as usual at the FBI as if Wilson's fall hadn't even happened.

The car door opened and Cavanaugh plopped into the passenger seat. "This better be good. Drive," Cavanaugh said.

"About accessing the code for the Sûr System . . . I made an executive decision."

"I've confirmed the link to another attack," Cavanaugh said, looking out his window and rubbing his thigh. "We're considering that a fifth incident happened back on June 30th at sixteen hundred hours. A Boeing 777 airplane crashed into the traffic control tower at the San Bernardino International Airport. You might have heard of it?"

"Absolutely."

"The NTSB is on-site investigating, but it will be months before they determine the cause of the crash. My guess is this was an act of terror and is related to the other incidents."

Jake's mouth dropped open. "Jesus. I remember thinking how aircraft like that don't crash into control towers." Jake tried again to imagine how such a modern, sophisticated airplane could make such a horrible error. During his thirty-year civil-engineering career, he had designed several airport layouts and had intimate knowledge of how air traffic was controlled. He enjoyed the idea of flying so much, he'd earned his private pilot's certificate ten years ago but hadn't flown often. He'd put flying on the back burner because of his work with the Super Six. Well, that and his tendency to get motion sickness. "I don't recall the details, how many fatalities?"

"Only twelve. The aircraft just had a maintenance crew on board. They were transferring the plane to LAX for routine work."

"And the black box, any transmissions or data that could prove helpful?"

"Box went missing. That's another problem for the NTSB."

"I think it's sad that we are saying things like *only twelve people were killed*." It astonished Jake how numb to death he had become in such a short time.

"Catastrophes change the way we look at things. Now let's get back to what the hell you mean by an 'executive decision'." Cavanaugh's eyes narrowed their focus onto Jake.

Jake merged into northbound traffic on a local street, driving around with no particular destination. "Any word from Carlie? Also, where am I going?" Jake asked.

Cavanaugh shook his head. "There's an out-of-the-way park down a couple of blocks. Let's stay focused here."

"Fine. In order to figure out who's behind this, I needed to access the source code that contains the algorithm I wrote, which lives on a certain high-security server, which meant—"

"No. No, no, no," Cavanaugh interrupted, "you didn't. Tell me you didn't hack into the federal mainframe."

"I told you yesterday I needed to get access to the algorithm."

"Shit. Nobody can hack the federal mainframe. It's impossible. I assumed that friend of yours had a copy of your program's source code somewhere." Cavanaugh rolled his eyes in disappointment.

"Well, technically *I* didn't hack into the federal mainframe." Jake had been searching for a way to test Cavanaugh. Was the guy truly trying to help, or was Cavanaugh merely a pencil-pushing robot bureaucrat who did everything by the book?

They came to a red light and stopped.

"C'mon, Jake, you're smarter than that. Do you have any idea how much more trouble we'll both be in if my superiors find out? I was very specific with you. I told you to keep your goddamned nose clean while you were out there, not commit a class-D felony."

"I'm not admitting to actually committing any felonies. The important thing is that we found what we were looking for. I found the backdoor and I have proof of who planted it."

Cavanaugh didn't look quite so pissed off now. "Someone we know?"

"So we're over the felony issue?"

"Yeah, yeah. Tell me what you found."

"The same guy we talked about yesterday, the guy who helped all six of us on the project. Viktor Johnston aka Viktor Engel aka Marion Engel."

"I knew it. I read a report this morning—signed off by Shankle—that Viktor Johnston died in the Long Beach fire with the others. You might not be the only living person who supposedly died in that damned fire."

The light turned green and they drove further west. "He's alive and he's involved. The Super Six was essentially six key experts, but most people were unaware that we had, in addition, over three hundred full-time staff who worked on the project. There's no way in hell we could've automated the freeway systems all over the country without those folks. We couldn't afford even the slightest hiccup in our work."

"Makes sense." Jake glanced at Cavanaugh, who was looking out the window, up towards the tall buildings. "I don't like this one bit." He slammed the inside of his door with a fist.

"He was a likable guy, almost too likable if you know what I mean. Like it was an act."

"Turn right at the next light. You say he was putting on an act. Not sure I follow."

"I'll give you an example," Jake said. "One day, some of us were wrapping up our meetings in DC, and when I exited the building, Viktor was outside waiting for me. I hadn't seen him since earlier that same morning, but he started talking about how he'd heard my mother had passed away nine years ago and how sorry he felt. He wanted to know what type of cancer she had, did she suffer, how it affected my daughter. Totally odd. People don't normally go into so much detail about that sort of stuff. Not sure how the hell he found out about her death anyway."

"Yeah, pretty weird."

"I tried to be polite and told him I didn't feel like talking about it. He was a great work colleague, but not the close-friend type, so I changed the subject to transportation and he was all too happy to showcase his latest work for me, which, from what I recall, was a key component to the algorithm. You guys probably have employment records. Maybe we can confirm he works at Caltech. He must've had a background check done before he worked with us."

"With this report, the official position at the FBI is that Viktor's dead, so it's gonna be a nightmare convincing someone to help us find a ghost."

"I'll bet you a dollar your file on Viktor is blank. In addition to deceased."

Cavanaugh turned toward Jake, then pointed to an empty

parking lot on their left. "Pull in here and park under the shade of that oak tree." Cavanaugh rifled through the digital files on his phone. "Son of a bitch, you're right. No additional paperwork on Viktor Johnston. No ADA's, either. File's empty, not even a photo we could use for facial recognition, which means someone on the inside is working against us. Our mole strikes again." He rubbed his chin, thinking. "This means he's probably alive like you say." He slapped the phone down onto the seat. "We already know someone's working for the bad guys because of that bomb threat we had at your safehouse. Either way, I don't know what to tell you, Jake. I have no idea how this could happen."

"Maybe the FBI is more incompetent than you think."

Cavanaugh replied, "If so, that's a bigger problem I need to deal with. Tell me more about this Viktor guy. Think about any reasons or motivations he might have for betraying your team."

Jake parked the car under the tree and shut off the engine. "I'm not sure about the motive, but I guess he had the means and opportunity. He worked with each member of the Super Six while we were developing the algorithm and implementation strategy for the automated driving system. I got the impression he knew most of the players already, so we just assumed he'd been cleared by the feds."

"Right, right, I know." The roar of a large jet flew overhead as it descended toward LAX. Sounded like a Boeing 777, similar to the one in June's San Bernardino crash.

"I want to get you in front of a sketch artist," Cavanaugh said. "Give us a physical description of the suspect."

"Not gonna happen. I barely remember his face. We did most of our communications on the phone and via email. I only met him twice, once over Skype and that time outside the meeting in DC. But wait—"

Jake pulled out his phone and sent a text to Everton.

"Maybe one of the other three hundred team members worked with the guy and would recognize him," Cavanaugh said.

"They never saw him either. His work was isolated from the rest of the team and he only worked with us six."

"The other five members are dead, so that doesn't help."

A tiny Mexican man pushed a food cart selling hot dogs and popsicles through the parking lot. Tinderbox music emanated from his umbrella-covered food box. He approached their car, and Cavanaugh waved the guy off while Jake tried to cover his face.

"There should be a record of at least the emails. Don't you FBI guys have techs who can go back and investigate where the IP addresses were and all that? How about a driver's license check?"

"We already searched the DMV records. Nothing. For the IP addresses, you're right, but we need clear details, dates, et cetera." Cavanaugh leaned back in his seat, his hands tightened into fists, and he crossed his arms across his chest.

Jake's phone pinged. Everton had sent a pic of the old yearbook photo of Engel. Jake zoomed in, showed it to Cavanaugh.

"It's old, but it's a start," Cavanaugh said. "How about his appearance?"

"I've worked with a ton of engineers from the Middle East, a lot of great people, really. But Viktor's shorter than me, maybe five-foot-eight . . . balding with some white hair . . . had a beard. He spoke with a stutter. Will never forget the stutter."

"How about his build . . . fat, skinny? Anything particularly noticeable about him?"

"Tiny frame with a potbelly. He's not a big man at all. Maybe a buck sixty in weight? He wore glasses."

Cavanaugh looked out the front windshield at two boys kicking a soccer ball. The hot sun beat down everything and a stiff breeze blew through the mulberry trees to Jake's left. One of the guys waved down the Mexican cart vendor and bought a cold drink.

"I tell you, the guy's a frickin' genius." Jake looked across the lawn to a playground next to where the two boys played. Empty save for three teenage gang-bangers leaning against a slide smoking weed. *No wonder moms don't bring their kids here to play.* That and the crazy heat. "Most people know a little about all sorts of things and a lot about a few. This guy was an expert in many different fields. In addition to what I told you a few minutes ago, he also knew as much or more than I do about some of the core civil-engineering fields, transportation systems, relational databases, and algorithmic programming. According to Dr. Mary Hart, the psychologist in the Super Six, Viktor knew as much as she did about psychology, social psychology, and sociology. That's saying a lot, because she's a national leader in her field."

"No shit."

"He helped her with the designs for the psychological and sociological impacts of having computers drive our cars for us on freeways. Now that I think of it, he was the one who came up with the panic-button idea so if you need to disconnect from the freeway network, you just—"

"We don't have time to get into those technical details," Cavanaugh said, waving his hand. "Talk to me about security clearance when it came to the code. You said he had access. I'm assuming there were different levels of administrative access to the server and its contents."

"True. He didn't—or at least wasn't supposed to—have access to the actual source-code files, either the beta version or the final product. But I was thinking that if one of the others gave him their username and password or if he somehow stole such information from one of us, he could've gained unlimited access to the entire project. Assuming that's true, he could've encrypted and uploaded the secret backdoor code in such a way that nobody would find it. Since he's a genius with coding too, I have no doubt he accessed the system and planted what looked like normal, benign code." Jake looked Cavanaugh dead in the eyes. "This snippet of code we found is written in such a way that it gives him access to the entire system. It opens up a backdoor large enough to drive a truck through."

CHAPTER 25

"Interesting theory, Jake," said Cavanaugh before over-exaggerating an exhale. "Let's get back to what you found earlier."

They both stared at each other for a moment.

Jake tried quickly to think of an analogy to help Cavanaugh understand how backdoors work.

"Remember that movie from the early eighties called *War Games* with Matthew Broderick?"

Cavanaugh thought a moment. "Yeah."

"I know that technology's outdated, and it's an exaggerated oversimplification of what's happening here, but the backdoor allows someone with the IP address of the federal mainframe to gain undetected access to the program and bypass any security firewalls in place. Just like in *War Games*, Broderick's character searched for and found a backdoor, the one that the original coder put there, and once inside the WOPR computer, he caused all those problems and nearly started World War III."

Cavanaugh agreed wordlessly. This guy was the king of nods. "Your theory is that this son of a bitch planted a secret way into the system months ago, maybe years ago, when he was part of your team. He's supposedly helping you guys but plants a digital door that allows him access to the system whenever he wants. Then what?"

Jake smiled. Good question. "That's where it gets interesting. Just because he has remote access to the mainframe doesn't necessarily mean he can make the system do anything he wants. The Super Six programmed the system so whoever makes changes would need a physical access point, where someone literally needs to be at the computer for the remote connection to become activated. Deductive logic dictates Viktor has to be working with someone else. In other words, he can't be sitting at his computer, hack in, and shut down a freeway. Someone on the inside needs to physically validate the action before the system will allow the change to start."

"Okay, before we jump into that, let me get someone started on an investigation into this Viktor Johnston working at Caltech. You're sure this guy is alive?"

"No, he's dead and we're investigating a corpse." Jake raised his right eyebrow for effect.

An ambulance siren whined in the distance and waned as Cavanaugh called someone to start a background check, then hung up. "Assuming Ivory Snow and Viktor Johnston are two different people, what did you dig up on Snow?"

"Ivory Snow's real name is M. Sanchez, and there's strong evidence to suggest that he's online buddies with Viktor Engel."

"Do you spell this guy's name with a 'k,' same as Viktor Johnston?"

Jake nodded. "As I said earlier, it's possible these two guys, Engel and Johnston, are one and the same."

Cavanaugh ran a hand through his thick, dark-brown hair.

"We had our best people working on Ivory Snow. No way you figured that out on your own."

Jake smiled and thought about keeping Dave a secret. *Ah, what the hell.* "I didn't. The hacker friend I met with did. He's a top dog in the hacking world. I promised him I wouldn't reveal his name."

"We don't have time for any of this bullshit. Stay focused on the big picture. Tell me his name so we run a check on him. We need to know he's on our side."

"He is, don't worry."

"Tell me his name."

Jake looked out his window, debating whether or not to violate the trust of his good friend. "I will if you give me your word you won't go after him. I asked him to hack into the mainframe, so I'll take full responsibility for the consequences."

"Yeah, yeah, okay, whatever, but I need to know who he is."

Jake thought about it for another second, not sure if he should trust Cavanaugh.

"His name is Dave Trainer. He helped—"

"Dave Trainer? The Slicer?"

"The what?"

"Dave Trainer's call sign's The Slicer. We busted him and turned him to work with us." Cavanaugh smiled. "I hadn't even thought about tapping into him as a resource for the investigation. Good call."

Jake made a mental note to give Dave a hard time about his nickname the next time they met.

The three thugs ran from the kiddie slide toward the Mexican vendor. In an instant, the tall one had a gun pointed at the old man's face while the other two opened the cart and helped themselves. Jake tapped Cavanaugh on his thigh and pointed to the crime in progress. Before Cavanaugh could get a good look, the three thieves were running away from them, heading toward a large group of trees to disappear.

Jake pulled out his burner phone, but before he could dial 9-1-1, Cavanaugh had placed his hand on the phone. "No, Jake, that's a problem for the local PD, but I'll call it in."

Jake blinked several times as he thought. "Before I forget, I received a text last night. Check out how the message has the words 'check' and 'brown' capitalized."

Cavanaugh held the phone and stared at the text before handing back the device. "I'm more concerned about how someone got hold of your number, especially if the text came from the terrorist. That's a brand new, off-the-record burner phone you're using, and I'm the only one who knows about it, or at least I thought I was. It's not like someone could just look you up in a phone book or online. Either way, tell me the time you got the text message so I can run a trace, maybe find out who sent it. And I'll check around to see how your phone number might have been leaked."

"You're doing a wonderful job building up my level of confidence in the FBI," Jake said. "If there's a mole at the FBI and he knows I'm alive, then he knows I have this phone. So do the terrorists."

Cavanaugh rubbed his chin.

"Regardless, the text came in early this morning around four o'clock."

As Cavanaugh called in the robbery, a low-pitched rumbling noise surrounded them and the tiny Ford shook. Cavanaugh's eyes opened wide and a woman screamed in the distance.

CHAPTER 26

Jake had figured out a long time ago that earthquakes and California went together like cheese and wine. While designing and constructing dozens of freeway bridges throughout the Golden State, he had studied many of the roughly two hundred potentially hazardous faults that splintered up, down, and across the land. Of course, the big daddy of them all, the San Andreas fault, ran north and south, near the coast through San Francisco and north Los Angeles County. In fact, the Mighty San Andreas sat less than a mile away from Jake's house, where two large tectonic plates, the Pacific and North American, have slid against each other for several million years. In the resulting mountain regions, Jake and his wife had hiked, camped, and made love under the stars many times. One of his favorite ranges was the San Bernardino Mountains, where Big Bear City was located.

Every California native had grown up with the little

quakes. Annually, Californians witnessed an average of two to three moderate-sized tremors registering at least 5.5 on the Richter scale. But it was the big ones that frightened even the most seasoned earthquake enthusiast.

Fortunately for ten million Los Angeles County residents, the 10:55 a.m. quake that rattled Jake and Cavanaugh as they prepared to leave the park was relatively small at 4.6. According to the USGS app on Jake's phone, scientists estimated the epicenter at forty-two miles east of the Staples Center, home of Jake's favorite NBA team, the Los Angeles Lakers.

After the rumble, the two men drove back to downtown L.A., then Jake pulled alongside a curb two blocks from the FBI building, the same place where he'd picked up Cavanaugh twenty minutes earlier.

"Tell the Slicer I said 'Hi,'" Cavanaugh told Jake as he exited the compact Ford.

"I'm going to meet Paige."

"Who?"

Jake gave Cavanaugh a high-level description of her, how she fit in, was Everton's daughter, et cetera.

Jake continued. "Need to do some brainstorming with her, but if you get anywhere with the search for Carlie, let me know. It's killing me we haven't found her."

Cavanaugh nodded, "I don't see your handlers anywhere. You're good to go," then shut the door.

✳

Jake headed on local streets in a northeasterly direction, then turned right on Melrose Avenue, where Paige was finishing a morning class at her favorite haunt, the Groundlings Theatre & School in West Hollywood.

She stood on the gum-strewn concrete sidewalk, chatting with some friends, leaning against the brick façade with ancient arches in the shade of pepper trees. Jake pulled up, she hopped in.

"We're gonna go meet Dave."

They drove east on Melrose.

"I've been thinking about this Viktor guy, or Marion, or whatever his name is, and his motivation for doing these things, and I mean, like, the reasons someone would want to kill so many people. Trying to figure out how someone can have that much hate in his heart."

"I'll bet he's just got a very low level of consciousness," Jake said, finishing her thought.

"Sounds like you've been talking with my dad."

"I suspect mental illness, so couple that with a powerful intellect and you get some pretty bad stuff, but we're going to stop him, don't worry." Jake shrugged, thinking more about how his discussion with Professor Everton challenged his notions of right and wrong, good and evil. But that low life scumbag had murdered his wife, so Jake could only accept one solution: *The guy's a dead man.*

Paige turned to Jake. "I can tell you're thinking about your wife, how wrong it is for her to be gone," she said.

Jake furrowed his brow. "You know me better than I do." He patted her on the knee. "It's not right."

"If it makes you feel any better, I believe in karma. He's going to have a huge karmic debt when his time's up and he leaves this world," she said, making a slicing motion with her finger across her neck.

"Let me run something by you that's been bouncing around in my head. You're still an engineer in my book, so maybe you can help me figure out a puzzle that's been bothering me."

"Go for it."

As they entered an uphill on-ramp to the freeway, Jake gunned their little Ford and she said, "Careful. You don't want to break the rubber band in this thing."

He smiled back. "Funny. Since math and physics are basically manmade models for interpreting the world around us, I'm wondering if we can use a physics equation to help us understand human behavior. You remember the equation for momentum?"

"Duh. It's like the mass of an object multiplied by its velocity."

"I've been thinking about applying that formula to the way human beings affect the world, an equation that accounts for their impact on the momentum of global consciousness. Maybe people with low levels of consciousness affect the world with negative spiritual momentum, while people with higher levels have a similar effect but in the opposite, positive direction."

Jake looked at Paige and saw the wheels spinning inside her head.

"Not sure I follow, but give me some time," Paige said. "I gotta let it soak in for a bit. Funny thing about thoughts, they're fragile and need us to, like, give them life. Everything manmade was, at one time or another, just a tiny frail thought in someone's head. Houses, roads, tech inventions, buildings, bridges, countries, the list goes on and on."

Jake agreed, exited the 101 freeway heading toward downtown Los Angeles, then asked Paige to text Dave to meet them at the Staples Center, little more than a mile southwest of Dave's current job as a cyber-security consultant in the financial district. In the past, Dave had not only been a good confidant, but his skeptical nature helped balance out Jake's innate sense of optimism.

Across the street from the home of the Lakers, Jake paid his five bucks to a parking attendant, then ran with Paige toward the meeting place, but as he approached, he noticed a makeshift memorial for the victims of the I-405 attack and stopped. Thousands of headshot photos lay intermingled among a car-sized bulge of white, red, purple, and orange flower arrangements, stuffed teddy bears, and candles of all sizes. The somber scene added to Jake's guilt, knowing his invention caused so much heartache and sorrow. He threw his head skyward and closed his eyes.

"Not your fault, buddy," Paige said, patting him on the ribcage with a motion to keep walking. "Let's go. I think I see Dave up ahead."

Dave joined them, then they all sat at an outdoor table between the Microsoft Theater and Smashburger, checking their surroundings to see if anyone had followed them. Clear.

Unable to sugarcoat his thoughts, Jake poured out everything that was on his mind, getting Dave up to speed. When finished, he said, "I want to run a theory by you two. It's crazy,

I know, but try to hear me out."

"Didn't get much sleep last night, but fire away," said Dave.

"OK." Jake began. "There has to be a logical sequence for these events."

"Totally agree, dude," Paige said.

"And according to the FBI, all five attacks happened without warning and on different dates." Paige and Dave waited for him to continue. "I know Viktor," Jake said. "His temperament is a rational thinker. Introvert. At his core he thinks logically, even though he exhibits all the classic signs of a psychopath."

"You some kind of psychiatrist now?" Dave asked.

"We had a bunch of training classes during the Super Six project. Had to learn to get in the mind of a terrorist. Several weeks, in fact, taught by professors at Harvard, Stanford—"

"Okay, sorry I asked," Dave said, crossing his arms and taking a confrontational stance.

"Think about it," Jake said. "He has a complete disregard for our laws or the rights of others and doesn't seem to feel any remorse or guilt for killing all those people. I worked with the guy, and I can tell you for a fact he's got an exceptional ability to mimic empathy with others, to trick them. I mean, he certainly has a charming, if somewhat quirky, personality. I'll give him that."

Paige thought about this for a split second. "Let's assume you're right. We need to go over the details again. You're saying he caused the SITS nightmare at intersections throughout California. Most people, including myself, are familiar with that, which could be considered, like, a random act of violence.

But he's targeting regular people—he killed nobody with any particular social status, no, like, famous actors, politicians, or high-profile people from the *National Enquirer*. People of all races, creeds, religions, et cetera."

"Got an idea," Dave said. He grabbed a napkin, borrowed a pen from Paige, and drew a quick sketch of a timeline. "Let's take a linear look at the timeline. Tell me how many days ago each event occurred."

Dave drew a simple table with columns for the attack name, number of days ago for each attack, and the time.

"The green-lights attack was forty-five days ago at four in the afternoon. The CDM attack was thirty-five days ago at four in the afternoon. The buses crashed into the horses fourteen days ago, also at four in the afternoon. The assassination attempt on Cardinal Mahoney was seven days ago, also at four in the afternoon. And the fire that killed your wife and colleagues was also seven days ago at seven at night."

"And this morning Cavanaugh told me more details about an airplane crashing into the air traffic control tower on June 30th at four in the afternoon at the San Bernardino International Airport. That's exactly three weeks ago."

Dave continued. "I'm thinking that's gotta be some specific effort on Viktor's part. He targeted that particular plane and made sure that it hit that particular target, a control tower."

"Okay," Paige said, looking down at the timeline table Dave had drawn on the napkin. "Look at the dates in terms of weeks. We have five weeks between the first two attacks, then four, three, two, and one. And with the Del Mar bus crash, even though thirty-eight people were killed, it's like he was more interested in trying to kill the horses for some reason. I have no idea why the hell he'd do that, unless the dude's got a thing against horses."

Another dud joke.

"No way to know for sure," Jake said. "I don't see how that attack relates to the attempt on Cardinal Mahony's life two weeks later."

They all turned and looked at each other, up at the blue sky, then back at the napkin, pondering the variables.

"Question," Paige said. "If all the vehicles in the CDM attack slowed at the same rate, even if they were only spaced at two feet apart, why didn't they just come to a nice gentle stop? No accidents. No death."

Jake stiffened his posture. "This guy's smart. He must have set the system to slow down every other vehicle on the freeway, in a checkerboard pattern. Half the vehicles braked, the other half accelerated. The speed differential is what caused the accidents."

Paige swiped the blue pen from Jake's hand. "Like a checkerboard?"

Jake nodded, then looked at Dave as Paige continued. "Check this out, guys. First, we have random people, then, like, a tower, then horses, then a cardinal." She grabbed a separate napkin and scribbled down her understanding of the timeline on the back. "If we could figure out a pattern in the dates and times, we could find out if there's a pattern to the types of events he's causing and when the next one will happen."

Crap. Jake needed to step up his game. "Hey, wait," Jake

said. "Last night I got a random text. Wasn't sure the wording meant anything." He whipped out his phone and showed the text message to his two friends. He'd forgotten to show them the message earlier. Normally he'd remember important things like that.

The scent of freshly popped popcorn meandered through the gathering area between the Staples Center and the shopping plaza to their north. A school bus full of children drove by.

Paige read the text. "*Next time you go surfing, Check your Brown board for one point five.*" She tapped her feet with excitement.

Dave said, "And with the words 'next', 'check' and 'brown' spelled with capital letters. Hmmm . . . I got no clue what the hell surfing has to do with any of this."

"Maybe it's a reference to the ocean and my research on modernized low-energy desalination plants," Jake said.

"Maybe the text isn't related," Dave said. "That's an FBI-issued phone, so maybe the message is for the previous owner or someone else entirely."

Jake ignored Dave's assumption, going over the keywords in his mind.

"This is definitely related." Paige grabbed her pen from Dave and drew a checkerboard with the words on another napkin. *Board. Check. Brown. People. Tower. Horses. Cardinal.* Staring at Paige's map, then back at the checkerboard, the epiphany hit Jake square in the head, like being struck by a high-speed train. "Chess." He looked at Paige, who was already nodding her head.

"Yup. Like pieces in the game of chess. I'll bet Viktor's

playing some kind of sick chess match with the FBI."

"And the American people are his pawns," Dave said, finishing the thought and scratching his right cheek with that familiar look of skepticism draped over his face. "Maybe, but the cardinal doesn't fit the pattern, per se."

"But he could represent a bishop," Paige said, checking her phone. "Says Cardinal Mahoney was promoted from bishop in May." She set her phone down and stared into Jake's eyes. "Which would mean Viktor's moving up the hierarchy of chess pieces, and the queen would be next."

"I don't know. Sounds like a pretty big stretch," Dave said. "The dates and times still don't make any sense."

"The object of a chess match is to capture the king, so assuming this is the pattern, the next piece—a queen, or possibly a king—would need to be killed sometime today, Tuesday, same as all the other attacks, and at four o'clock."

CHAPTER 27

Rays of sunlight came and went from behind fast-moving clouds which created alternating spots of sunshine and shade on the surrounding ground while the trio strategized.

"Now let's play hypotheticals." Jake loved to play hypotheticals. "Who would be the king, or queen, and what does he or she have to do with the color brown?"

Jake leaned over Paige's shoulder as she opened up the Google Chrome app on her phone and did a quick search for "brown" plus "king." Nothing. She changed "king" to "queen". Still nothing. She tried "brown" plus "royalty" plus "California." In the middle of the Google listings, a blog writer had a bunch of hits, so she clicked the link. Jake read down the page. *Blah blah blah* . . . then two paragraphs about Senator Brown at a ribbon-cutting ceremony today for the new High Desert Corridor opening in Victorville at 2 o'clock.

Jake grabbed her phone. "She's not a queen." He scrolled

through details of the ceremony announcement. "Says here they rescheduled. Original time was 4 p.m. Bingo. She's as close to anything royal we have. Says she'll be there because she helped secure federal funding for the project and wants to take credit."

"Dude," said Paige, taking her phone back, "what if Viktor plans on taking out Senator Barbara Brown at this ribbon-cutting ceremony?" She checked her watch. "Which starts in, like, less than three hours."

"Pretty thin, man. No way the dude's going after a senator," Dave said.

In Jake's mind, the equation balanced out on both sides, lining up perfectly with the timeline and the chess theory. "We gotta get up there." His heart pounded fast and hard, but he needed to get this information to the FBI. "We'll call Cavanaugh on the way up the hill."

Before he could take a second step along the sidewalk

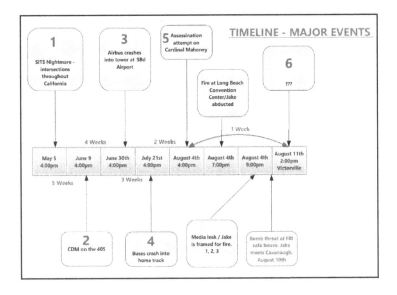

toward the parking lot, Paige hooked his arm, stopped him, and stood up from her chair, knocking it over. "Wait. We're not going to *do* anything. We're engineers, not terrorism experts. This is, like, totally outside our wheelhouse. We should just tell Cavanaugh and let the FBI handle this."

"She's got a point," Dave added, standing next to his two friends in the shade of the red-and-white striped awning.

Jake tented his hand across his forehead to block the morning sunlight. "I designed the geometrics for that interchange. If there's some way I can help Cavanaugh with an assessment of the bridge structures, likely places to strike or crash cars or whatever, I need to at least try." His phone rang.

"Speak of the devil," Jake said into the phone. "Cavanaugh, we think we've ID'd the next target."

"Jake, listen—"

"We know where the next attack will happen and when. It will be—"

"Listen to me," Cavanaugh said with urgency in his tone. "We just received word your daughter's in danger."

CHAPTER 28

"Does Carlie work at Cal State San Bernardino?" Cavanaugh asked Jake over the phone.

Running on a sidewalk away from the Staples Center, Jake skidded to a halt, a sense of foreboding erupting inside him.

"Jake? You there?"

Jake's mind spun like a whirling toy top and he realized he'd missed part of the conversation. "Um, yeah, last I heard, before I went to the safehouse, but I don't understand. You told me yesterday she was missing, so I assumed you'd already checked where she worked and you'd find her. Heck, I could've driven out there yesterday myself if it was as simple as going to her school. I trusted you."

Dave and Paige both drew closer to Jake. She put her arm around him.

A white limo passed by on Figueroa Street. A busty, bikini-wearing woman inside the vehicle stood, holding a sign that read "ISAIAH 13:9 DESTROY THE SINNERS I-405." The upper half of her body poked out the moon roof. She distracted Paige and Dave for a few moments while Jake took several steps toward the street.

"We did check her work," Cavanaugh said, "she's been out for several days and nobody knows where she is. But we hit a break. Anonymous tip to the San Bernardino PD. Someone saw a man crawling underneath a car in the parking lot at Cal State early this morning. Ran the plates, came back to her. Do you know if she recently had any car trouble?"

"No idea. I've been locked up at the damned safehouse for the last week. How the hell would I know that?" His face felt flush as the realization hit him how much he missed his little girl, his sweet angel. At six-foot-one, she wasn't a munchkin anymore by any stretch of the imagination, but in his mind, she'd always be his little princess.

"I know I told you yesterday to let me work on finding her, but now I'm telling you to help out and give her a call ASAP. You got her cell number?" Cavanaugh asked.

"I've been trying to text her, but she hasn't responded." His mind raced faster now to find a solution.

Jake waved his hands to his two friends, motioning for them to follow him, then he started to jog toward the parking lot. "I'll call her in a minute and drive out there myself if I have to. But, Cavanaugh, listen, we need to talk about Viktor's plan. I think we've figured out his next move."

Jake heard Cavanaugh talking with someone next to him, along with the word "bomb." After a second of rustling on the line, Cavanaugh returned. "We've just confirmed that an unexploded bomb was found planted underneath Carlie's car. She's apparently safe for now, but you need to get into contact with her ASAP."

"Jesus Christ," Jake said. He lowered the phone and told Dave and Paige, and Paige let out a yelp before covering her mouth.

"We can go over your terrorist theories after you get on the road," Cavanaugh said.

"No, I'm jogging to my car now. Let's talk at the same time."

"We've had a team of forty agents working night and day on this for weeks, and haven't come up with anything about what they're gonna try next."

Sometimes people act like insects, missing the big picture, Jake thought. "You asked for my help, and this is me trying to help you."

"Fine. Let's say, hypothetically, you did beat us to the punch. Tell me your reasoning."

He likes playing hypotheticals, too. Good.

"It's a chess match," Jake said, breathing heavily, waiting to hear what Cavanaugh thought.

After a long pause, Cavanaugh finally said, "A chess match? Not sure I follow."

"Picture this: first, there were the random people killed with the SITS nightmare. Second, more innocent people died in the CDM on the 405. All pawns. Third, the plane crash into the control tower at the San Bernardino Airport. Then those horses were killed. Knights. Fifth, we have the attempted assassination of the cardinal. All on Tuesdays, at reducing intervals of weeks. All at four o'clock. We discovered the cardinal had recently been promoted, and these guys are sometimes referred to as archbishops. Back in May, the guy was still a bishop. So that's the bishop and the rook."

"We know all this."

"The random people represented pawns on a chessboard. The airport tower represented a castle, horses were the knights, and the cardinal was a bishop. If the theory holds true, the terrorists would be hunting for a queen and or king to capture or kill."

Silence. Jake imagined Cavanaugh letting the idea settle in. Or maybe his phone died.

"But what if there are simply more pawns, another knight, or another bishop to kill? I'm not really buying this, to be honest. You've piqued my curiosity, though, so, since we're going down this hypothetical road, who do you think the so-called queen and king would be?"

Jake spotted his car in the parking lot, gave the ticket to the attendant, who scurried off to get his car. "Before I answer that, the other thing we noticed is the timeline, which your guys might not have found if they weren't using the Airbus crash from June. Without that, there's no pattern. With it, and using that text message I received last night, the one I showed you at the park, we got something."

"I'm listening."

"We've pieced this together. I'm thinking the word 'board' refers to a chessboard, and the reference to brown is not to the color, but rather to someone's name. And the word 'check,' as in 'checkmate,' a common chess phrase."

Jake explained the rest of their theory. "Bottom line, if

we're correct, there'll be an attack today involving Senator Barbara Brown, during the ground-breaking ceremony in Victorville at two o'clock for the opening of the new High Desert Corridor project."

"Are you sure Senator Brown's the next target? She's most certainly not a queen, but nevertheless, I'll need to inform the Secret Service on this if it's a potential threat to her." Jake wondered if Cavanaugh shared Jake's lack of fondness of politicians.

Paige hopped in the car and paid a tip to the attendant. Jake gulped as he sat in the driver's seat.

"Damnit, I told you to keep your head down and keep your personal contacts to a minimum. For your own safety. You can't tell everyone about our investigation."

Jake started the car and pulled out on the street, heading north.

Cavanaugh continued, "Look, I'll be honest with you. Assuming this is all true, we could use your help for this Victorville attack, but under no circumstances are you to physically go up there. I want you to focus on your daughter. What can you tell me about these ceremonies?"

Jake looked at Paige, then to Dave in the rear seat. "I've attended over a hundred ribbon-cutting events. Typically they'd be held on the newly constructed bridge structure, since it makes for a great photo op and good public relations for politicians. I might be able to help you understand the inner workings of the bridge, where the girders are, how they're constructed, how they connect to the bent-caps, et cetera, but now that I think about it, the highest bridge deck is vulnerable to attack, a weak point. Same thing with several of the main columns. Take one out and we have a dead senator. No traffic will be allowed onto the superstructures, but I'm thinking they might be planning to have a large bus or truck ram into one of the columns, or maybe a small bomb at the deck."

"Confirmed. I've just been told the event will be held on the highest bridge deck. You'd better be right about this."

"If I'm not, I'll buy you lunch."

"You'll buy me a case of Scotch! I'll figure out a way to get clearance from my director to dispatch a Critical Incident Response Group with the bomb techs and notify the Secret Service security detail for Senator Brown."

"Ten-four. I'm calling Carlie now." Jake ended the call and tried to remember if the number he'd been using for Carlie was correct. He wished to heaven he had his iPhone. Never been a fan of Androids. He dialed what he thought might be her number, but it kept ringing and did not go to voicemail.

What if there's a second bomb somewhere with Carlie's name on it? He'd never forgive himself. He weighed driving to Cal State San Bernardino versus up to the High Desert and ignoring Cavanaugh's command. If he had to choose between saving his daughter and some lame politician, he'd choose his daughter.

"Dude, talk to me," Paige said, bringing Jake back from his trance.

"I'm afraid the FBI might have a mole working with the terrorists, and, if so, he might have leaked that I'm alive. And one way to get to me is to hurt my daughter."

The mouths of both Dave and Paige dropped open in sync.

From the rear seat, Dave said he'd use his phone to open Google Maps. "Since the new auto-pilot freeway system is down, what normally would be a forty-five-minute drive to Cal State is now gonna take two hours with all the traffic. Of course, there are accidents on the 210, the 10, and the 60, so all three ways of getting out to the Inland Empire are congested."

"Cavanaugh told me yesterday she's missing and I've tried texting her, but she hasn't responded. I gotta get out to San Bernardino and search but she thinks I'm dead, so what about Victorville and helping the FBI save the senator?"

"No-brainer," Paige said with a knowing grin.

"Bent-caps?" Dave asked.

"Never mind," Jake said. "You're right. Who am I to think I could help the all-powerful FBI? It's a stupid idea. The senator will be fine. I'm going out to Cal State to find Carlie. You two should keep working to crack that algorithm. See if there's anything else of value you can mine from it. I'll drop you off somewhere and —"

"I want to go with you," Paige said. "Whether you want me to or not." She crossed her arms.

"You can drop me off at the next block," Dave said.

"Can you please find out what Carlie's number is?" Jake asked Dave.

"No sweat. I'll text you then keep working on the code. You two have a blast."

Jake pulled over, Dave hopped out, then turned back toward the window opening. Jake leaned toward Paige. "Please help Dave with chipping away at that code," Jake said. "He needs your powerful math mind. Plus, you'll be safe with him.

I couldn't live with myself if anything happened to you."

"Okay, fine. Whatever," she said, opening her door.

"See if you can find another clue to what we might have missed. That malware snippet we found in the algorithm was so well written, it's possible we overlooked another one somewhere."

Paige slammed the door shut, Jake zoomed away, then merged back into street traffic. His phone rang, he pressed the green button but didn't say anything. After a few seconds, a deep, gravelly voice on the other line said, "Ahh, Jakey Boy *is* alive and w-w-well."

Jakey Boy? Nobody had ever called him that, so demeaning, patronizing, but the stutter was unmistakable. The voice sounded different from the way Jake remembered, though, like a different personality altogether, and he knew exactly who this was.

"Viktor. How nice of you to call."

"You're one lucky son of a bitch. The last remaining m-m-member of the Super Six. You escaped the deathtrap I set for you and that sweet beauty of yours in Long Beach. You must be nestled snug in the praises of Allah. For now, at least. But I'm c-c-calling to ask you one simple question, Jakey Boy. Do you believe in God?"

The nerve of this guy. Jake wasn't sure if he should engage him. Maybe it would be better to hang up, or throw the phone out the window. At seventy miles an hour on an interstate freeway, the phone would shatter into a million pieces and blend in with the other trash on the shoulder. He felt trapped, and blood rushed to his face as if he were hanging upside down with a sunburn. He tried to stay calm, focusing on his breathing. "Not sure I follow."

A red-and-yellow motorcycle whizzed past him. The motorcyclist flipped off Jake.

"Do. You. Believe. In. God?" The man's voice sounded loud, irritated.

"The God I know is a loving God. You sound like one of those Middle-Eastern extremists who misquote the Quran. What do my religious beliefs have to do with any of this?"

"Everything. You and this country have grown weak, Jakey. Look at the symptoms. Gays are getting married, people are taking away your right to own guns, abortions are happening on every corner, your g-g-government murders innocent people in the name of peace. It's pathetic and will all soon come to a wonderfully artistic and violent end. We live in a nation of wimpy-ass whiners. B-b-before we know it, China or North Korea or some other country will be knockin' on your door, wanting to take over the place. I'm here to give everyone a nice little wake-up call, courtesy of my friends from Russia."

Jake had no idea what to say. He'd taken a training class years ago on how to deal with difficult people. They taught him to say, "I understand" when someone was upset.

Forget that crap.

Instead, Jake pried him. "I got your text."

"Allah has saved you. For what purpose, I don't know. But he is calling the shots. I'm not the one responsible for these beautiful and effective attacks, *He* is. I'm just a soldier in his army. He's cleansing the p-p-population, removing the damned, and rearranging things back to a world order so peace can reign supreme on earth."

Jake's heart pounded harder, faster.

"Let you in on a secret: I'm one of the g-g-good guys, Jakey. I'm doing this country a favor. This Christian country needs me to help set it free."

Jake tried to swallow but his mouth was dry. "Viktor, where are y—"

"You're g-g-going to shut the fuck up right now, Jakey Boy." The man's voice bellowed, seething with anger. "Now you listen to me carefully. You're going to stop whatever the hell you think you're doing and tell that Agent Cavanaugh jerk-off to do the same. Otherwise, I'm going to let my buddies have a private party with that pretty little daughter of yours. I'm looking at a picture of Carlie right now . . . mmm. She might end up like mommy if you're not careful."

Weaving in and out of traffic, Jake looked at his speedometer: ninety-five miles per hour. His stomach was pinned against his spine and rolled back and forth with each turn. Cars and trucks whizzed by on both sides. Part of his brain snapped. "My daughter has nothing to do with th—"

"Jakey, Jakey, Jakey. I'm not finished yet." He spoke slowly now, with a calm, condescending tone. "The Almighty Allah has instructed me and my friends to eliminate her from the equation unless you cooperate. He wasn't specific in his instructions to me, but my plan is to either turn that tender young thing into extra-crispy barbecue for a team of hogs to gobble up or cut her pretty little atheist body up into tiny pieces and send them to you in a cheap cardboard box. You have a preference?"

What the hell am I doing arguing with a psychopath?

During the briefest of moments that passed by like years, a wealth of feelings welled up inside Jake. Movies played in his head of the birth of his little baby girl, her soccer games, opening Christmas presents, birthday parties, and golfing when she was a teenager. The memories all blurred together, combined with sadness, anger, fear, remorse, revenge, and hatred. Everything rolled into one aggressive package. This new emotion gained strength like an avalanche. Rage. Pure unadulterated rage. Sure, he'd been angry a few times in life; who hadn't? But this dark energy was a whole new beast. Primitive. Animal-like.

With every cell in his body caught up in the fiery wrath, he surprised himself with how calmly he managed to speak. Like a wolf ready to strike. "You touch my daughter or come anywhere close to her, I will make it my singular goal in this world to hunt you down, rip your demented, disgusting head off, and crap down your throat. Do you understand me, you sick bastard?"

Viktor laughed, adding fuel to Jake's blazing fire. "I'm not the one who wants to harm Carlie. God does. The one true God. If you're angry, be angry at him, not me. I'm just one of his soldiers." His nonchalant response raised ire deep within Jake's belly. "Now, I can tell you that an important, historical event is going to happen t-t-today. In my city. My city, Jakey. It's a done deal. You can't stop it. Nobody can."

Jake panted. "I know what you're planning. The senator. Today at two."

Several seconds passed. "You think you do, but you seem

to be a bit on the slow side today, so let me make this very clear and fair for you," Viktor said. "Stop meddling or your daughter's dead. Period."

The call ended. Jake thought of texting a brief message to Cavanaugh that Viktor had called him, but not driving at a hundred miles per hour.

A deadly mixture of fear, rage, and invincibility flowed through his veins. His car vibrated, ready to fall apart any second with the torrent of air blowing by.

Jake tried to calm himself. He had learned over the years that when his primitive monkey brain took over as it had a moment ago, his powerful, logical, cognitive brain shut down. Three seconds inhale, five seconds exhale. Repeat. *This is a battle of wits. Calm down and think. He wants us to stop. He all but confirmed the imminent attack in Victorville when he said 'my city.' Twice. Ville means city in French, so the literal translation of Victorville is Victor's city or the city of Victor.*

With sweat drops oozing down his brow, Jake rotated his head and cracked his neck. Until this point in his life, he had done everything in his power to be a productive member of the interconnected world and to help, not harm all living creatures.

Screw it.

He gave up on being calm.

Like a raging tiger with its fur on fire, Jake said with clenched teeth, "Nobody threatens my daughter, especially the man who murdered my wife." A blood vessel popped in his nose as he grunted, balled his hands into fists, and hammered the steering wheel. He panted, scanning the road in front of him, as insanity tap-tap-tapped on the door to his brain.

To hell with him. No matter what it takes, no matter how long or how much pain I have to endure, I'm going to kill Viktor Johnston if it's the last thing on God's green earth I do.

CHAPTER 29

Underneath a scorching summer sun and a partly cloudy sky, Jake zoomed eastward toward the Inland Empire, weaving through the traffic on the 10 freeway. Out of nowhere, Dave sent a text and confirmed why Carlie hadn't responded to his texts: it *was* the wrong number. Jake had swapped the last two digits. His photographic memory had let him down. *Mental blocks occur during stress.*

He slowed to seventy and while swerving onto the shoulder, glancing up and down between the traffic in front of him, cell phone in his hand, he copied his previous text about her dad being alive and needing to talk with her, pasted it into a new one, hoping against hope she'd get it.

Two seconds later she called back.

"Carlie?"

"Whoever this is, I'm not laughing. My dad is gone. I—"

Sounds like Carlie, he thought, hesitant to feel real relief. "The Pfau Library. Your freshman orientation was at the Pfau Library. I stood next to you when you asked the question about how you were assigned to live in the black-scholar dorm. I made the joke about how you didn't belong there because you weren't a scholar." He knew this would get her attention because she hated that story.

"No way. No way! I don't . . . know . . . holy . . . you're alive?" He heard her sobbing.

"Yes, sweetie, it's me," Jake said over the phone, after accelerating back to over a hundred miles an hour, driving with one hand. "Tell me where you are. Right now. Very important."

"It's impossible. This is some sick joke. Randy, is this you? Not funny. I—"

"Carlie, no, it's me, I swear."

Silence. "Some reporter on the news is saying you killed Mom. How could you? I thought—"

"No, no, no, it's all lies. I'll explain everything when we meet. Tell me where you are."

"I was getting a lot of calls late last week from random, blocked numbers, I assumed spam, so I haven't been answering."

Probably why the FBI couldn't get a hold of her.

"I'm holed up in my friend's dorm. We unplugged for the last few days to de-stress, no phones. I swear, this week has been like one huge nightmare. I don't know who to trust or what to think, and I can't believe you're not . . ." The volume of her sobs grew louder.

"Carlie, I've always been there for you and I always will be. Trust me. Please, trust me. I've been trying to text you for a couple of days, but with all the stress, I had the wrong number. Plus, I've been—" He stopped for a second to gather his thoughts. "Doesn't matter. I need to see you right now."

"Someone sent me a video of you yelling at Mom, I guess when you were on the way to the ceremony in Long Beach. I've never seen you act that way."

Jake thought about the argument he had with Cynthia before the event, but they were still in their car. How could someone have made a video of that? He'd barely raised his voice, and Carlie had seen that behavior many times over the years. No excuse for the disagreement, but arguments happened. Doesn't mean he killed his wife.

"I'll explain everything."

"But I went to your guys' joint funeral. Maybe she's alive too and we can—"

"No. I understand how you might think that, but I'm sorry, you gotta trust me she's not." More sobs came through the speaker. "Carlie, I know this is a lot to absorb, but I need you to stay strong and stay focused. Tell me where you are. Someone placed a bomb underneath your car, and the police and FBI have been trying to get ahold of you." Jake tried his best to sound like a calm, confident father, though his heart raced at the same RPM as the whiny little compact Ford engine.

"I'm looking out the window now, must be what all those cop cars are doing in the parking lot. Geez, Dad, I'm not ready for any of this. I just want to—"

"It's a miracle you're still alive, sweetie, and I'll tell you everything when we meet."

"My friend's watching the news on ABC and she's saying that the plane crash in June at the San Bernardino airport as a terrorist attack. Tell me what's going on. We're all freaking out."

"I know. Meet me in the library on the top floor where you like to study. The place with the view of the foothills. Don't bring anyone. You understand?"

Carlie said with a crackling voice, "Yes."

"Stay strong. Library. Ten minutes."

They ended the call.

He blasted his way up the 15 and split off onto the 215 south, exiting at Kendall Drive in San Bernardino, before driving around to the north parking lot. After parking, he sprinted across campus, then to inside the library.

What am I gonna tell her? That her dad, who was blamed by the media for the deaths caused by the CDM attack, subsequently killed in a fire and held by the FBI for a week, agreed to work with the FBI to find the real culprit, who, by the way, is after her and is an extreme Muslim narcissistic psychopath who wants to convert the entire planet to Islam? Oh, and the psycho who killed your mom just threatened to kill you too, so watch your back?

Yeah, that'll calm her down for sure.

There was no point in telling Carlie everything. Maybe some.

He just needed to let her know he was framed and that he was now working with the FBI to track down the man who killed her mom, but she couldn't tell anyone. And she needed to stay close to her friends for safety.

He ran up five flights of stairs, making his way to their special place where he used to take her when she was younger and he was in grad school so they could both study. The entire fifth floor was deserted and quiet, with only the hum of the air-conditioner. He eyed his daughter standing near a large window. She wore white jeans shorts, a CSUSB T-shirt, and her favorite Nike jogging shoes he gave her last Christmas. Next to her stood a tall, slender man.

Jake approached, tapped her shoulder, and she turned around. Her eyes were red and puffy, with tears streaming down as she gave her dad a hug. She introduced the man standing next to her as her boyfriend, Michael. Jake purposely ignored the man's gesture to shake hands, then the three of them sat in opposing green-and-yellow faux-leather chairs. "Dad, I'm confused and feeling very anxious right now. Mom's dead, you were supposed to have been killed, but now you're not. Everyone's saying you killed her and . . . well, I found out this morning, from a random text message, about your affair with some lady. And how did someone get my phone number?"

Jake turned to Michael. "I'm sorry, but I'm not comfortable talking about personal family matters with you, young man. I'm sure you're a nice guy and all, but would you mind giving us a minute?"

Michael stood. "Sure, sure, I understand. Not a problem, Dr. Bendel." He looked down at Carlie, gave her a peck on the cheek, and wandered off.

"Show me," Jake said as he leaned over to Carlie. Blocked number. He clenched his jaw. Viktor.

Jake leaned back in his seat and furrowed his brow. "I need you to trust me. Someone put a bomb underneath your car, and a senator might be assassinated this afternoon up in Victorville, but I'm going to put those important issues to the side for a minute. Family first. Mom and I were waiting for the right time to discuss the affair with you. This has been an emotional roller coaster for us, and now that she's gone, I feel like the track disappeared and I've been freefalling. I need you to know that we'd reconciled everything. She forgave me, and we were working past my mistakes."

Carlie listened as her dad continued, describing other relevant details about Viktor and the Super Six.

She pushed her hair back and looked up to the vaulted ceiling. "Dad, I can't believe this is happening. I feel like crap right now. Just awful. I mean, I just went to your funeral on Saturday, and now you're here sitting with me having a conversation. Wait a minute." She leaned forward and wiped her cheeks with her hand, smearing several streaks of dribbled eyeliner. "Don't tell me Viktor's the guy who planted the bomb under my car."

Before he could answer, the FBI phone rang. Cavanaugh. "Jake, looks like you were right about Victorville. Whatever you do, do not go up there. There's a—" The line went dead.

"Hello? Hello? Cavanaugh?"

"What happened?" Carlie asked.

"I don't know. My guy at the FBI told me we were right about Victorville, but the line went dead."

"Crud," Carlie said, eyebrows furrowing then releasing.

Jake explained more about the possible assassination in Victorville, how he, Paige, and Dave figured out Viktor's plan, and how Cavanaugh had told him not to go.

"We have to try to stop this," Carlie said. "If there's even a remote chance we can save people from that monster, the same guy who killed Mom and tried to kill me. It's the right thing to do, Dad. You're one of the top civil engineers in the country, there's got to be a way to help."

"No way. I didn't tell you this crazy story so we could go run into the fire together. Great. My daughter, the hero." He stood, put his hands on his hips, and turned toward the large, expansive windows to get a view of the beige hillside to the north.

"You always taught me about the greater good, how important it is for our lives to have purpose. This is a real chance for us to do that."

He turned his gaze toward his daughter, impressed at her level of maturity, but drew a blank on how to respond. "I've already lost your mom, I don't know what I'd do if—" A wave of terror hit him as all the air left his lungs, and his pulse increased as he sat down in the chair.

Carlie stood, put her hands on his upper arms, and looked dead into his eyes. "Mom would want us to go. She wouldn't want more innocent people to die."

Images of Cynthia flashed in front of him, and he realized how much Carlie reminded him of her. Two strong women. Jake knew Carlie would be safe as long as she was with him. Sometimes emotion trumped logic. Sometimes.

"You're right. Let's go."

CHAPTER 30

The drive up to Victorville, California, from the San Bernardino Valley was normally quite pleasant when there was no traffic congestion or the lives of God-knows-how-many were not at stake. Jake flew past a sixty-five-miles-per-hour speed limit sign on the side of the 15 north as they drove up the Cajon Pass. He noticed how clean the air smelled as they rose out of the San Bernardino Valley to an elevation of 4,190 feet at the Cajon Summit. Thank God for the truck-climbing lane Caltrans built a few years ago, which moved all the slow trucks out of the way up that six-percent grade, a true example of engineering merit and efficiency while saving lives. *Nobody could ever hijack a truck lane and sabotage the rest of the freeway.*

"We need to go over this again," Carlie said. "I remember you mentioning several years ago that you'd worked a bit on the design of the High Desert Corridor. Tell me more so we can work on finding vulnerabilities."

As he drove like a maniac, knowing they'd arrive on scene within a few minutes, he summarized.

"Twenty miles of new freeway. Consulted with Caltrans

on the geometrics of the whole enchilada and twelve new interchanges. At the 15, there's a freeway-to-freeway interchange in the northern areas of Victorville and Apple Valley."

How happy he'd been when he worked on the HDC back in the nineties. Now, Jake's entire body stressed at the situation Viktor had created. Jake passed a black semi like it was standing still, while he speculated on the various ways a truck like that could possibly kill a senator.

He remembered how the High Desert Corridor was originally conceived in the eighties to help reduce the amount of truck traffic on the east-west corridors coming out of the ports of Los Angeles and Long Beach, since eighty percent of all imported goods entering the US arrived at one of those two ports.

"Goods are put on trains and trucks and then head east and north through San Bernardino County out to the rest of the country. Three freeway routes, Interstates 210 and 10 and State Route 60, all take the brunt of the heavy truck loads as they move through the Inland Empire."

"None of that information is relevant to the people who are about to die," Carlie said. "We need more specifics." As the words left her mouth, a view of the entire Victor Valley spread in front of them.

"I have the design of the interchange in my head, so if I can figure out a way to get inside Viktor's psychotic mind, we might be able to help." Jake thought about how the High Desert Corridor was designed to allow trucks to travel north on I-5, east to I-15, then out to the rest of the country and bypass the 10, 60, and 210 freeways altogether. A lot of good the interchange would do if Viktor destroyed it.

"I remember you taking me to a couple of ribbon-cutting ceremonies when I was younger. I'm guessing they'll have the ceremony where the new High Desert Corridor connects to State Route 18, several miles to the west of the I-15 interchange."

Carlie twirled a few strands of her long brown hair while bobbing her knees up and down. She'd done this since she was a little girl whenever she got nervous.

"No, not much to see there. They'll hold the event at the connection with I-15." He pointed to a place on the other side of the valley, ten miles in front of them, to the northeast. "Out there where those big bridges are." Jake added. "According to Cavanaugh's source in the Secret Service, the ribbon-cutting ceremony is scheduled to be held on the highest bridge deck. Reporters like good photo ops." He smiled, recalling some of the ground-breaking and ribbon-cutting ceremonies he had attended in the past. These events typically included politicians thanking themselves and taking credit for work the engineers and planners did.

Carlie leaned forward, trying to get a better view of the other side of the Victor Valley, but her attempt was interrupted when Jake swerved hard left to avoid an old lady in a white Buick Skylark.

"Tell me how we're going to get onto the bridge once we get there."

In his mind, Jake pictured the interchange he'd designed. "Assuming nobody at Caltrans changed my designs, the highest elevation ramp is the northbound 15 to westbound 18. If they constructed the ramp per the plans, it's up in the air about a hundred feet. We can get there from one of the southern entrances. I'll show you."

"I hope you know what we're supposed to do once we get to the site," said Carlie.

"Cavanaugh's flying there in a helicopter. I'm making this crap up as I go and thinking we can flag him down or try to spot Viktor."

"Lame. Sorry. We need a better plan than that."

Jake jumped in his seat when he felt his phone vibrate. He reached into his pocket and pulled it out. Cavanaugh.

"We're a few miles away," Jake said to Cavanaugh on the phone, steering with his right hand and holding the phone to his head with his left.

"After I told you twice not to go up there. Shit."

CHAPTER 31

"I'm here at the Victorville PD talking to you from a land-line, and before the phone goes dead again, listen to me. Turn around, there's nothing for you to do up there. Let us handle this," Cavanaugh said to Jake. "Any second now we're going to get cut off. The cell towers in the Victorville area are offline, everything's jammed, along with all radio communications—even HAM frequencies. Not sure how to stop this, but we've been unable to get word that those people are all in danger."

"Then I'm going to get there before the attack happens and pick up the senator in this piece-of-crap Ford compact."

"For heaven's sakes no. I'm getting intel there's a possibil-ity of a small bomb detonating on the upper deck. If your assumptions are correct about the vulnerability up there, I don't like this. Those people are like kittens sitting in a coyote den. Our bomb techs are still at least ten minutes out. Turn around now before your cell signal gets jammed. The sheriff's officers and other local law enforcement are scrambling now to evacuate everyone from the area. We really need your help in figuring out exactly what Viktor has planned. Our guys want to know what you think about the weakest point in the structure to hide a bomb and inflict maximum damage, but you don't need to be there physically. You better not still be headed north, goddamnit."

"I am. Just entered Hesperia."

"Shit, turn around," Cavanaugh said. "It's already one fifty-two. If the terrorists strike at two p.m. as you calculated, we've only got eight minutes to get everyone away. We don't have time to dick around. Put your bad-guy hat on for a second and tell me right now: if you were going to try to kill the senator at the ceremony on that upper deck, what would you do to cause the most damage?"

Images of the plans, profiles, cross-sections, bridge locations, and soil conditions montaged through his brain like snakes over hot Mojave Desert sand. He thought about the abnormal level of rainfall last season, which meant a higher-than-average water table. With the Mojave River relatively close by, there'd be the potential for liquefaction underneath the footings of the columns. If this were true, the structural designers would have taken it into account, so liquefaction would probably not be a factor. Viktor was an engineer, so he'd know all this anyway.

An idea hit Jake. "Got it. If it's a bomb, it will be buried next to the column that supports the section of connector bridge where the ceremony is. Above the spread footing but buried below the surface. Make sense?"

"Nope."

Jake put the call on speakerphone and, talking as fast as he could, he simplified a complicated engineering concept. "There's a huge chunk of reinforced concrete buried at the bottom of each column that holds up the bridge deck. If the soil underneath and around the footings is saturated with water, the soil would liquefy, and any type of lateral or horizontal force hitting the columns would be amplified. Even if there's no water there, that's the weak link. If you could blow up the area around the footing and displace it a few meters to the side, the column would become structurally unstable and suffer catastrophic damage."

"Ten-four. One more question, and this is the important one. If—" The line went dead.

Jake held the phone out in front of his face.

"Not again. He needs to get a better phone. Geez, that call dropped at the worst possible time," Carlie said.

He looked at the screen on the phone. "Not him, he's on a landline. It's me. No signal. Huh, normally this area has great reception. I guess—"

Carlie's phone vibrated. "That's weird," she said, clicking the green "talk" button without looking at the caller ID. Blocked number.

"Hello?" she said.

"I'm sorry, I must have the wrong number. This is Bridgette. I'm calling for Jake," the woman on the other end said. "Who's this?"

"This is Carlie." Carlie put the phone against her chest. "It's some creepy lady named Bridgette. She wants to talk with you."

Jake shook his head. Wait. *How did she get Carlie's phone number?* "Not now."

Carlie picked it back up and listened. "Tell him I want to see about grabbing a cup of coffee soon."

She put the phone back against her chest. "She's asking to get coffee with you."

No time for this chit-chat crap; gotta get to the ceremony site. *Stay focused, Jake.* "I can't talk right now."

Carlie responded. "He can't talk with you right—" She held the phone in front of her face and stared at it. "She hung up. Wait, no." Carlie fumbled with the phone. "Signal's gone again."

He put Bridgette out of his thoughts, needing to stay focused on his driving. A mile south, they sped toward the ceremony site on the three-lane northbound 15 freeway. "What time is it?"

"Couple minutes 'til two."

The beautiful new bridge structures peeked up over the horizon. Huge Caltrans bridges like that always impressed Jake, especially ones that were part of brand-new interchanges. He considered them amazing feats of engineering construction, human accomplishments at their finest.

The bridge site in the distance was business as usual for the people driving along the frontage roads on both sides, innocent civilians completely ignorant of any potential threat or fact that a major political event would be starting momentarily or that a bomb could detonate any second.

Jake slowed the Ford, remembering the endless hours of engineering on that interchange. He and his good friend

Ahmad had worked closely on the project to ensure the best possible engineering ideas went into the early designs. He'd enjoyed working with the other team members as well; he recalled it as a special time in his life. Unfortunately, the project momentum had slowed to a snail's pace due to good old-fashioned bureaucracy and an infestation of paranoia in the Caltrans culture. The original thirty-percent-completed plans were delayed several years because some jerk-off of an incompetent environmental planner with too much power threw a wrench in the works, causing unnecessary delays and costs to the taxpayers to the tune of tens of millions of dollars.

Jake witnessed the fruits of his labor unfold before his eyes as they approached the interchange. Amazing. But the project had barely made it to construction. A handful of experienced, knowledgeable managers at Caltrans had flexed their leadership muscle and took charge of the interchange project where he had left off. Competent engineering and environmental consultants had finished the design in record time. He held great admiration for the project and program managers who had worked closely with the federal government to procure a huge chunk of funding that had paid for the construction phase. Watching the interchange sprawl across the desert sand gave Jake goosebumps on his forearms.

Squinting at the highest peak of the tallest bridge, Jake saw a small blue tent nestled atop the bridge deck. A black helicopter with "FBI" painted on the side hovered fifty feet above the tent. Jake's heart raced, and beads of sweat dripped down his forehead.

From Jake's distance a mile south of the interchange,

people looked tiny, running in different directions away from the tent, waving their hands at the helicopter as it approached and attempted to land on the deck.

"At the top of the bridge deck. They're panicking," Carlie said.

As Jake and Carlie headed toward the interchange on I-15, they noticed a dozen or so people wearing black clothes near the bottom of the tallest bent, or column, of the highest connector bridge. There were two bulldozers, an excavator, and a loader scrambling around in the dirt.

Looks like they're digging.

CHAPTER 32

From the relative safety of his Cessna 182 aircraft crawling along at ten-thousand feet above the desert floor and a few knots faster than stall-speed velocity, Viktor evaluated the entire scene below. He used a belly-mounted ultra-high-definition camera with an internal wireless feed to his iPad.

Viktor zoomed in toward the blue tent atop the highest connector bridge and watched with eight-million pixel, sixty-frames-per-second detail as Senator Brown arrived late. Her driver pulled her shiny white 7-Series BMW into the entrance of the event. The CHP officer waved them through as one of the few vehicles allowed to drive directly up to the top of the overhead where the event would be held.

"Arrogant bitch," Viktor said to himself with a chuckle, watching his iPad.

She and her aide walked fifty feet to their assigned seats instead of over a quarter-mile like all of the non-electeds. The peasants. The pawns. Her driver stayed in the car, probably to keep the A/C running for her.

She took her seat in the front row—a white plastic chair with a small paper sign on it.

A helicopter appeared on Viktor's radar, flying beneath him and hovering over the crowd below. The black Eurocopter AS550 Fennec had the letters "FBI" painted white across its side. A man wearing black goggles and all camouflage stood hanging out the side of a large opening, pointing an MP5 submachine gun straight down at the ground.

The man waved his arm around, which caused confusion among the guests, probably because nobody could hear him yelling words of warning. Viktor assumed the senator considered the actions of this man inappropriate for the ceremony. From what he'd read about her, she knew that the people hired to protect her were normally more subdued and tended to blend in.

The man in the helicopter continued his attempt to get the attention of the crowd. Viktor smiled at the futility of it all. He assumed the helicopter pilot was probably trying to talk to the crowd through his loudspeaker, but Viktor knew the chopper was too far away, and the twenty-five-knot wind made hearing anything at that distance impossible to understand.

He envisioned the senator's heart jumping into her throat, her chest pounding. Good thing he scrambled the entire bandwidth for cell-phone frequencies—all of them—the entire 800 MHz and 1850-1900 MHz bands. If any of those losers tried to make a call, it would fail.

Tiny humans instinctively darted in all directions like

monkeys in a jungle fleeing a hungry lion. None of them could possibly comprehend that the same structure supporting them high in the sky would, in a matter of seconds, entomb them in a massive grave.

Fifty seconds into the fifty-ninth minute of the one o'clock hour on Tuesday, August 11, he shifted in his seat to get the perfect view of the entire scene below. The attendees were physically stranded one hundred feet above the ground, and Viktor smiled as panic infected them all. He gave the bird to everyone, said, "Die, you queen bitch," then pushed a red dynamite icon on his iPad.

CHAPTER 33

The clock on the car dashboard changed from 1:59 to 2:00. "My God," Jake said, "people are still on the bridge. They need to get off that thing now, and those guys at the bottom of the bent need to —"

Within a fraction of a second, a stadium-sized orange ball of fire appeared at the base of the column, the exact spot where Jake had anticipated, and an instant later, the fireball devoured the innocent victims atop the bridge. A cloud of sand, debris, and ash exploded upward, replacing the fireball before the massive gray concrete column supporting the entire upper deck shattered sideways into a million shards.

The blast tossed the helicopter outward, away from the bridge deck. But as quickly as the craft rode the shockwave away from the explosion, the vacuum sucked it back in and careened it to the side and down, into the cloud expanding in all directions at once.

In that instant Jake knew two facts: Viktor was definitely the man behind this, and he'd made good on his threat.

Before Jake could blink, the entire interchange was reduced

to a pile of debris, engulfed inside an elongated dust cloud, ascending toward the pale-blue desert sky and eventually taking the shape of a mushroom.

Jake released the accelerator, braked hard, and swerved off to the right side of the freeway about a half-mile southwest of the explosion. His mouth hung open and his eyes grew wide, and from the shroud of gray-beige muck, the deck emerged, falling in slow motion toward the desert floor.

"Holy Jesus, God," Jake said, regripping his fingers around the steering wheel. Inside the carnage, several human bodies jumbled around, tossed around like tiny black ants falling out of the sky, too many to count.

Carlie's hand covered her mouth and they both maintained their gazes of horror as the dreadful blast wave approached their car at nearly the speed of sound. An invisible wave of energy hit them three seconds after the initial explosion, with a painful, low-frequency rumble, slamming the tiny Ford so hard that the car bounced several inches off the ground. Jake expected the glass windows to break, but only a small crack formed on the front windshield.

Jake yelled to Carlie, "Rocks are coming at us. Duck!"

The ominous cloud attacked them like some creepy sand ghost.

Dust, sand, and rocks as large as his fist rained down on everything within the first minute. Jake and Carlie covered their ears to block the deafening sounds made by the debris hitting their car, which became covered with a layer of gunk.

"What—the hell—just happened?" Jake asked, his voice trembling. A wave of nausea hit him.

With a look of terror and disbelief glued to her face, Carlie tried to speak but obviously couldn't find the words. Finally, she blurted out, "What kind of bomb was that? It made a mushroom cloud, but it was too small to be nuclear. Way bigger than anything I've ever seen on TV."

A stiff breeze from the west helped dissipate the dust cloud into the surrounding air of Victor Valley. The bridge and all evidence of Jake's engineering marvel were gone. "We just witnessed several dozen people die," he said, tears welling up, trying to break free. "We're too late." He looked down at his lap.

"If we'd gotten here any sooner, we could've been on that deck with all those people. We would've been . . ." Her breathing rate increased and sounded like she might be hyperventilating from the shock.

His phone vibrated, and he thought the caller might be Viktor again. Adrenaline dumped into his system, turning images of the old man a raging red.

Jake opened the door and exited the car. Standing there, phone attached to his ear, he smelled a mixture of kerosene and damp earth. Emergency sirens drew near.

Jake answered. "Listen here, Viktor, I don't give a flying f—"

"Whoa there, Jake. It's me. Cavanaugh."

"You're alive. I saw a black helicopter crash and . . ."

"Not this time. I got lucky," Cavanaugh said with sadness seeping through the phone. Jake had a hard time listening because of the ringing in his ears, created by the deafening volume of the blast wave. "One of the bomb techs was in the helicopter. Just before detonation, he reported he found a semi-truck that had a covered daisy cutter in the trailer. Before you ask, these are fifteen-kiloton BLU-82B bombs, the largest non-nuclear weapons in existence. How the hell two managed to crawl onto American soil, I have no idea. Those things cost millions of dollars."

Jake put his hand above his brow to block the glare, remembering his dad talking about those back during Vietnam. The military used them to level hundreds of acres of trees to make way for camps and army posts. "The bombs took out the main column supporting the upper deck of the interchange. The heat on the reinforcing steel inside must've been intense enough to cause the other columns to expand and fail."

"Eyes in the sky say the blast created a crater the size of a football field. Nothing remains. The entire interchange evaporated."

Jake had no words.

"Two of my good friends were on the ground." Cavanaugh cleared his throat. "At least they died quickly."

"I'm sorry," Jake said. "Why the hell was cell service down?"

"Whoever did this wanted to keep us from communicating with each other. We couldn't warn the Secret Service or the senator."

"Viktor was behind this." Jake looked to the opposite side of the freeway where a light-blue ABC-7 van was parked. Two men were standing near the driver's side, arguing. One had a camera on his shoulder.

"I had a feeling you'd say that."

"He called me a little while ago and told me he had an event planned in Victorville. Historical-level proportion, he said. He also threatened to kill Carlie if we kept pursuing him. I was going to tell you but our call dropped. Remember when I told you he was a genius with several different technologies?"

"Yeah."

"I don't recall him ever discussing bombs or explosives, so I'm not sure how he pulled off this attack. But telecommunications and radio-wave technology are smack dab in the middle of his wheelhouse." Jake tried desperately to find some shred of strength to continue talking, even though he wanted nothing more than to crawl into a hole with Carlie and hold her tight. "It's Viktor, I know it. He killed the cell-phone communications. He worked on the networking algorithm for the Super Six, but we needed a wireless way for the vehicles to talk to each other, and he was a major part of developing the system we deployed. His radio frequency skill set is off the charts."

"Okay, I'm on board with Viktor as our main suspect. Shankle's not, but good work anyway. How's Carlie taking all this?"

"She's not with me. She's somewhere safe," Jake lied, in case anyone else was listening. He turned to Carlie and put a finger over his lips to make the "shh" sign.

"Good. I do think you two are in more danger now than before. Turn your car around, get the hell out of here, and meet me back at that same park where we met yesterday. I need to get the forensics team started up here, so I'll meet you in a few hours. Say six tonight?"

Jake didn't want to do anything or go anywhere but home. His mind wandered and he had trouble breathing. He grabbed a rag from the trunk and wiped his front and rear windows before he sat back in the car and slammed the door shut.

He rolled the window down. To his left, he noticed a camera crew from ABC-7 across the freeway. A black man in his thirties aimed a TV camera directly at Jake, one eye in the camera lens, the other closed, waving his arm at another man sitting in the baby-blue-and-white van. Jake assumed the man must have been filming the bombing scene, but *why the hell is his camera pointed at me?*

"Jake? Six tonight, okay?" Cavanaugh asked again.

Jake wanted to call it quits, but his daughter needed him to be strong, and he needed revenge for the innocent people who were just murdered. *Son of a bitch.* He tapped into that same roaring rage from earlier when he'd spoken with Viktor. He needed to get the bastard. "Sure. Park. Six o'clock."

"Roger that."

No sooner had he terminated the call when he received a text from a blocked number:

Jakey, Jakey, Jakey . . . what did you do now? Did you just blow up the Queen of California? Good for you. That atheist politician was totally useless. The good news is that now we can have some fun, ha-ha. Once the shepherd is gone, the flock will disperse. :)

Without sharing the text with Carlie, Jake pocketed the phone and drove across the median, flipped a U-turn and spewed dust from the explosion out from behind the spinning tires. When the car hit the pavement of the southbound shoulder, dust and rocks blew off the Ford, leaving a clouded trail. He glanced into the rearview mirror, through the cloud, to the cameraman still pointing his camera directly at Jake.

CHAPTER 34

Bobby Jones had worked as a field reporter at ABC-7 for five years before he realized he hated his job, especially when assigned to cover death-laden traffic accidents like the CDM attack. That day back on June 9th, the day he'd reported there from ground zero at the I-405 site, the day he'd for the first time witnessed massive death, something inside him broke. Add in the crazy hours, way too much freeway driving, rude interviewees, egocentric coworkers, and a skimpy salary barely enough to survive life in the L.A. basin, and he'd become one frustrated reporter.

But he considered himself a hard worker and enjoyed the celebrity aspect of being on TV. His ego beamed brightly whenever anyone recognized him at the grocery store or while shopping at BestBuy. His black-belt-level skills at editing clips put a fun spin on the challenge of polishing those turd stories into shiny gold. Lately, however, his career had languished, and instead of helping him climb the ladder, his producer continued to hand him the low-end assignments, the ones other reporters were happy to pass on.

With each passing day, the thought of quitting his job grew stronger. Maybe another career was waiting for him, one better suited to his needs and passions in life. He enjoyed base-jumping, but couldn't figure out a way to make a living at it. No money there unless he wanted to do a national show.

Bobby exited the news van, ran to Doug, and said, so excited he nearly shit himself, "Tell me you got that, Doug!"

"This ain't no amateur hour, boss. 'Course I got it. Bet you nobody else got the shot of that bomb, neither." Bobby fist pumped. "And I got something else, too," Doug said with an oversized, gleaming white smile splitting open his dark brown face.

Bobby's brain put two and two together, he lifted his arm and pointed to the south. "The guy driving that car, was that—"

"Million bucks says that was Dr. Bendel. Super Six project. Deceased." Doug made a slow bob of his head as he finished Bobby's sentence.

Bobby set his hands on his hips. *A massive explosion, senator assassination, and possible engineering conspiracy . . . all in one day.* The soon-to-be-famous reporter stood on the freeway shoulder, stunned, face going numb, watching the black car speed away to the south through a cloud of dust. He turned back to the smoldering pile of rubble to their north, then coughed. "No way, man. Bendel always had a beard."

Doug started packing up his camera gear. "Hello? Ever heard of a razor? I'd know that guilty piece of crap anywhere, even without the beard. His eyes. Very unique. Then his death, how he killed all those people . . . it's all we talked about last week, man. You must've been high the whole time."

With this I-15 interchange explosion, the potential for skyrocketing Bobby's celebrity status to a national level made his knees weak. His lucky break had finally arrived to give his career a steroidal shot in the ass. If he could become famous, on a national level, he'd finally be happy . . . and wealthy.

Earlier that day, he and Doug had originally been assigned to cover some lame-o story about a lost dog found at the pound, but his rival Nicole called in sick, so his boss, Carol, ordered Bobby in her whiny, high-pitched bitch-in-charge voice to instead cover the ribbon-cutting ceremony in Victorville. Whenever a US senator spoke at a public event, national news reporters were there en masse, and this event was no exception. NBC, CBS, Fox News, CNBC, CNN, all the major players.

Bobby's two-man ABC-7 crew had already set up a remote camera rig on the bridge deck before most of the other reporters had arrived. That camera would normally have captured the various speakers, including Senator Brown. But when the bomb exploded, Bobby and Doug were about a mile south shooting B-roll field shots of the interchange. Protocol dictated that field shots were to be gathered before an event, so the cameraman and reporter could be on location in time to film the ceremony. Call it good fortune or the universe or God stepping in, but Bobby switched the order of things around for the simple reason that Doug had taken too long in the bathroom before they'd left the news station. Doug had a fever and the runs, maybe the flu. But news and—Doug's bowel movements—never stop.

So instead of dying like all those other lame-ass reporters, Doug and Bobby had captured footage of an explosion that annihilated an interchange and, according to their police scanner, swallowed thirty-seven people, including a US senator. Even more exciting, before the two men could catch their breath, they'd also filmed the infamous Dr. Jake Bendel, the man whose photo had appeared on all the major news channels 24/7 since last week, with reporters speculating about his involvement in the CDM massacre and how he was killed in a fire, a story Doug wanted to cover. And now they'd filmed Bendel, driving a black compact Ford with some hot chick in the passenger seat, at the scene of a terrorist bombing.

Hopping on his toes like an overexcited puppy, Bobby said, "We need a game plan, man. Do we stay and cover this terrorist bombing bullshit or jump in the van and follow that black car with Jake Bendel escaping?"

"You know what I think. Not sure why you even asking," Doug said, hands on his hips, staring at the smoldering remains of the bomb site, not bothering to look at Bobby.

Bobby glanced at the smoking pile of rubble, then back at Doug. "Matter of fact, I don't know what you think, but I'd sure like your input, man, like now."

Doug crossed his arms. "Both. I'd stay up here. Cover this mess. But send the Bendel footage back to the boss at the station. Gonna make the single best conspiracy piece ever."

Bobby considered this for a second. Over the years, only a handful of reporters were fortunate to be in the right place at the right time. Some of the reporters who covered nine-eleven became national celebrities. Now was Bobby's turn. *That bitch*

Nicole will shit a brick when she finds out Mr. Stoner Bobby's hit a reporting trifecta: bomb, assassination, conspiracy. He'd died and gone to heaven.

I'm gonna get so stoned tonight it's not even funny.

Several of his competitors had been up there reporting on that bridge when it blew. Steve Hendrickson from Channel Four, Antonia Toledovitch from Channel 2. *Good riddance.*

"Dude, as much as I'd like to chase the assassin, I agree with you. We're staying here. We got enough footage of Bendel to start a conspiracy. Let's see how close we can get to the site to see the bodies. Keep rolling the whole time, baby."

They high-fived and went to work.

CHAPTER 35

"Dad, you know more than you're sharing. I want to know what the hell's going on," Carlie said.

Jake re-gripped the wheel with both hands, driving like he had the pole position in the final lap in the Indy 500. He stole a glance at Carlie and nodded, instincts pumping full bore to keep his baby girl safe from Viktor. *Now the monster's going to try to blame me for another atrocity.*

He showed her the phone, let her read the chessboard text message from Viktor, and waited for the look of pain to reappear on her face, the pain of having to doubt her father's innocence.

"I hope you weren't going to keep this from me."

"Doing the best I can. Not easy."

Carlie looked away, out her grimy window. "Blocked. I'll bet it's from that Bridgette chick. Probably working with Viktor."

"Not possible."

"How do you know?"

Jake changed the conversation direction. "We're assuming

the message has to do with a chessboard." The wheels in his head spun so fast, smoke puffed out of his ears. "Now he's taken the queen, he needs the king for checkmate to win."

"If the king's the shepherd of the flock, I wonder what flock he's referring to," she said, cupping her elbow in one hand while tapping her lips with the other. "Some random city? The people of California? The US?"

A piece of ice inside Jake's heart melted when he heard Carlie digging into the mystery instead of believing the lies the media had spread about him.

He swallowed hard. "Last week we had a meeting, then a ceremony to congratulate the members of the Super Six on a job well done. Everyone was there—staff, elected officials, Caltrans."

"Mom was with you?"

He nodded. "She knew how important this project was to me."

"And that's where she died."

"I'm getting to that." He explained about the fire, the four-teen deaths, and how he was the only surviving member of the Super Six.

"Oh, my God, Dad, that's horrible. But why did they drug Mom too?"

"No idea, but next I know, I'm in some FBI safehouse a thousand miles away. Turns out earlier that same day of the fire, someone leaked 'credible' information to the press that I was responsible for the CDM attack—which, of course, I wasn't—and that's why the FBI was on-site. Millions of people hate me right now, and if that news crew back there filmed me and they air video as proof I'm alive, it's gonna get ugly. These are seriously sick people we're dealing with. They think hurting you to get to me would be completely justified."

She stared out the murky front window in silence.

He continued. "So, for several days the American public thought I had not only killed about six thousand people, but I had also set fire to the convention center and killed your mom and my coworkers. The FBI planted evidence with the local police and press a couple of days later to make it look like I'd been killed too. The joint funeral last Saturday was all part of the cover-up. I'm sorry I wasn't there to help you know these things and you had to go through that, but I was stuck in the safehouse and had no idea what was going on."

She paused, taking it all in before saying, "I believe you, Dad."

Jake turned to his daughter, marveling at her maturity and intellect. A smile made its way to his lips. "Means a lot to hear you say that, Sweetie. Thank you."

Carlie looked out her side of the car. "Now you're working with the FBI to find Viktor."

"Find him and kill him. So far, I'm doing a crappy job tracking him down."

"You're not gonna kill anybody." Carlie turned her back toward her father.

"The hell I'm not. Eye for an eye. He killed Mom, all those innocent people, threatened you. He's got it coming."

Carlie rubbed the nape of her neck, crossed her arms, and kept quiet for a while.

Jake shook out his hands as an argument ensued inside his

head. Part of him, the rational part, second-guessed the angry decision he'd made earlier to kill Viktor. A much larger part of him wanted sweet revenge. Revenge was winning but clearly not impressing Carlie.

She broke the silence. "When my boyfriend, Michael, and I were watching the news he said he thinks you're guilty."

"You need to stay out of contact with that guy, can't risk it. Not even a text."

"I know. I can't believe this is all happening," Carlie said.

Maybe it was Jake's paranoia, maybe he was curious, but he said, "Tell me about Michael."

"We've been dating now for about four months. He's a really good guy, got a good soul."

Jake thought about whether to trust Michael. *Four months . . . when the Sûr System went online. Coincidence? Christ, I might have to take out her boyfriend. What if he's in on this?* "At this point, except for Dave, Paige, and my old professor friend, we can't trust anyone."

"He's an engineer," Carlie said. "Mechanical. Works in San Bernardino—and he loves me."

The way she said the words, he could tell she was in love. *Dammit, where's the time gone, and where have I been while my daughter is falling in love?*

"Where's he from?" Jake finally asked.

"Says he moved here from Mexico with his family when he was little." Carlie maintained her gaze out the side window while the commercial developments adjacent to the freeway blurred past.

"Do you trust him?"

"Dad, we're in love. Of course I trust him." She had a point, but at the age of twenty-five she tended to fall blindly for tall men. She'd probably trust any of the players in the NBA based solely on their height. Anyway, Jake needed to figure out a plan to keep her safe. A plan without Michael.

"We need to hide you somewhere safe while I take care of business."

They drove along the 10 freeway until 3:30 p.m. when Jake got a call on his cell.

"Jake, we need to talk," Bridgette said, hurried, hushed. "Just listen to me. Please."

He looked at Carlie and shrugged.

"I'm listening."

"You've known me since we were in college. I haven't had a chance to talk with you since the affair ended, and, well . . ."

As much as he fought it, his mind automatically flashed up images from their affair like an internal PowerPoint slideshow.

"I'm still here."

"I understand you're in mourning for your wife, but I still have feelings for you. I always have, and I'm worried about you with all this stuff going on. I need to see you. We have some issues to work through and need to talk."

Talking with Bridgette felt wrong, like he was betraying Cynthia. He was trying his best to save millions of people from an evil psychopath while protecting his daughter and avenging his wife's death. But before his mind could think of a rational reason, his mouth had already blurted out, "To be honest, I'm in the middle of a big project right now. I'll have to call you back. Maybe later tonight, but I have to go now." He ended the call with no intention of seeing her. *Too much on the line.*

For a moment, he tried to remember whether or not he had given Bridgette his FBI cell number. Then Carlie shook her head with disappointment. His thought disappeared.

"What?" he asked.

"I'm not blind. I know who that was." She turned away from him, crossed her arms, and stared out the side window.

CHAPTER 36

"Bobby, don't give me any of your shit," Carol, his producer, barked from the ABC-7 studios in Glendale. "We're getting calls and police reports and need info on the ribbon cutting and you haven't given us diddly squat."

Bobby's light-blue ABC-7 news van hit a rut and bounced its two passengers from their seats. "Slow down, Doug. Jesus. Carol, you haven't heard?"

"Heard what?"

"The bombing. The phone lines have been down, plus the ribbon cutting never happened. The story's now about a bridge bombing, with a dead senator in the middle of the pile. We need more time."

"Christ! What the hell's going on?" she asked.

Bobby held a sweaty hand out in front of the air vents which, until now, had been blasting out arctic wind, but at the moment, nothing but hot air. He hammered his fist on the dashboard. "Great. Our goddamned a/c is out. You can't keep giving me the shittiest van, Carol. I swear, you gotta treat us better. This is ridiculous, it's a hundred and twelve degrees out here."

"Tough luck, Bobby. Now answer my goddamned question."

"I'll be in touch with you in a bit." He ended the call.

As he and Doug filmed the bomb site from their van, circling the quarter-mile-wide crater over the next few minutes, Carol called several times, but Bobby ignored her. They drove as far off the paved road as possible before hitting soft, impassible sand. Doug grabbed his Sony PMW-300 4k video camera, hopped out, and grabbed more shots from the northeast quadrant of the former interchange.

Southwest of their location lay the charred, smoldering remains of the collapsed bridge, reminiscent of footage of the post-atom bombing of Hiroshima, Japan, at the end of World War Two. The site had an end-of-days vibe, for sure.

They climbed into the back of the van, which housed their portable video production room, then worked fast to finish compiling all relevant clips, trimming off the fat and making a finished, easy to absorb clip of the footage. Bobby normally enjoyed this part of the process, where he could really "sell" his story to viewers, but today, with the smell of charred kerosene and the sauna-like atmosphere in the cramped editing space, he only felt his pulse throbbing in his neck.

"Pull up the footage of Dr. Bendel and work your magic on this one, Doug. See how close we can get on his face. You and I might think that's him, and he's alive, but we gotta convince the rest of the world."

"It's him," Doug said as he linked his video camera to the digital in-feed and downloaded the entire video within seconds. Thank God for solid-state digital recording systems.

We'd never make the deadline with the old analog tapes, Bobby thought, as Doug fast-forwarded to their initial setup shot, scanned past the explosion, slowed through the scene with Jake, then rewound the film a few seconds. Pause.

Bobby pointed. "Zoom in here. I wanna see that asshole's face up close. Take a screen capture, then add a beard to the image."

Doug poked at the keyboard and jiggled the mouse till the screen zoomed in on Jake's face. Using a plugin from his photo editing software, he selected the brush tool, designated a photorealistic hair color to match Jake's, and made broad strokes with the digital brush around Jake's chin and mouth till a beard appeared.

Bobby pulled up several images of Jake from Google and found one used in the funeral publication last week that showed Jake—with a beard—standing in a similar pose, looking slightly left of the camera.

"Download this pic and paste it as a box into the frame. I want to edit the photo into the segment and show these two images side by side and let the viewers decide for themselves if this guy's really dead or not," Bobby said, chuckling under his breath.

Doug put the clips together into one cohesive piece, then Bobby pulled in voiceover recordings and put the final polish on the best segment he'd ever produced. A sense of confidence washed over him the moment they finished. That piece that would tell the story of the bombing, the senator's death, and, of course, how Dr. Jake Bendel was mysteriously intertwined with the worst terrorist hit since nine-eleven.

In order to make the 4:30 p.m. slot, they needed to submit by the deadline of 4:15. Under the assumption Carol would ask them to do a live shot on scene, Doug inched the van out of the sand, back toward Stoddard Wells Road, and they searched for a perfect spot to shoot. "Need a spot with a good backdrop. I'll finish the editing," Doug said. "Only need a few more minutes."

With beads of sweat dripping off the tip of Bobby's nose, he looked at his phone: twelve missed calls from Carol. He knew she held his ticket to fame because she was responsible for deciding whether to run Bobby's clip or to use that skanky reporter, Nicole Freemonte, who, according to her texts, was now miraculously feeling much better.

Approaching the other side of the crater, Bobby received another call from Carol and answered, bracing for the shit storm. He held the phone several inches away from his ear for thirty seconds as Carol barked a slew of words, some of which he couldn't even understand . . . unprofessional . . . last job . . . worst reporter ever . . . fired . . . blah, blah, blah. He looked at Doug and rolled his eyes. Finally, when the noise subsided, he spoke.

"I have an amazing piece here, Carol, if you'd just give me a chance to talk."

"You're already on thin ice after what you did last month with that teenager."

Ouch. While minding his own business, a fifteen-year-old female had approached him for no reason and started yelling at him. He lost his temper and while trying to calm her down, he'd grabbed her upper arm, but from the angle of the person taking the video, it looked like he punched her in the face. He denied it, but the video made her case, and she cast him as the instigator. Seeing is not always believing, but the fact that the girl happened to be black made things worse. He knew he could be an asshole sometimes, but he didn't have a racist bone in his body. Not that it mattered, because the video footage showed otherwise.

Now all he heard was Carol's heavy breathing. "Gonna totally make all that up to you. Not only do we have the bombing of the interchange—the actual explosion—but we edited an awesome senator-assassination piece *and* captured Dr. Jake Bendel on camera. He's involved with this, I know it."

"Wrong. That guy died last week. I went to the funeral with you, you idiot. I'm glad I helicoptered Nicole out there to do your job for you."

Bobby hated it when she patronized him. He lifted his forearm and wiped the sweat from his brow. "You're not hearing me. We have several seconds of footage of the guy. Yes, he's supposed to be dead, but I've got proof he's alive. The viewers are gonna bite into this story like a juicy hamburger."

She exhaled, then paused again.

Doug found a quiet nook to shoot the scene, parked the van and grabbed his tripod.

Bobby continued. "He was right across the freeway from us when the bomb went off, about a half a mile away from the bridge. He probably triggered the bomb from there."

With the phone pinched between his cheek and shoulder, Bobby snapped his fingers at Doug, who was setting up the camera. He made a "hurry-up" motion with his hand, who nodded and mouthed, "I know."

"Other than the footage, tell me what proof you have that it's him," Carol said.

"Stay with me here, Carol. The guy's supposed to have been some transportation engineering genius involved with the Super Six who caused the CDM attack on a freeway, blah, blah, blah, right? Well, I don't think it's too much of a stretch for us to assume he's involved with this attack, too."

"Fine. What's your angle?"

"I want to run with the conspiracy piece. I got a stationary shot of him looking directly into the camera, then I'll cut in a recent photo for a side-by-side, so we show viewers the before and after to let them decide."

"Not your call, plus I don't want you running both the bombing and Bendel stories, that'll confuse the viewers. Remember, they're like sixth-graders; you gotta spoon-feed them one story at a time." She paused again. "Nicole's gonna run with the senator's assassination. If you're lucky, I'll let you take the conspiracy piece. Maybe."

Doug hopped back into the rear of the van, which shook. Bobby covered the mouthpiece of the phone and said to Doug, "You have four minutes to finish and send that shit to Carol. Don't fuck it up." To Carol, he said, "No way. This is one huge, interrelated story. I'm already out here, I've already covered the main bombing and am seconds away from finishing the piece right now. I deserve to run this. It's my big shot, Carol, let me do this. I'm begging you."

"You get paid to report the news. I'm your producer. You do as I say. Period. Now send me what you have. Your clip was due two minutes ago, but I'll give you another five. I'm putting

Nicole in charge of running the bombing and assassination using your footage. We're going live with her in eleven minutes."

Bobby couldn't believe his ears. *Son of a bitch. Nicole? Are you fucking kidding me?!* He slammed his fist on the makeshift plastic table and hung up.

Doug spun his squat body around on the short stool. "That'll be the last time you piss off Carol. You'll be lucky if you only get fired."

Inside the back of the van, which reminded Bobby of how a turkey would feel inside an oven, he rotated his swivel chair and looked out the front windshield. "Finish editing what you can and send the piece to Carol, along with the clean feed." He looked at the time on his phone. "You got three minutes. Carol's going with Nicole for the live report."

"Oh, hell no. This is *our* story. We shot the explosion and—"

"Shut up and let me think."

Three minutes later, encrypted video files, billions of digital ones and zeros that would recreate the Victorville explosion, streamed through the airwaves from Bobby's van to the ABC-7 headquarters in Glendale, California.

"She still needs me to do the live conspiracy report. When we're done, that's it, we're going after Bendel."

CHAPTER 37

Jake and Carlie went to the vacant Bendel rental house in Pasadena to lay low for a couple of hours while Cavanaugh finished up in the high desert. At 5:55 p.m. they pulled into the parking lot of a soccer field at the Westwood Recreation Center where he and Cavanaugh agreed to meet.

They waited.

Multiple sirens screamed from different directions as Jake looked at the time on his phone: 6:05. With his heart pounding in his throat, Jake thought *Cavanaugh could be a no-show.*

A helicopter landed on the roof of the Federal Building two blocks away. Moments later, carrying a tan leather briefcase, Cavanaugh jogged across the parking lot.

Jake turned to Carlie. "Here comes Cavanaugh. Stay here in the car and be quiet. The terrorist we're dealing with is a psychopath, so nothing he does will make any sense, he could hit anytime and if he does, don't hesitate to run. If anything happens to me, you drive straight back to the Pasadena house and call Professor Everton." He took her phone, entered the professor's cell number, handed it back to her, and gave her a hug and kiss on her cheek. Looking into each other's eyes, they said goodbye without speaking a word before Jake climbed out of the Ford and walked a few meters away to a park bench.

Cavanaugh approached, placed the briefcase on the bench, leaned over and put his hands on his knees, out of breath. "Got to get back in shape." He straightened, locking his hands behind his neck and looked toward their car. "Jesus, Jake, you brought someone with you? Dammit, I specifically told you not to—"

"I found Carlie and want federal protection for her. And I'm not talking about some basement prison cell baloney. If this Viktor guy wants to hurt me directly, we need to hide her somewhere safe while we track him down."

Cavanaugh shook his head. "We can't just give federal protection to anyone." He took several breaths. "There's a ton of paperwork we have to fill out, I gotta get it all approved by Shankle, and you know we're already off the reservation with this whole investigation, so that's gonna be impossible; but more importantly, a sitting US senator was killed today. Everyone at the bureau's on full alert. Nobody's gonna give a shit about your kid."

Jake's mind went numb. *How could Cavanaugh not help to protect Carlie? He's completely ignoring the fact that her life was threatened by Viktor today. Twice. Her mother was killed by Viktor barely a week ago. Who gives a flying fart if there's some paperwork to do?*

"I don't give a gnat's ass about the senator," Jake barked back, waving an arm around and pointing a finger at Cavanaugh's face. "I didn't even like her. My priority right now is to keep my daughter safe. This psychopath kills my friends, tries to kill me, kills my wife, kills a senator, blows a two-hundred-million-dollar interchange to kingdom come, threatens my daughter, and now you say the feds can't help us because of too much paperwork?"

Cavanaugh looked down and crossed his arms. "That's not what I said, but either way, my boss doesn't even think Viktor's our guy. He thinks you made it all up and again, someone killed a senator today on our watch. On our watch! I'm sorry if you think your daughter's life is more important than the senator's, but management is fighting me at every turn. It's not always about what each of us wants, Jake. There are bigger issues here."

During his tirade, Cavanaugh's face turned several shades of red. A day ago, Jake would have felt guilty for raising his voice at the man who saved his life, but right now he viewed Cavanaugh as one more obstacle to getting his daughter to safety.

"Fine. You go tell my daughter." He pointed to the baby Ford. "She's right there. You tell her your paperwork crap is more important than her life. Go on." He shook his head.

Cavanaugh turned around, put his hands on his hips, and took a few steps away.

He turned back toward Jake, nodding. "Jesus. Fine. You're right, there's another way. Screw the paperwork. I'll make it happen, but we need to strategize our next move."

Jake put his foot on the seat of the bench and leaned over. "Thank you. Now, have your guys at the bureau been able to track down the purchase of the bomb or explosives used?"

"No way, that's not gonna happen for at least another few days. Our planes flew overhead and detected hyper-low radiation levels and confirmed the bomb was non-nuclear. Daisy cutter, just like we initially thought."

"How about the texts and calls to my phone?"

"Still working on it. So far, mostly dead ends. Good news, though, some of the security measures you Super Six people put in the algorithm worked as planned."

"Of course they did."

Carlie honked the horn and was making a "come here" gesture with her arms. Jake put up his hand, shaking his head.

Cavanaugh edged toward the car, but Jake blocked him.

"We figured out that during the CDM attack, the vehicle brakes were not immediately engaged," Cavanaugh explained, looking over Jake's shoulder at the car. "Every other vehicle slowed down over a three-second period, to about twenty-five miles per hour, before the brakes locked up and brought everything to a screeching halt. Here's the key: had the slow-down not happened, the death toll would have been higher. Way higher."

Jake looked up at the cloudy sky and closed his eyes, picturing the code in his mind as he crossed his arms and rubbed his chin.

Cavanaugh continued. "Whoever triggered the CDM attack could've easily made it much worse. I'm told that with a simple edit to the code, the brakes would've been applied at a hundred percent all at once. No slow-down. For some reason, the terrorist didn't make the attack happen like that."

Jake opened his eyes, looked at Cavanaugh. "You're saying Viktor could have killed more people if he wanted to?"

"You're the engineer, Jake. Calculate how many people

were driving on the road that day."

Jake closed his eyes again. Birds chirped from an oak tree behind them as he went into *the zone* to run the numbers in his head. His eyes burst open. "Sixty thousand fatalities. And over a hundred thousand injuries." He paused, still calculating. "And that's just on seven miles of freeway."

"I'm totally with you as far as pinning Viktor as the prime suspect, but my boss, Shankle, has the bureau looking at several other persons of interest, including you, I'm afraid. We're coordinating with the CIA and Homeland Security. Might be Hezbollah or ISIS, they're just not sure."

Jake put his hands behind his head and arched his neck back, looking out over the green soccer field grass.

"You mentioned earlier about a leak inside the bureau."

Cavanaugh took another step toward the little Ford. Jake blocked him again.

"Still looking into it. Someone inside my own agency is working against us. The terrorists seem to be ahead of us at every turn, so no way this is a coincidence. But tackling that issue is my job, not yours. Back to the CDM attack. Imagine if they went after us on a national level. During rush hour."

Jake ran more numbers in his head. "Nationwide, there are anywhere from sixty- to eighty-million commuter cars every workday on the freeways. Each vehicle is currently equipped with one of our networking devices, so theoretically . . . and as long as that back door is in the code . . ." A wave of panic filled Jake's body. "If Viktor sabotaged the Sûr System on a national scale, he could theoretically cause the mother of all terror attacks. Millions would die."

Someone coughed from behind Jake, and he turned around to see Carlie standing, her pale face looking as though she were getting sick. Before Jake could scold her for not following instructions to stay in the car, she put her hand out to shake Cavanaugh's.

"You must be the guy who let the senator get blown to a million pieces," she said, shaking his hand. She leaned toward her dad, put her hand up to her mouth in a feigned attempt to hide her next sentence from Cavanaugh. "A man in a suit always has something to sell you. Plus, I have to pee."

Jake couldn't hold back a small chuckle. *That's my girl, all right.*

But the thought evaporated, replaced by the national attack, marinating in Jake's mind for the next few moments.

"I'm not here to sell you anything, young lady," Cavanaugh said with a smirk. Cavanaugh ended the handshake with Carlie. "Seriously, nobody would ever be able to pull off a national-level attack." He stood tall and with confidence in his voice. "The system is shut down, we've already locked up the back door the terrorists used to get in, we're updating the security and in the next hour, we're going to pull the power to it. This can't possibly happen again."

Cavanaugh motioned for them to walk to the car. He set the briefcase on top of the hood and opened it. Inside was another burner phone, a black Glock 22, and two fifteen-round clips.

"Your old phone number will forward to this one."

Jake shook his head. "No way. I'm not taking a gun."

"You're taking the new phone and the weapon. End of discussion," Cavanaugh said.

CHAPTER 38

Bobby sat in the front passenger seat of his van, bursting an artery for not getting all the attention he knew he deserved. Nicole had stolen the 4:30 p.m. and 5:30 p.m. time slots, delivered the bombing and assassination airings and now stood a scant twenty yards from him, near the northern perimeter of the bombing site, ready to go live with the lead story at six o'clock—the bombing and assassination.

Carol had promised him she'd try to get him to run his conspiracy story at 6:00, that despite the senator's death and extensive coordination, she'd get Bobby some airtime. The entire broadcast consisted of stories of the senator's life and times, with backstory and political accomplishments sprinkled here and there among the footage of the blast area. The conspiracy had been cut from the lineup, so no Bobby at 4:30 p.m., 5:00 p.m., nor 5:30 p.m.

With her back to the crater, Nicole stood about a quarter mile northwest of where the bomb had exploded exactly four hours earlier. Her first live 60-second report had aired within an hour of the bombing and at a distance of two miles away from the site. The piece went national and looped on a nation-wide feed, cutting into regularly scheduled programming, which made her an instant celebrity, a status Bobby envied the same way a homeless guy would envy a briefcase brimming with cash.

Now closer to the site, Nicole stood with her lower back touching the yellow and black DO NOT CROSS tape, behind which over a hundred people—mostly uniformed officers from local law enforcement agencies—picked through the rubble searching for survivors. Dread filled her eyes when she spied Bobby and Doug standing next to her cameraman with only ten seconds before she went live.

"You're all over this, Nicole. You got this. You got it. It's all you. You're a national hero with my stories. Do it, baby." Bobby sneered.

Doug and Bobby were piped into the audio feed from Carol as her voice chimed in via the IFB earpiece wedged into Nicole's ear. "Nicole, darling, I need you to perk up a bit. You look scared. We need your strong face, our viewers want to watch a confident woman."

Nicole immediately lifted her chin and did some random facial stretches, opening and closing her mouth, sticking her tongue in and out like some damned lizard. She finally showed those sparkling iceberg-white teeth for all to see.

Carol counted down. "And we're going live in five, four, three, two . . ."

Bobby leaned into Doug, his hand covering part of his mouth, shaking his head, and said, "These bitches are colluding against us."

"We are live at the site where, at two o'clock this afternoon, United States Senator Barbara Brown was tragically assassinated during a massive bomb explosion. Sources confirmed the explosion was not an atomic or dirty bomb, but rather a tactical weapon not used by US forces since the Vietnam war. The military refers to this type of bomb using the nickname 'daisy cutter.' As you can see by the damage right behind where I'm standing"—she turned to point behind her as she looked back at the camera— "the blast was powerful enough to level the brand-new, two-hundred-million-dollar, freeway-to-freeway interchange on Interstate 15 that was scheduled to open to traffic tomorrow. We're now going to play a video of the explosion, an exclusive of ABC-7. We caution our sensitive viewers: this is very graphic in nature."

Bobby took a few steps toward the back of his van and peeked in to see what the studio played next. Carol cut to the prerecorded video he and Doug had produced earlier in the afternoon, with Nicole's voiceover describing the bombing.

After a short interview with the senator's office and another from the governor's office, the feed cut back to the live shot of Nicole. A breeze blew her stick-straight beige bangs in front of her face and she pulled her hair to the side while holding the blue-and-white ABC-7 mic below her mouth. "We are all saddened by this tragic and senseless loss of life. I'm told the governor has been in contact with the president to request any and all available federal resources to catch the person or people responsible for this. At this time, the FBI has no official comment, citing an ongoing investigation. Reporting live from Victorville, Nicole Freemonte, ABC-7 Eyewitness News."

The feed went back to the anchors in the Glendale news studio, each of whom had several comments and condolences. Doug stood behind his camera, hands adjusting knobs and buttons, as Bobby took the place of Nicole. Bobby fiddled with his earpiece., then jerked his head back and forth.

The light from Doug's camera helped pump Bobby up as he heard the anchorman say into his earpiece, "Okay, now for those conspiracy theorists out there, we have ABC-7's Bobby Jones, who's also out in Victorville reporting on an exclusive ABC-7 story you won't want to miss. Moments after the bombing, Bobby caught a man on video, a man we're sure you'll recognize, but let's let Bobby tell you more. Bobby?"

Bobby had taken some acting classes in high school and, for this segment, chose the emotion of "suspicious".

"Thank you, Dan. I'm also out here in Victorville and have a short story for our viewers. My cameraman and I were sent out earlier today to film the ceremony for the High Desert Corridor. Normally we would've been up on the deck of the upper-bridge structure filming, but as a matter of chance, we were getting wide-angle distance shots when the bomb went off. It was our footage you all just watched a minute ago, the one that Nicole reported."

"That fucking Bobby," Carol blurted from sixty miles away inside her studio. Bobby heard her outburst but simply smiled into the camera.

His blood pressure dropped, his breathing slowed, and he continued his report as though he were Ray Bradbury himself. "For several minutes, the entire area was dead quiet as the dust settled, but before we knew it, sirens approached from all directions, total chaos ensued, and we caught some footage of—well, something aside from the terror. We're now going to show it to you. It's of a man sitting in the driver's side of a small black Ford, with the door open. He's talking on a phone and is someone we're all quite familiar with, albeit a clean-shaven version. Here's the footage. Please take a look and decide for yourself."

Doug gave Bobby the thumbs up signal as the monitor screen switched to the video footage of Dr. Bendel. The camera zoomed in and paused on Bendel's face for all of America to see. The side-by-side image Doug had created earlier appeared on the screen, with the bearded version of Bendel on the right.

Bobby described the images. "The man you are looking at on the right is Dr. Jake Bendel, the man we've reported in previous segments as the one responsible for the CDM attack and who, we were told by federal officials, died tragically in the fire at the Long Beach Convention Center a week ago. If you're like us, you're probably suspicious whether these two men are one and the same. Guys, can we show the bearded photo to the viewers, please? Thanks. We've enhanced today's photo with a little video editing to add in a beard."

The image on the left now showed Jake with a beard.

"Less than a week after Dr. Bendel's funeral, we film a man who looks, at least to this reporter, exactly the same. Did we coincidentally tape Dr. Bendel's twin? Or have we stumbled onto a conspiracy with much deeper roots than government representatives and law enforcement agencies are telling us? We'll let you, the viewers at home, decide. Reporting live from Victorville, Bobby Jones, ABC-7 Eyewitness News."

They sent the video feed back to the anchors. The tan, white anchorman on the left said, "It sure looks like the same guy to me, Bobby. How can this even be possible?"

"Fred," Bobby said, "we captured the vehicle's license plate and are coordinating with the local sheriff's office to determine the owner, but when we find out, we'll be sure to let you know."

The tan anchorman scribbled some notes with his pen and looked up at the camera. "Okay, now for those viewers who are still getting up to speed, talk to us briefly about the crimes Dr. Bendel allegedly committed. How do we know he was involved and that he wasn't framed?"

"If he was framed, that would mean all of the video and photo evidence was fabricated by a genius."

Bobby continued to explain about the videos of bribery, planning the CDM, and more before they ended the report and cut the feed. Now off camera, Bobby heard Carol babbling something about the next segment, but he yanked out his earpiece and jumped up and down like a boy who'd opened his Christmas present to find exactly what he wanted. He shook his head and howled at the sky. *I nailed it. Booyah!* He looked at Nicole and flicked his tongue.

CHAPTER 39

As the evening drew to a close, Jake, Carlie, and Cavanaugh walked through a back alley that smelled like sewage, then entered the back door of a downtown Chinese food restaurant through a beige metal door. Once inside, a new agent greeted them.

"Guys, this is Agent Codling, my former partner at the LAPD and trusted friend. In fact, I trust him with my life. He's on board with everything." Introductions were made and Agent Codling, a tiny-framed, sturdy man with black caterpillar eyebrows and short salt-and-pepper hair, asked them to call him "AC." Codling escorted the trio upstairs to the third floor, to a two-bedroom apartment. Inside the main living room sat three red velvet chairs, a fifties-style teal Hughes sofa, oddball Chinese wall decorations, and a two-pane vertical sliding window with black cloth drapes. Jake looked out the window to the empty street below and his vision spun. He felt weak, physically and emotionally. He turned to Cavanaugh and shook his head. "I don't like it here. Doesn't feel safe."

"You're gonna have to trust me on this," Cavanaugh said. "It's important we keep a low profile while we put a plan together."

Jake massaged his temples. "Just get me to a computer." He pointed to the open laptop on the desk and looked at AC, who nodded in consent. Jake said to Carlie, "Could use your help."

"No, Dad, I'm exhausted. This is too much to process. I'm literally a wreck right now in my head, but maybe after I get some rest. I'm still crazy glad to see you." She smiled, gave him a hug and, holding onto his girl, the offspring of his loving wife, he felt a warm glow. In some odd way, he sensed Cynthia there with them.

"Sure, I understand." After they hugged, she walked into the north bedroom and crashed.

Jake wiped the sweat from his brow. "Too bad AC forgot to bring an a/c with him," he said before walking to the bathroom sink, splashing some water on his face to wake up while Cavanaugh and the other agent talked. He managed to hear something about "Shankle" and "next attack."

Jake sent a text message to Paige and Dave to notify them of his new phone number, then walked over and stood next to the two agents. "You're in capable hands here," Cavanaugh said. "I gotta run and untangle some of this mess, but I'll be back soon."

AC made a pot of coffee and gave a cup to Jake while he worked. Jake looked on Google Maps to find his location, and once the caffeine kicked in, began his research on intelligent transportation systems, or ITS's. He worked all night and a few hours into the morning of Wednesday, August 12, until a knock on the door brought breakfast from a local bakery. Jake grabbed a quick bite of a feast that consisted of hard-boiled eggs, orange juice, croissants, muffins, and more coffee. He wolfed it down and went back to his laptop to continue the research. He let Carlie sleep. God knows she needed the rest.

He thought of Cynthia and checked his internal flame of rage. Still burning.

Undaunted by his drained energy levels, he followed the long night with an entire morning of additional research. Already an expert on using ITS's, Jake had learned most of his niche skill set during training classes he took when the technology had debuted several years earlier. He wanted to learn all the juicy, intimate details that made the systems tick. What frequency did the modems operate on? Were the systems closed or open? What kind of cyber-security did they employ, if at all?

Viktor would probably have visited these same pages recently. The man's footsteps were practically embedded in them. Glaring straight at Jake was the very same information Viktor would have needed to hack in and cause that coordinated SITS attack back in May.

Carlie stumbled out of bed around noon, her disheveled hair curled out in all directions. She rubbed her puffy eyes and shuffled along, managing to mumble, "Mornin', Dad. Mornin', Mr. Agent," and aimed straight for what remained of the breakfast delivery. She sat, took a bite of croissant, then asked her dad, "I don't know what the hell happened the last few hours. I was totally out of it. Had a dream Mom was in a helicopter crash, but somehow you saved her." She looked up, rubbing her eyes. "Weird." She plopped down on the couch and looked up at her dad. "Tell me you found some hard evidence on this Viktor guy."

The agent sitting on the couch holding the business section of the LA Times looked up and down at her, noticed Jake was watching him check out the daughter, quickly looked back at the paper, snapped it back open and continued reading.

"Trying to put myself inside Viktor's mind right now. We know how he hacked into the federal mainframe to execute the CDM attack, and the FBI and Dave are working to find if we missed anything. But if I can determine how he hacked into the systems and caused the very first attack, the SITS green-lights attack on May 5, it might point us to a way of setting a physical trap for the son of a bitch."

Carlie took a swig of orange juice, tilted her head, and asked, "I still don't understand about this SITS green-lights attack."

He explained all the gritty details and her jaw dropped. "Oh, my God, Dad, I remember hearing about that. There's got to be something we can do to help."

Over the next six hours, Jake dove even deeper into intelligent transportation systems, trying to find answers and clues. His phone vibrated. Jake thought about not answering it, but he knew she'd keep calling. He had to answer.

"Jake, where are you? I need to see you right away," Bridgette said.

"I don't have time to—"

"I'm on your side, Jake, trust me. I'll tell you everything

when we meet. I have information that might be useful to you."

Jake paused, evaluating the variables. *Maybe she's working with someone on the inside at the FBI.*

But so are the terrorists.

"I'm listening."

"Jake, I put two and two together. I figured out that you must be trying to clear your name of those attacks you were blamed for, or maybe even trying to get revenge for your wife. I get it. I want to help."

Jake sipped his coffee. His fingers jittered as he compared his location to possible meeting places filed away in his memory. "Meet me near the entrance of the Los Angeles National Cemetery."

"The one next to the UCLA campus? Know it well. Should be nice and quiet. Meet you there in thirty minutes," she said in an over-the-top sexy voice.

He hung up and told Carlie and AC he needed to go out for some air.

"Bullshit. You're going to meet that woman," Carlie said. He gave Carlie a double take before turning to AC and hearing an earful about what Cavanaugh had said.

Jake picked up the gun from the couch, loaded a magazine, chambered a round, flipped on the safety and tucked it into the small of his back. "I don't trust Bridgette," Jake said, "but I need to see what she knows. Stay here, Carlie. You'll be safe. This guy makes a move on you," he pointed to AC, "you know what to do." He instructed AC to stay professional and keep his daughter safe.

The apartment above the restaurant and the cemetery were only two miles away from each other. An easy thirty-minute walk. The sun had already dipped down to the clouded horizon, and most of the day's heat had started to wane. The air smelled musty as a strong cyclone pushed eastward, inland from the Pacific.

CHAPTER 40

Jake walked at a brisk clip to the cemetery and when he arrived, Bridgette was already seated on a green metal park bench. He approached her, stood tall with his arms across his chest. No smile. All business.

"I didn't think you'd show up all alone," she said, patting the wire metal bench next to her.

He looked around and evaluated their location. Not a soul in sight. Only the sound of a stiff breeze churning through the nearby oak trees.

"I'll stand, thank you. We don't have much time, so I'd like to know how you got my cell number," he said, unsure how to handle his former girlfriend.

She smiled. He had forgotten how striking her blue eyes were. Crystal clear. She smelled amazing, like fresh roses on a spring morning. "Jake, I'm not exactly sure what you're mixed up in, but I want to help," she said as she touched her nose with the tip of her finger.

"Baloney. You know more than you're telling me. Spill it or I walk," Jake said, giving her his best poker face.

She maintained her smile, unfazed. "Do you remember the time we drove up the coast to Pismo and spent the weekend in that little hole-in-the-wall place? Ordering room service between orgasms."

He felt his face flush as the memories poured into his mind. "Don't change the subject. I swear, tell me why I'm here or I'm gone."

She stood and drew a line down his forearm with her index finger. "I think about that weekend all the time. It was probably the single best experience of my life."

Fifteen months ago, three months into his affair with Bridgette, he could no longer bear the guilt and had confessed everything to his wife. Now he hated what he'd let slither into his family's world.

"Like I said before, I'm mourning my wife and for all I know, you were involved with her death and the bomb planted under my daughter's car."

She tilted her head, narrowed her eyes, and took a step back. "I had nothing to do with your wife or daughter. I honestly only wanted the best for them. You have to believe me."

Before he could turn to run away, she lunged and grabbed his arm. He looked down at her and she said, "I don't know how else to say this, so I'm just gonna . . ." She let go of his arm and leaned forward with a nod and steady eye contact. "I never stopped loving you."

What if this is a diversion so they can get Carlie?

He put his hands in front of him. "I don't have time for this." He gulped, turned, and started to walk away, but she jogged up next to him.

"You have a lot going on right now, I get that, but I wanted you to know my feelings for you." Tears formed in her eyes.

"Your timing couldn't be worse. I'm a widower. I have a grown daughter and . . . Jesus," he stopped, then pointed at her face. "This better not be some goddamned trap. You people lay a finger on Carlie and I swear I'll—"

She reached for his hands with hers, but he pulled away. "You're confused, baby. Please listen to me. We're not starting anything. We're just continuing what we already had. Here, sit down." She motioned back to the bench.

Images of his wife flashed before him. No. Not today. Not like this. He sensed his wife's presence standing nearby, watching. *Being here is wrong. Wrong!*

He pushed Bridgette's shoulders away from his. "Dammit, Bridgette." Her eyes were a deep blue. He gritted his teeth and felt the gun rubbing against his tailbone, begging to be released. "You said you had some valuable info for me." He pulled out the gun and pointed it at her temple. "Tell me right now what that is, or I'm leaving."

She put her hands in the air. "Okay. Okay. Viktor won't stop until you and Carlie are dead," she said. "Tomorrow. Something's happening tomorrow. Thursday."

Jake thought about the previous attacks, dates, times, and how tomorrow fit with the chess theory.

She continued. "He has big plans for this country. At first

I bought into his rhetoric about the bureaucratic crap, the corruption, how the country needed a wake-up call, and all that, and once he actually started killing people, I wanted out, but it was too late. He knows where my parents and brother live. To say he's blackmailing me would be an understatement. I could be killing my family right now just by telling you this."

He tucked the gun back into his pants and turned away. "Unbelievable. I've got your number. I'll call you if I need anything." He swung around to head back to the hotel, confused as hell, but stopped when his phone pinged with a text from Dave that read, "Dude, I'm really close to a breakthrough, I can feel it."

He looked back at Bridgette, who was now in full breakdown crying mode. If it was an act, it worked because a tinge of empathy eked its way into his soul. "If you're telling the truth, we can't be seen together. Too dangerous. We need to separate ASAP."

Jake's instinct to return to Carlie burned strong inside him, but he couldn't head directly back to the hotel because Bridgette likely had a tail on her. No, he needed to take a circuitous route to confuse any potential follower. He made sure the gun was tucked in snug as he started a jog back in the general direction of the Chinese restaurant.

CHAPTER 41

Buried deep inside the cubicle-infested IT department at Caltech, the man following Allah's commands sat in his favorite office chair with extra lumbar support, in his dull gray office, working hard to eliminate millions of useless Americans.

Viktor's cubicle area was a mere six-foot-by-eight-foot rectangle and although during the day there were normally seven other people working in his area, they had all gone home for the night. The instant those hands on the shared clock above the secretary's desk hit four o'clock, off his coworkers ran, home to their perfect little lives and happy little children. *Stupid ungrateful fuckos.*

Viktor knew his psychopathic condition had been brought on by the accident with his mother long ago and he'd learned to control his impulses. He knew that he and other psychopaths could more easily fit into society, unable to form emotional attachments to anyone or anything but better than sociopaths at hiding it. Harder to pluck from a crowd. The feeling of empathy was a distant memory for Viktor. Whenever someone died, even a friend or close relative, oh well. No emotion.

He'd learned to overcome these differences by using his lack of emotion or empathy to use others' emotions to his advantage without remorse. His meds minimized the chances for a manic attack at work, but he'd learned to recognize the signs of an impending shift in his personality and would leave the office immediately whenever that happened. He needed to keep his cover intact and relished his uncanny knack for earning people's trust.

Despite his psychopathic schizophrenia, which his doctors long ago had diagnosed him with, Viktor's psychopathic side excelled at manipulation. His genius-level IQ meant the art of mimicking emotion came easily to him. In fact, he loved fooling people into believing he was normal, as he'd read was typical of most psychopaths who are well educated and have no problem holding down steady jobs.

Viktor had been employed at Caltech now for three years, had earned many admirers, and enjoyed knowing everyone assumed he had no mental condition whatsoever. The concept that murdering other humans was morally wrong, a concept taught to him by his Christian mother, no longer resonated inside his damaged brain. His work, these killings, all served a greater purpose. Their deaths were a necessary part of the grand scheme to cleanse the US of the sin-worshiping infidels in order to pave the way for an Islamic State. He knew Allah had called on him for this epic purpose because of his special set of skills, but with that redheaded bitch now questioning his motives . . . Viktor knew he had to take care of her. Nobody would ever get in the way of his plans.

Allah had planted the seed in Viktor's head four years ago,

guiding him along to the final stage of the *cleansing event.* Viktor's twelve followers had proven themselves dedicated men who welcomed martyrdom, willing to give the ultimate sacrifice for their leader, their god, and their cause. They also believed, as Viktor did, that the most powerful nation in the world needed a slap in the face. Allah's voice regularly told Viktor most politicians were narcissistic, selfish, greedy bastards who cared nothing for their constituents. This made deserving prey of the many dolts who were leading a nation to ruin. The test run with Senator Brown went off with the precision of an atomic clock. Viktor smiled.

The eyes of the mastermind focused keenly on his screen, typing inhumanly fast, manipulating code the same way he manipulated people, like a puppet master. The nervous twitch hit his right eyebrow every few seconds. *Those bastards have no idea what's coming.* As a true operational artist, a term the media had recently conjured up to describe possible motives behind certain terrorist attacks, Viktor had to make sure his impending spectacles of "performance violence" would change the world.

After wiping several crumbs from lunch from the surface of his gray beard, he focused on the impending reward for serving Allah, now only two days away, a deep, desperate desire to visit the great white light in the sky, sit on the knee of Mohammed, and be with his mother again. *I see the Promised Land*, he muttered to himself with a smirk.

His cell rang. Sanchez.

"Greetings, brother," Sanchez said. "I'm at the Cal Poly campus near the server farm, awaiting your orders."

For Viktor, the Caltech job provided him a perfect cover; he'd get his daily work done in the first thirty minutes of his eight-hour shift as a server maintenance supervisor, then have the rest of the day to hack into and set up the necessary systems, all the while looking like a productive IT guy.

"Excellent. I'll be inside their data center in one minute. Stand by," Viktor said.

He continued hacking into the server farm at the Cal Poly campus. *My dad, the man who'd adopted me, the one who championed me through school, pushing me to do my homework, helping my to do the very best I could, would have been proud,* he thought.

Viktor's screen showed "Login Successful" with a blinking cursor, and he knew exactly where to navigate next. A small vein on the right side of his forehead twitched and pulsed with adrenalized blood.

How many people would die? Dozens? Millions? *The more the better!*

The *cleansing event* would get the attention of that crazy bitch president for sure. Viktor thought about how people in the future, a hundred years from now, would sing his praises for bringing the mighty US of A to its knees, for starting the uprising that overthrew the bloated bureaucracy from hell. The new leaders might even put his image on the hundred-dollar bill. Get rid of that old Franklin guy. Useless. Put someone on there who deserved the credit: Viktor Johnston.

CHAPTER 42

In full panic mode, Jake hustled up the stairs to the makeshift safehouse. The lingering smell of old Chinese food wafted through the air as he pondered Bridgette's motive for luring him out of hiding. He didn't trust her and his gut told him that meeting was probably some trumped-up plot to snatch Carlie. AC answered the door and gestured him inside.

As the negative thoughts speckled his mind, Jake rushed to the bedroom and found Carlie sprawled out on the bed watching the news.

"Thank God, I thought maybe you'd . . . never mind," Jake said, forcing a smile. He wiped his brow, and the thoughts of her potential kidnapping disintegrated.

"Dad, the whole country's waiting to see who's behind the senator's assassination. This is all so crazy." She licked her dry lips. "But I can't stay cooped up like this anymore. I need some work to do. This place is driving me crazy."

He stepped toward her and sat on the bed. "I'm going to visit Uncle Mark and ask him about the chess analogy. He's the best psychiatrist I know, and he's a damned great chess player.

I'm hoping he can shed some light on this and help me figure out what we're missing."

Mark Rayhee was an old friend of Jake's who used to visit the Bendels several times a year when Carlie was young. Mark had studied at Stanford and quickly became licensed as a psychiatrist. His thriving practice in downtown Los Angeles had helped thousands over the last couple of decades and if anyone could help shed some light on the chess game Viktor was playing, Mark could.

"I love Uncle Mark. I'm definitely going with you."

"You'd be safer here."

"I don't care. I need to leave this place. Now."

"I'm not a hundred percent sure I wasn't followed back here. The bad guys might be setting a trap for us, are you sure—"

"Now." She turned and walked toward the door.

Jake trusted his daughter's instincts and they left the safe-house without AC. Once outside, they walked north on the sidewalk as the sounds of car horns and yelling echoed off the high-rise buildings. "His office is just a few blocks from here." Jake pulled his FBI-issued phone out of his pocket, but before he dialed, he looked up and spied the late Thursday morning gray clouds rolling into the area, darker than when he'd met with Bridgette. *Odd for this time of year.*

He dialed Mark's number, glad he remembered it after all these years. He punched the speakerphone button and waited.

"Hello?" Mark answered, clearing his throat. He sounded like he hadn't talked to anyone in several days. Mark's wife, Danielle, passed away a few years back. Now he and Jake were both widowers. Despite knowing the risks and helping many folks treat their alcoholism, Mark hit the bottle every day in memoriam to Danielle. Jake had assumed Mark would still be sober this early in the day. The man normally didn't put his first drink on ice till after noon. Only alcoholics have their first drink during the morning hours. Whatever.

"Mark, buddy, don't hang up," Jake said. He stopped walking and leaned against a brick façade. "This isn't a prank or anything. This is Jake Bendel."

Silence.

"Mark?"

"Listen, man, I don't know who the hell you think you are, but I'm going to hang up. Jake's dead. We buried the poor bastard and his wife on Saturday, for God's sake. Son of a—"

"Mark, no, it is me, I swear. Remember the time you and I went skiing? Well, I went skiing and you did that thing with a snowboard, and there was a blizzard the entire way up to Bear Mountain."

"Jesus. You were telling me you don't like snowboarders."

"Exactly. I don't like snowboarders, except for you, of course. I've always made an exception."

"Hmmm . . ."

"Your son's wedding. You and I got wasted. Hammered. You told me you had a threesome with those two chicks in Amsterdam." Jake hoped that snippet of truth would do the trick.

Carlie covered her mouth with her hand and laughed.

"Well, I'll be a stiff dick inside a tight hole," Mark said. "You're alive. What the hell, man?" Swearing made Mark feel good, like they were teenagers again. Possibly some kind of new-fangled treatment for alcoholism.

"I'm two blocks away from your office and need to meet you in person. I think my phone might be tapped."

"Done. See you in five."

Carlie and Jake walked several more blocks down Yale Street and made their way around to the back alley of a tall office building in downtown Los Angeles. The place was deserted save for a black homeless guy with a white beard sleeping against a green trash bin. A buzzing noise came from a door, then a click and a moment later, Mark opened the back door. He trotted to his old friends and after brief hugs and "holy shits," Mark took a step back, placed his hands on his hips, and said with a huge, adoring smile and chuckle, "Dude, this is tremendous. Absolutely frickin' nuts."

Jake explained what happened to Cynthia, how he was framed, working with the FBI, gotta keep everything on the down-low, et cetera.

"Two widowers. Jesus Cripplesticks. You know the details of how she died?"

"Long story."

"She was a good woman," Mark said, patting Jake's shoulder. "I remember she and Danielle got along great. That's a real loss, man."

Mark turned to Carlie, feigning a friendly punch to her gut. "How've you been, kiddo?"

"Great, except for all this crazy terrorist stuff."

Mark crossed his arms. "And you're working with the FBI. Great, man."

"Dad, maybe Mark can—"

"Sorry to be such an ass, but you two can catch up later," Jake interrupted. "I need your help to stay ahead of the bad guys. Everything I'm telling you is top-secret, so again, you can't repeat it. Any of it."

"Whatever it takes to, you know, avenge your wife's death. Murder. Fucking bastards. They practically shut our whole city down, man. People can't get to work, but nobody feels like working anyway. Everyone I speak with is depressed and still in shock. My parents now have PTSD thanks to the CDM. Whenever they see a freeway on TV or hear about it, they both have panic attacks. Sad, really. Some of the young kids in their twenties think all this shit is cool, but it's a goddamned nightmare," Mark said with a subtle slur in his speech and a hint of cognac, his favorite go-to drink, wafting out into the air. "If I had a chance to get the bastard who killed my wife, I'd totally do it—against my own professional advice, of course. I mean, if I were you, this is the right play to make, man, 'cause we're gonna do this. You and me."

Jake told Mark about the terrorists, their plot, and the chess-game analogy.

"So you want me to play the role of terrorist. Okay. Got it. Let's see," Mark said, looking up and crossing his arms. "Why the hell would I want to play chess . . . hmmm . . ."

A brief pause followed as Mark squinted, deep in thought. "Got it. Okay, this is just my theory, my two cents, if you will, but I think you're spot on with the chess-game analogy. I think the king," he said making hand quotes, "will be an attack you don't suspect. I'll bet your ass the king's not a single person, either."

Initially confused, wheels turned in Jake's head. "Multiple people?"

"Bingo. First of all, it doesn't make any sense to do all this just to kill one person. Even if it was the President of the United States. No, I don't think it's him . . . or her, rather. Still getting used to the whole woman-president thing."

"So if we go with your assumption they're going after a group of people," Carlie said, stepping into the conversation, "what's to limit them from attacking on a national scale? Why stay in California? I mean, if I were them, I wouldn't limit myself to just one geographic region."

Mark chuckled and pointed his finger at Carlie. "That's my girl. Exactly." He turned to Jake. "I'll bet these guys are out for massive blood. Thousands, tens of thousands, millions of people. We have to think national scale."

Jake backed away with raised hands as the thought of a national-level traffic accident hit him. "Oh, no. Please, God, no." Jake remembered the numbers he crunched earlier with Cavanaugh. "If you're right, millions of innocent people would die. But millions of people aren't a king. Doesn't make sense." He swallowed hard, crossed his arms to match Mark and looked back and forth between Mark and Carlie, who both averted his gaze.

"Think about it. In a democracy, who's the most powerful player? The people, right? The voters."

Right!

They talked for thirty more minutes about the details of what Viktor might be planning.

"Gotta run," Jake said. "You may have just saved the lives

of millions of people. You deserve a cold one."

"Okay, buddy, you stay safe and alive. When this all blows over, the first round's on you down at our old hangout," he said with a wink.

"Bye, Uncle Mark. I never want to hear about that three-some you had."

"Fine, be that way," Mark said, waving goodbye.

Jake and Carlie walked back to the safehouse, careful nobody was following them. "That was interesting," Jake said to Carlie.

"Mom would be proud of you right now."

A nice gesture, but Jake could tell her insides were all knotted up. She clearly hadn't made peace with what was happening.

As they approached the Chinese restaurant with the safe-house above, Jake called Dave, who as usual did not pick up, so he texted instead. "It's your fellow dancer, JB. Call me ASAP . . . new emergency."

Within a few seconds, Dave responded via text.

Dave: *Two back doors! More FBI news?*

Jake: *new threat: something big 2 happen – tomorrow!! Doesn't fit our Tuesday pattern, but need u to dig around.*

Dave: *10-4. Tell me what I'm looking 4 specifically.*

Jake called Dave and asked about the two back doors, maybe this was what his gut instinct had told him.

"The first one was nearly impossible to find, and the second was worse," Dave said. "But here's the thing: using the dark web and this digital tool called 'reverse observational coding,' I figured out that when anyone viewed the code, like we did last night, the system automatically revealed our IP address, via a secure text router, to the hacker. I stumbled on this when I spilled coffee on my keyboard."

"Are you freakin' kidding me? You spilled coffee and that's how you figured it out?"

"Well, sort of. As I grabbed the cup and saw the coffee drops floating through the air, an idea hit me about analyzing part of the code we hadn't really inspected in detail. As I finished mopping up the mess, I was staring at the line with fresh eyes and noticed that it, too, was in fact, a hidden snippet of code. So I coded a reverse observational algorithm and ran it on the system, and you'll never guess what happened."

"I'm waiting."

"When we originally examined the code two days ago, the system automatically, though unbeknownst to us, sent our IP address to a blocked cell phone number."

"So they know your home address?"

"Yes, but more importantly, I reached out to one of my underground buddies and ran a trace on the number. Guess where the number is registered?"

After hearing the name of the owner and location, Jake almost dropped his coffee cup. He thanked Dave for the info and hung up before texting him tidbits of what Mark explained, based on the napkin notes and his memory, then continued the digital conversation.

Jake: *go thru the algorithm again & look 4 details about another attack tomorrow*

Dave: *10-4, got several ideas for that shit. All over this*

Jake: *Call me when u get sumthing*

Before opening the rear door to the restaurant, Jake did a final scan of the area. Nobody had followed them. A few minutes later, Carlie and Jake were up in the safehouse and Jake let out a deep exhale. "Don't worry, sweetie. Everything's going to be fine. We won't need to be here much longer. I need a little more time to finish putting together a physical strategy to catch Viktor. He's up in Big Bear, I know it. Gotta figure out a way to get up there and catch him before he strikes again. Also, need to talk to Cavanaugh. We're gonna get this guy."

After checking in with AC, Jake grabbed a short power nap in one of the faux-leather chairs before pouring himself another cup of caffeine. The door burst open and Cavanaugh walked in. "We need to talk."

They sat on a couch next to a tiny coffee table and strategized how to catch the men behind the brutal killings.

"I want you to know that the FBI," Cavanaugh said, "in coordination with the CIA and Homeland Security, has officially named the man they feel has a strongest possibility of being responsible for these terrorist attacks, and I'm being told it's most certainly someone other than Viktor Johnston."

"No goddamned way." Jake felt his mind come alive. Forty-five minutes since his second cup of Folgers instant. "They're wrong. I'm positive it's Viktor. They have no evidence it's someone else. I'll bet they didn't even check the texts and calls from my phone yet."

"They're looking at a man named Syed Rezwan Farook. He showed up on the international terrorist list six months ago, our friends at the CIA have been tracking him since, and they've linked him to two other terrorist bombings in Europe and North Africa."

Carlie walked in from the bedroom and crossed her arms, listening.

"That has nothing to do with the SS," Jake said, standing and raking his fingers through his hair. AC stood in the corner like a stoic zombie.

"These bombings have everything to do with our current situation, and here's the scary part: nobody knows where he's at. They saw him five days ago in Paris, but after that he went totally off the grid. He's well-connected and well-funded, according to the CIA, possibly by an international group we know almost nothing about."

"Well, I hate to throw a monkey wrench into the plans of the mighty FBI here, Chief, but my research yesterday yielded proof positive that Viktor is involved."

Cavanaugh leaned forward, elbows on his knees, with narrowing eyes that drilled into Jake. "Tell me."

"I spent all night digging into the first attack. My theory was that if he was going to make a mistake somewhere, he'd screw up on his first try. Plus, I'm familiar with intelligent transportation systems. If anyone could figure this out, it's me."

Cavanaugh looked up and down at Jake, then leaned back in his chair. "Go on."

"In a nutshell, about two years ago, Caltrans took over the control of all signalized intersections on local streets that had more than a certain amount of daily traffic on them. Every intersection has a traffic signal when there's too many vehicles for a four-way stop," Jake explained. "In the old days, we used to set a traffic-control cabinet on one of the four corners of an intersection with a timer inside of it. Based on many different factors, a traffic engineer would set a certain amount of green time for one direction and a different amount of green time for the other direction. If there were turn pockets and other variations at the intersection, this would all have been considered and set into the controller."

Cavanaugh made a rolling motion with his hand. "You mentioned earlier about inductor loops. I remember that, but not sure what they are."

"When we started using loops in the pavement, a vehicle would drive over it, which sent a signal to the cabinet to tell it there was a vehicle there waiting for its turn. This all worked perfectly until we had so many vehicles driving on the roads, with signalized intersections spaced along roads one after another after another, it made sense to link them all together. This worked fine, too, until computers started getting more powerful. When the internet arrived in the late nineties and early two-thousands, the engineers figured it would increase efficiency to bring the control of these intersections in-house to a centralized computer system. This latest iteration could make changes from a distance using modems, so our technicians didn't have to go out and manually set the timing for each intersection."

Cavanaugh stood, walked to the table holding the food tray, ripped a piece from a croissant, buttered it up and threw it into his mouth. Chewing, he said, "All reasonable stuff, but hurry up and skip to the relevant part."

"Let me back up. Once each city and county had their own individual systems in place that controlled the timing of all major signalized intersections within their jurisdictions, the systems didn't play nice with one another. With the super-high volume of vehicles—"

"I don't know what that means, volume."

"The number of cars and trucks. Every road has a capacity to hold a certain volume of vehicles. When the volume is higher than the capacity, we get gridlock, traffic congestion, call it what you want. Nobody moves."

"Got it." Cavanaugh threw another piece of croissant into his mouth.

"Congestion sucks. It's bad for the environment, a huge waste of time and money for people, et cetera. So any deviation from a mathematically optimized timing scenario would prove disastrous from a traffic-congestion standpoint. All these agencies got together and gave full control to an agency in the State of California to oversee all of their systems. This way, in theory at least, everything would act together as one synchronized, well-oiled machine that would keep traffic congestion minimized on local streets."

Jake realized he'd just inundated Cavanaugh's brain with way too much technical information.

"Anyway, Viktor somehow hacked into this, so that's what I need to find more information about. He set all of the intersections at what we call 'simultaneous green.' Imagine driving down the road, you're approaching a signalized intersection and you have a green light. You think you have the right-of-way and assume that the cross traffic has red lights because it's your turn, right? No. Not in this case. On May 5 at four p.m., thousands of intersections across California had green lights *simultaneously*, green lights in all four directions. There were massive numbers of car accidents and over eighteen hundred people were killed."

Cavanaugh shoved his hands into his pockets and focused his gaze onto Jake. "I know all this, get to the point."

"When this hands-off approach was implemented, Caltrans was supposed to ensure a high level of multi-layered, heavily encrypted security, for obvious reasons."

"If the security was so solid, why are you assuming someone hacked in?" Cavanaugh asked, interrupting Jake's monologue.

Jake agreed. "Turns out they overlooked two critical things. Caltrans followed the same security protocols the banks used back in the day, maybe about ten years ago. It's what's called a two-step authentication process to access their system. They also disregarded the possibility of what is referred to as an injection vulnerability."

"I took a class on cybersecurity a few years back." Cavanaugh returned to his chair and shifted in his seat. "This sounds familiar, but I don't remember the details. Hurry up and get to the point. The next attack could be any hour now."

Carlie walked in. "Injection what?"

Jake noticed AC looking Carlie up and down again. He shoved his emotions aside. "The two steps were a PIN and a fingerprint. So theoretically, if someone had your PIN and your fingerprint, they could access the system. Do you know of anyone working in the industry who might have been kidnapped or bribed?"

Cavanaugh blinked and put his finger on his lower lip. He

thought for a moment and pulled up a new browser window on his phone and pecked at the screen. "Nope. But someone did get killed. A Caltrans guy." He scrolled through the text on his phone. "Yep, here we go. One week before the May 5 incident, a traffic engineer working on the system in Sacramento had his throat slashed and his right hand hacked off."

Carlie cringed.

Jake snapped his fingers and pointed to Cavanaugh. "That's gotta be it. Tell me who he was and where he worked."

Cavanaugh scrolled down. "Victim identified as Peter Mauricio. Worked at Caltrans. Fifty-three-years old. Full access to the traffic system."

Bells went off in Jake's head, and he walked in a tight circle, thinking. He remembered the lady he talked to at Caltech. *What was her name? Janel?* He wanted to make this right for so many people, and now he had one more.

"Check this out. If someone threatened Peter, got his PIN, then used his fingerprint from his dead hand to access the system, they could have set it all up to happen at 4:00 p.m. on the twenty-eighth. Clean. No loose ends."

"Interesting theory. I'm starting to question my judgment to save your life. You'd make quite an exceptional bad guy if you ever turned to the dark side."

"No plans to do that anytime soon. I'd rather focus on what's at stake right in front of us."

"Dad, I know I came a bit late to your little party here," Carlie interrupted, "but what does that have to do with Viktor? How do we know it wasn't this Syed guy Cavanaugh mentioned earlier who killed Peter?"

Cavanaugh looked at Jake and cocked his head.

"She has bionic hearing, like her mother. Don't ask," Jake said with a wink at his daughter. "Peter's widow works at Caltech in the IT department with the guy I told you about two days ago, Viktor Engel. I'm assuming you haven't followed up on that lead yet?"

"No, we haven't," Cavanaugh said, frustrated as he kicked the base of the chair and looked toward the curtains covering a window. "Dammit. We've been so focused on the senator's death, Shankle has us running all over the place chasing down leads." He walked to the window, pulled the curtains aside and looked out. "What's Peter's wife's name?"

"Janel Mauricio. I talked with her a couple of days ago when I went there looking for The Slicer. We now know her husband had access to the Caltrans SITS. He died over three months ago. She works in the same building as someone with the same first name as the guy we think is behind all this, Viktor with a 'k.' Don't forget, Viktor Johnston has called me and texted me on two different FBI phones, phones that you gave me, and has admitted he's the one behind the attacks."

Jake's paranoia kicked in and he sensed an odd vibe with Cavanaugh. He stepped toward his daughter, out of instinct, and stood in front of her.

"Don't look at me that way, Jake. I'm not the mole. I haven't been able to look into the communications because of how we issued you your phones. We're off the grid here, so I don't have access to my normal resources. But I will. Trust me."

"So you say."

Cavanaugh put his hands on his hips. "Think what you

want, but I'm on your side, for God's sake. Everything you've told me is circumstantial, so it could all be one huge-ass coincidence. No way I can take this to Shankle. Not until we have concrete proof. Hardcore shit."

Jake smiled at Cavanaugh.

"You got more. Tell me you do," Cavanaugh said.

"You want concrete? Well, early this morning, Dave uncovered an interesting piece of information about the CDM attack. Apparently, there were *two* back doors, not one, like the FBI had originally thought."

"Holy God."

Jake explained the story of how Dave found the second back door and the ping of their location in Pico Rivera to the blocked number.

Carlie sat in a chair next to Jake, deep in thought, twirling the tip of her hair with her fingers.

"Do you know the number?" Cavanaugh asked, leaning forward.

Carlie snapped out of her daze.

"That's the definition of blocked."

Cavanaugh raised his eyebrows and shot a look at Jake, waiting.

"Anyway, Dave, being the awesome hacker he is, reached out to one of his underground buddies and ran a trace on the number. Guess where the number is registered? A cabin in Big Bear, California, with title held under the name V. Engel." Jake handed his phone with the pic of the screenshot to Cavanaugh, sat back on the couch and crossed his arms.

"You're shitting me."

"Nope. I still think Viktor Johnston is the same guy as Viktor Engel."

Cavanaugh scratched his head. "Okay, I see a plan coming together."

"I'm no FBI agent, but if I were you guys, I'd pick him up, interrogate the hell out of him, and find out what the hell his plans are for the next attack. Maybe raid the cabin in Big Bear too while you're at it, if you think you can pull it off."

Cavanaugh slapped his hand on the wall. "This is solid work, worth jumping on right away, but I'm not going to risk running this by Shankle because we're on our own and he's hot and heavy on this Syed Farook dickhead. I'm gonna look into this personally."

Jake stood and poured himself another cup of coffee, but before he could take a sip, the hotel room door flung open. A tall, mustached agent hustled in, out of breath. "Agent Cavanaugh, we just found out they're going to—"

The agent turned to Jake.

"What the hell's he doing here?" he pointed his finger at Jake. "Shankle's looking for him. The entire division's looking for him."

CHAPTER 43

"Don't worry about it, Bob, just tell me what they're gonna do," Cavanaugh said to the new agent as they all stood in the middle of the makeshift safehouse. Cavanaugh walked toward AC.

Still out of breath and with his mouth hanging open, Bob said, "Cause a major attack across the US."

Jake sat in amazement as Mark Rayhee's suspicions came to life. He slammed his coffee cup onto the metal tray on the table next to him, spilling half onto the table, and considered how the implications of this attack fit into his chess theory.

"Do we know when?" asked Cavanaugh, sitting back down.

"Unfortunately, no, but according to the chatter, maybe sometime in the next two to three days, possibly sooner. We're coordinating with as many federal agencies as possible."

"Okay, thanks," Cavanaugh said, waving the man away. "And Bob, you didn't see anything here. Are we clear?"

Bob nodded, said, "Yes, sir," then left the room.

"If there's an attack coming on a national level tomorrow,

and all happened at four in the afternoon . . ." Jake stared at the ceiling, calculating more possibilities.

Cavanaugh raised his eyebrows in agreement.

"Tomorrow?" Cavanaugh said, realizing they didn't have much time left.

Cavanaugh's phone rang and he answered. He listened for a few moments. "Yeah, I heard about the cyclone, but listen, I need to call you back. I'm in the middle of some national-security crap. Okay." He hung up.

Jake tilted his head.

"Sorry, that was my younger—much younger—brother, Daniel. He's a fireman in Pasadena."

Jake nodded, walking to the window and looked outside.

"Anyway, so what I want you to do for now is just lay low. Stay here at the safehouse, take care of Carlie. I'll get some agents—two good guys I know I can trust—out to Caltech to talk with Janel and up to Big Bear to try to track down this Engel guy and bring him in for questioning. But we have no precise location to start looking up there, so I'll figure out a way to make it happen. Once we have him in custody, we'll smuggle you into the FBI building again and you can watch the interrogation."

"Ten-four. Call me when you find out anything," Jake said.

He watched from the window as Cavanaugh's car zoomed away north. As best he could, Jake spent the next several hours on the laptop researching server-farm designs and strategizing on ways to capture Viktor. Images of Bridgette distracted him, reminding him about how she had probably tricked him, none of what she'd said was true, and he couldn't trust her. He wiped his face up and down several times and did the best he could to stay focused.

His phone rang at three o'clock, he stood and walked over to the window as he answered. He wanted to keep working on a plan to catch Viktor, but, goddamnit, maybe he could get more information out of her.

"Hi, Bridg—"

"Jake, Jake! He's got me tied up and says you gotta come get me, but don't do it, Jake, don't—" Rustling noises came through the phone before a brief scream cut off and the call ended.

CHAPTER 44

Jake called the number back, someone answered.

"Bridgette, I'm coming. Where are you?" Jake asked.

A deep-bellowed laugh came through the line. "Jakey Boy. Looks like I have something of yours. T-t-tell me how much you want it back."

Jake's stomach turned at how Viktor could refer to a human being as a "thing," an object to possess, a piece of meat.

Goddamn this Viktor guy!

A licking sound, possibly lips smacking, came through the speaker and Jake recoiled in horror. This man had killed his wife. Now he was using Bridgette as bait for some crazy-ass manipulation game. Possibly a trap. *What the hell am I getting myself into?*

He knew what had to be done, but there was no logic to his plan. This man had to be stopped even if Jake went down in the process, a bargain price to save humanity, and with an added bonus: he'd get to be with Cynthia. He thought about the attempt on Carlie's life with the car bomb, his dead coworkers, and again about his wife's death, suffering in that horrible fire caused by the man on the other end of the phone.

"Tell me where you are, Viktor."

"Jakey," the mad man replied, "come down here to the construction s-s-site of the new 710 tunnel, and I'll trade her for you. It's that simple, your choice."

Jake knew Viktor had the advantage, so he thought carefully about what to say next.

"No way, you psycho-ass son of a bitch."

"Fine. The tramp dies and oh, I forgot to mention, I think dead people should be sliced into as many pieces as possible, so their souls have a way to find Allah's great kingdom of heaven. Would you agree?"

Jake kicked the wall, raised his chin high and responded, "The 710. Done. Tell me where." He recalled how state and local transportation officials had spent several decades planning to construct the tunnel on the Interstate 710 freeway between the 210 and 10 before funding finally became available. Once the project had cleared the environmental-review phase and received approval, civil engineers designed the new freeway, then construction finally began two years ago, or so he'd read in *Civil Engineering Today*. The six-point-three-mile project had a total estimated construction duration of more than six years and, when complete, will have cost the taxpayers over three billion dollars.

He definitely knew the layout of the project area, one possible advantage over Viktor.

"T-t-texting you coordinates right now," Viktor said. "You have one hour to get here from that shithole you and Carlie are staying at."

A truckload of fear slammed Jake and he fought back stronger waves of panic.

Viktor chuckled. "At four p.m. sharp, a bullet goes through her pretty little head. We'll slice and dice her and send the pieces down this nice wide maintenance shaft. Will be a fun way to kill this bitch, I'm sure." His voice sounded relaxed, not a care in the world, like someone explaining upcoming vacation plans to a friend.

Jake's pulse pounded in his neck, and by now his head felt warm. His palms glistened with sweat as he pictured Bridgette with a blindfold, tears dripping through it, shaking in fear, fully at the mercy of that crazy man.

"And as all us so-called b-b-bad guys say when we lure the hero to his death, if you try to bring in your buddy Cavanaugh or any other law enforcement, she dies." The phone went silent.

Jake evaluated his options, knowing he had no time to involve Cavanaugh. Plus, with a mole inside the FBI, he had zero trust with any other agent and had to protect his daughter. If he lost Carlie, life would be completely unbearable even if Viktor didn't kill him. He'd never regain his strength to carry on. *And Carlie doesn't deserve this. Any of it.*

Memories of his wife flashed in his mind, and the adrenaline was a welcome kick in the ass. He had to stop Viktor. Period.

Viktor knows we're here. I know this is a trap, but we gotta get the hell out of this apartment. Now.

He grabbed Carlie's arm and, before she could get in a word, threw open the door, flew past AC, ran them to the end of the hallway, and descended the stairs to the alley. They hopped into the car and sped east to the 10 freeway.

Jake told Carlie about Viktor and the hostage situation.

"Your car's impounded back at the San Bernardino police yard. We can't take you to the police, they'll just send us back to the FBI. We can't go to the FBI because I can't show my face there. We need to get you somewhere public for a while until I get this figured out."

"Starbuck's," she said, looking down at her phone. "There's one two blocks from here. Drop me off there and I'll call you in an hour."

"For now, fine. But call Dave and Paige and have them pick you up."

He sugarcoated an explanation to Carlie of what he was doing next, how he needed to try and get more information from Bridgette, but before Carlie could argue how bad the idea was, his phone rang.

"Dave, tell me you found the hidden code," Jake said, dodging a small gray Mercedes as he pulled into the parking lot at the Starbucks.

"Sounds like you're driving again. Tell me what's going on."

He wondered if he should confide in Dave after Viktor warned him not to tell anyone. Especially knowing his phone was probably tapped. *No time. I trust Dave, but not with Carlie still here.*

"Hang on." Jake pulled up to the curb in front of the Starbucks, Carlie hopped out and leaned back in.

"For the record, I don't think you should go. Mom wouldn't want you to go."

"I'm sorry, sweetie. I have to." He soothed her hand. "I'll be back. I promise. I love you." He waved goodbye, then took off south to get back on the freeway. He pulled out the gun from behind his waist and set it on the passenger seat.

"I just dropped off Carlie, she's going to call you. Viktor has a friend of mine, Bridgette," Jake told Dave into the phone. "And he's holding her hostage somewhere at the 710 tunnel construction site. He says he wants to trade me for her."

"You know it's a flippin' trap, man. Don't go."

"Of course it's a trap, but this is my chance to get closer to Viktor. The more I can talk with him, the more likely he is to give me a clue about the scale of the next attack, maybe some details, the time."

The speedometer read ninety-five miles per hour as he weaved his vehicle in and out of traffic, holding the cell to his ear with his left hand and explaining to Dave his history with Bridgette. "Keep plugging away at the code, man. I gotta get to Bridgette."

"Right. Of course, dude, but I gotta tell you something. Pretty bad-news shit."

"Tell me."

Jake slammed on his brakes and smoke plumed out from behind the Ford as he whooshed around an armored car, narrowly missing a blue Toyota four-by-four pickup.

"I know this is a shitty time to tell you this, but looks like the CDM attack was just a test run."

A practice run. Of course.

"Like you asked," Dave added, "I went through the original algorithm again, in even greater detail this time. Using a specialized read-only app, I located another snippet of hidden code in a totally different section, but the system won't let me in, so I'm unable to change the code. Anyway, once I decrypted the code, everything became crazy clear. There are instructions for another attack, a second CDM attack."

"Dammit Dave, get to the point."

"That is the point. A second CDM attack. Way bigger this time. Nationwide."

Jake remembered the second back door. Cavanaugh specifically said the experts at the FBI had buttoned everything up, but only the first back door.

"The FBI suspects the same thing. How sure are you?"

"Dude, I don't make mistakes. I'm one hundred percent sure I'm right."

"Holy crap," Jake said, running his fingers through his hair while reading a large green sign with white letters on the side of the elevated profile freeway section: "I-710 ½ Mile."

"It's gonna be massive in scale, all across the country. And remember how we figured out that the first CDM attack slowed down every other vehicle to twenty-five miles per hour first, then it hit the brakes?"

"Oh, no." He flinched before the news came through the phone.

"Jake, this next one is set to go one hundred percent on the brakes while everyone is traveling at sixty-five miles per hour, not twenty-five. You know what that means."

If thirty to forty million vehicles were all traveling at

sixty-five miles per hour with only two feet of space between their vehicles and the brakes of every other vehicle locked up, ten percent of the country's population would cease to exist within a matter of seconds.

Another sign up ahead indicated he was approaching the I-710 exit.

"Dave. Dave! The automatic computer controllers are all turned off right now. I'm driving like a madman and I'm on the freeway, which means everything's still set on manual driving mode at the main terminal. At least here locally. Can you check and tell me if all the freeways nationwide are set to manual too?"

"Ten-four. Stand by," Dave said. Jake heard him clicking away as he checked traffic conditions nationwide. If the system had been switched back to manual mode, meaning humans were back in control of their vehicles, then traffic congestion would be everywhere and Dave could verify.

A few seconds later Dave confirmed. "The computers aren't controlling anything. There's a shitload of congestion all over the nation, especially back east. It's smack dab in the middle of rush hour there."

Jake saw a glimmer of hope, but when he thought about Bridgette, the glimmer disappeared.

"As long as the feds keep all the freeways set to manual mode, Viktor can't activate a second CDM attack. We gotta figure out what his strategy is to turn the system back on to automatic."

Dave was quiet for a few seconds, probably thinking.

"Trying to figure out how he might do it, but I'm just the hacker," Dave said.

Jake ended the call with Dave and exited the freeway. At several minutes before four p.m., he pulled in to the I-710 construction site.

On that Wednesday afternoon, August 12, Jake observed construction in full swing on what project officials referred to as Segment Two, the middle two miles of the freeway extension project. He'd read a few weeks ago the southern two miles had been bored and sealed, which meant technically a fully functioning tunnel already existed. A paved roadway through the tunnel had yet to be constructed, and only a mix of dirt and construction debris, such as discarded concrete forms, nails, miscellaneous piles of gravel and unused concrete, were scattered along the bottom.

Two people stood about fifty yards away as Jake drove onto a temporary gravel road and immediately recognized Bridgette. The other person was a tall man wearing a black shirt and pants. Some sort of clown mask covered his entire face. Definitely not Viktor, he thought to himself. Too tall. The giant man had a pistol pointed at Bridgette's belly.

With a cloud of dust scooping up from behind him, Jake parked the car, stuffed the gun back into the rear of his waist, and climbed out slowly, hands raised. He scanned the site but didn't see Viktor.

Bridgette and her captor stood two feet from a seven-foot-wide vertical opening at the top of the tunnel structure he had read about in *Civil Engineering Today*. The hole was a maintenance shaft built for workers to enter and exit the tunnel from above. The thought of climbing down it turned his stomach.

White sailing rope was wrapped around her head and the

bottom half of her face, only her eyes visible. The masked man had Bridgette in a choke-hold. She stood between him and the hole. If the man wanted to, he could easily toss her into the shaft, a drop of at least fifty feet that would likely kill her. But not today. If he'd wanted to kill her that way, he would've already done it. Maybe clown-face had a more intricate plan for Bridgette. Jake admired the trap, but he had no plans to let Viktor win.

Jake flared his nostrils and cleared his throat, confidence growing he could save his former lover from a crazy man wearing a clown mask. At that point, Jake decided to sacrifice himself to save Bridgette, if it came to that. He imagined shoving the tall black toothpick down that shaft, maybe dying together. He cracked his knuckles and took a step forward as his heart rate and breathing stabilized. *Great, I must be getting used to this.*

The masked man motioned with hand signals for Jake to pick up his cell, which Jake felt vibrate, so he stopped walking and answered. The man spoke to him in English, but with a hint of a broken Spanish accent and not as deep a tone as Viktor's voice. Familiar, though. "Walk toward me, Jake. Slowly. Don't try anything funny or the bitch gets dumped down the drain."

The guy on the phone must be the guy standing next to Bridgette talking to Jake on a mic hidden inside the mask. He sounded nothing like Viktor, and called him by his true name, "Jake," not "Jakey Boy." Also, the man had no understanding of roadway construction, the hole next to them wasn't a drain. Viktor would have known the difference. A new terrorist altogether had now entered their game.

Jake pressed the phone tight against his ear as the man explained, "I'm giving this bitch two vials, one red and one green. When she gets to you, she'll give you the red one. You drink it. She'll take the green one. The slightest deviation from these simple instructions will result in me shooting both of you."

CHAPTER 45

"Confirm you understand," the masked man said.

Without rushing, Jake nodded his head in agreement, never taking his eyes off clown-face, then took a few steps toward Bridgette and her captor. The man in black pulled out a knife, put it to her face, cut the rope from her mouth, pushed her forward, and barked orders at her. Apparently, he wanted her to walk to Jake.

At least this guy is pushing her away from the shaft.

Jake stood forty feet away from Bridgette as tears dripped onto her flowered dress. With her arms tied behind her back and mascara running down her cheeks, dried blood dripped from the corner of both her mouth and several deep, angry scratches on her neck.

Walking, walking, walking. A two-foot-long piece of half-inch diameter rebar lay on the ground ten feet in front of him. He counted the wounds on Bridgette's body and multiplied that number by ten to calculate the number of times he planned to pummel that clown-faced asshole with the steel bar.

With Bridgette and Jake five feet apart, and the rebar near their feet, the man on the phone said, "Stop. Tucked in her bra, above the left titty, there is clear plastic baggie with two vials inside. You drink red and then give green one to bitch. Fail to follow these simple instructions and you die. Confirm."

Jake nodded in agreement for the man to see, but still held his hands up in the air.

Finally, within arm's reach of Bridgette, Jake mouthed, "We'll be okay." He forced a tiny side smile and she cocked her head, unsure. If she was in on the trap, she deserved an Oscar.

With gentle precision, he reached toward her chest then slid his right hand underneath her bra. Between the undergarment and her soft supple skin, his fingers stumbled on a coarse item that he assumed was the baggie. He pinched, then gently pulled out a clear, mini Ziploc bag containing two clear glass vials, each three inches long with rubber corks.

He extracted the green vial, the one intended for Bridgette, and her eyes widened, gazing deep into his soul.

Under her breath, she said, "Give me the red one, hurry." He gave her a curious look. "I know you don't trust me, but I'd never do anything to hurt you. I'm so sorry, Jake, I don't know how we ended up here. I was only trying to help. You must believe me."

Memories flooded his brain of their many intimate moments together during the affair. He did trust her at one time and did risk his life to save her. This was either a well-acted-out trap or she really did want to help, but he thought of Cynthia, who would want him to take whatever action would be in alignment with saving their lives. His mind froze. It's amazing, while grieving, how quickly someone can lean into a challenge and jump into danger.

Jake raised his arms back up, slow and steady, before turning his head to the man in the mask, who was waving the gun pointed at them. Jake realized clown-face was too far away to notice if they switched vials, but did it matter anyway? Both vials probably had poison.

And the shithead was too far away for Jake to get off a good shot with his gun, so instead of giving the green vial to her, he drank the bitter-tasting liquid himself. Down went the juice through Jake's esophagus and into his stomach, where it sat with the contents from an earlier snack.

Jake tilted his head down to the red vial in the baggie and looked at Bridgette, who nodded to him. He reached into the baggie and drew out what he assumed was a second vial of poison, but might possibly—*I'll give it a 10 percent chance*—be a placebo that would save Bridgette. His hand approached her open and waiting mouth, he poured the contents in, and with tears welling up in her eyes, she swallowed.

He oscillated his head, mouthing, "I'm sorry."

This is what I get for having an affair. We deserve whatever happens. I brought this onto myself. Gave Viktor an opening in my life to kill my wife.

He'd now ingested a liquid given to him by a man wearing a clown mask. Probably poison. *Way to save Bridgette, Jake. You're a real hero now!* He figured his heart would stop in a few minutes, and the world would remember him as a murdering bastard. Maybe it was his time to die.

But what about Viktor? He gets to win after killing Cynthia?

Panic exploded inside Jake and he curled his lips tight. The Universe had presented him with two opportunities: first, get his revenge on Viktor, and second, save people across the country from Viktor's crosshairs.

But the thought of failing at both endeavors wrenched his gut.

He looked between Bridgette's face and the ground.

A tear streamed down her cheek and he wiped it away with his thumb. "I'm the one who should be sorry," he said. *Christ, this is the way Viktor deserved to die, not us.* Assuming he had only seconds to live, he leaned in and gave her a solid hug. But as they stood in their embrace, the masked man fired a single gunshot that echoed throughout the site, forcing them to duck.

The man yelled, "You have three seconds to turn and walk to me, Dr. Bendel, or I swear to God—"

"Okay, okay!" Jake barked back. He stepped away from Bridgette. "I'm coming."

With the image of Bridgette's face burned into his mind one last time, Jake turned and walked with his arms up in the air toward the clown-faced man. With every step, Jake's target size grew and increased his chances of taking him out before the poison kicked in.

His heart slammed inside his chest, fueling an indescribable rage roaring deep in his belly, a fury he'd never experienced before. If he died soon, he knew his wife would be waiting for him wherever people go after they die, and he could apologize to her one final time.

After ten paces, before he could get into what he would consider a reasonable range for shooting clown-face, he turned to check on Bridgette, but several things happened all at once.

She crept toward Jake's car, where a shadowy object moved and rotated underneath the vehicle. Jake had a fraction of a second to process the shadow, maybe an animal or person, when the clapping thunder of a helicopter hit him. As he turned back toward the masked man, a black chopper came swooping by them so fast Jake dropped to the ground, covering his head. The craft must have been in the open trench portion of the future tunnel, lying in wait.

But how?

Clown man emptied his magazine at the aircraft, to no avail. Still on the ground and before he could whip out the pistol and take a shot, the man scurried down the interior ladder of the maintenance shaft.

Jake craned his head toward Bridgette, but turbulent swirls of dust gusted around him, reducing visibility and making it difficult to see her fifty feet away.

The helicopter made another pass, slowed, rotated and descended between them near where Jake had hugged Bridgette moments earlier. As the craft hovered above the ground, the rotating copter blades kicked up speckles of sand and dust, slapping Jake's face.

The craft touched the ground and throttled down the jet engine.

Cavanaugh hung out of the side door, jumped to the ground, weapon pulled, looking left and right before running toward Jake.

Jake stood, confused how the hell Cavanaugh knew precisely when to show up.

The two men stood toe to toe and Cavanaugh said, "Tell me what you're doing out here and who the hell that shooter was."

Jake stumbled, with Cavanaugh at his side, toward Bridgette to see if she was still alive. Jake dropped to his knees next to Bridgette and she coughed as he helped her sit.

"I was two steps away from shooting that guy in the knee," Jake said. "We could have questioned him about Viktor and the next attack, but you and this cavalry show up and—"

"Stay here," Cavanaugh said to them before taking off running toward the maintenance shaft, but Jake followed. They skidded to a stop, Jake's right foot caught the edge and dropped in. His left foot tripped on the lip of the shaft and he stumbled over the edge, one leg in the hole after slamming his kneecap into the concrete lip while grabbing the top rung of the inner ladder to stabilize himself. He cried out in pain and looked down the hole into pure darkness. The blur of a truck with bright headlights zoomed past below.

Two other agents arrived and helped Cavanaugh pull Jake out of the hole. Breathless, Jake said, "He's gone. Had a getaway truck at the bottom of the shaft."

One of the agents spoke into his radio. "He took off. We could try to follow in the chopper if we—"

Speaking through the radio to the copter pilot, Cavanaugh said, "Call it in to the local PD, but I doubt they'll catch him. Something else is at play here. I'll bet this place is rigged to blow like the interchange, so let's get these two to a safe distance." The agents jogged to the chopper and Jake hobbled behind them.

Jake and Cavanaugh knelt near Bridgette. "There was a second man under my car," Jake said. "And hey, I want to know how the hell you knew I was here."

Cavanaugh reached down to Jake's hip and tapped on his cell phone. "Like I said, for your protection." He smiled. "The tracking app on your phone uses GPS to tell us how fast you're going. We noticed you speeding at almost a hundred miles an hour and were heading east out of Los Angeles so I figured you were in trouble, and I commissioned two SWAT buddies of mine to fire up a copter for a ride. Considering your engineering background, I had a feeling right about now you'd need some backup."

"Jake," Bridgette said urgently.

"Sorry. Agent Cavanaugh, this is my friend, Bridgette Trukowski, professor of astrophysics at Caltech." They untied the ropes around her head and wrists.

"I was working with Viktor. He"—she coughed in quick succession—"has been . . . well, he told me the green vial was the placebo and wanted me to make sure you drank the red one so you'd finally die. He hates you, Jake." Blood covered the whites of her eyes and she labored with short breaths. "But I couldn't do it, Jake, I just couldn't. I truly fell in love with you and . . ."

As Jake leaned over her, she whispered, "Jake, Viktor, I'm sorry," coughing between words.

"Don't talk now, we'll do all that later, you just need to—"

"Jake, listen to me." Bridgette coughed and spewed specks of blood onto Jake's shirt. With her pale face whitening several shades lighter each passing moment, she leaned in close to

Jake and confirmed—in a whisper—the specifics of what Viktor was planning next, a national attack. And the time tomorrow.

Bridgette's face turned white, her eyes rolled upward and froze as her body collapsed into Jake's arms. Out of instinct, he grabbed her to prevent her head from landing hard on the ground. Jake yelled her name twice and shook her. No response. He placed two fingers onto her neck and felt a slow, weak pulse. He wondered if the same fate awaited him.

Cavanaugh leaned in and touched Jake's shoulder. "We gotta get her to the nearest hospital ASAP." He radioed to the pilot to keep the engine running and set a course for the USC Medical Center, just a couple of miles west. He made a whirling motion with his hand.

"Help me get her in the copter," Jake said, not caring about his motion sickness, and wondering how he'd made it through flight school back at Redlands.

They carried her to the copter, carefully laid her body across the back seat, then climbed aboard. Jake slid a green headset onto his head, reminding him of his flying school days. Within seconds they were airborne, ascending several hundred feet per minute, but even with their noise-canceling headsets on, the clapping of the copter blades was deafening. The copter ride was bumpy, and Jake had a hard time holding on to the outer rail. He tried checking her pulse again, but the vibrations from the ride made it impossible to tell if she was even alive.

Jake remembered why he no longer enjoyed flying. As he sat in the doorless copter climbing to a thousand feet above the

Cal State Los Angeles campus, held aloft only by the finger of God, the rapid ascent proved more than his motion-sickness-prone body could handle. He convulsed and puked—an interesting blend of nuts, raisins, and the green liquid—outside the craft.

Cavanaugh shook his head. "You're proving to be a lot braver than I expected, even if you can't seem to keep your stomach contents."

Jake mustered up the strength from deep within and explained, through the built-in headset mic, the vials scene to Cavanaugh, as each word caused a fresh wave of nausea. "Whatever's happening to her might happen to me any second now. I honestly don't understand the whole point of the meeting, unless they just wanted to kill me with poison."

"No way, that bastard had a gun. He could've just killed you with a bullet," Cavanaugh said, glancing between Bridgette and Jake.

Jake shook his head, unsure.

A few hundred feet above and south of the roof of the inpatient tower at the USC Medical Center on Marengo Street, the pilot radioed in to land. As they touched down on the helicopter pad, three crouched medical staff, including one doctor, wearing blue jumpsuits hustled to the copter and unlatched Bridgette from the back seat.

The copter's rotor wound down, Jake climbed out of the death trap, then helped the staff move Bridgette onto a clean white gurney.

Without blinking, Bridgette looked up at the gray sky with bulging eyes. Her breath slowed as she took one final inhale, exhaled the sound of death, and the pupils of her eyes dilated large, black.

The doctor placed a stethoscope onto Bridgette's chest. Helpless, Jake could only watch.

"No pulse. Get her inside stat," the doctor said.

But Jake knew the truth. Bridgette Trukowski was gone.

One more life lost on his watch.

As the medical team rolled her lifeless corpse into the hospital, Jake stayed near the copter and bent over, hands on his knees, trying to catch his breath and force the nausea away.

While walking into the building, he tried to relax his stomach, knowing with the green liquid out of his system and no symptoms of poisoning, nothing would likely happen to him now. By swapping the vials, Bridgette had sacrificed her life for his.

Smooth air cooled his sweaty face.

Cavanaugh stood by the sliding glass doors and popped a few antacid pills.

He chewed, swallowed. "Doesn't look good for her. We should get you checked out."

But Jake cringed, waving him off and walking past. "I'm fine."

They strode down the sterile-looking hallways until arriving at the door of the emergency room, where ten different doctors, nurses, and assistants attended to Bridgette. The team huddled in a circle around their patient, as she lay on a gurney next to a crash cart in the center of a vaulted-ceiling operating room. Tearing noises echoed off the walls as the nurses opened gauze baggies. A doctor in the middle wore a green gown with a green scrub hat on his head. The medical staff worked to resuscitate her.

Out of nowhere, a short pudgy nurse appeared, blocking the entrance. "I'm sorry, gentlemen, I'm going to have to ask you to wait outside. This is not the time or place to—"

Cavanaugh flashed his FBI credentials in the nurse's face. "We're going inside. Move."

She frowned, crossed her arms, and shook her head with confidence.

He pinched his eyebrows together. "Don't push me, lady. I'm not in the mood." Her face softened. "Get out of the way, or I'll arrest you for impeding a federal investigation, do you understand?"

She shot an angry glance at both men. "I don't care if you're the President of the United Fucking States, you're not going in. Period."

Cavanaugh clenched his jaw and looked up and down at the woman. "Fine. I gotta run anyway." He turned to Jake, put his arm around him, and guided him several paces away from the doorway. "Shit. I'm sorry about Bridgette. I really am, but Shankle's onto us, and he knows I'm here helping you." He glanced around the hallway. "Anyway, one of my agent friends is bringing my Ford from the construction site over to the parking lot here."

"Hold on, don't leave yet," Jake said, grabbing Cavanaugh's jacket and pulling him back. "I know when the next attack is."

CHAPTER 46

As Bobby and Doug pulled their news van into the ABC-7 studio parking lot in Glendale, Bobby received an email from a blocked address containing an MP4 video attachment, which he opened. "Carol's gonna shit when she sees this," he said, hopping out of the van.

Without knocking, they barged into Carol's office and stood in front of her desk, but she wagged a finger at Bobby as she spoke to someone on the phone, explaining details to them about the conspiracy. "Yes, we have multiple religious organizations publicly condemning Dr. Bendel for his attacks and—" she paused, listening and bobbing her head as her caller interrupted her. "If he's alive, he has some explaining to do and . . . no, we can't just do a public beheading, sir. Yes, okay, bye." Hanging up, she rolled her eyes, then leaned over her desk and stared at Bobby.

"Sounds like you're getting a lot of calls about my conspiracy piece," Bobby said with a smirk.

"It's deafening. Calls for justice are pouring in. We've been inundated with calls before, like with the OJ Simpson stuff, but this is beyond."

Carol's producer, a short, round black man with a goatee, wearing a faded, sweat-stained Dodgers hat, walked in and stood next to Bobby.

Bobby looked down at him. "I just forwarded you guys a video." They walked around Carol's desk as she opened the email on her laptop, then the four of them watched a five-minute, high-definition video of Jake Bendel walking toward a redheaded woman, in what looked like a hostage exchange. Jake and the redhead drank something, walked apart, and then a black helicopter, possibly SWAT or military, appeared out of nowhere and created a massive dust storm of sand and trash.

"That tall guy with the clown mask looks like he's shooting at the helicopter," Carol said.

The others mumbled a semblance of group agreement and watched the helicopter land and take off a few minutes later with two new passengers.

"Look," Bobby pointed to the screen. "There, under that black car. I'll bet that dark figure's a man. What the hell's he doing underneath the car?"

"It's time-stamped less than an hour ago and looks legit. I say we go with it," the producer said.

By the time they finished watching the video, the station had already gone live with the six o'clock news. The lead story covered the bombing investigation and the death of Senator Brown on Tuesday, news from two days ago.

"I'm going to show the entire uncut video, as is," Carol said. She told the others she had two other short segments scheduled to air before the first commercial break, but she switched the sequence and instructed the producer to have it ready to run at 6:15, right after they came back from commercial.

Bobby hung around the studio to watch them air the video. During the break, viewers were treated to a sales pitch for a stupid new dog leash, luxury features of the new Lexus mid-class, which he hoped to own soon, and a new twist on why milk is good for everyone to drink, except Doug, with his irritable bowel syndrome. The round-faced anchorman came back to the viewers and said, "For those of you following the ongoing conspiracy theory that Dr. Jake Bendel is still alive and might somehow be working with the government, we have a fresh new video clip for you sent to us by an anonymous concerned citizen. Take a look."

✳

Along with millions of other Southern California viewers, Viktor Johnston watched ABC-7 play the video on his phone while sitting at the Big Bear airport inside another one of his airplanes, a white-and-blue high-performance Cessna 172 with fully retractable landing gear. He'd already completed his preflight inspection and topped off the tanks with aviation gas.

When the video segment finished, he mumbled to himself, "Let's see if that ruffles up a few more pawns in our chess match."

Viktor had no intention of killing Jake during the hostage exchange. *What fun would that be?* He'd presumed Jake had some sort of tracking mechanism, an assumption that turned out to be spot-on.

He also knew a hero would come and save that useless bitch. Allah's voice had warned him. *She's going to ruin everything. Love, my ass, what a trumped-up, bullshit bunch of crap.* Viktor suspected she'd eventually fail to keep her emotions in check and make a fatal mistake. Allah had confirmed Viktor's suspicions, so Viktor had decided to test her loyalty. Given the choice, she would either try to switch the poisonous vials and kill herself, or she wouldn't and Jake would end up dead. If she had killed Jake, Viktor would've known she was a loyal follower and could hang his death over her head. Either way, Viktor would know for sure.

Syed Farook had reported she'd collapsed at the exchange with Mr. Sanchez and Jake had survived, which meant Bridgette had, in fact, betrayed Viktor. Knowing she had turned on him after all he had done for her made his blood bubble, but never again. No more backstabbing turncoats in his organization. He loved when the work of the mighty Allah trapped Satan's sinners.

The voice of Viktor's mother kept him on a path to righteousness, albeit stumbling, but Allah helped keep the plan on schedule. Allah's voice had already helped Viktor stay well ahead of his pursuers.

Viktor had initially set up the video camera at the perfect angle—behind where Mr. Sanchez and Bridgette ended up standing during the hostage exchange—before he fled the scene. Nobody would see the camera hidden in the shadow of that large inactive crane. The camera had captured everything in HD and sent its contents via a remote 6G wireless data network to Viktor's phone.

Viktor had planned all along to capture the video and reveal the FBI's involvement in a cover-up. That way, he could expose Jake as a confirmed killer—who was still alive—while simultaneously making the FBI look like a bunch of morons, fumbling around in the dark, bumping into each other. *What a joke.* A good conspiracy would add fuel to the perfect distraction while Viktor put the finishing touches on his plans to eliminate a tenth of the American population.

Indeed, the scheme worked well to throw people off guard and lead them down the wrong path away from the ultimate attack. The more distractions from Allah's true plans the better. Before he'd given the vials of poison to Mr. Sanchez, Viktor had made sure to dump in enough aconite to kill a horse. After all, if that's what Allah wanted . . .

He had thought about putting the aconite poison in *both* vials—no placebo—but he wanted to play with Jake a little more before the end.

Allah had also advised Viktor to make sure Syed Farook made the proper modifications to the black car Jake had been driving. Viktor hoped that with all the dust and debris flying around when the helicopter arrived, nobody had noticed Syed under Jake's car. He relished the confidence that Jake's fate was entirely in his hands. With Allah driving their bus of terror and destruction, Viktor knew his strategic plan would execute without a hitch.

Jake's death later that night would serve a higher purpose for all. Poisoning him earlier today would have prevented the opportunity to kill the infamous engineer and display his body on the grand stage for the entire world to see.

CHAPTER 47

"Before she passed out, Bridgette told me when Viktor was planning the national attack," Jake said.

Cavanaugh stopped walking, turned to Jake. "You can't believe anything she said."

"Her dying words were that Viktor is going to take the king, the voters. He's planning a massive attack for tomorrow between two and five, but she passed out before she could give me the exact time. I believe her. She saved my life, and we have to make sure her death means something." His eyes bored deep into Cavanaugh's.

"Fine, but it's critical we nail down the time in order to minimize risks. I need to go. We brought the black Ford here, it's in the basement parking," Cavanaugh said.

"Go. I'll call you in a bit," Jake said, and the two split, Cavanaugh jogging down the hallway, disappearing, while Jake walked back to the emergency room door and peered inside just in time to hear the doctor call the time of death at 4:47 p.m.

Jake kicked the door and hustled down a different hallway,

shunning eye contact with every soul he passed, because he knew he was casting a cold, flinty gaze. The only two lovers in his life were now dead. His mood pivoted between anger and self-loathing.

With tears streaming down his cheeks, he made his way to the ground floor and exited the front hospital doors, stopped and noticed the partly cloudy sky. Maybe it was his time to go too. He'd gambled with his life at the human exchange by drinking that green vial. He thought about how he and Bridgette had met eighteen months ago and how he'd been played. *I should hate her guts, yet . . . dammit.* He had so many questions to process as he wandered into the parking structure. He kicked in the headlights of some yuppie sports car, which set off an ear-piercing siren and pissed him off more, so he broke off the driver's side mirror with a downward thrust of his fist.

"Shiitake mushrooms!" he said to nobody. With the siren still blazing, he kicked the door of the stupid car for good measure. The conflicting thoughts and memories of Bridgette swirled like a vortex in his head until he felt dizzy and nauseous.

He wandered around in a mindless trance for several levels in the parking structure before realizing what he needed to do next. *Find the black Ford.* He walked down to the basement level where Cavanaugh said the car would be delivered and found it parked in the third stall, waiting for him with the key fob sitting on the seat. Since someone had placed a bomb under his daughter's car and he remembered seeing a shadow beneath this one, he did a quick sweep underneath just in case. He looked for anything out of the ordinary, maybe a small black box with curly wires taped to it like he'd seen in movies, but nothing jumped out at him, although he was a complete amateur when it came to searching for bombs.

Two women in business suits walked by, staring at Jake with his ass up in the air. *I'm not being paranoid.*

Once seated, he brought himself back to the human world and realized the only woman he loved who remained in his life was Carlie. He texted her and she responded.

Carlie: *I'm safe. Will call you in a bit. Bridgette?*

He texted some of the details of what had happened at the I-710 site.

Carlie: *I believe you. Mom would want you to keep fighting, catch Viktor*

With his daughter in a safe place, cheering him on, he decided to go to Pico Rivera and meet with Dave to find out more about the *CDM2*. Dave and Paige were the only friends he trusted.

As he drove eastbound along the 10 freeway again toward Dave's house, he cruised along at an average speed of thirty-five miles per hour in stop-and-go traffic. With the adrenaline wearing off, he sank back into a funk, reigniting his anger toward Bridgette, feeling nothing but confusion, and needing time to process her death and betrayal. Questions inundated his brain like four rivers converging into a flood-control channel during an El Niño event, but then the chess game popped back into his head. Viktor had snatched several key chess pieces, but the king, the citizens, remained. The goal of chess is to take the king of your opponent, but sometimes you needed to sacrifice pawns to do so.

Jake played out different chess-related scenarios as he parked, then walked up to Dave's door. Paige threw it open and ran through the doorway to give Jake a bear hug, which melted away a small fraction of his stress. He needed that. Bad.

During their embrace, he spotted Carlie in the living room as Paige said, "Jake, I'm so glad you're alive, but you, like, totally gotta get us up to speed on this fuster-cluck. We're running out of time. You better have a plan."

He shrugged and they entered the house. After greeting Dave, they all sat in separate chairs in what could be considered a living room.

Jake said, "Turns out Bridgette was working for Viktor. He used her as bait and tried to kill me, but she sacrificed herself. Viktor murdered her tonight, and I'm so confused right now." He fought back tears from flowing again and said, "Just before she passed, she told me Viktor's planning a national attack, probably this CDM2 that you're talking about, Dave, tomorrow sometime in the afternoon. But we don't know the exact time and we're assuming the voters are the king in Viktor's chess game, but not sure."

"Why not a global attack?" Dave asked. "Pair a CDM2 with something else in Europe at the same time? A bombing at the Eiffel Tower?"

Skepticism naturally flowed through Dave's veins like fish in a river, so he'd always see the absolute worst possible outcome, no matter what the facts were. If his favorite football team was winning forty-nine to nothing with only five minutes left in the fourth quarter, he'd still worry about losing.

Jake's gut told him Dave was totally exaggerating.

"Total shocker here, Jake. The lady saved your life, man," Paige said. She had a point. The ice-cold anger inside Jake began to melt.

Dave stood, staring at them both while pacing back and forth, fussing with his clothes and wetting his lips. "Maybe she lied," he said. "Seriously. Enough about that chick, we need to talk about the CDM2. I know the time." Paige and Jake darted stares at Dave.

Jake looked at the ceiling, then to Carlie, calculating variables.

Dave continued, "Haven't figured out how Viktor's gonna turn on the SS yet, but after we spoke earlier I did a little more digging into the algorithm, and I found the time of the next CDM attack. It was buried in the code. I'd say there's at least a ninety-five percent chance that the shit's gonna hit the fan tomorrow afternoon at four p.m. our time. Smack dab in the middle of rush hour traffic. Across the nation."

"And you have proof?"

He nodded, handing Jake a printout of code with some red, hand-written notes.

Jake studied the page and his nausea returned with a fresh wave of panic. Not motion sickness this time, though. The human mind was unable to handle this level of input, emotion, and energy drain. He was on the verge of shutting down completely. *Focus. Stick to the facts, it's what you do best.*

Logically, knowing the time of the attack would give them an advantage and a starting point to prevent tens of millions of people from dying tomorrow. He saw a pinhole-sized light at the end of the proverbial tunnel. "What exactly is this? I need to get it over to Cavanaugh ASAP, but I need to explain it."

They all hunched around Dave's screen. "We found the hidden code in the algorithm, right here," he said, pointing to the screen, "that instructed every other vehicle moving at sixty-five miles per hour to immediately slam on their brakes with a hundred percent force. I'm willing to bet the bastard was simply testing the back-door system during the first CDM attack."

Jake rubbed his chin. "Continue."

"Hate to say this, but your buddy, Viktor, is a goddamned genius." Dave used the cursor to highlight a different line of code on the screen. "Check it out. Right here. You're looking at the unencrypted version. I had to pull out all the stops and use some heavy-duty hacking tools to figure this out, but the guy embedded code inside another line of combo-embedded and encrypted code. It's like dual embedding with encryption. Like a digital Russian nesting doll, never seen anything like it. Nobody I know has."

Paige, Jake, and Carlie glanced at each other, knowing full well that Dave's comments went flying over their heads. They were mostly engineers, not computer geeks.

Dave put both hands in the front pockets of his surfer shorts while he gawked at the line of code the same way an artist would worship a Leonardo da Vinci painting in the Louvre. "Anyway, after decrypting the code, I found an instruction in that line set to execute the full brakes for every other car in that same checkerboard pattern as the CDM attack, at precisely twelve o'clock GMT Friday morning, which is four p.m. our time Thursday, tomorrow."

"But how do you know this is Viktor and not someone else?" Carlie asked.

Dave smiled and leaned back in his chair with his fingers locked behind his head. "Because, my young friend, in our world, we always leave digital signatures to claim our work. There's no point in creating havoc if we don't get no street cred."

Jake shook his head. "No idea what you're talking about."

"A calling card, if you will. Right here," Dave said, pointing to another line on the screen. "In my world, this is the same as a social security number or handwritten signature. It's Ivory Snow and we've already connected him to Viktor, so you have your man. Your proof." He pointed to the screenshot printout in Jake's hand.

Jake did not fully understand why or how Dave knew what he did, but he trusted Dave with his life. Jake leaned closer to the screen and squinted, as another wave of adrenaline kicked in, readying him to take this fight to the next level. *Viktor is going down.* Finally, the break they needed to stop the attack.

A crackle of thunder shook the house.

"Excellent work, Dave. I'll get this over to Cavanaugh right now. I can't send text messages because there's a mole at the FBI monitoring my phone."

Jake folded the paper and stuffed it into his jeans pocket, then cleared his throat. "You guys all stay here and keep working to see if you can figure out how Viktor's going to turn the SS back on. I'm gonna call Cavanaugh and set up a meeting somewhere safe and hand this to him in person. He's going to need solid proof to get this past that dickhead supervisor of his and convince him we're dealing with Viktor Johnston, possibly Viktor Engel, not some Al-Qaeda wannabe. If Bridgette can sacrifice herself for the cause, the least Cavanaugh and I can do is risk our own necks."

CHAPTER 48

Viktor received a text update from his mole at the FBI. They were closing in on Ivory Snow, but only with his partial identity. The FBI also knew the man as M. Sanchez and had no idea what his first name was or where to find him. Viktor ran his hands atop his balding head and grinned.

Using proprietary satellite phones, Viktor and his two brothers had been in continuous communication with one another and the other terrorist cells involved. Viktor called his two brothers, Syed and M. Sanchez.

Viktor remembered his fortuitous meeting several years ago with Syed, who had shared with Viktor about his birth in Syria, his birth name, and more.

Over the past several years, the three brothers had worked closely to bring their plan to fruition, with Viktor as the lead organizer and strategist. Viktor paid for a small portion of the expenses, but the bulk of the effort was funded by overseas groups affiliated with Syed. The brothers viewed the United States as a large canvas upon which they intended to paint a map of terror that would last for centuries. Now, each brother eagerly awaited the best part of their plan: the impending coup d'état.

Viktor knew he had impressed his biological brother, M. Sanchez aka Ivory Snow, with his genius when he came up with the ideas and various components of the technology needed for a traffic collision on a grand scale, at a national level. An attack completely new in the world of terror and wonderfully close at hand, all of which their software told him was right on schedule.

Each brother knew they needed only one final piece to fall into place. The automatic driving system needed to be turned back on. They needed to flip the proverbial switch from manual to automatic for their plan to work. Fortunately for them, they had a plan to make this happen and knew the time had come for action.

And Jakey Boy had no clue. Not that it would matter, with the special death they had set up for him.

Viktor replied to the mole:

GR8. Keep your head down and don't fuck this up, u know what we can do

CHAPTER 49

Agent Cavanaugh had voted for President McClintock during the last election. She'd won by the narrowest of margins but nonetheless had been elected the first female president in the history of the United States of America. A hard worker and gifted politician with a relatively high level of consciousness, most people rarely gave her superior intellect its due credit, probably because of her female status in the remnants of a male-dominated society.

Having worked at the bureau for the better part of two decades, Cavanaugh was all too familiar with protocol bullshit. McClintock was in charge of several bureaucracies too large for their own good. Valuable information often took longer than necessary to reach the top and, though McClintock did her best to appoint competent people to surround herself with, there were a few ding-dongs in the mix. One of them was appointed by her predecessor and unfortunately, directed the FBI. His name was Mr. Jim Bradley and he was like Shankle on steroids.

To be fair, when it came to politics, FBI Director Bradley

did have a gift. Cavanaugh had read that in college the director majored in religion and graduated from law school. As such, like most politicians, he had an exceptionally high level of arrogance when it came to making decisions outside his area of expertise—in this case, the question of keeping the Sûr System offline.

When Bradley's advisor called Cavanaugh to discuss the risks of turning the Sûr System back on, Cavanaugh stiffened with amazement at such a top-level call.

As he exited through the doorway of the Fourth Street Starbuck's in downtown L.A. with a half-gallon coffee cup full of sugar and caffeine, Cavanaugh raised his voice to ensure the guy on the phone understood him with crystal clarity.

"You're telling me the system is shut down, no power whatsoever, but it's still operational? How the hell can it be both?" Cavanaugh asked the advisor, his sense of wonder quickly morphing into frustration.

"That's the problem. ADIC Shankle is saying our system is turned on, using a server farm, and he wants to leave it on. He said we can turn the SS off if we want to," the man on the phone said.

"We're gathering credible intel there's gonna be another attack soon—tomorrow. Way worse. Total nightmare scenario and the possibility of that happening only exists if the SS is active, which we simply can't have."

Cavanaugh ducked into an alley and looked up between two tall brick buildings to the gray clouds swirling in a circle above. "Jesus, you guys in Washington have absolutely no clue. I can tell you this: if you don't figure out how to turn that system back off, a lot of people are gonna die. You can forget about retiring on some beach somewhere. We'll all end up in prison or coffins."

"No need to get personal here, Agent. We have no idea where the server farm is that's controlling the Sûr System. Whoever is controlling all the freeways right now is running a top-notch trace-blocker. It will take us days to untangle the digital mess and reveal the location of the system."

"Can't you just cut the power to the server farm?"

"Agent, you're not listening. We. Don't. Know. Where. The server farm. Is."

Cavanaugh kicked a trash bin before he shot back. "I don't even know why you called me." He paused. "Find that system—"

The advisor ended the call. Cavanaugh threw his phone against the brick wall. It shattered into hundreds of various electronic components and landed in a mud puddle.

Realizing he no longer had a working phone, Cavanaugh squeezed his eyes shut, let out a primal grunt, threw his coffee cup onto the asphalt and, before running back to his car, swiped the SIM card from the remains of his phone.

CHAPTER 50

Jake drove back toward the City of Angels, with smog lingering on the horizon as the sun went to bed. A sea of red lights blazed in front of him and six lanes' worth of vehicles crammed into four lanes of the I-10 freeway, as he remembered why he worked so hard to develop the self-driving vehicle network and how much he hated driving—crawling—on the Southern California freeways.

He slowed, a Corvette cut him off without signaling, Jake honked, then the driver flung his arm out the window and gave him the bird. *Son of a bitch. How do dickheads like that end up with such nice cars?*

"Hope you die, asshole." He surprised himself at his level of anger.

Rolling along the freeway, Jake had tried several times to call Cavanaugh, but they kept going to voicemail. He took a risk and left a message even though the mole might hear it. This information carried too much importance. Too many lives depended on him talking to Cavanaugh.

He flipped on the red-and-blue lights to play pseudo-cop

again. He'd used them while driving down the Cajon Pass two days ago and had arrived at Cal State San Bernardino in record time. But as he weaved in and out of traffic, his mind turned to the deaths of his wife and now Bridgette. The questions hit him again. Hard. He slumped over in his seat, his level of contentment plunging fast and his zest for life disintegrating. He wanted to quit. In all his forty-nine years, he never once had such a feeling of complete failure. The brief excitement he'd experienced while at Dave's house had vanished, replaced with a dark cloud of doom.

Then he thought to himself, *I'm a civil engineer. Why the hell am I wrapped up in this? I don't have to take this anymore.* Fear took over, he made up his mind to quit and strategized a way to get Carlie out of this mess while handing over the reins to the feds to figure out a solution. That's their job, what those guys were supposed to be doing. *Not my problem.*

Nothing could stop him. If people died, that wasn't his problem. *I gotta take care of myself and Carlie. Nothing else matters.*

*

At 8:05 p.m. a small blue-and-white Cessna 182 circled at 1,150 feet above Jake's Ford as he drove westbound amongst thousands of cars on the Interstate-10 freeway toward Los Angeles. The air was hazy but clear enough to see the freeway below. The sun drew itself behind the horizon and scattered clouds for another night's sleep. Only one man remained who could save the entire country from destruction, and the pilot's imminent plan was to detonate the bomb planted underneath the guy's car.

As Viktor piloted his small craft just above stall speed at a mere sixty-five knots and twenty degrees of flaps, he plodded along parallel to the I-10, directly above Jake's black Ford. He'd taken a new dose of meds to keep the seizures at bay. For now. He verified his location with a glance down at an iPad, attached at his leg, displaying the sectional map. As part of their aviation education, all airmen learned that flying was noticeably different than driving a terrain-based vehicle. In a car, when driving on a road, there are two dimensions, but in the air, there are three. Viktor noticed his speed up at seventy-five knots. He throttled back and pitched up to reduce the speed of his aircraft back to sixty-five, effectively "bleeding" off speed.

Another skill Viktor had mastered was how to read an aeronautical map. Like a normal road map, it indicated major roads, such as the I-10 freeway, and showed compass bearings, which meant north was "up" and south was "down," though aeronautical maps have two different north arrows. When flying an airplane, roads were used only for establishing a ground reference and were, therefore, shown on the map in subdued colors. Viktor aligned the thick black line on his map with the interstate freeway below him, unlike the prominent colors used on road maps.

He also used ground references like towers, city lights when flying at night, buildings, and natural terrain features like lakes and mountains to determine his location relative to the ground. Some aeronautical maps offered a pittance of information, like the ones for terrain in the middle of nowhere. Other maps were so crammed with details they were a challenge to read. The sectional map Viktor used covered the foothills of the San Gabriel Mountains and was jam-packed with so much information that an untrained eye would fail to recognize the map as one of Southern California. Viktor read the map like a pro, but Jake was the only true terrestrial detail he cared about right now.

The Los Angeles International airport, designated LAX, sat relatively close to anywhere Viktor could have flown to eliminate his nemesis. He had read the major airport typically saw more than 1,500 daily flights jumping into the sky, so any normal pilot would need to comply with the floors and ceilings of the class-bravo airspace. Viktor knew the maximum altitude he could fly without contacting the air traffic controller varied along his route from 2,500 feet to 4,000 feet above sea level, which meant his chosen altitude of 1,150 was perfect to maintain direct visibility of Jake's car below, among the sea of hybrids. It also kept Viktor flying "below the radar" of any numb-nuts controller at the LAX tower.

Viktor had also turned off his transponder to avoid the risk of detection. Those dolts could only see him using their primary radar system, which had limited effectiveness, especially for such a small plane flying so low to the ground. Of course, this violated a host of federal regulations, but Viktor didn't give a holy crap. *Screw all those jack-off federal laws.* After all, he had a civil engineer to kill, someone who could, although not a great risk at this point, figure out the duplicate server farm location and code and stop his plans to bring the mighty US of A to its knees. No, Jakey Boy had only a small chance in hell of stopping the plan. *This is more for me, because I want to kill him. I need to watch him die.*

Viktor used a modified navigational flying app on a separate Android tablet via wi-fi hotspot and GPS link that showed a blinking red dot lying on top of an interactive moving aeronautical map of the area. This allowed him to "see" where Jake was at all times. While Jakey Boy had been distracted with that whole Bridgette mess near the I-710 freeway, Viktor's brother, Syed, had planted a combo homing device/IED underneath Jake's car that transmitted a signal to Viktor's tablet as a blinking red dot. Syed was a master craftsman when it came to making exploding devices.

While Syed and their brother worked hard to fine-tune details for tomorrow's terrorist attack, Viktor stalked his prey like a bald eagle hovering above a helpless kangaroo rat. He'd officially had enough. Each time he thought about Jake, Viktor's mind flashed images of his mother's decapitated head—and merged them with Jake's face, which enraged Viktor. He hated the way his mother had died and he hated Jake even more. Civil engineers created the bedrock for civilized, organized societies, the very opposite of the chaos Allah intended for mankind. Every time the engineers constructed a new bridge, new water system, more electrical infrastructure, or a new building, Viktor knew it would be that much more work for him to tear down.

He was finished playing with Jake and the time had come to take out his chess-pawn. The voice of Allah confirmed suspicions now was the time for Jakey Boy to die. How fitting for Viktor's nemesis to meet his end on one of the freeways the engineer loved so much. Not that anyone loved the I-10 freeway and the constant traffic nightmare it produced when humans were in control.

Viktor pressed the little red "talk" button on the wire connected from his headset to his cell.

"Confirm we are a go for tomorrow," Viktor said to Syed.

"Yes, my brother. Allah is looking down on us favorably and"—Syed replied over the phone line—"we are green light for tomorrow. Working on the finishing touches now."

Viktor looked down at the dense matrix of cars beneath him on the I-10 freeway and made sure Jake's Ford was still below him using the augmented reality app. Jake's car lit up on the screen as a blinking target, even though the engineer was weaving in and out of lanes every few seconds. The red-and-blue flashing lights were on, and Jake accelerated, but Viktor couldn't care less.

"Tell me how brother Sanchez is doing."

"He's getting into position. We will be ready at the designated time."

Viktor terminated the call. Time to fly in for the kill.

*

Carlie had texted earlier she would call him, but she hadn't. Jake needed to call her and talk about disappearing, so he accelerated to over a hundred miles per hour with the intention of getting off at the next exit, turning around, and heading back to Dave's house.

But the moment he looked at his phone screen, his car jolted like it had hit a deep pothole. A loud, continuous hammering thud echoed throughout his car, like a laundry dryer with a brick tumbling around inside.

He doubled his grip on the steering wheel while glancing

in the rearview mirror. Bright orange flames spilled out from the back of his vehicle.

"Holy crap!" He slammed on the brakes, but as he decelerated through forty miles per hour, the rear of his car launched straight up like a rocket and the car flipped rear over front.

After hovering in the air for a second, the Ford slammed the full weight of itself onto the roof, all four side windows exploded outward under the stress, and the front window collapsed, shooting glass chunks inward, pummeling his body.

The ceiling slammed into his head and the door smashed into his ribs. The smell of kerosene filled the interior, along with a cloud of choking smoke and flames spewing all around him. Now, hanging upside down, Jake could only watch in terror as the Ford slid upside-down for more than a football field, spinning on its top, giving off a deafening screeching of tearing sheet metal. Trapped by his seatbelt, he tried to open the door despite great stabbing pain from his ribs, but it was cramped shut. His world warped inward as thoughts of dying inside a compact Ford coffin created a new level of panic. Entombed in a burning car, he felt his consciousness slipping away as he came to an abrupt stop in a shallow drainage ditch on the right side of the freeway. The upside-down sign for Dave's exit came into view. So close. He tried again to open the door, but everything went black.

✻

One minute earlier, as Viktor flew above Jake at precisely 8:12 p.m., he peered down at the car, chuckled to himself, and pushed the orange "boom" button on his app. The small square icon had a little image of exploding dynamite in the center. A radio signal transmitted and detonated the bomb underneath the Ford. All according to plan.

But the sum total of Viktor's hopes for splattering millions of pieces of civil engineer across four lanes of freeway were erased when only a small fraction of the Semtex detonated. Instead of turning Jake and the car into a pile of smoldering ash, flames the size of a campfire burst out of the Ford's trunk, only enough to flip the car over.

Viktor turned the plane around, headed back toward the Big Bear airport, then called Sanchez.

"The FBI is closing in. Switch to the clone server farm tomorrow morning—nationally—at two o'clock. I mean, turn the entire system back online. They won't know what hit 'em, plus that give us two hours until the shit hits the fan."

CHAPTER 51

Cavanaugh walked along a deserted sidewalk, two blocks outside the Federal Building, underneath an umbrella. Raindrops pelted his plastic shield.

He turned to his supervisor, also underneath an umbrella, and said in a raised voice, "For God's sake, we need more resources on this case. Lives are at stake here."

Cavanaugh had overheard his coworkers occasionally refer to Shankle's leadership skills as "horrendous," and one time someone said when things went well, he "took all the credit about as often as a dog licks his balls."

Although Cavanaugh had made it clear he had no idea how the guy had made it up that high on the government ladder, some shred of his prior-to-rogue self knew he should at least try to follow orders. He had studied and respected the chain of command, the backbone of any solid bureaucracy, but when the shit hit the fan, Shankle seemed to make sure the staff took the blame because, as everyone knew, the man had self-esteem issues. The result: the vast majority of people working under Shankle had no detectible level of respect for him and Cavanaugh knew it. *Screw him.*

The two agents stood on the sidewalk, distant lightning strikes every few seconds, as Cavanaugh continued his tirade of insubordination. "Rumor has it something happened to your family, but I don't give a shit. Without more men to investigate these homegrown terrorists, we're in for one hell of a wake-up call. The clock is ticking, goddamnit. Why the hell can't you see this? It's so obvious."

Shankle crossed his arms and took a wide stance. "Let me tell you a little story. Back in the eighties, when I was a young pup fresh out of Quantico, the boss assigned me one of the first cyber-terrorist cases on record. Worked with some folks at Cal Poly and dug deep into the suspect list. I mean deep. Questioned everyone. Did my job, and you know what? We never caught the raving lunatic. Well, we figured it out and by the time we could get a warrant to search his house, the son of a bitch had bolted. Engel was his name. Never forgot." Shankle looked at the sidewalk. "Point is, Cavanaugh, when it's a homegrown domestic terrorist, I have a gut instinct that puts up a red flag so big you could see it from space. But not this case. This case here screams foreigner. Nothing about it says one of our own citizens is involved."

"Bullshit," Cavanaugh fired back, even though the name Engel rang a bell. "We follow the goddamned evidence and it all points to someone here. A local guy."

"I'm not gonna say this again: stay focused on ISIS. We are *not* looking for a domestic terrorist, and certainly not someone who grew up in Southern California. No. The focus needs to stay on Syed. People love to hear about the evil ISIS empire."

"Jesus, Shankle, talk to me and tell me what's really going on. Are they blackmailing you? Tell me. They have your wife or kids held hostage somewhere? Tell me I'm wrong. Tell me."

Shankle looked away but admitted nothing. Cavanaugh read him like a magazine article. "I knew it. If they have her, let's work together. We're the FBI, this is what we do, man."

"No, you don't understand. Just do your fucking job and get Syed."

"Wait a second. You're the one who sent that helicopter after us in the High Desert when we first left the safehouse on Monday. And the bomb threat. Viktor didn't know about Jake being alive at that point. You must not have told him yet," Cavanaugh said, taking a confrontational stance.

Pause. "You have a pretty vivid imagination. But even if you were right, you'd know how hard it would be to work off the grid using burner phones, ducking in and out of the Federal Building, keeping a low profile, and diverting attention away from the real terrorists. You'd know how hard it would be to put the finishing touches on what would be a traitor-laden plan to use Syed as the scapegoat so Viktor could get away unscathed, and save my family. Hypothetically."

"You're right, I would know."

"You'd also know that until three days ago, nobody knew that Syed and Viktor were brothers and both part of the same ISIS terrorist cell. Or that an hour ago, I might have figured out their stupid plan. Maybe they intended to use *me* as the scapegoat. But since none of that is real, this conversation is over," Shankle said, starting to walk back toward the Federal Building.

With time nearly out, Cavanaugh ran after Shankle and grabbed him by his jacket.

"This crap is real. One day. That's all we have left. In less than one day, millions of people die. We're out of time. You need to get more men on this. Now. If you don't, I'm going over your head and calling Bradley myself."

"You threatening me? Good. I know all about what you've been doing the last couple of days with Bendel and his daughter. Aiding and abetting terrorists." His chubby cheeks gave way to a partial, forced smile. "Do it, and you're history." He swiped his coat from Cavanaugh's hand and kept walking.

CHAPTER 52

Sanchez knocked on the motel room door where Syed was staying. The door opened and Sanchez walked to the TV in the corner of the main room and turned it on. Together, they watched the video of the explosion of Jake's car from the aerial footage shot by Viktor. After the seventh viewing, Syed heaved the TV up and slammed it onto the floor. Sanchez knew Syed had messed up and why.

"Tell me what happened, my brother," Sanchez said, playing dumb.

Syed squinted and turned around, shouting an explanation about how he had planted the bomb underneath the rear of the black Ford, but his creation exploded differently than designed. He normally tinned the ends of all his wiring connections, but that goddamned Viktor had rushed him.

"I stripped ends and just twisted together, which, normally, would work fine, but somewhere between the Bridgette hostage situation and the infidel driving on the I-10 freeway toward LA, the wires came loose. That bastard Jake still has breath in his lungs because two tiny wires were not soldered together." He paused. "Damn it!"

Sanchez pinched his lips together and clenched his jaw as he stepped close to Syed. "In your haste to create the IED targeted to kill Bendel, you have failed our father, the great Allah. Now Viktor will have both our heads. This is unacceptable."

✳

Jake found himself sitting on a park bench along the shore of a quiet lake surrounded by evergreen trees with a gentle breeze blowing. He turned to his left where Professor Everton sat holding a fishing pole with a thin line angled away from the shore. After turning the reel a few times, Everton looked at Jake. "Tell me what you've gotten yourself into now, my boy."

Jake rubbed his chin and explained, in an uncertain tone, to the professor about the week's bizarre events. "Sitting here trying to figure out what to do." Jake's gaze turned downward, but his legs were missing. Odd.

Dave tapped Jake on the shoulder, startling him. Jake turned to find Dave holding a shotgun, butt tucked under his cheek, one eye closed, aiming to the lake.

"You ever wonder where ideas come from?" Everton asked.

"Random firings among neurons in our human brains," Jake said.

"Ha! Are they? What if they originate from some other source similar to the way transmitters emit radio waves? What if ideas—always present, floating around us in the ethereal—were somehow captured by a part of the brain that served as an antenna? Human egos believe each of us creates our own ideas. Maybe we have it all backward! We don't come up with ideas; ideas are given to us by God or the universe or some omnipotent being. Native Americans believed trees made the wind. Logical. Trees swayed back and forth only when the wind blew. You wave a leaf in your hand, it 'makes' the wind. False. Wind is created by differences in air pressure and temperature. Wind causes the trees to sway, not the other way around."

Jake had never thought of ideas that way.

Everton continued. "Remember: there's always a way. Focus and stay positive, I can tell you that much. No matter how bad things appear, always remember: optimism isn't easy, but it's better."

"I don't understand. Why do people do this, Professor? How do some people see the glass half full all the time? There's so much hate in the world." Jake trembled in frustration at the whole idea of someone like Viktor having enough resources and power to even conceive of a plan so sinister.

Dave cocked the shotgun hammer.

The professor smiled as a fish jumped out of the pond and dove back into the water. "You have a superior intellect and powers of reason. You're an educated civil engineer. Use your knowledge to stop Viktor. You have everything you need to stop him before he strikes again and kills more innocent people. Partner with Cavanaugh. Find the way. Find Viktor Engel. Find Viktor . . ."

A loud boom echoed the entire scene.

"Viktor Engel. Viktor Engel," Jake mumbled, half-coherent as he regained consciousness at the sound of the beeping and the smell of rubbing alcohol. His eyes pried open to the sight of a blurry clock on the wall: 10:03 a.m., and he found himself lying in a bed at the exact same hospital Bridgette had died in sixteen hours earlier.

"Dude. You're awake." Paige said, rushing to his side, all smiles.

Groggy, Jake said, "Whoa. Was having the weirdest dream with your dad." He grabbed Paige by her shoulders and pulled her close. "What happened? Is Carlie alright?"

"Somebody blew up your car last night, or tried to, at least. You're on some heavy-duty pain meds." Paige leaned over him and pushed his hair over his left ear. "You're the luckiest dude on the planet. Been out of it for, like, over twelve hours." She looked down. "Not sure where Carlie is, though."

A nurse walked by, popped her head in, smiled, and said, "Looks like Mr. Brownstone is awake. I'll go get the doctor."

Jake started to regain a slippery grasp on reality. *Mr. Brownstone? Are we still in this nightmare?*

Paige leaned in further and whispered in his ear. "Cavanaugh thought it best if we kept your ruse in full swing. Dude said he's taken care of everything, whatever that means."

Jake lifted his eyebrows and with some help from Paige, sat up and rubbed his eyes to try to get the grogginess out. It didn't work.

"Last thing I remember is some dickhead in a yellow Corvette flipping me off. Next thing I know, I'm here with you. Jesus, my ribs are killing me." He licked his dry lips in a failed attempt to bring moisture to his cottonmouth.

Paige bit her fingernails. "Dave said he thinks all we've done so far is dig ourselves a few nice graves," Paige said.

"Sounds like Dave." Jake, exhaled, shifted himself in the bed to get a better position.

"Dude has a point, I mean, we've added all kinds of stress to our lives, and now people are trying to kill you. Not sure that was the best choice, but you're the one who's always been trying to save the world. Now's your chance, assuming you'll get one. Not sure, though. I mean, dude, someone blasted that piece of shit Ford into the next dimension, man."

"Thanks for the cheerful analysis, Paige," Jake said.

After an awkward moment when the nurse came in and checked the pan beneath Jake's ass, Professor Everton shuffled into the room.

"Is this where patient 'Brownstone' currently resides?" the professor said in his joking way. He looked at Jake. "A36 . . ."

"101," said Jake, nodding.

"Dad." Paige ran up to give him a hug. "I'm so glad you came. Jake was mumbling about Viktor Engel just before he woke up."

Jake pushed his eyebrows together and asked Paige to repeat herself.

"I said, you were mumbling about Viktor Engel and . . ."

Jake's energy level surged. He felt restless, needed to get moving. Deep in the recesses of his subconscious, he remembered the Everton pep talk and knew what he needed to do. He rotated a few of his limbs to test his joints, his elbows and knees, and they seemed to work pretty well—better than they had in years. Or maybe that was just the painkillers.

"Yes. Professor, I just had a weird . . . well, never mind. I have a feeling someone named Viktor Engel is involved in this whole thing. I'm positive Viktor Engel is the same as Viktor Johnston. He goes by both names. Johnston knew an incredible amount of all the various tech—"

"Wait. Wait a minute, Jake. Viktor Engel. Oh, goodness," the professor interrupted.

Jake glanced at Paige and back at the professor. "Clock's ticking here, Professor."

"Do you remember me telling you on Monday about my coworker back in the eighties who was considered one of, if not the first, cyber-terrorists?"

"The guy who planted the virus in your structural-engineering software. The one who disappeared. Yeah."

"Precisely. His last name was Engel too. Dr. Marion Engel." The professor started to pace with his arms crossed. He moved his lower jaw from side to side as he thought. "If I recall, back then I remember chatting with one of the FBI agents and he told me that after Marion's dad died, his mom went nuts with fundamentalist Christianity and the Bible. Both were born again and tried to do what they thought was the right thing, but apparently, somewhere along the line Marion started hearing voices from God and told his mom about the voices. They talked with their pastor, but he told them there's no such thing as mental illness, psychology is a bunch of hocus-pocus, science is the devil's work, and Marion just hadn't been praying hard enough. I guess the pastor was wrong. Was right before his mom died in a car accident, too."

"Professor, if you're saying what I think you're saying, we can now confirm Viktor Johnston is Viktor Engel is Marion Engel, the guy you used to work with."

The professor snapped his fingers and pointed at Jake. "Bingo. I just remembered another key piece. As I recall, their family had a cabin in Big Bear."

"The FBI already flagged the Big Bear area as a possible location for Viktor, but they don't have a definite location. Need Cavanaugh to run a background check on Engel, search for properties in the Big Bear area, and see if the system comes up with anything we can use, like a specific address."

Jake scratched his head, thinking. Feeling more lucid with each passing minute, he cocked his head back. "I know it's him, I know what he's planning. I need to find Viktor and confront him before it's too late, but now I'm stuck in this place for God knows how long. Where the hell's the doctor? And what about the printout? Did it make it to Cavanaugh?"

Paige shrugged her shoulders.

Jake gained more speed as his brain came online, explaining to the professor about the second CDM attack planned throughout the entire country. "Dammit. At least there won't be a CDM2 if the system stays turned off. This is what I was going to tell Cavanaugh before the bomb. Crap. I need to talk with him ASAP and make sure he keeps the system off."

Paige handed Jake his phone. "I've texted Carlie to let her know you're okay. Now call Cavanaugh."

Jake dialed Cavanaugh's cell, but the call went straight to voicemail again. As he set the phone on his lap, out of the corner of his eye he noticed a TV hanging from the ceiling on the opposite side of the room. The volume was muted, but he saw a female newscaster giving a report about the weather. Jake asked Paige to turn on the volume.

"We are officially on storm watch. A large subtropical cyclone is already starting to inundate the Los Angeles basin with scattered thunderstorms. We're expecting up to ten to fifteen inches of rain in the next several hours, with even more rain in the foothills. This is a welcome break from the recent fires and the ongoing drought, but with saturated ground conditions, mudslides and debris flows are all but certain, especially in the burn areas near Pasadena."

She continued. "In better news, there are mixed reviews coming in about the National Self-Driving Network, or Sûr System, having resumed operation. Officials were unavailable for comment." A reporter interviewed one driver who was ecstatic the system was back online. "I hate traffic, but now I can use the freeways again without having to stop all the time. It's wonderful, but at the same time, I'm worried because of the CDM. We don't want nothing like that happening again," the woman said on the TV. The next interview showed a less enthusiastic man. "Bad government. Big brother don't need to know where I am. I ain't gonna drive on no automatic freeway no matter what. Don't trust 'em. Don't need 'em. That tech they usin' is like playin' with fire. They gonna kill us all if we ain't careful."

Jake blinked rapidly and sat up further in his bed. "Holy Christ," Jake said. His visitors turned toward him. "The SS is back on? I thought they pulled the power to the server. Cavanaugh knows about the impending attack today." He looked down at his hands, scraped and bruised. "I breathed life into a technological monster. I'm the one who fought to give it such a high level of unparalleled control over so many human lives. Should've never done that. We need to kill that thing before it's too late."

"Another breaking news story for our viewers is about the conspiracy surrounding Dr. Jake Bendel." Paige grabbed the remote and turned up the volume. The screen showed the various pictures of Jake at the High Desert Corridor bombing, with a photo of a screenshot of the I-710 hostage situation from yesterday pasted in the corner. The next frame showed a photo from last night of paramedics pulling Jake's flaccid body out of the upside-down Ford. The announcer added, "This video, shot yesterday evening on Interstate 10, is of the same black Ford that our crews spotted two days ago near Senator Brown's assassination bombing. A man matching Bendel's description was pulled from the wreckage."

Jake's gut wrenched as he watched the workers pull his body from what remained of the car. His face flushed with blood as anger returned and his head pounded harder.

"Again, if you have any information on the whereabouts of this man, we urge you to contact our hotline at the number shown on your screen." The TV displayed the photoshopped picture of Jake from two weeks ago, sans his beard, with a toll-free number scrolling across the bottom of the screen.

"Guys, I need to get out of here or I'm gonna lose it," Jake said with a rising voice as panic swelled inside him.

Jake grabbed the remote from Paige and turned off the TV.

Paige nodded, but before they could act, the doctor walked in, unfolded the aluminum case, looked at the patient chart inside and asked, "So . . . Mr. Brownstone, that was quite the accident you were in last night." He leaned forward with a miniature flashlight in his hand to check Jake's eyes. The doctor smelled like a donut store. Jake imagined the three-hundred-pound medical professional surrounded by pastries.

The doctor performed additional routine checks on Jake's heart, lungs, and reflexes. "Well, Mr. Brownstone, for the magnitude of the accident you were in, you came out quite all right other than two bruised ribs, your left seventh and eighth, and you're going to have a headache once the pain meds wear off. The ribs will cause you pain when you cough and breathe deep, so try to take it easy for the next few weeks. No jumping, running, or jarring of any kind."

"Thanks for your advice, Doc, but I'm checking myself out. Get me a release form."

"X-rays and CAT scan don't show any skull fractures or internal bleeding or swelling on your brain, but I'd like to keep you here the rest of today and overnight for observation."

As Jake lifted his legs up off the bed and placed them onto the floor, motivation hit him dead center. He wanted to kill Viktor. He needed to. He felt in his gut the guy was hiding up in Big Bear, so he told himself to make it happen, whatever it took.

"Now," Jake shouted as he stood, pain shooting from his ribs, and forcing the doctor out.

After the nurse unhooked Jake from the various monitors that kept track of his vitals, Paige handed Jake a fresh set of clothes she had retrieved from his house. His friends waited outside while he dressed in his favorite jeans and blue short-sleeved checkboard dress shirt, then the nurse slid into the room with the release papers. The pen felt like it weighed ten pounds as he signed them. She ripped free his copy and attached it to several other disclosure papers, all held together by a standard oversized paperclip.

She handed him the printout with the proof. "Thought you might need this."

Once he met his friends in the hall, they headed into the stairwell on their way to the parking lot, but as Jake stepped forward, the paperclip popped off and the documents scattered across the floor. With his mind focused on what to do next to catch Viktor, he stopped, grabbed the paperclip, scraped up the papers from the steps, and headed down. As the group stepped down the stairwell, the lights at the hospital flickered and the staircase went dark.

CHAPTER 53

Carlie knew Paige had told her to go to Starbuck's and wait, but after six hours of people-watching, she got frustrated and drove to the family rental house in Pasadena. While staring out the living room window, dark clouds and rain rolled through a blackened sky.

Every passing moment of her confinement, the anxiety grew stronger. As an extrovert, she needed to talk with people, in any medium possible, whether texting, talking on the phone, or face-to-face. She wanted to help and needed something—anything—to do, even if it meant violating her dad's advice to lay low. Paige had told her he was recovering in the hospital but had advised against coming in to see him since he was still unconscious. Not worth the risk.

The internal emptiness rubbed her raw, like carpet on a knee. She missed her friends. She missed her boyfriend. She tried to relax, but the thought of her dad lying unconscious in a hospital bed only made things worse. He'd survived a car bomb, a fire, and potential poisoning. What if next time luck failed to shine down on him so graciously? *What if that Viktor guy winds up getting the best of him?*

She found it impossible to answer any of the dozens of questions floating around in her mind, so when she received a text from her best friend, Kristen, she grinned. Carlie had told Kristen on Wednesday she would be staying in Los Angeles for a few days for job interviews. She thought about telling her about her dad but decided against it. To Kristen and the rest of the world, he was already dead.

Kristen must have shared the same restlessness and said she missed Carlie as well, so she thought they'd get together for some girl time and to catch up on all things female. Kristen lived in North Los Angeles, which on a normal day without any traffic would take about fifteen minutes, but with traffic congestion, over an hour. Fortunately, with the heavy rain, fewer people were out driving. And when you're twenty-five-years old and want to see your BFF, potential threats to your life tend to get ignored.

Carlie talked Kristen into coming over to the rental house for a visit. Kristen told her she'd be "right there."

The Bendel rental house was located in the Pasadena foothills near the Jet Propulsion Laboratory, north of the Rose Bowl and east of the thirteen hundred-acre Hahamongna Watershed Park. The east-west road three blocks west dipped perpendicularly across an eighty-foot wide, fifteen-foot deep southern-flowing flood-control channel that, again according to her dad, had been pushed through to approval, for political reasons, over fifty years ago. The engineering firm turned out to be corrupt and did a crappy design. Her dad had told her that to be fair, at that time most roads were built for drivers to drive across the flow of water in the channels. This made it easier, faster, and cheaper to build dips in the road instead of bridges, which would be more expensive and safer.

The brunt of the cyclone had not yet hit the foothills, but heavy rain fell, still not traditionally the norm for August. As Kristen talked to Carlie via Bluetooth, she told her she was approaching a dip in the road—the flood-control channel—and she stopped. She told Carlie about the water and asked whether she should go for it or not.

"Do it, girl. I'm going crazy here without you," Carlie advised.

A few moments later, Kristen pulled into Carlie's driveway. Carlie ran out in the downpour and gave a big hug to her long-lost companion whom she hadn't seen in forever.

Well, two days.

"Oh my god, Carls, it's so good to see you," Kristen said, raindrops falling on their heads. "The last week here in L.A. has been just terrible. Everyone's acting weird, like the end of the world is coming. It's been really creepy and I've been, like, scared to drive anywhere. Today's my first day driving since the CDM."

"You're here now where it's safe. It's been too long. We have so much to catch up on."

Kristen agreed. "Let's get inside before we get soaked. It's really starting to come down."

They hustled toward the front door, and a loud clap of thunder rattled the area, startling them both to screams.

They entered the rental house and sat on the leather couch. All the lights were off. Power outage. The Bendels' TV did not work, either, so the girls gossiped about the latest scandals with their friends, who cheated on who, who might be getting married soon, and which ones were pregnant.

A half-hour into their conversation, Carlie's phone rang.

"Hey, baby, where you at, girl?"

"Hi, Michael. I'm here at my family's rental house in Pasadena. Kristen just got here," Carlie said.

He paused.

"You two had lunch yet?"

Carlie put the call on speaker so Kristen could hear. She nodded her head and said, "No, yeah, we need to eat. You in the area?" Carlie was curious why Michael would call out of the blue like this. She thought he'd been born without a spontaneous bone in his body. Especially on a crazy rainy day like today.

Carlie hoped Michael would remember the address of the rental. They had gone to a party nearby a few months back and stopped at the rental beforehand for a quickie.

"I'm just around the corner, be there in a few."

That's weird.

Several bright flashes of light appeared, followed closely by multiple loud claps of thunder.

"It's been raining non-stop for hours and now it's really coming down, never seen it pour like this. Wow." Kristen chuckled.

"Must be getting closer," Carlie said. "My dad says that if you count after the lightning, each five seconds represents a mile since the sound of the thunder travels so much slower than light."

Fifteen minutes later, someone knocked on the front door. The two girls popped up off the couch, trotted over, and when Carlie opened it, Michael stood in the doorway completely drenched.

CHAPTER 54

After the main lights went out, the emergency battery lights in the stairwell at the USC Medical Center switched on. The dim, focused light beams shot from multiple incandescent bulbs, providing a minimal amount of light, reflecting off the baby-blue walls and hybrid concrete-and-steel steps. Generators were installed at all hospitals in preparation for a power outage. After all, life-support machines need electricity; people die without power.

Jake overheard a security guard running up the stairwell, yelling into his walkie-talkie about a lightning bolt that had struck the top of the roof. That must've caused the flickering of the lights.

"Take my car, Jake. I'll grab an Uber back to my house in Claremont, no worries," Professor Everton offered. The professor stopped on the step beneath Jake and Jake bumped into him. The professor reached into his jeans pocket, pulled out the keys to his '65 Mustang, looked up at his former student, handed them to Jake, and gave him a big hug. "You take care of my baby while you're out there, y'hear?"

"I hope I do better than I did with the FBI car," he said, trying to infuse some humor into an otherwise dreary situation. "Paige, you ride with me up to Big Bear. We'll call Cavanaugh on our way and update him and find out if he has anything for us."

Paige nodded with a wink. They blasted through the door from the stairwell to the parking structure and hustled across the concrete to the old Mustang, which sat impossibly close to the VW next to it. No way Jake could open his door.

"I hope I can drive this thing better than you can park it," Jake said to the professor.

"Stay safe, you two," the professor said, giving his daughter a brief hug before nudging her toward the Mustang.

"We'll give Dave a call, too," Jake said as he walked toward the passenger side. "Need to get him up to speed and figure out a way to keep hacking at the code. He said he has a read-only program to view the decrypted code and needs to find the spot to turn off or prevent the CDM2. And we need to figure out how the hell the system was turned back on."

"He said there's no way to get write access, it's not normally possible—"

Jake stopped. "Paige, please. Let's give him a call. If he finds some evidence in the code, that would be huge."

Paige rolled her eyes as Jake flung open the passenger-side door, realized how much it hurt to move, crawled in and over the console, then plopped into the driver's seat.

"Hold on," Paige said. "You were in a massive car accident last night. An explosion. You're on heavy pain meds, have bruised ribs, and have a crazed look in your eyes."

Jake stopped, turned to her. "So?"

"So I think I should drive."

"I'm fine, really," he said, climbing in. She grunted, did the same and yanked her door closed.

With Paige riding shotgun, Jake bolted out of the parking structure. The skies were a dark gray, practically black, and large globs of raindrops splashed the car while flashes of lightning lit up the sky every few seconds, followed by booming claps of thunder. "Hope this old car doesn't leak," he said.

"My dad babies this thing. Runs just like new. I'm surprised he even offered it to us. He must, like, super trust us and think we'll be able to get this dude. So what's this secret code between you and my pops?"

"It's silly, really, just the standard steel-alloy, A36, combined with the class number I was taking when I first met your dad: Engineering 101."

"Men," she said, shaking her head.

Jake dialed Cavanaugh to let him know about Viktor, but he didn't answer. Again.

Paige asked Jake about his dream back at the hospital. Jake explained how her dad came to him at a lake and explained some pretty trippy spiritual stuff. He told her Dave was there with a shotgun and he blew away some ducks just before he woke up. *What the hell does that mean, anyway?*

"Bizarre. Even in your dreams, Viktor's following you," she said.

"Not sure there's any truth to it. Just some dream. Speaking of which…"

He called Dave, who answered. *At least someone answers their phone.*

Jake talked for several minutes and brought Dave up to speed. An idea suddenly hit him. "I've been thinking. If the Sûr System is still online, but the federal server farm that runs it is unplugged and offline, Viktor must have figured out a way to clone the whole enchilada."

"Jesus, God, that would be a monumental undertaking. He'd have to hack in, which we know he can do, cloak everything on a new server farm, somehow upload all the files—the entire app—to the new servers, reroute and connect all of the systems nationally, and operate the cloned system without anyone detecting or tracing the location of the servers."

"Exactly. But it's the only logical explanation. Tell me you can find power data-usage footprints for multiple IPs," Jake said.

"Of course, man. This ain't no amateur hour," Dave said.

"I'll bet Viktor put the server farm somewhere here in Southern California. Can you search all IP addresses and narrow down the list based on their footprint usages? Then cross reference to the electrical service point for their server farm?"

"I'll have it to you in ten minutes."

"Make it eight."

Multiple lightning bolts struck in front of them in the distance.

Today, Jake was on a mission. When he entered what his friends referred to as "the zone," they knew to look out. Few people in the world could match his skill at solving problems with logic, especially one as complex and intricate as this one. There was a drawback to being in the zone, though. When his mind became so focused on a given task, his other senses stopped working.

"Looks like you're back in your zone now," Paige said, with a death grip on her door handle. "Go with it. I've seen you like this before. You probably can't even hear me right now." She paused, waiting for a response. Nothing. "Tell you what. If it were theoretically feasible for someone—anyone—on the planet to figure out where Viktor was hiding the cloned system and prevent him from killing tens of millions of people, you'd be the guy."

A tractor trailer rig blurred by carrying dozens of cows, with bits of hay floating away behind the rear.

"Tell me what's going on in that genius brain of yours," Paige said.

Jake zoomed out from his focused effort, back to human-talking mode. "Assuming I'm correct, if Viktor is as mentally deranged as we think, used to work at Cal Poly Pomona back in the eighties and was able to clone the Sûr System, he might be using the new server farm at Cal Poly."

Paige shook her head. "No way. They'd totally find that out. The power draw would be enormous and it would attract all sorts of attention."

Jake nodded. "The SS takes a massive surge when it's initially booted up, but it only lasts three hours and two minutes."

Paige bit her lip and did a slow head shake. "Not sure how the hell you know that."

"My wife's birthday is . . . was March 2nd. Three-two. For some reason, I remember each time we fired up the system during testing. It always took three-two. Three hours, two minutes before the power surge dropped off. Send it to Dave in a text."

They left another message for Cavanaugh as they drove east on Interstate 10 toward San Bernardino. Dave responded via text, and Jake handed the phone to Paige. She rotated the phone several times to read the attachment.

"Looks like a list," she said.

"Find the IP address for Cal Poly and the electrical service point for their server farm, then see what the power footprint looked like this morning. If it was three-two and there's a hundred-twenty-three terabits per second, that's where Viktor is hiding the cloned system."

Paige scanned the document, zooming in and out for several minutes, until finally she said, "Holy server system, Batman. Here it is. Black and white. The son of a bitch is running the cloned system from Cal Poly. You were right."

Jake called Dave. "You need to jack into the Cal Poly servers."

"Hold on," Dave said, clicking noises in the background. "Can't. There's some sort of industrial-strength firewall. Never seen anything like it. You'll need to go there and actually plug in a cable, hard-wire yourself in to access the server."

Jake looked at Paige. "No, *you* need to go to the campus and plug in. We're headed to Big Bear to find Viktor."

"Dammit, you know I'm agoraphobic. I'm not leaving my house. Have someone else do it."

"Dave, I need you to dig deep on this. Pick up your junk and get over there now. I'll ask Everton to meet you there. He has security access to the server room."

After a long pause, Dave said, "No way. Can't do it. Sorry."

Paige leaned over to Jake and yelled into the phone, "I'll give you free tickets to my next show at the Improv if you leave in the next thirty seconds."

Rustling noises came through the phone. "Fine," Dave said before hanging up.

Jake left several messages for Cavanaugh over the course of the next hour. They had driven out of LA and were heading into the Inland Empire on the I-210 toward State Route 330 when Cavanaugh finally called back.

"Cavanaugh, thank God. Urgent news about Viktor. Need your help."

"Funny you should say that."

Jake exited the I-210 and merged onto the 330 north in Highland. They had officially left the valley and were heading up into the mountains to Big Bear. The cyclone and accompanying scattered thunderstorms hadn't hit this part of Southern California yet.

"We dug up some solid leads from Viktor's background," Cavanaugh said. "But tell me what you've got first."

"I'm heading up to Big Bear and might get cut off any second, so I'll make it brief." He informed Cavanaugh of the server farm at Cal Poly. At first Cavanaugh did not believe him, but as he explained the details, his logic, Cavanaugh agreed. "I need you to meet Dave and Everton at the Cal Poly server farm. They'll be there in a few minutes."

"Headed there now. Got anything else?" Cavanaugh asked.

"Yes. It all makes sense now. According to Professor Everton," Jake reported, "a guy named Dr. Marion Engel worked with him at Cal Poly about thirty years ago. You guys should have a file on him." Jake explained Marion had changed his name to Viktor, probably to start a new life. "It looks like the Engels own a house or cabin in Big Bear, so I need you to do a title search for the address."

"You took some of the thunder out of what I was gonna tell you. Already found this out. In fact, Marion Engel was one of the very first cyber-terrorists," Cavanaugh said. "Viktor's two stepbrothers died a couple of years after the car crash, the one that Viktor lost his mom in. The brothers died under suspicious circumstances and Viktor was a suspect, but never formally charged because the local PD couldn't come up with enough evidence."

"Viktor killed his stepbrothers? Great," Jake said.

"Our criminal profiler says there's a high probability the two siblings blamed him for their mom's death and were probably a bit nuts themselves, even though they weren't Viktor's blood."

Jake passed through several tight horizontal curves, each with black-on-yellow curve warning signs posted.

"Also, we didn't find a birth certificate for a Marion Engel, so that fits the theory of him being adopted or brought in to the country illegally when he was young."

"Put it on speaker so I can hear," Paige said. He did.

"Jake, I have more news. A bit disturbing."

"Here we go."

"I convinced a couple of guys on our cyber-research team here—close, trusted friends of mine—to do off-the-record digging and found out something interesting about your daughter's boyfriend. Remember when you told me your guy Dave found out Ivory Snow was a guy named M. Sanchez?"

Jake put it together before Cavanaugh could spit it out. "Don't tell me. The 'M' stands for Michael?"

"One and the same. There're a ton of guys in California with that first and last name, but we ran his fingerprints and reviewed the background check he did when he applied for a job last year at a power company in SoCal. Exact match to the prints we pulled of the bomb underneath Carlie's car."

Jake's heart jumped into his throat. "I need to call Carlie right now to tell her. Are we done?"

Pause.

"Jake, there's one more thing. Sanchez has an older brother from Syria, and he's on our top ten most-wanted list of international terrorists. These two guys are involved with Viktor, and I've got two of my CIA buddies digging deep into their backgrounds. Our theory is that the three of them orchestrated the attacks as part of a cell, and I'll bet there are more cells across the country."

Paige slowly mouthed the F-bomb.

"Tell me you're joking. Viktor might be working with two Syrian terrorists on this and one of the guys is my daughter's boyfriend?" Jake asked as his pulse pounded in his neck. *I was planning on killing Viktor nice and quick, but now . . .*

"I gotta find Carlie!"

CHAPTER 55

Bobby glanced at his watch: 2:29 p.m.

Standing outside the USC Medical Center, he prepared to report on the latest breaking news update at ABC-7 about the Bendel conspiracy, his baritone voice sending test words into the mic for Doug to check the decibel reading. Rarely in his career did he get this excited about a story.

To give the viewers an update that afternoon, Carol had told him she'd squeeze him in during three minutes between shows, the next scheduled to start at 2:30 p.m. called *Puppet Masters: How to Make Your Own Politician Puppets.* He knew only a few people were watching TV with the blackout still spread across most of Southern California.

Bobby envisioned his golden-brown face sending a strong, confident image to Carol's monitor back at the station. He stood ready to report live from the top step outside the front entrance, intending his interview to be quick with a short, stocky nurse who had called the hotline with a tip. He and the nurse stood together as Doug, the cameraman, looked into the viewfinder of his trusty Hitachi 4k, set up on the tripod and ready to send the live feed to Glendale.

Carol talked to Bobby via his earpiece and counted down from five. "Four . . . three . . . two . . ."

Bobby smiled. "We are here live at the USC Medical Center in downtown Los Angeles this afternoon with Lauren McSteril, a nurse who has some rather interesting information to share with us. Go ahead and tell the viewers what you saw, Lauren."

Lauren shifted her hefty mass from one foot to the other. It was her first time on live TV. Any TV. Earlier, Lauren had shared her two concerns with Bobby. The first was what her girlfriend would think, and the second, how she might have a hard time coming up with a good way to tell her story.

Bobby's response to both concerns was, "Don't worry about it, babe, just be yourself."

As expected, Lauren gave a stereotypical uneducated response to his simple question. "Well, um, I work in the emergency room, right? And so, we've all been working twenty-four-hour shifts since the CDM. People be on edge and angry and stuff, so I just try to focus on my job and—"

"Right, now let's fast forward to the part we talked about," Bobby interrupted.

"Oh, right, sorry. So there was this guy that came in last night who kinda looked like the guy you been followin' on the news. That Bendel guy, right?"

"Uh-huh, keep going," Bobby prodded.

From behind the camera, a bead of sweat rolled down Doug's nose and dripped off the tip. Bobby hoped the woman would spit out the good stuff soon.

"Yeah, okay. Well, he was in this really bad car crash," Lauren said. "But the police wouldn't tell us where, which I thought was weird. Then these three guys showed up from the government, flashing around FBI badges and demanding the man's things before we could get his clothes off him. They wanted his wallet, I assume for his ID, which they never gave to us. They told the doctor to admit him as Mr. Neil Brownstone."

"Neil Brownstone?"

"Yeah."

"You're sure of this?"

"Yeah. So anyway, we ran a bunch of tests and stuff, and the guy discharged himself."

"He did? This morning?"

"Uh-huh. And so I'm like thinking this was all really weird, right? So then when I saw him walking out of his patient room, I knew something was up, so I snapped a picture of him."

Bobby imagined Carol back at the studio, posting the photo on the screen for all the viewers to see. It was a tad blurry but clear enough to make out the face.

"Thank you, Lauren," Bobby said, turning toward the camera. "Now, for our viewers at home, what you're looking at is the exact photo that Lauren took four hours ago. We've had our graphic artist at ABC-7 clean it up for comparison."

Below Doug, on the monitor, an updated photo popped up with the other two photos they had from the previous report on Tuesday. All three photos of Jake appeared side by side on the screen.

"Now, of course, you can decide for yourself, but in this reporter's opinion, we're looking at the same guy: Dr. Jake Bendel. The questions we now have for the FBI are, why are you covering this up? If Dr. Bendel is responsible for killing everyone with the CDM attack, why not arrest him and bring him to justice?" Bobby knew this story would vault him to the top. He hoped Carol would get a call any minute from the national news stations.

"We did contact the FBI with a request for comment. Our request was denied, with the excuse that they cannot comment on an ongoing investigation," he said. Bobby paused for a moment. Normally at that time, he would wind up and send it back to the studio.

But the call to glory was strong.

Bobby heard Carol speak to him in his earpiece. "Don't do it. Don't go in for the kill. Not this time. Please."

He ignored her. "If you happen to see this man, I urge you to call the authorities or, if you have a chance, stop him and ask him why he's doing these things. Let him know that we have a right to know what's going on." Bobby's face beamed with immense satisfaction over his ballsy request to the public.

"Cut the feed," he heard her say to her producer. "Go to commercial. Successful conspiracy or not, one more stunt like that and your ass is fired."

CHAPTER 56

"Who's ready for some food?" Michael asked with his winning smile.

"Michael, I'm super excited to see you, but I thought you were working in San Bernardino today. It's Thursday."

"Geez. Twenty questions. I had a training class in Glendale and we got out early, so I figured I'd try to catch you and I got lucky. Hope I'm not interrupting." He maintained his smile, out of breath, as he rubbed his nose.

She smiled back. "With all this rain, I'm not sure if anything's even open right now, especially with the blackout." The ominous sky spoke to her, hinting to stay indoors.

"Nah, it's fine, just a sprinkle," Michael said, still smiling.

She and Kristen grabbed their jackets and hurried outside into the deluge. A tiny river flowed in the gutter, at the base of the driveway. Carlie smelled the moist air and remembered one of the rainy soccer games her dad made her play when she was eleven, and how much fun she'd had getting all muddy.

Carlie also remembered her dad explaining the signifi-cance of intense rain: a heavy cloud-burst of rainfall coming down on the order of several inches per hour can cause major damage to the infrastructure. She suspected this might not be the best time to drive around, but pushed aside the thought.

Michael held the hood of his jacket over his head as loud drops of rain splattered onto the nylon material. He said, "Hey, Carlie, I gotta run to a meeting after we're done, so I'm just gonna follow you in my truck."

Michael drove a dark gray four-wheel-drive GMC 2500 diesel with a four-inch body lift. Carlie knew Michael liked his manly truck; it had the power he craved.

"We'll take Kristen's Neon. See you at Subway. It's just a few blocks west of here, so hang a left on Lincoln."

Michael nodded and climbed up into his truck.

As the two ladies entered the Neon, droplets of rain snuck in and splattered all over the upholstery. Kristen turned on her windshield wipers and backed up, splashing through the gutter water. They drove down the cul-de-sac and turned right onto the street with the large flood-control dip. Michael followed in his oversized gray beast. A moment later, the girls entered the dip, and Kristen skidded to a stop on the steep downward slope, the front of her car aimed straight at the flowing debris.

She gasped as her mouth fell open. "Oh, my God, Carlie, look at all that water and mud. Is that a tree trunk floating downstream?"

What flowed as a soft trickle of water not thirty minutes earlier had turned into a raging river of mud, tree branches, and floating debris traveling downstream from right to left in front of them at about ten feet per second. Carlie had learned

382 | J. LUKE BENNECKE

to estimate water velocities from her dad. The flow was maybe three feet deep, about half the height of their car. Carlie told Kristen to back up and go around and avoid the crossing altogether.

Rain crashed onto the windshield, and over the noise of the wipers flopping back and forth at full speed, Carlie heard the faint sound of rocks tumbling inside the flow. Carlie's mom had warned her long ago never to cross flooding water, even if it might seem possible. She realized she had made a mistake advising Kristen to cross the stream when she'd called earlier.

She darted a look at Kristen. "We're gonna have to find another way around; this ain't gonna happen."

Kristen's eyes were wide open with fear.

"Get us outta here, Kristen, I don't like this. I don't like this one bit."

Carlie felt herself overreacting, and Kristen followed suit. Kristen's breathing became heavy as she kicked the Neon into reverse gear and turned her body around to start a backup maneuver.

But Michael's headlights were right behind their tiny white car, his bumper no more than a foot away from their trunk.

"Dammit. Michael's blocking us." Kristen honked the horn a few times. Nothing. Then she held it down for ten seconds. "What's wrong with him? He needs to get out of the way so we can go find a bridge crossing." Kristen hopped up and down in her seat while waving both her hands like a confused mental patient.

With the car in reverse, Carlie hoped Michael would see the back-up lights and take a hint. After a few seconds, he hadn't budged. Maybe he couldn't hear the car horn over the rain, so she tried to call him. She saw through his windshield that he was already on the phone with someone and didn't pick up her call. A surge of adrenaline dumped into her gut, increasing her heart rate.

Who the hell is he talking to?

✳

"Yes, sir, I was gonna knife her at her house like you told me to, but her stupid bitch friend was there, so I'm improvising. Then her friend wouldn't leave, so I had no choice. Gonna take both of 'em out. I'm in my truck and they're both in some stupid little car in front of me, about fifteen feet away from the flood," said Michael Sanchez. "Don't worry, sir, I'll take care of her."

"This storm is Allah's way of supporting our plan, my young brother. He truly wants to help us. You'll see. Do what you need to do," Viktor instructed Sanchez over the phone.

Viktor and Michael had been plotting to kill Jake's only daughter for some time. Viktor wanted to rip Michael a new one when he heard the police discovered the bomb Michael planted under Carlie's car at the CSUSB parking lot earlier in the week. But not this time. They had her. Michael had finished with the last of the setup work for their grand finale, the greatest terrorist act—a thundering cluster of traffic collisions—in the history of the world; then Viktor released him with instructions to follow Carlie and go in for the kill when appropriate.

Thanks to intel from Bridgette before she went on her permanent vacation to Allah, Viktor knew where Jake and Carlie had been staying in the downtown safehouse above the Chinese restaurant. They waited, biding their time. Viktor knew Carlie's death would enrage Jake to the point of making a mistake. Since Jakey Boy survived the car bomb, Viktor would continue to toy with him.

Michael had been on a stake-out across from the Chinese food restaurant for two days, waiting for Carlie to leave. When Carlie left in an Uber, Michael followed her all the way to Dave's house, then to the Pasadena rental house. He told Viktor how the two bitches had swallowed his line about going to lunch and how "Chicks these days are so stupid and gullible," and how he trailed them to the flood-waters crossing.

Michael ended the call, slammed the front of his truck into the rear of the Neon and pushed.

CHAPTER 57

The screen on Jake's FBI cell blinked. Incoming call. He recognized the number immediately. Carlie. His hands shook and he grabbed Paige's forearm.

"Cavanaugh, Carlie's calling me right now. Get to Cal Poly. Help Dave. Find the address for the cabin in Big Bear and get it to me ASAP." He simultaneously hung up on Cavanaugh and answered Carlie's call. Screams and cries came through.

"Daddy! Daddy, Michael's pushing us into the flood!"

✳

Over the last hour, Bobby's cameraman, Doug, had shot some of the most amazing rescue scenes from the Sky 7 Chopper. Now, after listening to a dispatch call from the fire department about a possible car stuck in a Pasadena flood-control channel, the pilot and Bobby searched the area below while Doug fiddled with the camera settings.

Through the thick curtain of rain and heavy mist from the thrust of the blades, Bobby spotted the scene below their hovering craft. "There! A halfmile east," he said to the pilot, pointing toward a blackened sky to their right. Moments later they were above the scene.

Rain poured hard all around. Officials on the radio had classified the cyclonic energy as an extended five-hundred-year storm, so Carol had advised Bobby against flying until later. Either way, a hefty storm like that was rare for Southern California, especially during the summer season. The outside temperature read eighty-two on the copter's digital readout, so the air felt muggy, the ground was saturated, and the rain came down in relentless buckets.

A mother with an umbrella and small children ran along a sidewalk about a block away, but there were no other pedestrians near the site. A GMC truck sat on the inclined pavement with what looked like a Chrysler Neon in front of it.

The reverse lights of the Chrysler Neon shone bright white, and a gray GMC truck spun all four of its wheels as it pushed the Neon, stopped for only a moment, and then moved forward as though the Neon were nothing more than a giant cotton ball. The big gray beast had fully rammed the tiny Neon into the floodwaters with little effort. Puffs of diesel exhaust the size of basketballs spewed out from the truck's tailpipe, propelling the makeshift killing machine toward the channel.

From the helicopter, Doug zoomed in on the vehicles and watched the scene unfold via their 4k monitor inside the cockpit. The mudflow sucked the Neon like a Snickers bar down a toilet bowl. The GMC truck bumper licked the floodwaters, then reversed back up the hill.

✳

Out of instinct, Carlie and Kristen tried to push open their doors, but the outside water pressure had trapped them inside as the water level splashed onto the windows. With rasping breaths, they screamed from inside Kristen's car. Their windows were up, which kept the inside dry. For now.

Carlie yelled into her phone to her dad, begging him to come save her. With astonishing speed, the muddy water rushed over the car and the engine died. The dashboard lights flickered briefly and went black. The two women were stuck in a slow-moving vehicle, plodding downstream, off of the pavement, and down another several feet into the earthen channel that abutted the dip. The fierce momentum of the flow shoved the Neon sideways, perpendicular to the roadway. The noise of the gravel and fist-sized rocks hitting the side of the car made a deafening noise, and the air smelled of wet earth. Carlie looked up to a blue helicopter floating above them.

The chocolate-milkshake-colored water climbed up over the top of the side and front windows. If they stayed in the car, it would entomb them within minutes.

Carlie could not hear anything her dad was saying, so she dropped her phone and tried to find a way out, hoping, praying for a miracle.

CHAPTER 58

"Carlie? Carlie?!" Jake yelled. A tidal wave of fear blasted him to numbness as the line went dead and a full body tremor hit him. He squeezed his eyes shut, then pulled his foot off the gas. Paige grabbed the wheel, guiding them onto the shoulder and up onto a weed-infested embankment before the coming to an abrupt stop. In rapid sequence, images of his little angel flashed before his eyes as a constant stream of memories flowed through him starting with when she first popped out of Cynthia. They were both so beautiful that day. Anything seemed possible. All of her soccer games, reading at night, jammy time, going out to their favorite pizza place, high school dances, homework, college admissions, college graduation. Tears broke through and slid down his cheeks. *Is this the end of my sweet baby girl? No!*

I need to go back.

Jake opened his eyes, grabbed the wheel, floored the accelerator and lunged the car forward, pulled off the hill and made a U-turn.

Paige told him to stop. "Dude, what the hell are you doing?"

As the adrenaline pumped through his veins, he managed one word. "Carlie."

Even with Jake's well-trained mind, even after all he had been through in life, all of the education he had, all of the training, all of the experiences, none of it helped at that moment. Jake Bendel had failed his daughter.

Every cell in his body wanted to save her, but he knew deep down it would be impossible to travel the sixty-mile gap in any reasonable amount of time. He pondered how he had let this happen.

Without looking at Paige, he drew in a deep breath and blathered how Carlie was trapped and Michael, one of Viktor's accomplices, was pushing her into a flood in Pasadena.

"I know you don't want to hear this, but look at it logically," Paige said. "There's nothing you can do. We're over an hour away from Pasadena right now." She tried to sound empathetic but failed miserably. He appreciated her effort. "We need to try to stop Viktor. Save millions of people. There's a bigger picture here, Jake. You know it."

Jake covered his face with his hands and moaned. His exhausted body told him to run to Carlie.

"You're asking me to make a decision between saving my daughter and saving millions of people?" No way he could engineer a solution to that.

Fear, anger, dread, and remorse ran haywire with random thoughts of Carlie's past, his marriage, the Sûr System, and Viktor, overwhelming him. For a moment he went into a trance, his heart raced, and his stomach felt heavy as his brain took over the situation to figure out a plan.

Jake's old friend logic had been good to him over the years. Better than his experiences in dealing with emotions. He trusted logic. He knew, for example, that getting emotional would shut down the frontal part of his brain, which was the powerful, logical, intelligent part. Getting emotional served no purpose. Feelings would do no good right now. *Stay focused, stay alert.*

Logically, he knew Paige spoke the truth. At sixty miles away from Carlie, even if he could wave his magic wand and get into a small airplane, flying an average speed of 120 miles per hour, it would still be a thirty-minute trip to get to Pasadena. By that time, Carlie would be dead. The feelings and emotions welled up again and he shoved them back down.

He had become ensnared in Viktor's trap. Viktor's face appeared as an indelible image plastered in front of him.

Jake had only one course of action available but didn't want to believe it. Daughters were precious gifts to dads. He'd focused too hard on catching Viktor.

Time slowed and Jake remembered his dream—Everton's theory about where ideas come from.

One appeared: Cavanaugh had mentioned yesterday about his younger brother being a fireman. Where did he work? Maybe the guy was on duty.

He snapped back to reality, called Cavanaugh, and for once he answered right away. A miracle.

"Tell me where you are," Cavanaugh said.

"Carlie's in Pasadena near our rental property, at the flood control channel, being pushed into a flood. Contact your brother to save her. You said he worked in that area."

"They're out in the fire truck looking for rescue opportunities. I have her cell number. I'll run a trace . . ." *static* hit the line, ". . . then give Dan a call then and text *static, static* the address of Viktor's house."

Unbelievable.

He tossed the phone to Paige and said, "Hope he said what I think he said. Total torture. Let's keep heading up the hill." He skirted onto the highway, then floored the Mustang.

Over the next thirty minutes, he twisted his way through extreme mental anguish, thoughts of Carlie consuming him. He could tell Paige wanted to talk, but she knew he was a nervous wreck. His hands still shook as an angry fire raged deep in his belly.

The phone vibrated. Paige looked down. Missed call. Must've been out of range.

Jake kept driving. East of the dam was State Route 18, a windy road with lots of back-and-forth turns. Not the ideal conditions for getting somewhere fast.

"This is where the sick son of a bitch is operating from, I can feel it." Pine trees flew by as Jake sped and wound his way along the mountain highway.

"Got a voicemail from Cavanaugh. Shitty-ass reception up here," Paige said as she put the phone on speaker and played the message.

"Tracking Carlie's location, put a call in to my brother. Found the property, will send a text of it to you in a sec. Was owned by the Engel family trust back in the eighties. Deed of trust paid off in eighty-two . . . no bank liens on the property. Here's something weird, says it was sold four years ago to a

corporation, a subsidiary of an LLC owned by a separate offshore corporation. Still trying to crack the code and stop the CDM2. I swear we've got half the bureau's IT experts working on this right now. Call me when you get this message."

"Crap," Jake said. "The CDM2 is scheduled to happen in less than thirty minutes."

A text message came through. Paige looked down at the phone. "You're never gonna believe the address. No flippin' way this is a coincidence. It's gotta be him."

CHAPTER 59

Professor Everton greeted Cavanaugh outside the server farm in the center of the Cal Poly campus.

"Ah, yes, you must be the young FBI Agent Cavanaugh," the professor said, putting his hand out.

"Get me inside. Now," Cavanaugh said without shaking. "Your guy, Dave, he inside already?"

Everton nodded as he swiped his security badge over the scanner reader. A red light turned green, the device made a beep, and the door clicked.

Cavanaugh shoved the door open and spied the inside of the massive room the size of a basketball court, with white paint on the walls and server racks, load balancers, routers, and redundant data-storage devices jammed from floor to ceiling. Tiny white, red, green, and yellow lights blipped on and off by the thousands, covering the front of each rack. The air inside was easily forty degrees cooler than outside, and, as Cavanaugh stepped toward the closest rack, he found Dave sitting on the tile floor with his laptop, a blue cable hard-wired into one of the servers.

A cold shiver came over Cavanaugh. He noticed the entire lower rear of Dave's head was a sloppy mop of tangled hair and sweat.

"Nice to see you again, Slicer," Cavanaugh said, strolling over to Dave's makeshift work area.

Without looking up, Dave made a grunting noise and continued typing inhumanly fast.

"Tell me where we're at," Cavanaugh said.

Over the hum of hundreds of fans, Dave said, "We've confirmed this is where the cloned system is operating from and there's a jamming device somewhere close by that's preventing any of us from using our cell phones. But I'm gonna try using the outbound internet connection here to chat with Jake. I'm almost in, but won't know exactly what we need to do to shut the system down for a bit."

"I'm going to unplug this whole thing and be done with it. Too risky," Cavanaugh said.

Dave stopped typing, looked up at him, shaking his head. "Not an option, dude. I suggested that to Jake, and he said there's a dead man's switch."

Cavanaugh waited for an explanation.

"According to the algorithm on this cloned system, if we try pulling the plug, the system will automatically run the death snippet and we'll have CDM2, so to avoid that, we do not, under any circumstances, pull the plug." Dave looked back at his computer and continued typing.

"Christ Almighty," Cavanaugh said, spinning around with his hands on his hips. He whipped out his new cell phone and checked the signal strength. Zero. He rubbed his forehead, thinking of what to do next. He was no help to Dave, and without his cell phone, he was unable to communicate with the other members of his rogue team, so he decided to leave.

But before he could take a step toward the door—at 3:46 p.m.—fourteen minutes before the scheduled unfolding of what would, by any measure, be the worst human disaster in the history of mankind, David "Dave" Cornelius Trainer achieved a hacking milestone.

"Got it!" Dave yelled, stopping Cavanaugh. "I've reverse-engineered a double-encrypted, triple-security layered subset of the code and revealed the proverbial ticking time bomb. Unfortunately, I have no way of altering the code. Two minutes ago I discovered the system requires positive digital identification, a fingerprint from one of the members of the Super Six."

"You're joking. Five of the team members are dead, and Jake's fingers are somewhere up in Big Bear sixty miles away."

Dave shook his head and texted Jake.

Cavanaugh kicked one of the servers. "Is the fingerprint all we need?"

"Essentially," Dave said. "I rewrote a portion of the algorithm that would have effectively eliminated Viktor's instructions for the CDM2. This is like doing digital surgery to eliminate a tumor, but unfortunately, I don't have a write-level security clearance and without it, I can't access the original script and overwrite it. Basically, I know exactly what to do, but I'm at a dead-end without write-level access, so right now there's no way to stop the CDM2."

"So that's it then, we just give up? There's got to be

something else we can do. Think, man, think. You're the Slicer!" Cavanaugh said.

Dave stood, rubbed his face with his hands, and hammered his fist onto a small desk stuffed in a corner. He looked desperate to find a possible solution. "I need Jake's fingerprint and we have a window of fewer than fourteen minutes. God help us."

An idea hit Cavanaugh. "Maybe I can go get one of the bodies of the other five. Scan one of their fingerprints and send it to you."

Dave cringed. "Dude, no way, not enough time. Plus, the news said they were all burned beyond recognition anyway."

Beads of sweat formed on Dave's brow, dripping down past his eyelids and into his eyes. He wiped the perspiration away with his forearm as he stared at the screen. Precious minutes ticked away. The two men stood inside the server room and searched for a solution.

Nothing.

Checkmate.

CHAPTER 60

In the server farm, Cavanaugh stepped toward Dave. "Tell me Jake has an idea. Please."

Nine minutes remained until the scheduled trigger of the CDM2 attack. "He does. Just messaged me back." He read the message as he spoke. "Jake says he's driving around in Big Bear, but what if he could somehow get a digital image of his thumbprint to us? This would take Jake's location completely out of the equation. If we're lucky, the security system would analyze it the same as a live print." Dave rubbed his chin. "He's right. I do know quite a bit about how modern fingerprint scanners work—they take a high-res photo of a fingerprint and compare the loops, whorls, and arches to determine the identity."

Everton stuck his head inside the room and yelled in a panic, "Three angry men are coming down the hall with what looks like automatic weapons!"

Cavanaugh ran to the door and looked down the hallway.

As soon as one of the men, Shankle, made eye contact with

Cavanaugh, the ADIC barked, "There he is!" The other two men, dressed in black jeans and long-sleeved black shirts, sped from a jog to a full sprint.

Cavanaugh recognized the three agents as his boss and two agents loyal to Shankle. Both crooked as an arthritic finger and mean as shit, they opened fire as they ran.

Cavanaugh grabbed Everton by his shirt, yanked him into the room behind him, pulled the Glock 22 from inside his jacket, and fired off all fifteen rounds in his magazine before slamming the door shut and locking it.

"Jesus! You're not helping, Mr. Agent Man," Dave said, fingers shaking.

Cavanaugh jogged to Dave and shook his shoulder. "What you said a second ago about the fingerprint idea. All the security training I've had, that should work. Now hurry up and do it. Do something!"

Dave went back to work on his laptop, talking aloud, clearly nervous. "I remember a snippet of code I wrote a couple of months ago as part of a hack for a corporate client." He typed so fast his fingers were only a blur, but he talked while he searched for the files.

"Professor, please tell me this door is bulletproof," Cavanaugh said.

The professor shrugged. "No idea. I work in the civil engineering department, I—hey, wait a sec. Yes, it is. I helped design this building. Yes. Yes! My goodness, I almost forgot."

Cavanaugh checked the lock. He felt the agents on the other side banging on the door, working the handle.

One of the agents yelled through the door, "You dumb ass!

You shot Shankle! You can't stay in there forever. You only have a few minutes left until . . ."

Dave talked mostly to himself in the background as he worked. "They asked me to remotely break into their mainframe. Of course, with my skill set and experience, it was a breeze. The program fit like a perfect little key and unlocked the database to the entire company. It worked super smooth, and I'm gonna try to use it here. If not, we're screwed, gambling with the lives of thirty million people and with the odds totally against us. No pressure." He wiped the sweat out of his eyes with his wet forearm.

Cavanaugh dropped the empty magazine, reloaded a fresh one with fifteen more rounds, and chambered the first. He walked to Dave and stood behind him.

Every second counted. With bloodshot eyes, and the weight of so many lives in the balance, Dave explained—as he typed—to Cavanaugh each step as he hunted for and found the old file he had worked on, opened the code, and tweaked it into a self-installing app. He messaged Jake.

"Shit. What are we going to do now? It's three fifty-five." Cavanaugh's instincts told him to open the door and waste the two losers outside. When he was done, he'd find Viktor and shoot him dead. *Jesus, did I shoot my boss? He had it coming. Doesn't matter.*

Dave closed his eyes for a moment.

"Try again. Send the message again. Keep doing it. Go," Cavanaugh told Dave.

Jake replied via instant message:

Dave, we got five minutes left. What the hell is this app?

What am I—

Dave replied: *The app will run on your Android FBI. Click and let it automatically install. Then click the big green button and put your right thumb in front of the camera lens, about ½". The app will do the rest . . .*

Everton joined the huddle and the three men waited for Jake to respond.

✳

"What's going on? Like, what does he want us to do?" Paige asked.

"He sent me an app that will take a picture of my thumb-print to get access to the cloned server," Jake said, knowing full well he was the only remaining soul on earth with security access to make modifications to the algorithm. "Probably why Viktor wanted me dead."

While his body trembled, he rubbed his right hand down his leg, then read the big white numbers on the dashboard: 3:57. His heart skipped a beat. Paige had proven herself an exceedingly competent navigator as they arrived at the base of a dirt road that led to a cabin in Sugarloaf, just outside Big Bear.

Jake had tried calling Cavanaugh several times to find out if Carlie was alive, but it went to voicemail each time.

They turned off the paved highway and wended their way up a rutted, curvy, unmaintained dirt road to an area nestled in the foothills between the relatively flat area of Sugarloaf and Moonridge. Ford Mustangs were not designed for off-roading, but the car performed like a beast. Jake parked about fifty yards away from the southern-facing side of the house for the address Cavanaugh had given them: 1776 Christian Way, where a medium-sized poo-brown log cabin with a pine-green asphalt roof sat in the center of the tree-cleared property.

Dust billowed all around them, the storm hadn't arrived yet in Big Bear. Jake hunched over and studied his phone. The app installed itself and opened twenty seconds later, but Jake didn't see a green button. There was only a red button on the screen.

"Oh no, there's no frickin' green button."

Paige leaned over. "Click the red one, that's got to be the right one. We're totally out of time."

Jake clicked the red button while holding his right thumb in front of the camera, which flashed bright light for an instant. The screen went black for several seconds, then came back on with a rainbow-colored whirling circle in the center. He assumed data was being processed. Jake swiped the app up, then opened his texting app.

Jake: *Done. Tell me what 2 do next*

Jake received no response from Dave.

Jake: *Dave, you still there?*

Jake opened the fingerprint app again. Still only the whirling circle.

His jaw shivered.

Nothing.

CHAPTER 61

With a paltry sixty seconds remaining until thirty million people met their doom, Jake stared at his screen and that stupid whirling icon.

Paige looked at him with wide, darting eyes. "We gotta do something! We can't just sit here."

Jake noticed several drops of sweat descending the side of his flushed face, his heart pounding hard and fast. Adrenaline surged through his veins but had nowhere to go and nothing to do, other than wait with the phone in his lap. No ideas came to mind.

"We need to boost the signal. Here," Paige said, grabbing the phone and climbing onto the roof of the car with her arm straight up in the air.

Jake shook his head, heart racing as four o'clock approached.

A deadline to end all deadlines.

*

Dave received the fingerprint moments later and grabbed a quick glance at his clock. 3:59. *No time.*

Dave opened the fingerprint JPEG image and uploaded it to the security system in an attempt to trick it into thinking Jake's fingertip was physically at a non-existent fingerprint terminal.

Cavanaugh stared at the screen, smoke emanating from his recently fired Glock.

Tick. Tick. Tick.

Cavanaugh thought about the millions of people all over the country zipping along in their cars at sixty-five miles per hour across thousands of miles of automated freeways as part of their daily commute home. None of them—not a single one—knew that their lives were in danger of ending in seconds.

On Dave's screen, a small orange "continue" button popped up. "I'm in," he said.

"Go. Hurry!"

Dave copied and pasted his modified code—the clean code—without Viktor's hellfire instructions for a CDM2 into the cloned system, then pressed the "enter" key to formally submit the change. A small hourglass showed up on his screen and rotated slowly. Dave alternated his focus between the hourglass and the clock on his computer, back and forth, back and forth. A moment later, his computer clock updated to 4:00 p.m., but the hourglass was still spinning.

"Goddamnit. Too late!" Cavanaugh kicked the server again and again and again.

Three full seconds later, a slow-motion eternity, the hourglass stopped rotating.

"Holy. Shit. I didn't make it. People are crashing all across the country right now because of three lousy seconds."

Dave's breathing increased even faster. "I don't feel so well," he said, lying back, down on the glossy concrete floor. He screamed up at the ceiling, "If hell exists, this must be it. I had the responsibility to save those people, and I failed them all. So close." He audibly wept.

Cavanaugh's phone rang. What the . . . ? He answered and someone spoke to him. After a few seconds, Cavanaugh said to the other agent on the phone, "You found the jamming device. Excellent work." A pause. "What do you mean?" Cavanaugh snapped his gaze to Dave. "Get up! I need you to check something."

"It's too late."

"Maybe not."

*

Paige climbed down and sat back in the parked car on the unkempt dirt driveway at the base of the driveway to a run-down cabin in Big Bear. The clock on Jake's phone turned to four o'clock.

Half in a trance, Jake turned to Paige. She knew they hadn't made it. They were powerless to help all of those people. He knew his ideas would have worked if they'd had more time. Those poor people would all die while Jake sat on his ass and waited. A real hero.

The sheer number of deaths was a hard pill to swallow, impossible to comprehend thirty million people dying in a matter of minutes. As smart as Jake claimed to be, wrapping his head around the number proved futile. He figured most people would never believe such massive casualties could occur. Thousands? Maybe. Hundreds of thousands? Probably not. Dozens of millions? No way. He quantified it for himself: about half the total number of people killed in World War Two, dead in a matter of minutes.

Jake maintained his gaze on Paige as the stress hit him. He lowered his chin to his chest and closed his eyes.

That was that. Done. "Viktor wins. Our country loses," Jake said, hanging his head. The walls of a panic attack caved in, and he struggled for air as thoughts of losing his daughter and succumbing to the terrorists filled his mind. He exited the car and slammed the door shut. Two yards from the driver's side of the car, he looked to the sky, put both fists in the air, and yelled as loud as he could, "No!"

Paige had Jake's phone in her hand when it rang. She answered with speakerphone and turned the volume to MAX.

"Jake. I'm back now. Cavanaugh's here with me. Says the cell phone jamming devices have been dismantled. Initially, we missed the cut off by three seconds. Three goddamned seconds, but . . ."

After a brief pause, Jake stepped back toward the car, leaned into the open window and responded with a dry voice. "Still there?"

Jake jumped into the car and he and Paige sat frozen in their seats, listening to the speakerphone, not daring to breathe. Loud, incomprehensible static noise came through the phone, then the call dropped.

"Viktor's still out there somewhere, and"—an infusion of adrenaline hit him when he thought about Carlie—"I still don't know if Carlie is alive or not."

He tried calling Cavanaugh, but the phone read zero bars. Jake slammed the steering wheel with his palm.

Paige looked at Jake. "The prick might be inside this old cabin. C'mon."

Jake drove up the driveway, parked near the Engel family cabin—or at least what used to belong to the Engels—and looked with Paige toward it, as additional anger ignited deep in his soul. He went to the trunk of his car and, with his mind focused on Carlie, grabbed a crowbar. *Nobody kills my wife and daughter, slaughters 30 million Americans, then lives.*

CHAPTER 62

In the pouring Pasadena rain, a fifty-three-year-old woman was in the middle of her daily walk when she heard tires screeching near a flood-control ditch. She whipped out her phone, took a photo of a dark gray GMC 2500 backing up and fleeing the scene of what she assumed to be a traffic accident before a white Neon got sucked into the flood debris. She sent the photo to nine-one-one and texted that the Neon needed help. A dispatch operator had notified the County Fire Department of this, which lead Cavanaugh's brother to call him.

Cavanaugh answered. "Not now, Danny, I gotta—"

"Listen to me, bro, we located a white car at the spot you said to check," Daniel told him. "Plus a call came in over nine-one-one with a photo of the license plate of a gray pickup that apparently fled the scene. I'm heading there now."

Back at his desk at the FBI building, Cavanaugh zoomed in on the photo of the truck, entered the plates into their database, and discovered it belonged to Michael Sanchez. *I knew it!* Cavanaugh flagged the truck as a high-priority target, a possible terrorist subject known as Michael Sanchez, aka Ivory Snow.

A CHP unit driving on the I-210 spotted the truck and before long, a high-speed chase ensued on various Los Angeles freeways.

The FBI ordered the cops to capture Sanchez alive—possible hostage situation, figuring Carlie might be with Sanchez—but Cavanaugh knew every single man with a badge and gun wanted him dead. Every last one of them. These were local cops from the Los Angeles area, the ones on the front lines when fifty-seven hundred drivers were killed in the first CDM attack the previous month. They were the ones who dealt with the grieving families, the loss, the tragedy of it all. That attack hit home on a deep, personal level, and they wanted revenge. Badly.

As a co-conspirator of one of the FBI's most-wanted terrorists, Michael had been an integral part of the plot to kill millions of innocent Americans. The FBI told the cops this guy was involved in the CDM attack too, so Cavanaugh knew the wall of testosterone and rage chasing Michael Sanchez flushed any chance of him living down the toilet.

✳

Viktor sent Michael a text at 4:03 p.m. saying his part of the plan had failed.

Viktor: *We're compromised by FBI*
Thx for your work brother
Last 4 years been great

Know you want 2 relish fame & martyrdom
but play it safe
get out of country
We will rise again
and be glorious 4 Allah!

✳

Hovering in the ABC-7 chopper above the I-605, Bobby and Doug followed the action, sending a live feed back to the station.

"Roger that," the FBI helicopter pilot said over the emergency COM frequency, as Bobby listened in. "Suspect heading south on the 605 in a dark gray GMC 2500 truck." The message went out to more than fifty squad cars and two additional police helicopters in the pursuit of terrorist Michael Sanchez. A minute later three LA County Sheriff and LAPD helicopters joined the chase.

Now that the power outage had ended, Carol told Bobby about the record number of viewers watching the scene, which was like the O.J. Simpson chase on steroids.

"This is our big chance, Doug. We need to zip down there and get my face in front of a million viewers." Bobby checked his hair in a hand mirror. "Tell me again how these guys found out about this S.O.B," Bobby said into his headset to the helicopter pilot.

"I've been listening to the scanner all day, and this Sanchez dickhead was spotted by the CHP doing over ninety miles per hour on the paved shoulder of eastbound I-210. While they chased him, the officer punched in the plates, and within minutes four other patrol cars joined in. Now look at them. Half the cops in SoCal are chasing that stupid little shit."

Bobby sensed a shocker of a story as the chase wound through the Baldwin Park area on the I-605, with the cops pursuing one of the deadliest terrorists to ever inhabit American soil. *Police live for this shit.*

"My sheriff buddy told me some FBI dude named Cavanaugh had provided all local law enforcement agencies critical information so they'd know who they're up against." Bobby watched the monitor inside the chopper as Doug captured the unfolding events with his camera beneath their copter. Whatever level of education or training the man driving the GMC truck had, nothing could have prepared him for his new role of being hunted like a fox by more than fifty bloodhounds.

"Negative. No other passengers in the truck. Single passenger only. Repeat, single passenger only," someone on the police scanner said.

Sanchez took the Beverly Boulevard exit, two law enforcement helicopters followed him, and Bobby imagined the sweat squirting from the guy's facial pores like a leaky faucet, dripping down his cheeks onto his lap as he drove.

The terrorist sped eastward into the hills, drenched from the downpour, probably in search of a fire road.

"They always think they'll have a chance to flee the damned cops if they make it to the foothills," Doug said. "He'll kick in the four-by-four and haul ass up the fire road where some overhanging trees might block our view of him, but that's all temporary."

"Total moron, this guy. No matter, we're gonna be famous

thanks to him," Bobby said with a high five.

From the ABC-7 chopper, Doug captured a close-up as Michael slowed and rounded a corner. The man's eyes were wide open, and he gripped the steering wheel with white knuckles.

The cops chased Michael, racing through the north end of Whittier, as he approached a yellow gate. Mud and debris kicked up behind him as he slammed head-on into the barrier, which kicked to the right, shattering the windshield of the police car behind him and forcing the black and white to roll off the road into a drainage ditch.

Doug said, "Yes, I got that," before Bobby could ask.

The lone terrorist wound his way up the curve-laden fire road into Hellman Wilderness Park, increasing the distance between him and the cops.

"They better not be getting cold feet," Bobby said.

"They ain't," Doug said, pointing down to a large hole in the ground in front of the entire chain of flashing blue and red.

"We've got a problem," one of the helicopter pilots reported on the police band. "The dirt road you're following is flooded out a few hundred yards in front of the truck. That kid ain't gonna make it. Get ready."

A chunk of road had been completely eroded away, with vertical jagged walls and cave-shaped craters. Water drained over the sides into a dark brown soup, exposing layers of clay and cobbles that hadn't seen the light of day in centuries. The open-faced hole made the road impassable.

Michael's truck approached the pit without hitting the brakes, and Bobby's stomach went into his throat when the truck leapt off the edge. The muddy earth disappeared from under Michael's monster tires, the truck dropped like a lead weight, and the truck's nose slammed into the opposite ledge of the crater, the back end of the gray pickup jutting into the air.

Debris exploded across the mini-ravine below as the truck landed vertically on a mound of thick mud, rotated about its lengthwise axis, then slammed down onto its right two tires.

Apparently not wearing a seatbelt, Michael slammed his face against the windshield, cracking the glass into a thousand places, likely shattering every bone in his face.

"Fly around to the side there so we can get a better view of that shit," Doug instructed the pilot as he zoomed in to capture the grisly details of the steering wheel crushed into the driver's chest.

From the looks of the collision and based on Bobby's extensive experience studying and covering car crashes, he guessed Michael Sanchez had lost consciousness within a second and suffered massive internal injuries. "No way he makes it out alive," Bobby said to Doug and the pilot.

Bobby heard Carol in his earpiece. "Dammit, Bobby, start talking. We ain't getting another shot at this. Stop dickin' around."

Bobby cleared his throat, clicked his TV mic on, and began his live report of the scene.

"Two dozen sheriff, CHP, and local PD are jogging with their guns drawn, converging to the accident site. Folks, if you have a weak stomach or children are watching, I recommend you turn away, this is going to get violent."

The camera captured every gritty detail as hundreds of rounds punctured the terrorist's vehicle, many of them sailing through various parts of Michael's limp body.

The copter pilot flew north, then swung around for a better view as Doug zoomed in through the windshield to highlight Michael, now lying across the seat, with dark-red blood spilling out onto the interior of the once-shiny truck. The bullets had hit each of Michael's four limbs, turning his torso into Swiss cheese.

"According to our anonymous source, this man played an instrumental part in planning and implementing what would have been the worst terror attack in our country's history. It appears that this terrorist is now dead."

An army of officers approached the truck, reloaded their guns as they stepped, crouched and cautious, down into the hole next to the truck. Several cops peered inside.

"It appears officials below are satisfied this threat has been neutralized. Bobby Jones reporting live from Air-7, now back to you."

CHAPTER 63

A faint trace of smoke lifted from the cabin's river-rock chimney toward the crystal-blue sky. Overgrown California wild roses intertwined with fireweed, cow parsnip, and other naturally growing weeds in a small meadow out front, and the place looked unkempt for decades. Pine trees surrounded the entire perimeter of the property, so the cabin had no worthwhile views from the interior. No neighboring houses could be seen either. Jake assumed there were neighbors out there somewhere, but none within shouting distance, for sure. A sense of foreboding came over him and the hair on his forearms stood up.

He thought back to one of his classes at Cal Poly when he fell in love with structural engineering in Timber Design. All that could be done with wood fascinated him. As he stared at the home, images popped into his mind of the interlocking log corner, the lapped lock notch, and the sheer strength of the glued logs, and he calculated a rough ballpark for the insulating factor of the walls. Nobody outside the structure would hear a muffled scream from inside.

"I hope Viktor's in there," Jake said, snatching the pistol from the rear seat, then stuffing it into the small of his back.

Paige exited the car and stood in front of Jake. "Wait a sec. Someone's watching us. I don't like this." Paige turned and peered at the cabin. "I don't know, dude. If this is Viktor's war room, he might just want to let everyone think it's not his anymore. We should call the cops."

Jake looked at the phone. "Still don't have a signal. I'm going to keep dialing Cavanaugh while I walk up to the front door."

"Wait," Paige said, grabbing his arm. "I know you have a crazy amount of anger and vengeance in you right now, but are you sure you want to kill him? Take another man's life? You do and that shit's gonna haunt you for the rest of your days." She took a step closer. "We need to recalculate your end game here. Instead of you and me with this old school vigilante shit, let the FBI bring this asshole to justice."

He swiped his arm away from her grasp, stormed away from the car, kicked a rat-sized rock into the floral abyss, then took a few steps on the dirt driveway—but pain shot up from his knees. The drive up had taken over two hours, and the car accident yesterday made every joint stiff and painful to move. He drew in a big gulp of air, pumping more oxygen into his lungs, knowing his tight muscles would need the energy to beat the living crap out of Viktor.

But he stopped and, with fists tight, fingernails biting into his palms, walked back to Paige's side of the car. "Get back in the car." He opened her door and she sat. "Stay right here. Roll up the windows and lock the doors. Keep trying Cavanaugh on your phone. Here are the keys. If I'm not back in two minutes, call nine-one-one and drive back down the hill."

"But—"

Jake put his hand up and bared his teeth. She understood.

He turned and walked toward the front porch, almost eager to break the neck of the man responsible for all his pain. It felt good. Like scratching an itch. Revenge had marinated deep into every cell of his being and his focus was razor-sharp.

It was time to checkmate his opponent and end this sick game.

As he turned the corner, out of Paige's sight-line, the smell of rotting flesh hit him. A dead cat lay off to the side of the porch, hundreds of flies buzzing around it.

He stepped up an old set of wooden stairs, each one making a creaking sound. His phone showed one signal bar. He decided to dial Cavanaugh one last time, but instead of a regular voice call, he used the video chat app, thinking that might get Cavanaugh's attention. With the phone held in his left hand, it rang as he scanned the area. A rustling noise came from around the corner where the car was parked and he assumed Paige was walking around. *Gee whiz, I told her to stay put.* He took a step back toward the corner of the porch, but before he could see the car, the front door of the cabin flew open and a man poked his head out.

Jake turned to the man, but when he jumped back onto the top step, his foot punctured through rotten wood, he lost his balance and waved his arms to keep from falling onto his butt. After catching his balance, he turned to the man in the doorway, who had a calm appearance. Not Viktor.

Instinct told Jake to run, but he pulled his foot up from beneath the broken step and held his ground. The man had curly black hair and a well-trimmed beard, wore a white T-shirt with the words "IN MY DEFENSE I WAS LEFT UNSUPERVISED," and smelled heavily of Polo cologne.

"Can I help you?" the man said in a deep-pitched, smoker tone, breathing harder than Jake would have expected. His English was good, but since Jake had worked with thousands of Middle Eastern engineers over the years, he knew the accent the moment he heard it: Syrian.

"I'm sorry to bother you, sir, my name is Mike Smith. I'm working with some real estate investors in the area and was wondering if you were interested in selling your house." Jake had to figure out a way inside. He knew this guy was working with Viktor somehow. Perhaps a low-ranking grunt.

Before Jake could formulate a plan, the man put out his hand to shake. "We are. Thank you for coming by. I'm Amir Jones."

Out of habit, Jake put his hand out. The man's hand was cupped more than expected for a typical handshake.

"Hello? Hello?" came through Jake's phone. In his nervousness, he'd failed to notice Cavanaugh had picked up the face-chat call. Jake put the phone up to his ear rather than look at the video feed of Cavanaugh's face on the screen while shaking Amir's hand.

"Hi, Cavanaugh, it's me. Great timing! I'm up at the cabin you're interested in buying." When he tried to pull his hand back away from Amr, the man continued to squeeze—hard—and held an extra few seconds. Another surge of adrenaline dumped into Jake's bloodstream.

The smile on Amir's face disappeared, replaced by a scowl.

"Jake, we found Carlie, she was trapped in the car underwater and is—"

A numbness started in his hand, then his wrist, then his forearm, inching its way up to his neck, then down his other arm. The hand holding the phone fell to his side.

Amir ended the shake and pulled back his right hand, which had a small, wet-looking piece of paper in his palm. A full suite of panic symptoms hit Jake.

Three men appeared from behind Amir, who stepped out of the doorway, then stood next to Jake. Each man wore black-and-gray camouflage pants and jackets, kneepads, and gloves. With their assault rifles aimed at Jake, they stepped slowly toward him, but he was initially unable to move. Fight, flight, or freeze. Apparently, his primitive brain chose freeze and only his knees shook. Without realizing it, Jake stumbled backward, then tried to take a sidestep toward the stairs, but the numbness had worked its way down through his quads, calves, and toes.

His heartbeat slowed as a sense of queasiness came over him, along with a strong urge to sleep. Without hearing another word from Cavanaugh about Carlie, the phone slid from Jake's hand, spanked a wood plank of the patio deck, bounced, and rotated, landing on its back. Struggling to keep his eyelids open, Jake looked into Amir's eyes. Somehow, Jake kept his balance, standing, wavering—barely.

With labored breathing, he sent orders to his legs, arms, neck, or mouth, but nothing happened. No movement. He tried to lift his arm up behind him to pull out the pistol, but it, too, failed to respond. His eyelids felt like stones were tied to them, pulling them down.

Amir laughed in his face, but Jake only heard weird echo-chamber noises. "Now you have high dose of my custom paralytic in your infidel veins, injected with nano-paper here." Amir revealed the paper in his hand. "It cut many holes into your skin, just deep enough to do the job."

"Perimeter's clear, Syed," said one of the para-military grunts to Amir.

With a squint, Syed nodded. "Please, Dr. Bendel, say hello to my friends from your federal government. You need to see what you are up against. Stupid insect." Syed looked into Jake's eyes, smiled, and lightly shoved him.

Jake collapsed like a stringless puppet onto the dusty wood porch.

CHAPTER 64

Inside the locked Cal Poly server vault, Cavanaugh stood next to Dave and the professor, all three gawking at Cavanaugh's phone as the entire Big Bear scene unfolded from the vantage point inside Jake's phone on the porch. They had a front-row seat, but looking up from the steps made for an odd view.

Cavanaugh recognized the man opposite Jake as Syed Farook, the Syrian funding partner of Viktor Johnston. He also recognized the three men in black—all former colleagues of his, all paramilitary contract mercenaries, or 'mercs' as they liked to be called. All loyal to Shankle.

An ISIS cell was in Big Bear, with three traitorous ex-federal agents.

✳

Syed had resisted Viktor's idea of playing the chess game with the infidels and thought it quite absurd, totally unnecessary. He'd foreseen the Allah-haters who ran the corrupt, sinful, and disgusting country figuring out the chess references for the attacks—to the pawn, rook, bishop, knight, and queen. He wondered if they'd guessed the reference to the king.

Syed found true joy in watching his enemies slaughtered. After he'd witnessed his parents get blown to pieces by US troops when he was a young boy, the seed of hatred grew each time another obese, entitled, arrogant American smiled at him. Blood, death, and suffering fed the fire of his inner hatred. One night years ago, Allah had spoken to him in a dream, telling him he had two biological brothers, they would work together to bring down the infidel, and the jihad would be won.

The next day he'd begun his search for Viktor, spending countless hours over several years, and taking detailed steps to recruit his older brother to their cause, only to find Viktor was a sinning maniac and crazy as battery acid. Viktor had funding partners, so Syed went along with the hope Allah would give praise to their cause. Syed and his ISIS brethren only wanted to fight the jihad and score a victory for Islam, the one true religion on Earth.

Now, on the cabin porch, he looked down at Jake's limp body. "Please help pull this shit inside." Syed directed the three ex-federal agents, two former DEA, one former ATF, all well-paid mercenaries, to each grab ahold of Jake.

Veins popped out on Syed's arms as he grabbed Jake's legs at his ankles and, with the help of the agents, pulled Jake's body inside the cabin. They dumped him next to the woman on the floor. After Jake had left his helpless female companion alone, two of the ex-agents had lured her out of the Mustang with their counterfeit badges, overpowered her, and eliminated her from the equation with a dose of chloroform doused on a handkerchief. Syed knew she'd be easy to approach, way too trusting. All women were idiots that way. *Typical stupid Christian bitch.*

Standing inside the cabin with the front door open and two bodies lying on the living room floor, Syed instructed two of the mercs to get back outside on guard duty while he called Viktor. As much as Syed wanted to blast bullets through the skulls of the two drugged heathens, he knew Viktor had a secret plan. At least for Jake.

He called Viktor. "Jake and the bitch are subdued. They caused enough headache for us, my brother. It is time for wood chipper."

"Allah is shining down on us today, brother Syed," Viktor responded. "No wood chipper. I have something far more glorious in store for them, and you shall be rewarded for your efforts. I'll double your fee."

"Tell me where to take them so I can be done and over with this."

"We are truly blessed and are in his grace. B-b-bring them to me, alive, at the Big Bear airport. Thirty minutes. I'll have the plane f-f-fueled and ready to go."

"As you wish, brother. Allah is the one true God." Syed ended the call and turned to the ex-agent standing next to him. "Wait here while I get truck. Watch these two. Shoot in legs if they move."

The agent nodded.

Syed hustled out the front door, jogged to the north side of the house and into the woods where he'd hidden their green Toyota Tundra. A squirrel stood perched on an old rotten tree trunk and cocked his head, curious, but Syed whipped out his .357 and scared it away.

He threw open the driver door, jumped in, fired up the engine, and raced to the house. Mud kicked up underneath as he backed up the truck and parked it perpendicular to the front porch. Inside the cabin, he grabbed his duffle bag from the floor, removed a ball of twine, and tossed it to a former agent.

"Tie her hands behind her back and stuff red foam ball in her mouth," Syed told one of the mercs as he wrapped a burka around her head before swiping the car keys from her pants and pocketing them. Once finished, the two men picked her up. As they carried her out toward the truck, her head slammed against the entryway. The lack of response confirmed she was still unconscious, and they tossed her limp body into the truck bed.

Syed radioed the two ex-agents posted outside. "Any signs?"

"Negative," the digital voice responded.

"Stay alert. These two idiots found us, assume more shall follow soon." Syed rushed back inside the cabin with a merc to get Jake. They looked down at the unconscious engineer. The twine he used to tie Paige's hands would probably not work on Jake. Again, Syed scooped up his duffle bag from the corner, dug inside, and pulled out a set of handcuffs.

The two men wasted several precious minutes jostling the unconscious body in order to get Jake's hands behind his back. Syed grunted with frustration.

In the interest of time, he secured Jake's hands in front, locked the handcuffs around his wrists, then shoved the same type of gag ball into his mouth as he'd used for the woman.

The two men heaved Jake's limp body over their shoulders, carried him out to the truck, and slammed Jake ass-first on the tailgate before unfolding his torso backward and letting his head bash down onto the truck bed. Underneath the porch, Syed found and pulled out two blue, spider-infested tarps. He threw them on top of the two bodies and, with the help of the merc, used bungee cords to tie the four corners to the truck-bed hooks. He stopped and pondered what to do with the Mustang.

"Here," Syed said, tossing the car keys to his favorite merc. "Get your men and follow to airport." Syed climbed into the Tundra and headed down the dirt road with the two bodies rolling around in the back of his truck. He figured by the time anyone discovered what happened to the two infidels, he, Viktor, and his brother Michael Sanchez would be safe back in Syria.

CHAPTER 65

Jake always dreamed of taking a Bahaman cruise with his family. While spending a lazy day at the pool on the upper deck, he relished how good life had been to them. *Man, that sky is so blue. Crazy blue.* A deeper hue of blue than he'd ever seen before.

He turned to ask Carlie if she'd ever seen a sky so radiant, but she had disappeared. Only an empty lounge chair remained. He looked around. The deck was void of all passengers. He turned his head back to the sky, and the color blossomed ever bluer. The sound of a calm ocean breeze morphed into the clankity-clank of the back of a pickup truck.

The dreamy mirage slipped away as his physical world gave way to a new reality and he regained consciousness. His body sloshed back and forth in a truck bed, underneath an opaque blue tarp. The truck tossed him around like a number-ten bowling pin. A soft, smooth object was jammed into his mouth and he labored to breathe through his nose.

With a tingling sensation in his extremities, he tried to move his legs. No response. They felt like two large lead logs.

A few moments later, his toes and fingers awoke, ready to accept his commands. A painful tightness cramped his wrists, and although his arms were intact, they still failed to respond.

His most recent memory appeared of the man at Viktor's cabin. *Syed.* Jake had never met him or seen a photo of him, but he knew. The way their eyes had met during the handshake. The cold, murderous gaze of a twisted, mass-murdering terrorist.

A massive, two-and-a-half-inch-long black widow spider dangled inches from Jake's face, trying to grab hold of his nose. *Jesus!* Jake's eyes opened wide in panic. Several white cotton-ball egg sacs clung to the tarp nearby, bundled next to their mother.

Don't panic. Slow breaths. Stay calm.

He tried focusing on feeling the subtler sensations of the ride. A bump here, a bump there, a turn here, a turn there. Gravel kicked up by the tires splattered underneath the bed of the truck as they barreled down some road. Seconds later the noises smoothed out, the frequency of the tires rolling on the road increased, the volume decreased and, compared to the dirt road, the ride became silky. He guessed they had transitioned onto pavement, so he pictured a map of the Big Bear area and recalled the dirt road they'd driven up to Viktor's cabin. The driver quickly accelerated, and Jake estimated they were doing about fifty miles per hour. Only the main road had design speeds that fast, so he deduced if he'd been unconscious for less than five minutes, they must be on Highway 38. Based on the new pitch of the truck, they were driving on a descending grade, which meant they were probably heading north toward the lake.

With the black widow hovering in front of his face, his mind wandered, trying to figure out what to do, but the grogginess made it difficult. He worked to control his breathing. *Nice and slow.* If he started to thrash, he would trigger panic and end up with hypoxia, because mucous would form in his nose, then block the airflow of oxygen through his nostrils. *Slow and steady.*

Eventually Jake felt his arms and legs waking from their slumber. His legs felt free of any bindings.

Paige. Where is she? And Carlie? Is she alive? What about the CDM2? What happened? His breathing increased again and he struggled with the effort to regain his calm.

Airplane pistons and props roared, increasing in volume, twirling at high revolutions per minute, biting through the air. The truck approached what Jake assumed to be the airport.

He knew little about Syed, but if he was anything like Viktor, he was a psychotic extremist hell-bent on casting a death net over the country.

The tip of Jake's left foot sensed an object. Rubber? Foam? He tapped on the item a few times, which felt like a heavy sponge. His arms now alive, he moved his hands up toward his face, batted the spider away, removed the gag, then lifted his head to get a better view of the object adjacent to his feet. A migraine panged the rear right of his skull.

Dim gray sunlight filtered through the tarp, casting a blue hue over the pale cheeks of his friend, Paige. He tried to wake her by shoving her left shoulder with his feet. Out cold.

With no response from Paige, he waited, a weighed-down feeling covering his entire body, his mind racing through various scenarios. Viktor probably had plans to kill him; the only question was how.

The truck's speed bled off, and then they hit a quick dip in the road that bounced the truck nose to tail, rocking-horse style like they'd entered a driveway. The driver downshifted again, then the truck cruised forward in a lower gear till they came to a full stop. What sounded like a gate rolled open. The truck jerked sideways as it drove onto what he assumed would be the tarmac. After what felt like a quarter mile, the truck stopped and the driver turned off the engine. Another vehicle pulled up beside the truck bed.

The truck's driver-side door opened as the man got out and slammed the door shut, wobbling the truck. "They're here, under tarp."

A familiar voice said, "Good to see you, my b-b-brother." A voice that sounded exactly like Viktor, but without the lacing of anger and frustration.

Jake closed his eyes and played dead, figuring this would give him the best chance at survival, but he still lacked any plan for escape. Air whooshed over him as the tarp lifted open. Through his closed eyes, the light changed from a blue hue to bright red as it passed through the blood in his eyelids. A spider landed on his cheek, started crawling toward his ear, and every cell in Jake's body wanted to move, run away, scream, but he overrode his instincts and remained motionless.

"In Allah's glory," Viktor pronounced, holding up the tarp like a museum curator unveiling an ancient sculpture. "Syed, you have done well to b-b-bring two of Satan's children to me. Behold, the world-famous civil engineer responsible for all those domestic, deadly attacks on America. I have a fitting d-d-death planned for this sin-worshiper. He will be dropped from this plane, down onto a famous interchange in the middle of LA called 'The Stack,' one of the first multi-level interchanges b-b-built by the infidels back in the forties."

"You have great way with symbolism, my brother," Syed said as he opened the tailgate.

"It will be a fitting end to this man's p-p-pursuits," Viktor replied. "An old interchange and a dead civil engineer. The media will assume someone f-f-found and murdered him out of revenge for killing thousands on the 405."

"I still wish we used full brake for the first attack," Syed said. "Would have been better. Would have killed sixty thousand infidels."

The spider crawled onto Jake's earlobe and stopped. With great discipline, Jake continued to play dead.

"It was n-n-not Allah's will to do so, brother." Viktor snapped his fingers. "You three, help Syed g-g-get this body into the airplane so he can stare into the face of Satan firsthand."

"You want us to stand guard here, sir?" said a man in perfect American English.

"Yes, you stand guard while we m-m-move these two into the airplane," Viktor said.

Jake listened as the five men walked away. With his head near the cabin of the truck and feet touching the tailgate, he flicked the spider off his ear, pinched it to death with the tarp, then snuck a peek down over his legs. A plane taxied in the distance a hundred yards to his south, and the two military men stood in a fifteen-yard perimeter, guns aimed at the ground.

Jake lifted his torso and grabbed a quick glance over the side of the truck bed to confirm his captors. The truck was parked several yards away from the door of a twin turboprop, where Viktor, Syed, and one of the men from the cabin stood near the airplane door, talking.

When three of the men returned a moment later, two of them, one probably Syed because he was taller and stronger than Viktor, hopped up onto the truck bed and lifted Jake under his armpits. Jake squinted his right eye for another peek as the camouflage guy grabbed his legs. With his cuffed hands lying on his lap, Jake let the two men carry him out of the truck bed and up three stair steps into the fuselage of the King Air. After they propped him into one of the two rear seats, he purposely leaned to his right to convince them the drugs were still in effect. One of the men pushed him upright and fastened the seatbelt over his waist.

"Why put his seatbelt on?" Syed asked the man. "He's going to die soon."

"Sorry. Habit."

Jake slumped over with his eyes closed, pretending to be drugged, while he subtly tested muscles throughout his body to make sure the paralyzing effects of the drug were fully withdrawn.

The plane wobbled as two men entered.

"Here's the bitch, Viktor."

Three men stood next to Jake. "This woman infidel, we need to send her st-st-straight to hell. I know you want to take her back to the cabin and get rid of her using the w-w-wood chipper to eliminate all evidence. But she's going to die alongside her engineer friend here. It is Allah's will," Viktor said in a cold, unemotional voice.

"If it is Allah's will," Syed said with a head bow.

"Before Bridgette died, she did a b-b-background check on our little friend here," Viktor said. "Turns out her father is a civil engineer at Cal Poly and was involved with the FBI investigation into me back in the eighties. If that man had not called the police, none of this would have ever happened. In a way, I guess I should thank him. But we'll send him a nice m-m-message anyway by dropping his daughter onto the same interchange with Bendel."

A new pain emerged from Jake's jaw as the three men exited the aircraft, leaving Jake alone with Paige.

Jake tried to move his jaw around, recognized the sensation, and stopped. This was the second time he'd hurt his jaw. The first was during a high school football game. *Great, a migraine and a bruised jaw. A nice pairing with my bruised ribs.*

Jake opened his eyes and surveilled his new surroundings. Paige sat next to him on his right, still unconscious. Six beige leather seats filled the plane's interior, two for the pilot and copilot and four for the passengers. Six circular windows lined the fuselage, three on each side, and the only way out was through the open door behind him to his left. He looked around for anything to use as a possible weapon. Not a damned thing. A small table jutted out from the side of the plane into the passenger area, presumably designed to hold a map, a cup of coffee, or a snack. Several parachutes lay piled on the floor next to a lumpy gray wool blanket. Out the window, he read a small guide sign with the words "Big Bear Airport." He'd flown fifteen hours in a similar model aircraft when getting his instrument rating seven years ago.

He reached behind him for the pistol. Gone. He thought about doing a surprise attack. Stand next to the door and jump on whoever came through next. *They have guns and I have no weapon, plus I'm handcuffed, and they might kill Paige. Long odds, but I have no other choice.*

His heart leapt from his chest, providing the energy he needed to prevent them from killing Paige. He'd roped her into this mess, so surprise attack it was.

But before he could act, the thump-thump-thump of a helicopter echoed all around the plane, reminding him of the sound he heard yesterday at the I-710 after Bridgette drank the poison.

"Stay where you are, do not move," a man called on a loudspeaker. "Drop your weapons and move away from the truck. This is the FBI. You are all under arrest."

Jake's instincts told him to make a run for it, but he couldn't leave Paige behind.

"Go. Go, Viktor, get rid of the engineer. We don't have time. We make our stand right here against the infidels," Syed said, pushing Viktor toward the plane, before turning toward the three mercenaries near him and barking orders to get into position for a gun battle. "We get these sinners," Syed said. "Wait 'til they see the two AK-12 Kalashnikov rifles and four extra drum magazines with hundred rounds each." He let out a low, bellowing laugh. "Go. Now."

Over the thunder of the helicopter chop and the crackle of semi-automatic gunshots, Jake felt the plane wobble again as

Viktor ran up the airplane steps. Head down, Jake slit one of his eyes open while Viktor closed the hatch, then walked between Jake and Paige, around the table toward the cockpit, holding a pistol in his left hand.

The high-pitched whine of airplane engines starting up was followed by more automatic weapon fire from multiple guns, then the frequency of the two turbo-props increased in pitch.

Viktor slid a green headset onto his head.

From the window on his left, Jake spotted two black FBI helicopters, one landing to the side as several armed agents hopped out, all decked out in full SWAT gear, firing toward the truck.

To have any chance at overpowering Viktor, Jake needed to get out of the handcuffs. He looked down at them—Peerless brand—and scanned the floor and seats of the airplane for anything he might use to pick the lock.

Like an arrow hitting its target dead-center, a memory flashed into Jake's head of the paperclip from the hospital paperwork. He adjusted the cuffs higher on his arm so his fingers could reach to the bottom of his left shirt pocket, then withdrew the thin metal item. He straightened the paperclip, inserted the clip into the keyhole of the handcuffs, and bent the tip ninety degrees. This made a small "L" shape at the end of the clip. When Carlie was in middle school practicing for a magic show, they'd done the maneuver hundreds of times and perfected it.

Jake twisted the clip so it released the internal latches, then pop, the jaw of the left cuff opened. He repeated the same procedure for the right cuff as the engine hum from outside shrouded out any noise Jake made with the handcuffs. He leaned down, grabbed the old blanket, and used it to hide his uncuffed hands.

But the instant he leaned back in his chair, the window to Jake's left exploded, followed by a surge of white-hot pain in his left shoulder.

"Attention G-men in the helicopters. This is Viktor Johnston. I have two hostages and will be taking off now. Get your copter out of my way or I put a b-b-bullet in each of their skulls. You have five seconds. Four. Three . . ."

The plane's engines roared, revving up to full speed. Warm liquid oozed from Jake's shoulder, flowing down the outside of his left arm. He peeked at the dark red blood, which looked like his shoulder had a nosebleed. *Shot by the FBI! Broken window won't affect Viktor taking off, but without pressurization can't climb to more than eleven thousand feet.* Jake jerked backward in his seat as the plane lunged forward across the tarmac. Viktor taxied the trio toward runway two-six, an airstrip Jake had used dozens of times as a pilot. The volume of the gun battle decreased.

Jake shifted in his seat to prepare for takeoff, calculating whether or not to charge Viktor, but with the pistol in the hand of the psycho, the attempt from a distance would be too risky. He needed close quarters. Hand-to-hand. But with only one useful arm, also risky.

In an effort to put the agonizing pain out of his mind, he focused on his wife and daughter, and a wave of renewed energy flowed through him.

The two five-hundred-fifty horsepower Pratt and Whitney

engines thundered as the mass-murderer pilot revved the engines spinning the four-blade props.

Jake's body gravitated back against the leather seat as the aircraft accelerated westward down the runway. At what felt like ninety knots, Viktor pulled back on the yoke to rotate the plane up, and the airplane jumped off the runway, ascending into the sky.

CHAPTER 66

As long as Viktor piloted the plane, Jake would never be able to take control of the situation. He needed to get Viktor out of the cockpit—and soon—if he had any chance for success, so as they climbed through what Jake estimated to be about ten thousand feet over the San Bernardino Mountains, he moaned and cocked his head back but kept his eyes partially open to simulate coming out of the effects of whatever paralysis drug Syed had given him.

Viktor turned around, pointing his pistol at Jake. "Well, well, well, Jakey Boy. Didn't expect you'd be awake just yet." Then he faced front. "Didn't expect you to be awake again. Ever."

"Vkt, I tht yood, ahh . . ." Jake mumbled through a sore jaw, purposely incoherent.

"I loved my father, well, step-father. Was killed by a civil engineer. Never found out which one, exactly, but you represent all the evil that civil engineers do onto this world."

"Wha—"

"Jakey, I'm gonna level the plane, slow it down to a hundred knots, trim it, and set the automatic pilot to descend to f-f-four-thousand five hundred feet."

Good for you, you sick son of a bitch.

Viktor stood, hunched over to avoid hitting his head on the low-ceiling, then stalked toward Jake. "You know why?"

Jake shook his head, slowly.

Viktor continued. "You get to be famous all over again. But this time, as a dead engineer. Not sure how you stopped us, b-b-but Allah's not happy with you."

The news both froze Jake's heart and simultaneously adrenalized it, knowing the possibility existed that Dave's efforts an hour earlier saved the lives of millions. *But was Viktor telling the truth?*

"Allah, buh I?" Jake asked with a slur, eyes barely open.

"The moral spine of this country will continue to d-d-decline into Satan's abyss. There's no escape for you. Any of you. Four years of planning, and you robbed me of my grand finale." He walked past Jake, still pointing the gun at him, then over towards the door. "Well, I guess we can rejoice in knowing the spirit of your dead daughter is now with Allah. My brother, Michael, pushed her into a flood and she drowned, just like I promised you yesterday." He grabbed the handle and plunged open the hatch behind Jake's seat.

Jake expected the pressure in the cabin to drop, but with a window already out of commission, the pressure remained constant. The outside air rushed by at the same speed as a hurricane wind, increasing the noise level.

Viktor returned to Jake, leaned over his prisoner and laughed, all the while keeping the gun aimed at Jake's torso.

Yelling over the noise of the rushing air, Viktor said, "The gas tanks are half full. I'm flying us out to LA. Once the autopilot drops us to four thousand five hundred, you lose. You get two in your chest, and I'm going to send a message to the world by dumping your dead carcass out the d-d-door so you'll splatter all over one of your favorite interch—"

"Tell me why," Jake slurred, loudly.

Viktor grinned. "You Americans should be g-g-giving your lives to the great Allah, the one true god, instead of p-p-utting your lives in the hands of some artificial intelligence system. People like me will always be here to expose your flaws. You can't engineer your way out of t-t-traffic congestion any more than you can dig your way out of all the other problems your country has."

"It was about saving lives. Saving money. Saving lives."

"And look how wonderful that turned out for you, J-J-Jakey B—"

Without another thought, Jake grabbed at the gun with his only working arm and fought to get the advantage over Viktor. With the lives of both men in the balance, the gun fired. The bullet missed Paige's nose by inches, and a middle window on the opposite side of the plane exploded while the two men battled.

Jake glanced at Paige to see if she was conscious. Not yet. Viktor drove against him with greater strength than he expected. Jake elbowed Viktor in his gut.

They pushed each other from one side of the airplane to the other until Viktor grabbed Jake's working wrist and twisted clockwise. Jake bent over in a feint and then thrust his torso upward, striking Viktor, knocking him against a seat. Viktor pounded on Jake's gunshot wound. Jake howled, then head-butted Viktor's face, which busted open like a water balloon full of blood. A surge of pain bolted through Jake's jaw.

But Viktor lost his balance, grabbing the ceiling to stabilize himself. The gun dropped to the floor and slid to the back of the plane. Jake kicked Viktor's knee from the side, grabbed him by the front of his shirt, and pulled his assailant down as he fell.

Staring down at Jake with his bloody face, Viktor's hands went for Jake's throat. Jake struggled for air as he grabbed Viktor's balls and twisted till Viktor released his grasp on Jake's neck, crying out several obscenities before falling sideways to the floor.

Jake stood, coughing, sucking in gulps of air as he kicked Viktor twice in his gut before turning, lunging toward the rear of the plane and grabbing the gun.

He pointed the weapon at Viktor, who put his left hand up. "You got me, Jakey Boy." He grinned a yellow-toothed smile before spitting a mouthful of blood and mucous onto the leather seat.

Every cell in Jake's body wanted to pull the trigger and waste his enemy, the man who'd murdered his wife and daughter. Jake had fought so hard to get to this point, but now the moment had arrived, before he could shoot, his wife's voice spoke to him, softly. "You're better than this, honey. I know you're hurting, but don't become the darkness you hate. Killing Viktor will not bring us back."

Jake slammed into his own sense of self, so consumed with the desire to erase Viktor from his life that he'd lost track of who he was inside. Professor Everton's advice about good and evil all pelted him at once.

Jake Bendel is not a murderer.

Jake began to lower his arm, but the psychopath sensed weakness and lunged at him one last time. The gun still in his right hand, Jake crunched his right knee into Viktor's stomach. The old man let out a low guttural noise and stopped. Jake shoved him forward toward the seats, where he crashed against the back of the rear seat before dropping onto the floor near the pile of parachutes.

A pocket of turbulence jolted the plane, forcing Jake to his knees, toward the rear of the craft. He lost sight of Viktor, but only for a second.

By the time Jake rose and faced Viktor, the man's right arm had become wrapped outside the open door. The air sucked his torso out the plane, bent him over at the waist, keeping his lower body in a horizontal position inside, trapped. Viktor's legs kicked along the fuselage wall for traction.

Paige's mouth flew open and she let out a gasp. *She's awake!*

Viktor was horizontally scissor-wrapped in the doorway. Hundred-mile-per-hour winds pushed the top half of his body toward the rear of the plane.

I'm not a murderer. Viktor had cast considerable evil onto the planet and inflicted pain to many, many people. He deserved to die, but not right now. Not if Jake could save him. *Let karma take care of him.*

Jake reached down to grab Viktor's left foot and pull his enemy back into the plane, but when he did, Viktor kicked Jake as though he didn't want to be saved, only to be set free.

Jake took another grab and Viktor thrust his foot so hard into Jake's bloody shoulder that he knocked him on his ass, then the air sucked Viktor's body out of the plane. One second the psycho's legs were there dangling on the wall, the next instant, his entire body: Gone.

CHAPTER 67

Jake leapt to the fuselage doorway, grabbed ahold of the frame, and watched Viktor's spinning body fall toward the earth.

Nothing I could do . . . I tried to save him for the sake of my own integrity. For my wife. For Carlie. For justice.

With a solid heave, Jake tried to pull the door closed and reset the lock, but the air pressure differential combined with high-velocity winds prevented him, so he let go, knowing he'd have to land the plane with the door open. The blustery swooshing noise pounded his eardrums as he bent over and caught his breath near the pile of parachutes. The pile had toppled over. Jake or Viktor must have kicked it during their struggle. Jake counted the parachutes. Three. *Were there originally three parachutes or four?*

He stood over Paige, peeled off the gag, untied the twine around her wrists, and nudged her shoulder. Her eyes bolted open. She grabbed both armrests with a death grip, looked up at Jake.

"Jesus. My head's frickin' killing me," she said, rubbing

her temples. Jake gave a Cliff's notes version of how they ended up on the plane. She gave him an urgent gaze and said, "So tell me you know how to fly this thing."

The plane now floated at a low, near-stall speed somewhere above the southern face of the foothills near the San Gabriel Mountains with nobody at the controls, only the autopilot computer in charge.

"Once a pilot, always a pilot. Come on. Need a copilot." He motioned to her and she stood, followed him to the cockpit, and the two sat.

After they'd taken the front two seats, he thought about putting a parachute on each of their backs and making a jump for it.

Not today. They had zero parachute training, so risking their lives to jump out of a perfectly good plane was an example of living, breathing insanity. He could land this baby. Probably.

One thing he knew for certain: flying a multi-engine airplane required more experience than flying one with a single engine. He'd completed hundreds of successful landings in smaller craft and knew the various factors involved, but with only a handful of hours flying multis, he calculated the risk level as high.

He knew he might be a rusty pilot with nausea, a headache, two bruised ribs, a bruised jaw, and a bleeding, throbbing gunshot wound in his left shoulder, but he hoped his flying skills would come back fast. They *needed* to come back fast.

As Jake locked in the shoulder harness, he decided to

contact air traffic control with a mayday signal, the international distress signal derived from the French m'aidez, meaning "help me." *Wish it was a day in May when I was back on the ground instead of in this flying deathtrap.*

He adjusted the seat, cautious to avoid hitting or touching sensitive controls, and slid on a headset. Viktor had set the airplane's controls on autopilot, but Jake was unfamiliar with how that system operated.

He faced the six-pack, the vital, most basic level of instruments needed for safe flying: airspeed indicator, heading, vertical speed indicator, turn coordinator, attitude indicator, altimeter. *Familiar. Good.* Like riding a bike.

The frequency on communications radio number one—COM1—read a sequence of numbers. Pilots usually stuffed a laminated cheat sheet somewhere within reach, so he fumbled his hands below, searching under the seat, nothing, then inside the pocket on the left interior wall. Success! He found one down near his left foot, noted several SoCal Approach frequencies, then tuned the radio to the top one on the list: 124.50 Mhz. A woman's voice came over the radio into his headset. ". . . heavy, descending through one-zero-five, with delta . . ."

The aviation industry frowned upon pilots who stepped on or interrupted other pilot communications, but this emergency took priority.

With the shoulder pain throbbing hard, he shifted in his seat and pushed the red 'talk' button on the yoke. "Mayday. Mayday. Mayday. This is Jake Bendel, I'm flying over what looks like maybe West Covina, about fifteen miles east of Los Angeles in a twin-engine airplane, Beechcraft, two souls on board, holding steady at vector two-seven-zero, altitude seven thousand, autopilot engaged. Request landing assistance to nearest runway, please. I have a private pilot's license but haven't flown in several years. Our pilot is . . . no longer on board."

Seconds passed without a reply. Maybe he had the wrong frequency? He tuned the COM2 to the dedicated emergency frequency of 121.5 and repeated his plea for help in an uncertain tone. Nothing.

He turned to Paige. "They're supposed to plow the field when a pilot calls in a mayday." He squished his eyebrows together and glanced around the cockpit.

After switching back to COM1, he pushed the talk button again and spoke into the black mic near his mouth. "I am working with FBI Special Agent Jose Cavanaugh. We took off from Big Bear and need assistance with landing. This is not a joke or stunt. We need help now. Anyone copy?"

The two engineers floated along for another minute. He noticed a sliver of sun peeking out from behind a wall of dense rain clouds, then looked down at his shoulder. A fresh wave of blood was trickling down his arm.

"Dr. Bendel, roger that," a deep male voice said. "This is SoCal Approach. My name is Richard. We have you on radar and will be handling your landing to LAX. We've confirmed with Agent Cavanaugh. Stand by for further instructions."

"Roger," Jake replied, his mind flooding with memories of airplane jargon that experienced, safe pilots used every day to communicate with each other.

After an eternity, Richard's voice returned and asked Jake if there was an operating manual in the wall pocket next to his left ankle. He recalled how all planes always need to have this with them for emergencies exactly like this one, as he dug around and found a one-inch-thick, white paperback with the words "Pilot's Operating Manual," a black outline of the Beechcraft C90 on the cover, and blue-and-red stripes. "Got it."

"What does it say on the front cover? I need to know which type of Beechcraft plane you're flying. Copy?"

"Roger." He held up the book and flipped through it. "Beechcraft King Air C90." Jake alternated between glancing at the key velocities table in the book and the horizon in front of him.

The rays of sunshine widened through various cloud openings below, which provided a brief series of peeks to the fabric of land below.

"Stand by, we're pulling up those specs right now."

"Roger that." Jake pictured the man as an elderly Neil Diamond, with a thick black mustache and a half-smoked cigarette in his hand. He imagined having a beer with him and Cavanaugh when this fiasco was all over, sharing "close-call" stories and laughing till they got good and drunk.

Some light turbulence hit the airplane and Jake's anxiety kicked up a notch. He looked at Paige, who'd covered her face with her hands.

"I'm back," said Richard. "What's your current airspeed?"

"One hundred five knots."

"Great. You need to stay above seventy-eight, that's your stall speed. Do you see the two black knobs to your lower right?"

Jake scanned the cockpit panel, adjusted his headset, then winced at a fresh pang from his shoulder. "Yes."

"Those are your two engine throttles. Move them up and down, just like you would for a Cessna, which I'm assuming is what you were trained on."

"Yes, just like a Cessna, keep them the same. Roger that." Jake wiped his brow with his forearm.

"If you need more throttle, push them forward. To throttle back, pull them back down toward you. Copy?"

Jake's toes nestled against the two foot pedals, and he tested the yaw by pushing each one in an alternating sequence. The plane's nose pointed more left, then right, then straight again.

"Yes, ten-four."

"Now, Jake, you're going to turn off the automatic pilot. The basics of flying the plane you're in are just like a Cessna. Slow the plane down by pitching up, increase the speed by pitching down. Use the throttle sparingly when you're landing. You've probably had hundreds of landings. It's a similar procedure when coming in for an extended final approach. Do you understand?"

"Right, so no downwind or base, just final. You're just gonna set me on a vector to come straight into one of the runways at LAX, correct?" His jaw gave him a reminder of its condition with every word he spoke.

Paige pulled her knees up to her chin and wrapped her arms around her shins.

"Exactly. Disengage the automatic pilot. Below the center console, between the two seats, there's a button labeled

A-P-E-N-G. That stands for autopilot engage. I want you to press it one time and confirm."

Jake found the small rectangular black button with a yellow backlight down to his right and pushed. The backlight turned off, but nothing happened. He pushed the yoke in and the plane pitched down. He pulled it back to correct, rotated the yoke left and right to get a feel for the plane, which felt like a heavy Cessna. "Okay, autopilot disengaged, my controls."

"Excellent. Now I want you to slowly turn toward a heading of two-two-five. Keep her level, same speed, nice and easy. I have you on radar, don't worry," Richard said.

"Turning to heading two-two-five," Jake said as he slowly rotated the yoke to the left while keeping his altitude level. The airplane rotated toward the left, and the horizon turned to a ten-degree angle in front of them. An increased g-force pulled him down into his seat and another pang hit his shoulder.

With the aircraft now on the proper heading and tracked by air traffic control, Richard continued his instructions. "Excellent work, Jake. In about three minutes, we'll have you turn onto your final heading of two-five-zero. Right now, I want you to pull the throttle back to twelve hundred rpm and pitch down a bit until you are descending at four hundred feet per minute with an airspeed of one hundred knots."

Jake's field of vision began to spin. He'd lost too much blood.

"Paige, I need you to take off your belt and tie it around my shoulder before we get too much closer to landing," he said.

"Thought you'd never ask," she said, not missing a beat. As Paige half-stood, pushing her hand into her seat back, she undid her belt buckle and slid out the thin, red-leather belt from around her waist.

Jake responded to Richard. "Roger that, pulling throttle back to twelve hundred."

His right hand grabbed hold of both black throttle knobs and slid them down until the engine rpm's slowed to twelve hundred. "Pitching down . . . vertical descent at four hundred."

Jake leaned forward and Paige reached over to his left arm and attempted to wrap her belt around his shoulder just above the bullet wound, but she lost her balance and fell onto Jake's back, which pushed the yoke forward. The plane pitched down and for a second they felt weightless. Their rate of descent increased to over a thousand feet per minute. Jake's stomach jumped up into his throat as he tried to pull back on the yoke, but his left arm had gone numb. He pulled with his right hand, trying to keep the plane level, but Paige had lost her balance and was pushing him forward with her entire body weight.

Jake winced. "Get off! We're gonna be in a nose dive if you don't get off me."

"Almost got it," she said as she finished tying off the belt around his shoulder. "There." She pushed one final time off Jake's back and sat back in the co-pilot's seat.

Jake pulled back on the yoke and leveled the plane, but they had lost over five hundred feet in precious altitude.

He turned to Paige. "You got one hell of an ability to concentrate. Jesus." She grabbed a second headset hanging in front of her, plugged the jack into the dashboard, put the headset over her ears, brought her knees back up to her chin and assumed her sitting fetal position.

"Talk to me, Jake," Richard said. "You lost altitude."

"We didn't want to make this too easy for you," Jake replied. The plane had leveled off, then Jake continued his controlled descent.

"Roger that," Richard said.

Every few seconds Jake's eyes switched between the digital clock readout on the dashboard and the watch his wife had gifted him for their twentieth anniversary. The first minute passed by like a full moon rising above the eastern horizon, and he found himself rocking in place, rechecking the six-pack instruments in clockwise sequence: airspeed, horizon and pitch, alt, vertical speed. The second minute he wanted to crawl out of his skin, lean back and kick his feet through the windshield. He could barely keep his ass nailed to the leather seat. At least the sweat trickling down his spine created enough glue to hold him in place. That and his desire to keep every bone in Paige's body intact.

After another minute of mind-numbing silence, Richard came back on the radio. "Jake, I now want you to turn slightly to your right to bearing two-five-zero. This will be your final approach to LAX. Any second now you should see the runways. There are two of them. Pick either one. We have all traffic holding until you land. The entire airport is yours."

"Well, that's sure nice of them," Paige said.

"Okay, turning right to heading two-five-zero." He rotated the Beechcraft toward LAX and again the horizon turned at an angle, giving him a view of the miniature residences and office buildings on the ground. Surrounded by passing pockets of opaque clumps of mist hanging from the sky, Jake swerved his craft around them like dodging floating land mines.

On the proper heading, descending at a suitable rate through three thousand two hundred feet above sea level, he estimated his location at about ten miles east of LAX. By now he should have had a clear view of the LAX runway, but saw only sparkling rays of sunshine refracting through the sporadic haze. He scanned the earth in front of him, searching for parallel lights on the runway. Still nothing, not one runway. The remnants of the storm had left a cloud cover and some pelting rain as he descended toward what he hoped would be LAX in the distance.

"SoCal Approach, I am on a heading of two-five-zero, but I do not see the runways. Repeat, do not see runways. A large cloud formation is blocking my view."

Every ounce of Jake's body told him not to fly into the cloud. Jake had only been certified to fly with Visual Flight Rules—VFR—where the FAA had strict rules that prohibited flying through clouds. Unless the pilot was instrument rated. He'd wanted to continue getting his instrument, or IFR, rating, which would have trained him to fly through clouds—a perfect skill to have right now—but with family and work, he had never found the time.

"Will have to do a go-around," Jake said, fighting the urge to squeeze his eyes shut as the dark cloud approached.

"Jake, you gotta do this," Paige said. "We can be on the ground in one minute. Just fly through those damned things."

"I want to be on the ground too, just not in a million pieces," Jake said.

"Negative. Do not go around," Richard said. "The runways are on the other side of those clouds, I promise you. You're doing a great job, you are on the proper heading and flying the plane like a pro. You're going to fly right through those clouds, you understand?"

Jake heard the man from ATC say to fly through, but an instinct to stay alive throbbed strongly inside. He throttled back, thinking of Cynthia. *What should I do? I wish you were here with me.*

Without saying a word, he received Cynthia's message to trust the ATC. *Fly through the clouds. Land the plane. Be strong. Do it for her.*

Jake sat up in his seat, refocused his eyes on the clouds dead ahead, and overrode the will of his physical being.

"Roger that, flying through the clouds now." As the plane entered the dark mist, everything outside—the city streets below, the warehouse district, the mountain range in the distance to the right—all disappeared, replaced by pure gray haze in the front and side windows. Without visual confirmation of the plane's movement, Jake felt like they were still on the ground, not moving, flying blind.

His vision narrowed further, which only made his heart beat faster as his anxiety level spiked, and he blew out a series of short breaths to gain control before a full-blown panic attack hit him. With immense determination, he focused on the six-pack to make sure he kept the plane steady, but dizziness came over him. Even with the homemade belt tourniquet, he knew he'd lost too much blood, and time was short before he'd lose consciousness from lack of oxygen.

Turbulence tossed the plane around like a pair of jeans in a dryer and jolted him back to reality.

The dark gray clouds began to disintegrate, turning to pale gray that eventually gave way to a gentle fog and mist on the windshield as the lights from LAX came into view. Flight training taught him what the appropriate glide path looked like, and the plane was dead on, which boosted his confidence. He straightened his posture and stared at the two welcoming, gigantic, well-lit runways waiting to take him into their arms. He lined up the plane on the perfect vector with the left runway. At two miles out, he read the writing on the concrete at the front of the runway: "25L," meaning the left runway at heading two-five-zero, or 250 degrees clockwise from zero, or north. He descended out of the sky toward the ground and took a deep, calming breath to stay focused. *You got this, Jake. Almost there.*

"Nice and easy, Jake. That's one big-ass runway in front of us. Take your time," Paige said.

When their plane was a mile away from the runway, Richard chimed in, "Continue descending at four hundred feet per minute, and once you are above the runway numbers, pull the throttle back to idle and coast in. Don't rush it, just let the airspeed bleed off. Keep your nose up the whole time. You have plenty of runway. Confirm."

"Roger."

Jake had been busy making micro-adjustments to the yoke and rudder with the foot pedals. Richard was correct, flying this plane was like the smaller ones on which he'd trained. Down, down, down the craft went, lower and lower, until he sensed what pilots referred to as the cushioning of the "ground effect."

The plane floated for a few seconds, and when the wheels chirped onto the runway, he started to breathe again and he knew Paige would live to see another day. But he relaxed too soon and the plane jumped back up off the runway. A second later, the wings lost their lift, a stall warning buzzer blared into his ears, then the wheels of the plane slammed onto the runway. Hard. Not his best landing, but back on terra firma in one piece.

He pulled all the way back on the yoke, remembering to steer the plane using the foot pedals now that the plane was on the ground. When he pushed the tops of the brake pedals with his toes, the nose of the plane rocked forward and down, and the front wheel crushed onto the runway.

Jake applied even brake pressure with his feet, watching with amazement as the airspeed indicator rotated counter-clockwise from eighty knots to zero, which meant no more forward motion. Full stop. *We're still in one piece. Holy crap.* He knew there were probably a number of different buttons and switches he needed to click before he killed the engines, but screw it. He slid both throttles all the way down to idle, rotated the ignition key to the "off" position, and listened as the engines shut down.

"You son of a bitch," Paige said. She shook Jake's good shoulder with excitement.

Fire trucks, ambulances, and an assortment of other emergency vehicles approached their plane from all directions, lights flashing red and amber.

"That was fun," Jake said.

"I can't wait to never, ever do that again," Paige said.

CHAPTER 68

"We need to get outta here." Jake took Paige's arm and helped her hobble out of the plane.

Gratitude filled his entire body as he stepped onto the pavement, but his knees gave out. Like a Muslim praying toward Mecca, he put both hands on the pavement, bowed his head, and kissed the wet asphalt.

When he tried to stand, his eyes rolled up into his head and he felt a strong urge to pass out.

The sirens wound down and the sounds of quick-paced footsteps hit his ears. At least a dozen black-clothed, fully armed SWAT officers surrounded the plane. Confused and unsure if they were there to help or arrest him, he sat still with his gaze faced downward but didn't care either way. Several trotted past him and boarded the plane.

One agent stuck his head back out of the plane. "The plane's empty, sir."

Jake looked up. Cavanaugh. The agent strolled up to Jake with his hands on his hips, shaking his head. He stared at Jake and, with a curt nod, said, "The guy's a goddamned magician.

I know that sick son of a bitch was with you when you took off from Big Bear, and now he's not on the plane."

"You'll need to recover the body."

"We need to find Viktor and—holy crap, you've been shot." Cavanaugh waved to the paramedics.

Paramedics rushed over to attend to his gunshot wound.

"Somewhere above West Covina, I think." He looked up at Cavanaugh and read the confusion wrinkling his brow. "He fell out of the plane."

"Jesus!"

"I came to," Jake said. "We fought. Was me and Paige or him. I chose us. His gun's still on the plane." Jake ran his fingers through his hair.

Cavanaugh dialed a number into his cell. "Yeah, fire up a search team out to West Covina to look for a body . . . Uh-huh, the body of Viktor Johnston, aka Viktor Engel aka Marion Engel. Give me an update every hour on the hour until he's found. We need confirmation that this guy is dead."

Still catching his breath, Jake asked, "And the CDM2?"

"I think I'll let the Slicer tell you what happened," Cavanaugh said, turning, as Dave strolled up from behind.

"Holy Jesus, it worked, dude. Oh, my God. Right after our call ended, the system showed everyone still going sixty-five miles per hour. No brakes were applied. No chessboard pattern. Every shred of Viktor's code was officially wiped from the system."

"So we prevented a second CDM attack?" Jake asked, still out of breath. He still had no idea of Carlie's condition and knew Viktor was still out there somewhere, but preventing millions of innocent deaths allowed a shimmer of light into an otherwise dark and dreary moment.

"For a minute there I didn't think we made it."

Paige patted Jake on the back. "Nicely done, gentlemen. You guys saved the lives of countless Americans. National hero time. Wow."

Jake looked up toward Cavanaugh as the medics kept working on his shoulder, cleaning his wound with water and hydrogen peroxide. "I heard a ton of gunfire at the terminal in Big Bear. I'm assuming that was you and your guys."

"The little shit and his three hired mercs put up a good fight. But in the end, they were outnumbered. Even though they had automatic weapons, they fought against over a dozen fully armed and well-trained FBI agents. That stupid-ass Syed ran away from the truck and tried to take cover behind a wall of the hangar. The thing with hangar walls is they're pretty thin. We simply out-gunned his ass and shot right through the wall. Filled him full of holes."

"And apparently one of your bullets went astray and hit my shoulder. Thanks so much. Gives a new meaning to 'taking one for the team,'" Jake said.

"He's lost a lot of blood, sir, but he'll live," said the paramedic as he cleaned off Jake's left forearm and inserted a thick IV needle attached to a saline solution.

"We took out two of the mercs and wounded the third. Bastard's lucky to be alive and knows what kind of shit he's in. We can't get him to shut up."

With Viktor out of the picture, the CDM2 attack averted, and the safe return of Paige to terra firma, his thoughts turned again Carlie.

"I need to know what happened to Carlie, with the flood. If she went quickly. Our call was cut off. Have they been able to recover her—"

"Ask her yourself."

Carlie came running toward him from the terminal, both arms extended in front. "Dad. Daddy!"

The sweetest sound a father could ever hear. He loved it when she called him that, no matter how old she was.

He struggled to stand before she plowed into him, hugging his waist and putting her head across his chest, just like the old days when she was little. She kissed his forehead and cheeks while he squeezed her with what little energy remained in his right arm. Welled up with joy, tears flowed down from Jake's eyes and in his exhausted mind, he was hugging his wife and daughter at the same time.

As he relished the fact his daughter was alive, a blue reporter's van came skidding to a halt not twenty feet from the group, two men jumped out, one with a camera with a bright light on top, and ran toward Jake. The other guy had a mic.

"Let me handle this," Cavanaugh said to Jake before turning to confront the reporter, flashing his FBI creds at the cameraman. "No comment. This is an active crime scene. You need to please leave. Now," he snapped.

The reporter stopped but otherwise ignored the agent's request. He spoke into his ABC-7 microphone: "I'm Bobby Jones with ABC-7. Just a quick word with Dr. Bendel. Why all the secrecy? Why the cover-up? The people have a right to know."

Cavanaugh extended his arm and started to push the two

men back, but Jake intervened. "It's okay, I'd like to talk to this gentleman," Jake said. Cavanaugh stopped and turned to Jake. "Okay, you're the man."

Carlie stood next to her father.

Bobby asked Jake several more annoying questions, including one about the blood streaming down his left arm, but Jake answered with a question of his own. "You're the reporter from up in the High Desert? You filmed us during the senator's assassination, the explosion. The one who didn't help anyone except yourself. Ran the conspiracy piece about me while I was still grieving for my wife, who was murdered by the terrorists," Jake said.

"Yes, when the federal government tries to cover up the death of—"

"The reporter who put his career before the safety of not only my life but the lives of my daughter and my friends?"

Bobby lowered the mic. Carlie stepped in front of her dad, kneed Bobby in the groin and connected a punch to Bobby's nose, likely breaking it into several jagged pieces of cartilage and bone, forcing him to stumble back several steps before kneeling on the ground and spitting gobs of blood onto the pavement.

Cavanaugh pulled Carlie away before she could hurt the sleaze-ball reporter more. "Go on. Get your sorry asses out of here before I have you arrested," Cavanaugh said to the two men, who gathered their equipment and scurried back toward their van.

"That was the move Mom taught you when you were little. Glad you still remember it," Jake said.

Carlie smiled, shaking the sting out of her hand.

"You little shit, I didn't know you could fly." Cavanaugh patted Jake on his good shoulder. The paramedic applied a hefty patch of gauze and tape to Jake's wound.

Cavanaugh had switched gears to a friendly, warmer tone, one Jake hadn't heard during any of the time they'd spent together over the last four days since meeting at the FBI safehouse.

For the first time in years, he felt home again, whole again.

Carlie hugged her dad again. "Careful, sweetie."

Her eyes opened wide and she gasped at the bandage on his left shoulder. "Holy crap, Dad."

"Don't worry, just a scratch." Jake ended the hug, tears streaming now. He stared at his daughter with an outstretched arm. "Carlie, I thought you were—"

At that moment, he made a vow to himself to never lose sight of the most precious thing in life: Family.

"I know. I thought that was the end too, but a few minutes after Michael left us for dead, a fire truck showed up with an extension ladder. A brave fireman named Daniel Cavanaugh risked his life to save me." She looked up to Agent Cavanaugh.

Shaking his head with disbelief, Jake said, "So you escaped unharmed? What about Kristen's car?"

"It's a goner. Buried under several feet of mud. Daniel pulled Kristen up first and, right before her car got sucked away downstream, Daniel pulled me up onto the ladder. Oh my God, Dad, I was hanging there by his arm above that rushing water and, oh, holy crap, he's so strong, he pulled me up onto the ladder like Superman. It was amazing."

Cavanaugh crossed his arms and gleamed like he knew something. Jake turned toward him.

"What?" Jake insisted.

"My little bro. All in a day's work for that guy. I must have done something right raising that pain in the ass."

Jake squinted. "So it's a done deal, the Sûr System—our version on our server—is back online and fully operational and there's no chance in hell of being hacked again?" As much as Jake relished the hefty benefits of having the system in place, the multi-billion-dollar economic stimulus, three thousand lives saved every month because of no more human-caused fatalities, he questioned, again, whether the benefits outweighed the risks, whether mankind should put the lives of so many humans in the digital hands of an artificial intelligence system.

With an upturned face, Cavanaugh leaned in. "And you'll never guess what else we discovered. Our Assistant Director in Charge, Shankle, was the mole. The west coast ISIS terror cell blackmailed him to cooperate with them. They'd kidnapped his wife and told him if he didn't steer us in the wrong direction, they'd slit her throat, but the assholes killed her anyway. The bullet I hit him with was non-fatal, a through-and-through above his left lung. The son of a bitch is gonna live, but he's a goddamned mess. His career's over and he's going to prison for a while."

Jake's eyes went wide. "You shot your superior?"

Cavanaugh nodded. "I can understand why he did it, but he's still facing serious charges," Cavanaugh said. "I called in a favor to an old friend of mine at the AG's office in DC, told him what happened, and asked him for the inside scoop. Turns out Shankle had already been under investigation for the last several months. That was way too close. He'd almost gotten away with treason. After we suck as much useful info out of him about the remaining terrorists, we won't see his ugly face for a long time."

Most of the SWAT team had dissipated, replaced by a new team checking the plane for evidence.

Jake smiled to his buddy Dave, as more footsteps approached. Professor Everton joined the group, embracing Jake and Paige in a big cluster hug. Dave punched Jake in his good shoulder and ruffled Paige's hair.

"Seriously, dude, you have no idea how close we came to missing the deadline on the CDM2. A microsecond. Totally stressed me out. I'm never working with you again." He laughed.

"Dave, we make a pretty good team." Jake wanted to make sure Dave got the proper credit he deserved in front of the FBI. "My logic and ideas combined with your hacking skills saved millions of people. I don't have a brother, but if I did . . ." Jake said, giving his friend another hug.

"The FBI owes you big time. All of you." Cavanaugh turned to Carlie, Paige, and Dave, and said, "Each of you has earned the appreciation of your government and many, many families. Not thirty minutes ago I briefed the President myself and mentioned several of your names. I think you're gonna be visiting DC soon for a more formal appreciation."

"What about all that crap in the news about this being my dad's fault?" Carlie asked. "Sounds like you were maybe able to somehow clear his name?"

"It's all over the news right now how Viktor framed him with the deep fake videos. We issued a national press release that said you were alive and part of an undercover operation essential to national security. Worked like a charm."

"Anything more about Viktor?" Jake asked.

Cavanaugh nodded, saying, "Viktor's birth name was Mohammed Rezwan Farook and he'd been sold as a baby to Mr. and Mrs. Engel, a white Christian family from Houston, Texas. They'd renamed him Marion in honor of his new mother's grandfather. The Engels moved to California when Marion was ten, raised him as their own in their fundamentalist Baptist family, with their two biological sons, until the father was killed in a car accident. While working as a professor at Cal Poly Pomona, he terrorized the country with a computer virus, and ultimately disappeared before we could find him. Shankle worked that case back in the eighties. Figures the guy would get away. Anyway, he changed his name to Viktor Johnston after his mother was killed, also in a car accident."

"So much hatred towards me."

"The working theory is since both his parents died in car accidents, in his twisted mind all civil engineers are to blame. For some reason, he focused in on you. Possibly because of your fame, not sure."

"He eluded to that."

Cavanaugh added, "But that chess theory of yours, Jake . . . you were spot on with who the supposed king was."

"Thanks, but that was my buddy Rayhee's theory. I owe him a lobster dinner and a ton of beers."

EPILOGUE

Two weeks later, while Jake and Carlie waited in line to check their baggage at Port Canaveral, Florida, excitement built inside him in anticipation of boarding their nine-hundred-foot-long ship designed to hold over two thousand passengers. Jake wanted to live and experience the Bahamas for real, unlike the dream he'd had while tumbling around the back of Syed's truck. Jake had invited Carlie to join him on a seven-night, all-expense-paid Bahama cruise to help celebrate Cynthia's life, and to start a healing process necessary for them both to move on with their lives.

Jake had read in the brochure that Port Canaveral was created in the mid-twentieth century to serve the community and provide economic opportunities for the folks in the area. It was located several miles south of the famed Cape Canaveral, which had launched thousands of rockets and missiles since 1950.

The Bendels wore matching blue-and-yellow tank tops and baseball caps, and each toted two large pieces of luggage to check.

Jake turned toward Carlie, and her ecstatic smile said it all. Neither of them had ever been on a cruise before or visited the Bahamas. The weatherman said he expected the weather to be warm, clear, and humid, which would be perfect.

As they shuffled along in the baggage-check line and neared the counter, Carlie turned to her father, took his hands into hers, and said, "Dad, I want to tell you how amazingly proud I am of you. You've always been my hero, and now you're a hero to millions. Guess I'm gonna have to get used to sharing you."

He looked into her eyes with deep admiration, but before he could respond with something profound and return the compliment, his phone rang. "Just a sec, sweetie. Speaking of sharing me with others, I gotta take this," he said, leaving Carlie in line and walking to a more secluded area of the terminal. With sweat drizzling down the center of his back from the Florida humidity, he answered. "Agent Cavanaugh, to what do I owe the pleasure?"

"I know you're on your vacation with Carlie. Good for you guys. I thought you might like to know we've concluded our initial search for Viktor but were unable to find a body. We've gone over this before, but are you absolutely sure the plane was over West Covina when he jumped?"

Jake paused for a moment, gathering his thoughts and memories of the flight. An image of the parachutes popped into his mind. "Maybe there really were four parachutes. I'd been drugged, so maybe my mind was playing tricks on me."

"So there's a possibility he might have grabbed a parachute before he jumped and somehow managed to put it on while falling to earth at over a hundred miles an hour."

"Well, when you put it like that." Jake paused. "He couldn't have made it. No way. His body's out there somewhere, probably just hidden in a bush or tree. Maybe he fell in a lake."

"We can't officially close the file on him until we have a body, and I'd like you to come back and help us with the investigation. We'll all rest a lot easier once we find that damned body."

"I'm in line right now to board the cruise ship. Another week won't hurt anything."

"If you think of anything else, let me know."

"Roger that."

Jake hung up, but when he turned toward Carlie, she'd disappeared from the line. His heart rate quickened again, his pulse throbbing in his neck. *Not again.* He'd thought she'd died in the flood and not enough time had passed since, especially without confirmation Viktor was dead and gone. Jake's dad instincts revved into full hyper-mode.

He stood on his toes and scanned the entirety of the terminal, reviewing the faces, searching for her blue-and-yellow tank top. Nothing. No Carlie.

In a different line, he noticed someone with a similar colored tank top, a fit blonde with a black bikini bottom waiting to board the vessel. She flashed her million-dollar smile at Jake, but he ignored her as a voice in the distance yelled his name. To his left, Carlie waved at him from the baggage-check area. She stood next to a tall, tan man with dark hair.

Jake sighed, relieved, as he hurried to her.

She said, "Dad, this is Daniel Cavanaugh."

Daniel faced Jake and put his hand out to shake, but Jake gave him a solid hug instead, left shoulder still tender, but healing. "Honor to meet you, sir," Daniel said.

"Right back at you. She wouldn't be here right now without you."

They chit-chatted for a few minutes.

"Well, babe," Daniel said, turning to Carlie and giving her one last kiss and hug, "I just wanted to see you off before you left on your cruise. I'll be here waiting for you when you get back. Gonna visit some old college buddies of mine while you're out soaking up the sun." Daniel said his goodbyes to the two Bendels and started walking back toward the terminal entrance.

"Babe?" Jake gave Carlie his best overprotective dad look.

"I have a good feeling about him, Dad. I don't know if it's because he saved my life and I'm suffering from one of those psychological syndromes like the Florence Nightingale effect or whatever, but he's super sweet, tall, and handsome as hell, and great in bed."

"Too much information!"

"Sorry," she said, chuckling. "I'd love to find the right guy and get married and have kids. Maybe you'd like a few grandchildren, Grampa Jake."

Jake liked the sound of that. "Seems like you've really got it bad for this guy."

"Yep." She continued staring at Daniel as he walked away.

Jake dug into his knapsack and pulled out his ticket. As much as he longed to spend the next week talking, healing, and catching up with Carlie, he had a better idea. He went to the ticket counter and managed to convince the cruise line—after a bit of haggling and agreeing to pay extra—to essentially swap his ticket in exchange for one for Daniel.

He handed the new ticket to Carlie, who showed her palms and shrugged. "Why are you doing this?" she asked.

"So you two can go on the cruise. Cruises are a great place for romance."

Her eyes grew wide, that gorgeous smile beamed bright, and she jumped and gave him a bear hug.

"I'm so happy to be your father, Carlie. I know Mom was very proud of the woman you've become."

"Love you too, Dad."

Jake handed her a wad of cash. "For Daniel, so he can buy some clothes, toiletries, whatever."

She ran after Daniel, waving at him and calling his name. Moments later Daniel was back in line next to Jake.

"Are you sure about this, Dr. Bendel?"

"Do you love my daughter?"

Daniel looked into Carlie's eyes, then back to Jake, nodding. "I do."

"Then yes, I'm sure."

Daniel shook Jake's hand, Carlie tugged him into line, and they both waved back at him before turning toward the luggage check.

With the two lovebirds on their way, Jake wandered back to the parking lot, knowing his sacrifice would be a good start toward regaining his daughter's trust.

Lost deep in thought, he walked between rows toward his rental car. All the loose ends were tied up, except one, a critical, missing puzzle piece to what the press now referred to as—a phrase coined by Bobby—the "CTG" incident, which stood for Civil Terror Gridlock. No matter how hard he focused, Jake failed to draw a logical conclusion about whether Viktor was dead or alive, his intellect simply unable to reconcile the facts about what occurred aboard Viktor's plane.

He approached his rental car and beeped it.

"Thought you could use a lift back to California on your favorite plane," Cavanaugh said, standing next to Jake's rental car.

Jake stopped, startled, tilted his head to the side and, with pursed lips, said, "The hell you doing here? Thought you were in LA?"

"Had a feeling you'd give your ticket to my bro."

Jake calculated the odds of Cavanaugh's assumption being correct. Slim to none.

"The FBI jet I threw up on? No way. Never."

Cavanaugh put his arm out as a black Charger pulled up in front of them. "We're all fueled up and ready to head back to California." He opened the car door for Jake. "You can't take a commercial flight anyway. I'm surprised you made it out here to Florida without too much paparazzi."

"It's amazing how effective a hat and sunglasses can be," Jake said as he entered the black beast. They both sat in the back with a driver up front.

While driving toward the airport, curiosity overcame Jake and he wondered how Cavanaugh could show up at exactly the right time. "I didn't expect you here. How in God's name did you know I'd give my ticket to Daniel?"

"I could've told you I'm an FBI agent. A master detective. It's what I do, but honestly, I had no idea you'd do that." He chuckled. "I was all set to join you on the cruise to keep an eye on you and make sure nothing happened. That was such a nice gesture, though. You're a good man and it's an honor to know you."

Huh.

Cavanaugh patted Jake's knee. "Now let's go find Viktor's body."

THANK YOU

Thank you for reading *Civil Terror: Gridlock*, the first in a series of three full-length thrillers. I sincerely hope you enjoyed the story!

The self-driving vehicle revolution is here and it's important for our society to have honest discussions about where we're headed. The more people who read this book, the more likely we are to avoid an actual terrorist attack like the one described in this story.

Getting book reviews will help get this important message out. If you have a minute, please go to the online store where you purchased this copy and enter a five-star review, along with any comments you feel appropriate.

Thank you!

Sincerely,
J. Luke Bennecke, Author

Website: www.jlukebennecke.com
Email: jason@jlukebennecke.com

BESTSELLING AUTHOR OF *CIVIL TERROR: GRIDLOCK*

WATERBORNE

A JAKE BENDEL THRILLER

A NOVEL BY

J. LUKE BENNECKE

WATERBORNE
A JAKE BENDEL THRILLER

AVAILABLE APRIL 2021

FACTS

1 Light-water reactors, used at both the Chernobyl and Fukushima disasters, are the most common type of nuclear reactor in use today. The United States Department of Energy oversees the operation of 99 light-water nuclear reactors, providing 20% of U.S. electricity.

2 Molten Salt Reactor technology was developed in the 1950s, consumes existing spent nuclear fuel, and will not melt down.

3 California has a population of 40 million people, each of whom uses 109 gallons of fresh, pure drinking water every day during summer months.

4 In 2015 CRISPR gene editing technology matured to the point where biologists could accurately change the genome of living organisms, including viruses.

CHAPTER 1

Mass murder can be complicated. But profitable. From a vacant corner of the Chili's parking lot, behind a four foot-high wall of cropped manzanita shrubs, Gunther Pertile scanned the area for civilians. Not a soul in sight. He whipped out his Glock 9mm—with suppressor—aimed at each of the two main overhead lights and squeezed off two muffled rounds. Glass shattered, falling to the ground as the entire scene went dark.

He dismounted his jet-black Harley, then slid off his helmet to reveal the short, curly hair he'd recently bleached to no longer be the dark-haired, dark-eyed killer on the FBI's most wanted list.

Running his fingertips along each of the four loaded mags inside the pocket of his leather jacket, he calculated the time to empty all sixty rounds. At three rounds per second and another three seconds to swap each mag, he could finish in just over half a minute.

One dead every half second.

Not bad.

But he tossed aside his mass shooting fantasy, forced himself back to reality, drew a deep breath and relished the security of his weapon. After two decades as a sniper, he knew tonight's assignment—his actual job—would succeed.

Piece of cake.

His weapon holstered, he glided through the front door of the restaurant and took a window seat.

A flash of blue pulled into the parking lot. The target—a civil engineer named Jake Bendel—wore a gray fedora hat, jeans, a light blue dress shirt and plaid charcoal sport coat as he exited a Tesla and strolled toward Chili's carrying a laptop, several rolls of paper, and a three-ring binder. Inside, the hostess escorted him to a booth on the room's opposite side. Physically, the target's height and weight matched the profile the boss had provided. At a height of just above six-one, maybe two hundred pounds, Gunther evaluated the level of effort to accomplish the abduction.

Within tolerance.

After Bendel sat, he ordered dinner and worked, checking his Apple Watch every few minutes.

Gunther took a slow sip of ice water, studying the mostly vacant dining room of the restaurant.

Eventually, the target's food came and he ate—still checking his watch. Gunther smiled.

The other members of the assault team had already taken care of Jake's friend, Dave, who most definitely would not be dining at Chili's tonight.

Or anywhere ever again, for that matter.

Gunther finished his water and set the glass on the table. His Android read 11:55 p.m.

Perfect.

He dug a hand into his pants pocket and wrapped his fingers around a syringe filled with enough Trihypnol to subdue a professional wrestler. With the quarter-inch-long needle capped at the tip, he'd avoid accidentally injecting himself with the hypnotic drug.

Trihypnol was the perfect concoction for tonight's events. Once administered, the victim would remain fully awake, but in a highly suggestible and altered state of consciousness— alert and fully mobile for up to four hours. The famous Dr. Jake Bendel would later crash like a pelted pigeon and sleep for half a day, with zero memory of the evening's activities.

Bendel stuffed the last piece of halibut into his mouth, chewed, and washed it down with a final swig of beer. *Game time.*

CHAPTER 2

Jake shifted in his seat, alone in an oversized padded booth, as he stabbed the last dry bite of cold halibut with his fork. From inside his leather folder, he slid out his favorite pen, the one personally awarded to him by the Governor for his previous efforts. Inscribed on the side, above a line with his initials "*J.B.*" read: *Sûr System - Moving America Forward without Traffic Congestion.*

While scanning the construction plans sitting off to the side of the table, he wrote several notes for himself, focusing on the remaining year of scheduled tasks—hundreds—all accurately displayed in the form of bar charts, dates, and percentages of completion. After setting the pen onto the plans, he raked his fingers through his thinning hair, wishing he'd worn his comfy construction boots instead of the black leather dress shoes pinching his toes. He took a long swig of Budweiser, then rubbed his eyes, trying to relax.

One final survey of the inside of the restaurant for Dave Trainer, his longtime friend, yielded nothing. Still no sign. If Dave wasn't coming, Jake could get more work done at his home office than in this restaurant.

As he packed up the multi-paged schedule, Jake's mind churned through potential solutions to the project delays and he waved the waitress over.

Jake's waitress strolled up then slipped the check and its black plastic tray next to the napkin dispenser. He plucked his wallet from his jeans and tossed an American Express onto the tray.

After closing a manila folder stuffed full of the latest progress reports, he thought about the largest water treatment plant. Three months behind schedule—unacceptable on a five billion dollar project. The construction delays needed serious reining in, for sure, to keep the governor off his ass.

A tall order.

Maybe with twelve-hour shifts per day, seven days a week. Jake blinked rapidly, running the numbers in his head. The shit ton of overtime would totally obliterate the already bulging budget.

But the governor demanded excellence, especially from her project director. She'd brought Jake on board to solve California's drought by finishing all five plants in record time. At her request, Jake had engineered the concept of pumping and treating seawater with energy created by a new form of cheap, safe nuclear power. The clean water would provide a basic human resource to most of California's booming population for decades.

Now, only three of the five plant combos were finished and ready to go online.

Jake piled up his used silverware on his plate, glad he hadn't ordered steak. He'd thought about it a few times the last couple of years, but ever since the infamous Los Angeles auto crashes and terrorist threats two years ago he hadn't been able to eat red meat. Partially because he'd seen too many of the victims. Partially because his wife was one of them. And partially because the press had initially blamed him for the carnage.

Too much death.

That's why he planned to meet Dave here tonight. As a master computer hacker, Dave had played a key role in stopping the terrorists responsible for the crashes. Coming head-to-head with evil like that had messed them both up pretty bad, so Jake had invited Dave to a seafood dinner as part of their ongoing healing process.

But now the guy had stood him up.

No text. No phone call. Nothing.

As he waited for the waitress to bring his card back, he noticed a muscular black man with short, bleached blond hair and a salt and pepper half-length ZZ-Top beard sitting alone across the room, nursing a clear drink. Vodka on the rocks, perhaps.

Jake checked his watch: two minutes after midnight. He needed to go home.

The waitress returned, he picked up his card, threw on his fedora hat and rose to leave.

As he walked toward the door, the bearded man also rose to leave. A credit card slipped from his hand and landed in front of Jake on the low-pile carpet.

Jake bent, scooped the card up off the ground, and jogged after the man.

✳

Gunther strode across the parking lot as Bendel raced after him.

So far so good.

"Excuse me, sir! I think you dropped this."

Gunther smiled and turned around. "Thanks, bro." Jake gave him the card and spun toward his Tesla.

As Jake extended his arm to open the driver's door, Gunther pulled out the syringe from his pocket and closed the distance between them while placing a thumb snugly on the plunger. Before Jake could open the car door, Gunther lunged forward, bumping the engineer forward while injecting the Trihypnol into the meat of his neck.

Jake stumbled but caught his balance. Gunther stabilized his target, saying in a drunken, slurred tone, "Sorry, dude, didn't mean to—"

Jake whirled around and stepped back, eyes blinking. He shook his head, brushing imaginary dust off his arms. "Watch where you're going, man, I—"

Gunther said nothing, instead turning his gaze to the corner of the parking lot and motioning toward the target. Headlights popped on as the unmarked black van parked in an opposite corner of the lot sped forward and pulled up next to Jake.

The side door swooshed open and the rest of the abduction team, two men wearing dark green ski masks, black jackets, and leather gloves, leapt out and surrounded Jake, who stumbled sideways in a failed attempt to escape. The largest of the abductors jabbed a stun gun and ten thousand volts into Jake's rib cage, then heaved him into the van.

As Gunther hopped into the cargo space of their vehicle, another man jumped out and dashed toward the Harley. Gunther slid the door shut and nodded to the driver who hurled the van onto an empty street and accelerated west.

The abduction had taken less than ten seconds.

Another success.

Two of the masked men secured Jake's wrists behind his back with 3/8-inch yellow nylon rope. Same with his ankles. Jake's aggressive efforts to free himself eventually gave way to slow, clumsy movements as the Trihypnol coursed through his veins.

Gunther thought of his boss and the several dozen Jihadist souls sent to Allah two years ago because of Jake's actions. But now the Almighty had called on their sleeper cell as chosen ones, to send yet another message to the American infidels. One final, symbolic act of religious supremacy before the heroes would ascend to the Kingdom of God.

And those 99 virgins, or whatever.

What a bunch of extremist Allahu Akbar bullshit. Gunther was in this for the money.

And the unbeatable rush.

The sense of control.

Power.

The assassin pulled up Jake's torso, sitting Jake's drugged body upright on the van floor as Jake's head flopped around like a fishing bobber. "He's all yours."

The woman in the passenger seat unbuckled her seatbelt, climbed to the rear of the van, leaned forward, and lifted Jake's chin as she stared into his half-open eyes.

She slapped his cheek, but he only smiled. "Whew. Just a nightmare." He chuckled, glancing around the van before taking a second look at Gunther.

"Glad you think this is funny," the woman said. "Good news is you won't remember a damned thing."

The van drove across a deep pothole, forcing everyone to bounce. Jake gave a weak shake of his head, likely trying to clear the fog and regain clear focus.

She continued. "You're going to do me a favor." She brought her face to within an inch of his. "Jakey boy."

Jake's face morphed into a distant, confused daze. "I understand your daughter, Carlie, has a three-month-old son. Living in New York. Would be a shame if anything were to happen to them."

He furrowed his brow, tilting his head.

She finally had his attention.

The van turned a corner and sped up as streetlights streaked by in a blur before the team entered the I-5 north, ultimately headed toward the coast to put Jake to work.

"You tousha my family," Jake said, still slurred, to the woman, "and I'll hunt your seck ass down and bash in that pretty li'l face of yours."

"Sounds like we have an understanding then," she said, smiling, leaning back and crossing her arms. "Tonight, you'll live. But you're going to wish we'd killed you."